Nora Roberts is the *New York Times* bestselling author of more than two hundred novels. A born storyteller, she creates a blend of warmth, humour and poignancy that speaks directly to her readers and has earned her almost every award for excellence in her field. The youngest of five children, Nora Roberts lives in western Maryland. She has two sons.

Visit her website at www.noraroberts.com.

Nora Roberts

Summer with You

MILLS & BOON

This edition published in Great Britain 2015
by Mills & Boon, an imprint of Harlequin (UK) Limited,
Eton House, 18-24 Paradise Road, Richmond, Surrey, TW9 1SR

SUMMER WITH YOU © 2015 Harlequin Books S.A.

One Summer © 1986 Nora Roberts
Island of Flowers © 1982 Nora Roberts

ISBN: 978-0-263-25416-7

029-0715

Printed and bound by
CPI Group (UK) Ltd, Croydon, CR0 4YY

One Summer

Chapter 1

The room was dark. Pitch-dark. But the man named Shade was used to the dark. Sometimes he preferred it. It wasn't always necessary to see with your eyes. His fingers were both clever and competent, his inner eye as keen as a knife blade.

There were times, even when he wasn't working, when he'd sit in a dark room and simply let images form in his mind. Shapes, textures, colors. Sometimes they came clearer when you shut your eyes and just let your thoughts flow. He courted darkness, shadows, just as relentlessly as he courted the light. It was all part of life, and life—its images—was his profession.

He didn't always see life as others did. At times it was harsher, colder, than the naked eye could see—or wanted to. Other times it was softer, more lovely, than the busy world imagined. Shade observed it, grouped the elements, manipulated time and shape, then recorded it his way. Always his way.

Now, with the room dark and the sound of recorded jazz coming quiet and disembodied from the corner, he worked with his hands and his mind. Care and timing. He used them both in every aspect of his work. Slowly, smoothly, he opened the capsule and transferred the undeveloped film onto the reel. When the light-tight lid was on the developing tank, he set the timer with his free hand, then pulled the chain that added the amber light to the room.

Shade enjoyed developing the negative and making the print as much as, sometimes more than, he enjoyed taking the photograph. Darkroom work required precision and accuracy. He needed both in his life. Making the print allowed for creativity and experimentation. He needed those as well. What he saw, what he felt about what he saw, could be translated exactly or left as an enigma. Above all, he needed the satisfaction of creating something himself, alone. He always worked alone.

Now, as he went through each precise step of developing—temperature, chemicals, agitation, timing—the amber light cast his face into shadows. If Shade had been looking to create the image of photographer at work, he'd never have found a clearer statement than himself.

His eyes were dark, intense now as he added the stop bath to the tank. His hair was dark as well, too long for the convention he cared nothing about. It brushed over his ears, the back of his T-shirt, and fell over his forehead nearly to his eyebrows. He never gave much thought to style. His was cool, almost cold, and rough around the edges.

His face was deeply tanned, lean and hard, with strong bones dominating. His mouth was taut as he concentrated. There were lines spreading out finely from his eyes, etched there by what he'd seen and what he'd felt about it. Some would say there'd already been too much of both.

The nose was out of alignment, a result of a professional hazard. Not everyone liked to have his picture taken. The Cambodian soldier had broken Shade's nose, but Shade had gotten a telling picture of the city's devastation, of the waste. He still considered it an even exchange.

In the amber light, his movements were brisk. He had a rangy, athletic body, the result of years in the field— often a foreign, unfriendly field—miles of legwork and missed meals.

Even now, years after his last staff assignment for *International View,* Shade remained lean and agile. His work wasn't as grueling as it had been in his early years in Lebanon, Laos, Central America, but his pattern hadn't changed. He worked long hours, sometimes waiting endlessly for just the right shot, sometimes using a roll of film within minutes. If his style and manner were aggressive, it could be said that they'd kept him alive and whole during the wars he'd recorded.

The awards he'd won, the fee he now commanded, remained secondary to the picture. If no one had paid him or recognized his work, Shade would still have been in the darkroom, developing his film. He was respected, successful and rich. Yet he had no assistant and continued to work out of the same darkroom he'd set up ten years before.

When Shade hung his negatives up to dry, he already had an idea which ones he'd print. Still, he barely glanced at them, leaving them hanging as he unlocked the darkroom door and stepped out. Tomorrow his outlook would be fresher. Waiting was an advantage he hadn't always had. Right now he wanted a beer. He had some thinking to do.

He headed straight for the kitchen and grabbed a cold bottle. Popping off the lid, he tossed it into the can his once-a-week housekeeper lined with plastic. The room was clean, not particularly cheerful with the hard whites and blacks, but then it wasn't dull.

After he tilted the bottle back, he chugged the beer down, draining half. He lit a cigarette, then took the beer to the kitchen table where he leaned back in a chair and propped his feet on the scrubbed wood surface.

The view out the kitchen window was of a not-so-glamorous L.A. It was a little seamy, rough, sturdy and tough. The early-evening light couldn't make it pretty. He could've moved to a glossier part of town, or out to the hills, where the lights of the city at night looked like a fairy tale. Shade preferred the small apartment that looked out over the unpampered streets of a city known for glitz. He didn't have much patience with glitz.

Bryan Mitchell. She specialized in it.

He couldn't deny that her portraits of the rich, famous and beautiful were well done—even excellent ones of their kind. There was compassion in her photographs, humor and a smooth sensuality. He wouldn't even deny that there was a place for her kind of work in the field. It just wasn't his angle. She reflected culture, he went straight for life.

Her work for *Celebrity* magazine had been professional, slick and often searing in its way. The larger-than-life people she'd photographed had often been cut down to size in a way that made them human and approachable. Since she'd decided to freelance, the stars, near-stars and starmakers she'd photographed for the glossy came to her. Over the years, she'd developed a reputation and style that had made her one of them, part of the inner, select circle.

It could happen to a photographer, he knew. They could come to resemble their own themes, their own studies. Sometimes what they tried to project became a part of them. Too much a part. No, he didn't begrudge Bryan Mitchell her state of the art. Shade simply had doubts about working with her.

He didn't care for partnerships.

Yet those were the terms. When he'd been approached by *Life-style* to do a pictorial study of America, he'd been intrigued. Photo essays could make a strong, lasting statement that could rock and jar or soothe and amuse. As a photographer, he had sought to do that. *Life-style* wanted him, wanted the strong, sometimes concise, sometimes ambiguous emotions his pictures could portray. But they also wanted a counterbalance. A woman's view.

He wasn't so stubborn that he didn't see the point and the possibilities. Yet it irked him to think that the assignment hinged on his willingness to share the summer, his van and the credit with a celebrity photographer. And with a woman at that. Three months on the road with a female who spent her time perfecting snapshots of rock stars and personalities. For a man who'd cut his professional teeth in war-torn Lebanon, it didn't sound like a picnic.

But he wanted to do it. He wanted the chance to capture an American summer from L.A. to New York, showing the joy, the pathos, the sweat, the cheers and disappointments. He wanted to show the heart, even while he stripped it to the bone.

All he had to do was say yes, and share the summer with Bryan Mitchell.

"Don't think about the camera, Maria. Dance." Bryan lined up the forty-year-old ballet superstar in her viewfinder. She liked what she saw. Age? Touches of it, but years meant nothing. Grit, style, elegance. Endurance—most of all, endurance. Bryan knew how to catch them all and meld them.

Maria Natravidova had been photographed countless times over her phenomenal twenty-five-year career. But never with sweat running down her arms and dampening her leotard. Never with the strain showing. Bryan wasn't looking for the illusions dancers live with, but the exhaustion, the aches that were the price of triumph.

She caught Maria in a leap, legs stretched parallel to the floor, arms flung wide in perfect alignment. Drops of moisture danced from her face and shoulders; muscles bunched and held. Bryan pressed the shutter, then moved the camera slightly to blur the motion.

That would be the one. She knew it even as she finished off the roll of film.

"You make me work," the dancer complained as she slid into a chair, blotting her streaming face with a towel.

Bryan took two more shots, then lowered her camera. "I could've dressed you in costume, backlit you and had you hold an arabesque. That would show that you're beautiful, graceful. Instead I'm going to show that you're a strong woman."

"And you're a clever one." Maria sighed as she let the towel drop. "Why else do I come to you for the pictures for my book?"

"Because I'm the best." Bryan crossed the studio and disappeared into a back room. Maria systematically worked a cramp out of her calf. "Because I understand you, admire you. And—" she brought out a tray, two glasses and a pitcher clinking with ice "—because I squeeze oranges for you."

"Darling." With a laugh, Maria reached for the first glass. For a moment, she held it to her high forehead, then drank deeply. Her dark hair was pulled back severely in a style only good bones and flawless skin could tolerate. Stretching out her long, thin body in the chair, she studied Bryan over the rim of her glass.

Maria had known Bryan for seven years, since the photographer had started at *Celebrity* with the assignment to take pictures of the dancer backstage. The dancer had been a star, but Bryan hadn't shown awe. Maria could still remember the young woman with the thick honey-colored braid and bib overalls. The elegant prima ballerina had found herself confronted with candid eyes the color of pewter, an elegant face with slanting cheekbones and a full mouth. The tall, athletic body had nearly been lost inside the baggy clothes. She'd worn ragged sneakers and long, dangling earrings.

Maria glanced down at the dingy Nikes Bryan wore. Some things didn't change. At first glance, you'd categorize the tall, tanned blonde in sneakers and shorts as typically California. Looks could be deceiving. There was nothing typical about Bryan Mitchell.

Bryan accepted the stare as she drank. "What do you see, Maria?" It interested her to know. Conceptions and preconceptions were part of her trade.

"A strong, smart woman with talent and ambition." Maria smiled as she leaned back in the chair. "Myself, nearly."

Bryan smiled. "A tremendous compliment."

Maria acknowledged this with a sweeping gesture. "There aren't many women I like. Myself I like, and so, you. I hear rumors, my love, about you and that pretty young actor."

"Matt Perkins." Bryan didn't believe in evading or pretending. She lived, by choice, in a town fueled by rumors, fed by gossip. "I took his picture, had a few dinners."

"Nothing serious?"

"As you said, he's pretty." Bryan smiled and chewed on a piece of ice. "But there's barely room enough for his ego and mine in his Mercedes."

"Men." Maria leaned forward to pour herself a second glass.

"Now you're going to be profound."

"Who better?" Maria countered. "Men." She said the word again, savoring it. "I find them tedious, childish, foolish and indispensable. Being loved…sexually, you understand?"

Bryan managed to keep her lips from curving. "I understand."

"Being loved is exhilarating, exhausting. Like Christmas. Sometimes I feel like the child who doesn't understand why Christmas ends. But it does. And you wait for the next time."

It always fascinated Bryan how people felt about love, how they dealt with it, groped for it and avoided it. "Is that why you never married, Maria? You're waiting for the next time?"

"I married dance. To marry a man, I would have to divorce dance. There's no room for two for a woman like me. And you?"

Bryan stared into her drink, no longer amused. She understood the words too well. "No room for two," she murmured. "But I don't wait for the next time."

"You're young. If you could have Christmas every day, would you turn away from it?"

Bryan moved her shoulders. "I'm too lazy for Christmas every day."

"Still, it's a pretty fantasy." Maria rose and stretched. "You've made me work long enough. I have to shower and change. Dinner with my choreographer."

Alone, Bryan absently ran a finger over the back of her camera. She didn't often think about love and marriage. She'd been there already. Once a fantasy was exposed to reality, it faded, like a photo improperly fixed. Permanent relationships rarely worked, and still more rarely worked well.

She thought of Lee Radcliffe, married to Hunter Brown for nearly a year, helping to raise his daughter and pregnant with her first child. Lee was happy, but then she'd found an extraordinary man, one who wanted her to be what she was, even encouraged her to explore herself. Bryan's own experience had taught her that what's said and what's felt can be two opposing things.

Your career's as important to me as it is to you. How many times had Rob said that *before* they'd been married? *Get your degree. Go for it.*

So they'd gotten married, young, eager, idealistic. Within six months he'd been unhappy with the time she'd put into her classes and her job at a local studio. He'd wanted his dinner hot and his socks washed. Not so much to ask, Bryan mused. To be fair, she had to say that Rob had asked for little of her. Just too much at the time.

They'd cared for each other, and both had tried to make adjustments. Both had discovered they'd wanted different things for themselves—different things from each other, things neither could be, neither could give.

It would've been called an amicable divorce—no fury, no bitterness. No passion. A signature on a legal document, and the dream had been over. It had hurt more than anything Bryan had ever known. The taint of failure had stayed with her a long, long time.

She knew Rob had remarried. He was living in the suburbs with his wife and their two children. He'd gotten what he'd wanted.

And so, Bryan told herself as she looked around her studio, had she. She didn't just want to be a photographer. She was a photographer. The hours she spent in the field, in her studio, in the darkroom, were as essential to her as sleep. And what she'd done in the six years since the end of her marriage, she'd done on her own. She didn't have to share it. She didn't have to share her time. Perhaps she was a great deal like Maria. She was a woman who ran her own life, made her own decisions, personally and professionally. Some people weren't made for partnerships.

Shade Colby. Bryan propped her feet on Maria's chair. She might just have to make a concession there. She admired his work. So much so, in fact, that she'd plunked down a heady amount for his print of an L.A. street scene at a time when money had been a large concern. She'd studied it, trying to analyze and guess at the techniques he'd used for setting the shot and making the print. It was a moody piece, so much gray, so little light. And yet, Bryan had sensed a certain grit in it, not hopelessness, but ruthlessness. Still, admiring his work and working with him were two different things.

They were based in the same town, but they moved in

different circles. For the most part, Shade Colby didn't move in any circles. He kept to himself. She'd seen him at a handful of photography functions, but they'd never met.

He'd be an interesting subject, she reflected. Given enough time, she could capture that air of aloofness and earthiness on film. Perhaps if they agreed to take the assignment she'd have the chance.

Three months of travel. There was so much of the country she hadn't seen, so many pictures she hadn't taken. Thoughtfully, she pulled a candy bar out of her back pocket and unwrapped it. She liked the idea of taking a slice of America, a season, and pulling the images together. So much could be said.

Bryan enjoyed doing her portraits. Taking a face, a personality, especially a well-known one, and finding out what lay behind it was fascinating. Some might find it limited, but she found it endlessly varied. She could take the tough female rock star and show her vulnerabilities, or pull the humor from the cool, regal megastar. Capturing the unexpected, the fresh—that was the purpose of photography to her.

Now she was being offered the opportunity to do the same thing with a country. The people, she thought. So many people.

She wanted to do it. If it meant sharing the work, the discoveries, the fun, with Shade Colby, she still wanted to do it. She bit into the chocolate. So what if he had a reputation for being cranky and remote? She could get along with anyone for three months.

"Chocolate makes you fat and ugly."

Bryan glanced up as Maria swirled back into the room. The sweat was gone. She looked now as people expected a prima ballerina to look. Draped in silk, studded with diamonds. Cool, composed, beautiful.

"It makes me happy," Bryan countered. "You look fantastic, Maria."

"Yes." Maria brushed a hand down the draping silk at her hip. "But then it's my job to do so. Will you work late?"

"I want to develop the film. I'll send you some test proofs tomorrow."

"And that's your dinner?"

"Just a start." Bryan took a huge bite of chocolate. "I'm sending out for pizza."

"With pepperoni?"

Bryan grinned. "With everything."

Maria pressed a hand to her stomach. "And I eat with my choreographer, the tyrant, which means I eat next to nothing."

"And I'll have a soda instead of a glass of Taittinger. We all have our price to pay."

"If I like your proofs, I'll send you a case."

"Of Taittinger?"

"Of soda." With a laugh, Maria swept out.

An hour later, Bryan hung her negatives up to dry. She'd need to make the proofs to be certain, but out of more than forty shots, she'd probably print no more than five.

When her stomach rumbled, she checked her watch. She'd ordered the pizza for seven-thirty. Well timed, she decided as she left the darkroom. She'd eat and go over the prints of Matt she'd shot for a layout in a glossy. Then she could work on the one she chose until the negatives of Maria were dry. She began rummaging through the two dozen folders on her desk—her personal method of filing—when someone knocked at the studio door.

"Pizza," she breathed, greedy. "Come on in. I'm starving." Plopping her enormous canvas bag on the desk, Bryan began to hunt for her wallet. "This is great timing. Another five minutes and I might've just faded away. Shouldn't miss lunch." She dropped a fat, ragged notebook, a clear plastic bag filled with cosmetics, a key ring and five candy bars on the desk. "Just set it down anywhere, I'll find the money in a minute." She dug deeper into the bag. "How much do you need?"

"As much as I can get."

"Don't we all." Bryan pulled out a worn man's billfold. "And I'm desperate enough to clean out the safe for you, but…" She trailed off as she looked up and saw Shade Colby.

He gave her face a quick glance, then concentrated on her eyes. "What would you like to pay me for?"

"Pizza." Bryan dropped the wallet onto the desk with half the contents of her purse. "A case of starvation and mistaken identity. Shade Colby." She held out her hand, curious and, to her surprise, nervous. He looked more formidable when he wasn't in a crowd. "I recognize you," she continued, "but I don't think we've met."

"No, we haven't." He took her hand and held it while he studied her face a second time. Stronger than he'd expected. He always looked for the strength first, then the weaknesses. And younger. Though he knew she was only twenty-eight, Shade had expected her to look harder, more aggressive, glossier. Instead, she looked like someone who'd just come in from the beach.

Her T-shirt was snug, but she was slim enough to warrant it. The braid came nearly to her waist and made him speculate on how her hair would look loose and free.

Her eyes interested him—gray edging toward silver, and almond-shaped. They were eyes he'd like to photograph with the rest of her face in shadow. She might carry a bag of cosmetics, but it didn't look as if she used any of them.

Not vain about her appearance, he decided. That would make things simpler if he decided to work with her. He didn't have the patience to wait while a woman painted and groomed and fussed. This one wouldn't. And she was assessing him even as he assessed her. Shade accepted that. A photographer, like any artist, looked for angles.

"Am I interrupting your work?"

"No, I was just taking a break. Sit down."

They were both cautious. He'd come on impulse. She wasn't certain how to handle him. Each decided to bide their time before they went beyond the polite, impersonal stage. Bryan remained behind her desk. Her turf, his move, she decided.

Shade didn't sit immediately. Instead, he tucked his hands in his pockets and looked around her studio. It was wide, well lit from the ribbon of windows. There were baby spots and a blue backdrop still set up from an earlier session in one section. Reflectors and umbrellas stood in another, with a camera still on a tripod. He didn't have to look closely to see that the equipment was first-class. But then, first-class equipment didn't make a first-class photographer.

She liked the way he stood, not quite at ease, but ready, remote. If she had to choose now, she'd have photographed him in shadows, alone. But Bryan insisted on knowing the person before she made a portrait.

How old was he? she wondered. Thirty-three, thirty-five.

He'd already been nominated for a Pulitzer when she'd still been in college. It didn't occur to her to be intimidated.

"Nice place," he commented before he dropped into the chair opposite the desk.

"Thanks." She tilted her chair so that she could study him from another angle. "You don't use a studio of your own, do you?"

"I work in the field." He drew out a cigarette. "On the rare occasion I need a studio, I can borrow or rent one easily enough."

Automatically she hunted for an ashtray under the chaos on her desk. "You make all your own prints?"

"That's right."

Bryan nodded. On the few occasions at *Celebrity* when she'd been forced to entrust her film to someone else, she hadn't been satisfied. That had been one of the major reasons she'd decided to open her own business. "I love darkroom work."

She smiled for the first time, causing him to narrow his eyes and focus on her face. What kind of power was that? he wondered. A curving of lips, easy and relaxed. It packed one hell of a punch.

Bryan sprang up at the knock on the door. "At last."

Shade watched her cross the room. He hadn't known she was so tall. Five-ten, he estimated, and most of it leg. Long, slender, bronzed leg. It wasn't easy to ignore the smile, but it was next to impossible to ignore those legs.

Nor had he noticed her scent until she moved by him. Lazy sex. He couldn't think of another way to describe it. It wasn't floral, it wasn't sophisticated. It was basic. Shade drew on his cigarette and watched her laugh with the delivery boy.

Photographers were known for their preconceptions; it was part of the trade. He'd expected her to be sleek and cool. That was what he'd nearly resigned himself to working with. Now it was a matter of rearranging his thinking. Did he want to work with a woman who smelled like twilight and looked like a beach bunny?

Turning away from her, Shade opened a folder at random. He recognized the subject—a box-office queen with two Oscars and three husbands under her belt. Bryan had dressed her in glitters and sparkles. Royal trappings for royalty. But she hadn't shot the traditional picture.

The actress was sitting at a table jumbled with pots and tubes of lotions and creams, looking at her own reflection in a mirror and laughing. Not the poised, careful smile that didn't make wrinkles, but a full, robust laugh that could nearly be heard. It was up to the viewer to speculate whether she laughed at her reflection or an image she'd created over the years.

"Like it?" Carrying the cardboard box, Bryan stopped beside him.

"Yeah. Did she?"

Too hungry for formalities, Bryan opened the lid and dug out the first piece. "She ordered a sixteen-by-twenty-four for her fiancé. Want a piece?"

Shade looked inside the box. "They miss putting anything on here?"

"Nope." Bryan searched in a drawer of her desk for napkins and came up with a box of tissues. "I'm a firm believer in overindulgence. So…" With the box opened on the desk between them, Bryan leaned back in her chair and propped up her feet. It was time, she decided, to get beyond the fencing stage. "You want to talk about the assignment?"

Shade took a piece of pizza and a handful of tissues. "Got a beer?"

"Soda—diet or regular." Bryan took a huge, satisfying bite. "I don't keep liquor in the studio. You end up having buzzed clients."

"We'll skip it for now." They ate in silence a moment, still weighing each other. "I've been giving a lot of thought to doing this photo essay."

"It'd be a change for you." When he only lifted a brow, Bryan wadded a tissue and tossed it into the trash can. "Your stuff overseas—it hit hard. There was sensitivity and compassion, but for the most part, it was grim."

"It was a grim time. Everything I shoot doesn't have to be pretty."

This time she lifted a brow. Obviously he didn't think much of the path she'd taken in her career. "Everything I shoot doesn't have to be raw. There's room for fun in art."

He acknowledged this with a shrug. "We'd see different things if we looked through the same lens."

"That's what makes each picture unique." Bryan leaned forward and took another piece.

"I like working alone."

She ate thoughtfully. If he was trying to annoy her, he was right on target. If it was just an overflow of his personality, it still wouldn't make things any easier. Either way, she wanted the assignment, and he was part of it. "I prefer it that way myself," she said slowly. "Sometimes there has to be compromise. You've heard of compromise, Shade. You give, I give. We meet somewhere close to the middle."

She wasn't as laid-back as she looked. Good. The last

thing he needed was to go on the road with someone so mellow she threatened to mold. Three months, he thought again. Maybe. Once the ground rules were set. "I map out the route," he began briskly. "We start here in L.A. in two weeks. Each of us is responsible for their own equipment. Once we're on the road, each of us goes our own way. You shoot your pictures, I shoot mine. No questions."

Bryan licked sauce from her finger. "Anyone ever question you, Colby?"

"It's more to the point whether I answer." It was said simply, as it was meant. "The publisher wants both views, so he'll have them. We'll be stopping off and on to rent a darkroom. I'll look over your negatives."

Bryan wadded more tissue. "No, you won't." Lazily, she crossed one ankle over the other. Her eyes had gone to slate, the only outward show of a steadily growing anger.

"I'm not interested in having my name attached to a series of pop-culture shots."

To keep herself in control, Bryan continued to eat. There were things, so many clear, concise things, she'd like to say to him. Temper took a great deal of energy, she reminded herself. It usually accomplished nothing. "The first thing I'll want written into the contract is that each of our pictures carries our own bylines. That way neither of us will be embarrassed by the other's work. I'm not interested in having the public think I have no sense of humor. Want another piece?"

"No." She wasn't soft. The skin on the inside of her elbow might look soft as butter, but the lady wasn't. It might annoy him to be so casually insulted, but he preferred it to spineless agreement. "We'll be gone from June fifteenth until after Labor Day." He watched her scoop up a third piece of pizza. "Since I've seen you eat, we'll each keep track of our own expenses."

"Fine. Now, in case you have any odd ideas, I don't cook and I won't pick up after you. I'll drive my share, but I won't drive with you if you've been drinking. When we rent a darkroom, we trade off as to who uses it first. From June fifteenth to after Labor Day, we're partners. Fifty-fifty. If you have any problems with that, we'll hash it out now, before we sign on the dotted line."

He thought about it. She had a good voice, smooth, quiet, nearly soothing. They might handle the close quarters well enough—as long as she didn't smile at him too often and he kept his mind off her legs. At the moment, he considered that the least of his problems. The assignment came first, and what he wanted for it, and from it.

"Do you have a lover?"

Bryan managed not to choke on her pizza. "If that's an offer," she began smoothly, "I'll have to decline. Rude, brooding men just aren't my type."

Inwardly he acknowledged another hit; outwardly his face remained expressionless. "We're going to be living in each other's pockets for three months." She'd challenged him, whether she realized it or not. Whether he realized it or not, Shade had accepted. He leaned closer. "I don't want to hassle with a jealous lover chasing along after us or constantly calling while I'm trying to work."

Just who did he think she was? Some bimbo who couldn't handle her personal life? She made herself pause a moment. Perhaps he'd had some uncomfortable experiences in his relationships. His problem, Bryan decided.

"I'll worry about my lovers, Shade." Bryan bit into her crust with a vengeance. "You worry about yours." She wiped her fingers on the last of the tissue and smiled. "Sorry to break up the party, but I've got to get back to work."

He rose, letting his gaze skim up her legs before he met her eyes. He was going to take the assignment. And he'd have three months to figure out just how he felt about Bryan Mitchell. "I'll be in touch."

"Do that."

Bryan waited until he'd crossed the room and shut the studio door behind him. With uncommon energy, and a speed she usually reserved for work, she jumped up and tossed the empty cardboard box at the door.

It promised to be a long three months.

Chapter 2

She knew exactly what she wanted. Bryan might've been a bit ahead of the scheduled starting date for the American Summer project for *Life-style*, but she enjoyed the idea of being a step ahead of Shade Colby. Petty, perhaps, but she did enjoy it.

In any case, she doubted a man like him would appreciate the timeless joy of the last day of school. When else did summer really start, but with that one wild burst of freedom?

She chose an elementary school because she wanted innocence. She chose an inner-city school because she wanted realism. Children who would step out the door and into a limo weren't the image she wanted to project. This school could've been in any city across the country. The kids who'd bolt out the door would be all kids. People who looked at the photograph, no matter what their age, would see something of themselves.

Bryan gave herself plenty of time to set up, choosing and rejecting half a dozen vantage points before she settled on one. It wasn't possible or even advisable to stage the shoot. Only random shots would give her what she wanted—the spontaneity and the rush.

When the bell rang and the doors burst open, she got exactly that. It was well worth nearly being trampled under flying sneakers. With shouts and yells and whistles, kids poured out into the sunshine.

Stampede. That was the thought that went through her mind. Crouching quickly, Bryan shot up, catching the first rush of children at an angle that would convey speed, mass and total confusion.

Let's go, let's go! It's summer and every day's Saturday. September was years away. She could read it on the face of every child.

Turning, she shot the next group of children head-on. In the finished spot, they'd appear to be charging right out of the page of the magazine. On impulse, she shifted her camera for a vertical shot. And she got it. A boy of eight or nine leaped down the flight of steps, hands flung high, a grin splitting his face. Bryan shot him in midair while he hung head and shoulders above the scattering children. She'd captured the boy filled with the triumph of that magic, golden road of freedom spreading out in all directions.

Though she was dead sure which shot she'd print for the assignment, Bryan continued to work. Within ten minutes, it was over.

Satisfied, she changed lenses and angles. The school was empty now, and she wanted to record it that way. She didn't want the feel of bright sunlight here, she decided as she added a low-contrast filter. When she developed the print, Bryan would "dodge" the light in the sky by holding something over that section of the paper to keep it from being overexposed. She wanted the sense of emptiness, of waiting, as a contrast to the life and energy that had just poured out of the building. She'd exhausted a roll of film before she straightened and let the camera hang by its strap.

School's out, she thought with a grin. She felt that charismatic pull of freedom herself. Summer was just beginning.

Since resigning from the staff of *Celebrity*, Bryan had found her work load hadn't eased. If anything, she'd found herself to be a tougher employer than the magazine. She loved her work and was likely to give it all of her day and most of her evenings. Her ex-husband had once accused her of being obsessed not with her camera, but by it. It was something she'd neither been able to deny nor defend. After two days of working with Shade, Bryan had discovered she wasn't alone.

She'd always considered herself a meticulous craftsman. Compared to Shade, she was lackadaisical. He had a patience in his work that she admired even as it set her teeth on edge. They worked from entirely different perspectives. Bryan shot a scene and conveyed her personal viewpoint— her emotions, her feelings about the image. Shade deliberately courted ambiguity. While his photographs might spark off a dozen varied reactions, his personal view almost always remained his secret. Just as everything about him remained half shadowed.

He didn't chat, but Bryan didn't mind working in silence. It was nearly like working alone. His long, quiet looks could be unnerving, however. She didn't care to be dissected as though she were in a viewfinder.

They'd met twice since their first encounter in her studio, both times to argue out their basic route and the themes for the assignment. She hadn't found him any easier, but she had found him sharp. The project meant enough to both of them to make it possible for them to do as she'd suggested—meet somewhere in the middle.

After her initial annoyance with him had worn off, Bryan had decided they could become friends over the next months—professional friends, in any case. Then, after two days of working with him, she'd known it would never happen. Shade didn't induce simple emotions like friendship. He'd either dazzle or infuriate. She didn't choose to be dazzled.

Bryan had researched him thoroughly, telling herself her reason was routine. You didn't go on the road with a man you knew virtually nothing about. Yet the more she'd found out—rather, the more she hadn't found out—the deeper her curiosity had become.

He'd been married and divorced in his early twenties. That was it—no anecdotes, no gossip, no right and wrong. He covered his tracks well. As a photographer for *International View,* Shade had spent a total of five years overseas. Not in pretty Paris, London and Madrid, but in Laos, Lebanon, Cambodia. His work there had earned him a Pulitzer nomination and the Overseas Press Club Award.

His photographs were available for study and dissection, but his personal life remained obscure. He socialized rarely. What friends he had were unswervingly loyal and frustratingly closedmouthed. If she wanted to learn more about him, Bryan would have to do it on the job.

Bryan considered the fact that they'd agreed to spend their last day in L.A. working at the beach a good sign. They'd decided on the location without any argument.

Beach scenes would be an ongoing theme throughout the essay—California to Cape Cod.

At first they walked along the sand together, like friends or lovers, not touching but in step with each other. They didn't talk, but Bryan had already learned that Shade didn't make idle conversation unless he was in the mood.

It was barely ten, but the sun was bright and hot. Because it was a weekday morning, most of the sun- and water-seekers were the young or the old. When Bryan stopped, Shade kept walking without either of them saying a word.

It was the contrast that had caught her eye. The old woman was bundled in a wide, floppy sun hat, a long beach dress and a crocheted shawl. She sat under an umbrella and watched her granddaughter—dressed only in frilly pink panties—dig a hole in the sand beside her. Sun poured over the little girl. Shadow blanketed the old woman.

She'd need the woman to sign a release form. Invariably, asking someone if you could take her picture stiffened her up, and Bryan avoided it whenever it was possible. In this case it wasn't, so she was patient enough to chat and wait until the woman had relaxed again.

Her name was Sadie, and so was her granddaughter's. Before she'd clicked the shutter the first time, Bryan knew she'd title the print *Two Sadies*. All she had to do was get that dreamy, faraway look back in the woman's eyes.

It took twenty minutes. Bryan forgot she was uncomfortably warm as she listened, thought and reasoned out the angles. She knew what she wanted. The old woman's careful self-preservation, the little girl's total lack of it, and the bond between them that came with blood and time.

Lost in reminiscence, Sadie forgot about the camera, not noticing when Bryan began to release the shutter. She wanted the poignancy—that's what she'd seen. When she printed it, Bryan would be merciless with the lines and creases in the grandmother's face, just as she'd highlight the flawlessness of the toddler's skin.

Grateful, Bryan chatted a few more minutes, then noted the woman's address with the promise of a print. She walked on, waiting for the next scene to unfold.

Shade had his first subject as well, but he didn't chat. The man lay facedown on a faded beach towel. He was red, flabby and anonymous. A businessman taking the morning off, a salesman from Iowa—it didn't matter. Unlike Bryan, he wasn't looking for personality, but for the sameness of those who grilled their bodies under the sun. There was a plastic bottle of tanning lotion stuck in the sand beside him and a pair of rubber beach thongs.

Shade chose two angles and shot six times without exchanging a word with the snoring sunbather. Satisfied, he scanned the beach. Three yards away, Bryan was casually stripping out of her shorts and shirt. The sleek red maillot rose tantalizing high at the thighs. Her profile was to him as she stepped out of her shorts. It was sharp, well defined, like something sculpted with a meticulous hand.

Shade didn't hesitate. He focused her in his viewfinder, set the aperture, adjusted the angle no more than a fraction and waited. At the moment when she reached down for the hem of her T-shirt, he began to shoot.

She was so easy, so unaffected. He'd forgotten anyone could be so totally unselfconscious in a world where self-absorption had become a religion. Her body was one long lean line, with more and more exposed as she drew the shirt over her head. For a moment, she tilted her face up to the sun, inviting the heat. Something crawled into his stomach and began to twist, slowly.

Desire. He recognized it. He didn't care for it.

It was, he could tell himself, what was known in the trade as a decisive moment. The photographer thinks, then shoots, while watching the unfolding scene. When the visual and the emotional elements come together—as they had in this case, with a punch—there was success. There were no replays here, no reshooting. Decisive moment meant exactly that, all or nothing. If he'd been shaken for an instant, it only proved he'd been successful in capturing that easy, lazy sexuality.

Years before, he'd trained himself not to become overly emotional about his subjects. They could eat you alive. Bryan Mitchell might not look as though she'd take a bite out of a man, but Shade didn't take chances. He turned away from her and forgot her. Almost.

It was more than four hours later before their paths crossed again. Bryan sat in the sun near a concession stand, eating a hot dog buried under mounds of mustard and relish. On one side of her she'd set her camera bag, on the other a can of soda. Her narrow red sunglasses shot his reflection back at him.

"How'd it go?" she asked with her mouth full.

"All right. Is there a hot dog under that?"

"Mmm." She swallowed and gestured toward the stand. "Terrific."

"I'll pass." Reaching down, Shade picked up her warming soda and took a long pull. It was orange and sweet. "How the hell do you drink this stuff?"

"I need a lot of sugar. I got some shots I'm pretty pleased

with." She held out a hand for the can. "I want to make prints before we leave tomorrow."

"As long as you're ready at seven."

Bryan wrinkled her nose as she finished off her hot dog. She'd rather work until 7:00 A.M. than get up that early. One of the first things they'd have to iron out on the road was the difference in their biological schedules. She understood the beauty and power of a sunrise shot. She just happened to prefer the mystery and color of sunset.

"I'll be ready." Rising, she brushed sand off her bottom, then pulled her T-shirt over her suit. Shade could've told her she was more modest without it. The way the hem skimmed along her thighs and drew the eyes to them was nearly criminal. "As long as you drive the first shift," she continued. "By ten I'll be functional."

He didn't know why he did it. Shade was a man who analyzed each movement, every texture, shape, color. He cut everything into patterns, then reassembled them. That was his way. Impulse wasn't. Yet he reached out and curled his fingers around her braid without thinking of the act or the consequences. He just wanted to touch.

She was surprised, he could see. But she didn't pull away. Nor did she give him that small half smile women used when a man couldn't resist touching what attracted him.

Her hair was soft; his eyes had told him that, but now his fingers confirmed it. Still, it was frustrating not to feel it loose and free, not to be able to let it play between his fingers.

He didn't understand her. Yet. She made her living recording the elite, the glamorous, the ostentatious, yet she seemed to have no pretensions. Her only jewelry was a thin gold chain that fell to her breasts. On the end was a tiny ankh. Again, she wore no makeup, but her scent was there to tantalize. She could, with a few basic female touches, have turned herself into something breathtaking, but she seemed to ignore the possibilities and rely on simplicity. That in itself was stunning.

Hours before, Bryan had decided she didn't want to be dazzled. Shade was deciding at that moment that he didn't care to be stunned. Without a word, he let her braid fall back to her shoulder.

"Do you want me to take you back to your apartment or your studio?"

So that was it? He'd managed to tie her up in knots in a matter of seconds, and now he only wanted to know where to dump her off. "The studio." Bryan reached down and picked up her camera bag. Her throat was dry, but she tossed the half-full can of soda into the trash. She wasn't certain she could swallow. Before they'd reached Shade's car, she was certain she'd explode if she didn't say something.

"Do you enjoy that cool, remote image you've perfected, Shade?"

He didn't look at her, but he nearly smiled. "It's comfortable."

"Except for the people who get within five feet of you." Damned if she wouldn't get a rise out of him. "Maybe you take your own press too seriously," she suggested. "Shade Colby, as mysterious and intriguing as his name, as dangerous and as compelling as his photographs."

This time he did smile, surprising her. Abruptly he looked like someone she'd want to link hands with, laugh with. "Where in hell did you read that?"

"*Celebrity*," she muttered. "April, five years ago. They

did an article on the photo sales in New York. One of your prints sold for seventy-five hundred at Sotheby's."

"Did it?" His gaze slid over her profile. "You've a better memory than I."

Stopping, she turned to face him. "Damn it, I bought it. It's a moody, depressing, fascinating street scene that I wouldn't have given ten cents for if I'd met you first. And if I wasn't so hooked on it, I'd pitch it out the minute I get home. As it is, I'll probably have to turn it to face the wall for six months until I forget that the artist behind it is a jerk."

Shade watched her soberly, then nodded. "You make quite a speech once you're rolling."

With one short, rude word, Bryan turned and started toward the car again. As she reached the passenger side and yanked open the door, Shade stopped her. "Since we're essentially going to be living together for the next three months, you might want to get the rest of it out now."

Though she tried to speak casually, it came out between her teeth. "The rest of what?"

"Whatever griping you have to do."

She took a deep breath first. She hated to be angry. Invariably it exhausted her. Resigned to it, Bryan curled her hands around the top of the door and leaned toward him. "I don't like you. I'd say it's just that simple, but I can't think of anyone else I don't like."

"No one?"

"No one."

For some reason, he believed her. He nodded, then dropped his hands over hers on top of the door. "I'd rather not be lumped in a group in any case. Why should we have to like each other?"

"It'd make the assignment easier."

He considered this while holding her hands beneath his. The tops of hers were soft, the palms of his hard. He liked the contrast, perhaps too much. "You like things easy?"

He made it sound like an insult, and she straightened. Her eyes were on a level with his mouth, and she shifted slightly. "Yes. Complications are just that. They get in the way and muck things up. I'd rather shovel them aside and deal with what's important."

"We've had a major complication before we started."

She might've concentrated on keeping her eyes on his, but that didn't prevent her from feeling the light, firm pressure of his hands. It didn't prevent her from understanding his meaning. Since it was something they'd meticulously avoided mentioning from the beginning, Bryan lunged at it, straight on.

"You're a man and I'm a woman."

He couldn't help but enjoy the way she snarled it at him. "Exactly. We can say we're both photographers and that's a sexless term." He gave her the barest hint of a smile. "It's also bullshit."

"That may be," she said evenly. "But I intend to handle it, because the assignment comes first. It helps a great deal that I don't like you."

"Liking doesn't have anything to do with chemistry."

She gave him an easy smile because her pulse was beginning to pound. "Is that a polite word for lust?"

She wasn't one to dance around an issue once she'd opened it up. Fair enough, he decided. "Whatever you call it, it goes right back to your complication. We'd better take a good look at it, then shove it aside."

When his fingers tightened on hers, she dropped her gaze to them. She understood his meaning, but not his reason.

"Wondering what it would be like's going to distract both of us," Shade continued. She looked up again, wary. He could feel her pulse throb where his fingers brushed her wrist, yet she'd made no move to pull back. If she had... There was no use speculating; it was better to move ahead. "We'll find out. Then we'll file it, forget it and get on with our job."

It sounded logical. Bryan had a basic distrust of anything that sounded quite so logical. Still, he'd been right on target when he'd said that wondering would be distracting. She'd been wondering for days. His mouth seemed to be the softest thing about him, yet even that looked hard, firm and unyielding. How would it feel? How would it taste?

She let her gaze wander back to it, and the lips curved. She wasn't certain if it was amusement or sarcasm, but it made up her mind.

"All right." How intimate could a kiss be when a car door separated them?

They leaned toward each other slowly, as if each waited for the other to draw back at the last moment. Their lips met lightly, passionlessly. It could've ended then, with each of them shrugging the other off in disinterest. It was the basic definition of a kiss. Two pairs of lips meeting. Nothing more.

Neither one would be able to say who changed it, whether it was calculated or accidental. They were both curious people, and curiosity might have been the factor. Or it might have been inevitable. The texture of the kiss changed so slowly that it wasn't possible to stop it until it was too late for regrets.

Lips opened, invited, accepted. Their fingers clung. His head tilted, and hers, so that the kiss deepened. Bryan found herself pressing against the hard, unyielding door, searching for more, demanding it, as her teeth nipped at his bottom lip. She'd been right. His mouth was the softest thing about him. Impossibly soft, unreasonably luxurious as it heated on hers.

She wasn't used to wild swings of mood. She'd never experienced anything like it. It wasn't possible to lie back and enjoy. Wasn't that what kisses were for? Up to now, she'd believed so. This one demanded all her strength, all her energy. Even as it went on, she knew when it ended she'd be drained. Wonderfully, totally drained. While she reveled in the excitement, she could anticipate the glory of the aftermath.

He should've known. Damn it, he should've known she wasn't as easy and uncomplicated as she looked. Hadn't he looked at her and ached? Tasting her wasn't going to alleviate any of it, only heighten it. She could undermine his control, and control was essential to his art, his life, his sanity. He'd developed and perfected it over years of sweat, fear and expectations. Shade had learned that the same calculated control he used in the darkroom, the same careful logic he used to set up a shot, could be applied to a woman successfully. Painlessly. One taste of Bryan and he realized just how tenuous control could be.

To prove to himself, perhaps to her, that he could deal with it, he allowed the kiss to deepen, grow darker, moister. Danger hovered, and perhaps he courted it.

He might lose himself in the kiss, but when it was over, it would be over, and nothing would be changed.

She tasted hot, sweet, strong. She made him burn. He had to hold back, or the burn would leave a scar. He had enough of them. Life wasn't as lovely as a first kiss on a hot afternoon. He knew better than most.

Shade drew away, satisfying himself that his control was still in place. Perhaps his pulse wasn't steady, his mind not perfectly clear, but he had control.

Bryan was reeling. If he'd asked her a question, any question, she'd have had no answer. Bracing herself against the car door, she waited for her equilibrium to return. She'd known the kiss would drain her. Even now, she could feel her energy flag.

He saw the look in her eyes, the soft look any man would have to struggle to resist. Shade turned away from it. "I'll drop you at the studio."

As he walked around the car to his side, Bryan dropped down on the seat. File it and forget it, she thought. Fat chance.

She tried. Bryan put so much effort into forgetting what Shade had made her feel that she worked until 3:00 a.m. By the time she'd dragged herself back to her apartment, she'd developed the film from the school and the beach, chosen the negatives she wanted to print and perfected two of them into what she considered some of her best work.

Now she had four hours to eat, pack and sleep. After building herself an enormous sandwich, Bryan took out the one suitcase she'd been allotted for the trip and tossed in the essentials. Groggy with fatigue, she washed down bread, meat and cheese with a great gulp of milk. None of it felt too steady on her stomach, so she left her partially eaten dinner on the bedside table and went back to her packing.

She rummaged in the top of her closet for the box with the prim man-tailored pajamas her mother had given her for Christmas. Definitely essential, she decided as she dropped them on the disordered pile of lingerie and jeans. They were sexless, Bryan mused. She could only hope she felt sexless in them. That afternoon she'd been forcibly reminded that she was a woman, and a woman had some vulnerabilities that couldn't always be defended.

She didn't want to feel like a woman around Shade again. It was too perilous, and she avoided perilous situations. Since she wasn't the type to make a point of her femininity, there should be no problem.

She told herself.

Once they were started on the assignment, they'd be so wound up in it that they wouldn't notice if the other had two heads and four thumbs.

She told herself.

What had happened that afternoon was simply one of those fleeting moments the photographer sometimes came across when the moment dictated the scene. It wouldn't happen again, because the circumstances would never be the same.

She told herself.

And then she was finished thinking of Shade Colby. It was nearly four, and the next three hours were all hers, the last she had left to herself for a long time. She'd spend them the way she liked best. Asleep. Stripping, Bryan let her clothes fall in a heap, then crawled into bed without remembering to turn off the light.

Across town, Shade lay in the dark. He hadn't slept, although he'd been packed for hours. His bag and his equipment were neatly stacked at the door. He was organized, prepared and wide-awake.

He'd lost sleep before. The fact didn't concern him, but

the reason did. Bryan Mitchell. Though he'd managed to push her to the side, to the back, to the corner of his mind throughout the evening, he couldn't quite get her out.

He could dissect what had happened between them that afternoon point by point, but it didn't change one essential thing. He'd been vulnerable. Perhaps only for an instant, only a heartbeat, but he'd been vulnerable. That was something he couldn't afford. It was something he wouldn't allow to happen a second time.

Bryan Mitchell was one of the complications she claimed she liked to avoid. He, on the other hand, was used to them. He'd never had any problem dealing with complications. She'd be no different.

He told himself.

For the next three months, they'd be deep into a project that should totally involve all their time and energy. When he worked, he was well able to channel his concentration on one point and ignore everything else. That was no problem.

He told himself.

What had happened had happened. He still believed it was best done away with before they started out—best that they did away with the speculation and the tension it could cause. They'd eliminated the tension.

He told himself.

But he couldn't sleep. The ache in his stomach had nothing to do with the dinner that had grown cold on his plate, untouched.

He had three hours to himself, then he'd have three months of Bryan. Closing his eyes, Shade did what he was always capable of doing under stress. He willed himself to sleep.

Chapter 3

Bryan was up and dressed by seven, but she wasn't ready to talk to anyone. She had her suitcase and tripod in one hand, with two camera bags and her purse slung crosswise over her shoulders. As Shade pulled up to the curb, she was walking down the stairs and onto the sidewalk. She believed in being prompt, but not necessarily cheerful.

She grunted to Shade; it was as close to a greeting as she could manage at that hour. In silence, she loaded her gear into his van, then kicked back in the passenger seat, stretched out her legs and closed her eyes.

Shade looked at what he could see of her face behind round, amber-lensed sunglasses and under a battered straw hat. "Rough night?" he asked, but she was already asleep. Shaking his head, he released the brake and pulled out into the street. They were on their way.

Shade didn't mind long drives. They gave him a chance to think or not think, as he chose. In less than an hour, he was out of L.A. traffic and heading northeast on the interstate. He liked riding into the rising sun with a clear road ahead. Light bounced off the chrome on the van, shimmered on the hood and sliced down on the road signs.

He planned to cover five or six hundred miles that day, leading up toward Utah, unless something interesting caught his eye and they stopped for a shoot. After this first day, he saw no reason for them to be mileage-crazy. It would hamper the point of the assignment. They'd drive as they needed to, working toward and around the definite destinations they'd ultimately agreed on.

He had a route that could easily be altered, and no itinerary. Their only time frame was to be on the East Coast by Labor Day. He turned the radio on low and found some gritty country music as he drove at a steady, mile-eating pace. Beside him, Bryan slept.

If this was her routine, he mused, they wouldn't have any problems. As long as she was asleep, they couldn't grate on each other's nerves. Or stir each other's passion. Even now he wondered why thoughts of her had kept him restless throughout the night. What was it about her that had worried him? He didn't know, and that was a worry in itself.

Shade liked to be able to put his finger on things and pick a problem apart until the pieces were small enough to rearrange to his preference. Even though she was quiet, almost unobtrusive, at the moment, he didn't believe he'd be able to do that with Bryan Mitchell.

After his decision to take the assignment, he'd made it his business to find out more about her. Shade might guard his personal life and snarl over his privacy, but he wasn't at a loss for contacts. He'd known of her work for *Celebrity*, and her more inventive and personalized work for magazines like *Vanity* and *In Touch*. She'd developed into something of a cult artist over the years with her off-beat, often radical photographs of the famous.

What he hadn't known was that she was the daughter of a painter and a poet, both eccentric and semisuccessful residents of Carmel. She'd been married to an accountant before she was twenty, and divorced him three years later. She dated with an almost studied casualness, and she had vague plans about buying a beach house at Malibu. She was well liked, respected and, by all accounts, depend-able. She was often slow in doing things—a combination of her need for perfection and her belief that rushing was a waste of energy.

He'd found nothing surprising in his research, and no clue as to his attraction to her. But a photographer, a suc-cessful one, was patient. Sometimes it was necessary to come back to a subject again and again until you under-stood your own emotion toward it.

As they crossed the border into Nevada, Shade lit a cig-arette and rolled down his window. Bryan stirred, grum-bled, then groped for her bag.

"Morning." Shade sent her a brief, sidelong look.

"Mmm-hmm." Bryan rooted through the bag, then gripped the chocolate bar in relief. With two quick rips, she unwrapped it and tossed the trash in her purse. She usually cleaned it out before it overflowed.

"You always eat candy for breakfast?"

"Caffeine." She took a huge bite and sighed. "I prefer mine this way." Slowly, she stretched, torso, shoulders, arms, in one long, sinuous move that was completely un-planned. It was, Shade thought ironically, one definitive clue as to the attraction. "So where are we?"

"Nevada." He blew out a stream of smoke that whipped out the open window. "Just."

Bryan folded her legs under her as she nibbled on the candy bar. "It must be about my shift."

"I'll let you know."

"Okay." She was content to ride as long as he was content to drive. She did, however, give a meaningful glance at the radio. Country music wasn't her style. "Driver picks the tunes."

He shrugged his acceptance. "If you want to wash that candy down with something, there's some juice in a jug in the back."

"Yeah?" Always interested in putting something into her stomach, Bryan unfolded herself and worked her way into the back of the van.

She hadn't paid any attention to the van that morning, except for a bleary scan that told her it was black and well cared-for. There were padded benches along each side that could, if you weren't too choosy, be suitable for beds. Bryan thought the pewter carpet might be the better choice.

Shade's equipment was neatly secured, and hers was loaded haphazardly into a corner. Above, glossy ebony cabinets held some essentials. Coffee, a hot plate, a small teakettle. They'd come in handy, she thought, if they stopped in any campgrounds with electric hookups. In the meantime, she settled for the insulated jug of juice.

"Want some?"

He glanced in the rearview mirror to see her standing, legs spread for balance, one hand resting on the cabinet. "Yeah."

Bryan took two jumbo plastic cups and the jug back to her seat. "All the comforts of home," she commented with a jerk of her head toward the back. "Do you travel in this much?"

"When it's necessary." He heard the ice thump against the cup and held out his hand. "I don't like to fly. You lose any chance you'd have at getting a shot at something on the way." After flipping his cigarette out the window, he drank his juice. "If it's an assignment within five hundred miles or so, I drive."

"I hate to fly." Bryan propped herself in the V between the seat and the door. "It seems I'm forever having to fly to New York to photograph someone who can't or won't come to me. I take a bottle of Dramamine, a supply of chocolate bars, a rabbit's foot and a socially significant, educational book. It covers all the bases."

"The Dramamine and the rabbit's foot, maybe."

"The chocolate's for my nerves. I like to eat when I'm tense. The book's a bargaining point." She shook her cup so the ice clinked. "I feel like I'm saying—see, I'm doing something worthwhile here. Let's not mess it up by crashing the plane. Then, too, the book usually puts me to sleep within twenty minutes."

The corner of Shade's mouth lifted, something Bryan took as a hopeful sign for the several thousand miles they had to go. "That explains it."

"I have a phobia about flying at thirty thousand feet in a heavy tube of metal with two hundred strangers, many of whom like to tell the intimate details of their lives to the person next to them." Propping her feet on the dash, she grinned. "I'd rather drive across country with one cranky photographer who makes it a point to tell me as little as possible."

Shade sent her a sidelong look and decided there was

no harm in playing the game as long as they both knew the rules. "You haven't asked me anything."

"Okay, we'll start with something basic. Where'd Shade come from? The name, I mean."

He slowed down, veering off toward a rest stop. "Shadrach."

Her eyes widened in appreciation. "As in Meshach and Abednego in the Book of Daniel?"

"That's right. My mother decided to give each of her offspring a name that would roll around a bit. I've a sister named Cassiopeia. Why Bryan?"

"My parents wanted to show they weren't sexist."

The minute the van stopped in a parking space, Bryan hopped out, bent from the waist and touched her palms to the asphalt—much to the interest of the man climbing into the Pontiac next to her. With the view fuddling his concentration, it took him a full thirty seconds to fit his key in the ignition.

"God, I get so stiff!" She stretched up, standing on her toes, then dropped down again. "Look, there's a snack bar over there. I'm going to get some fries. Want some?"

"It's ten o'clock in the morning."

"Almost ten-thirty," she corrected. "Besides, people eat hash browns for breakfast. What's the difference?"

He was certain there was one, but didn't feel like a debate. "You go ahead. I want to buy a paper."

"Fine." As an afterthought, Bryan climbed back inside and grabbed her camera. "I'll meet you back here in ten minutes."

Her intentions were good, but she took nearly twenty. Even as she approached the snack bar, the formation of the line of people waiting for fast food caught her imagination.

There were perhaps ten people wound out like a snake in front of a sign that read Eat Qwik.

They were dressed in baggy Bermudas, wrinkled sundresses and cotton pants. A curvy teenager had on a pair of leather shorts that looked as though they'd been painted on. A woman six back from the stand fanned herself with a wide-brimmed hat banded with a floaty ribbon.

They were all going somewhere, all waiting to get there, and none of them paid any attention to anyone else. Bryan couldn't resist. She walked up the line one way, down it another, until she found her angle.

She shot them from the back so that the line seemed elongated and disjointed and the sign loomed promisingly. The man behind the counter serving food was nothing more than a vague shadow that might or might not have been there. She'd taken more than her allotted ten minutes before she joined the line herself.

Shade was leaning against the van reading the paper when she returned. He'd already taken three calculated shots of the parking lot, focusing on a line of cars with license plates from five different states. When he glanced up, Bryan had her camera slung over her shoulder, a giant chocolate shake in one hand and a jumbo order of fries smothered in ketchup in the other.

"Sorry." She dipped into the box of fries as she walked. "I got a couple of good shots of the line at the snack bar. Half of summer's hurry up and wait, isn't it?"

"Can you drive with all that?"

"Sure." She swung into the driver's side. "I'm used to it." She balanced the shake between her thighs, settled the fries just ahead of it and reached out a hand for the keys.

Shade glanced down at the breakfast snuggled between very smooth, very brown legs. "Still willing to share?"

Bryan turned her head to check the rearview as she backed out. "Nope." She gave the wheel a quick turn and headed toward the exit. "You had your chance." With one competent hand steering, she dug into the fries again.

"You eat like that, you should have acne down to your navel."

"Myths," she announced, and zoomed past a slower-moving sedan. With a few quick adjustments, she had an old Simon and Garfunkel tune pouring out of the radio. "That's music," she told him. "I like songs that give me a visual. Country music's usually about hurting and cheating and drinking."

"And life."

Bryan picked up her shake and drew on the straw. "Maybe. I guess I get tired of too much reality. Your work depends on it."

"And yours often skirts around it."

Her brows knit, then she deliberately relaxed. In his way, he was right. "Mine gives options. Why'd you take this assignment, Shade?" she asked suddenly. "Summer in America exemplifies fun. That's not your style."

"It also equals sweat, crops dying from too much sun and frazzled nerves." He lit another cigarette. "More my style?"

"You said it, I didn't." She swirled the chocolate in her mouth. "You smoke like that, you're going to die."

"Sooner or later." Shade opened the paper again and ended the conversation.

Who the hell was he? Bryan asked herself as she leveled the speed at sixty. What factors in his life had brought out the cynicism as well as the genius? There was humor in him—she'd seen it once or twice. But he seemed to allow himself only a certain degree and no more.

Passion? She could attest firsthand that there was a powder keg inside him. What might set it off? If she was certain of one thing about Shade Colby, it was that he held himself in rigid control. The passion, the power, the fury—whatever label you gave it—escaped into his work, but not, she was certain, into his personal life. Not often, in any case.

She knew she should be careful and distant; it would be the smartest way to come out of this long-term assignment without scars. Yet she wanted to dig into his character, and she knew she'd have to give in to the temptation. She'd have to press the buttons and watch the results, probably because she didn't like him and was attracted to him at the same time.

She'd told him the truth when she'd said that she couldn't think of anyone else she didn't like. It went hand in hand with her approach to her art—she looked into a person and found qualities, not all of them admirable, not all of them likable, but something, always something, that she could understand. She needed to do that with Shade, for herself. And because, though she'd bide her time telling him, she wanted very badly to photograph him.

"Shade, I want to ask you something else."

He didn't glance up from the paper. "Hmm?"

"What's your favorite movie?"

Half annoyed at the interruption, half puzzled at the question, he looked up and found himself wondering yet again what her hair would look like out of that thick, untidy braid. "What?"

"Your favorite movie," she repeated. "I need a clue, a starting point."

"For what?"

"To find out why I find you interesting, attractive and unlikable."

"You're an odd woman, Bryan."

"No, not really, though I have every right to be." She stopped speaking a moment as she switched lanes. "Come on, Shade, it's going to be a long trip. Let's humor each other on the small points. Give me a movie."

"*To Have and Have Not.*"

"Bogart and Bacall's first together." It made her smile at him in the way he'd already decided was dangerous. "Good. If you'd named some obscure French film, I'd have had to find something else. Why that one?"

He set the paper aside. So she wanted to play games. It was harmless, he decided. And they still had a long day ahead of them. "On-screen chemistry, tight plotting and camera work that made Bogart look like the consummate hero and Bacall the only woman who could stand up to him."

She nodded, pleased. He wasn't above enjoying heroes, fantasies and bubbling relationships. It might've been a small point, but she could like him for it. "Movies fascinate me, and the people who make them. I suppose that was one of the reasons I jumped at the chance to work for *Celebrity*. I've lost count of the number of actors I've shot, but when I see them up on the screen, I'm still fascinated."

He knew it was dangerous to ask questions, not because of the answers, but because of the questions you'd be asked in return. Still, he wanted to know. "Is that why you photograph the beautiful people? Because you want to get close to the glamour?"

Because she considered it a fair question, Bryan decided not to be annoyed. Besides, it made her think about something that had simply seemed to evolve, almost unplanned. "I might've started out with something like that in mind. Before long, you come to see them as ordinary people with extraordinary jobs. I like finding that spark that's made them the chosen few."

"Yet for the next three months you're going to be photographing the everyday. Why?"

"Because there's a spark in all of us. I'd like to find it in a farmer in Iowa, too."

So he had his answer. "You're an idealist, Bryan."

"Yes." She gave him a frankly interested look. "Should I be ashamed of it?"

He didn't like the way the calm, reasonable question affected him. He'd had ideals of his own once, and he knew how much it hurt to have them rudely taken away. "Not ashamed," he said after a moment. "Careful."

They drove for hours. In midafternoon, they switched positions and Bryan skimmed through Shade's discarded paper. By mutual consent, they left the freeway and began to travel over back roads. The pattern became sporadic conversations and long silences. It was early evening when they crossed the border into Idaho.

"Skiing and potatoes," Bryan commented. "That's all I can think of when I think of Idaho." With a shiver, she rolled up her window. Summer came slower in the north, especially when the sun was low. She gazed out the glass at the deepening twilight.

Sheep, hundreds of them, in what seemed like miles of

gray or white bundles, were grazing lazily on the tough grass that bordered the road. She was a woman of the city, of freeways and office buildings. It might've surprised Shade to know she'd never been this far north, nor this far east except by plane.

The acres of placid sheep fascinated her. She was reaching for her camera when Shade swore and hit the brakes. Bryan landed on the floor with a plop.

"What was that for?"

He saw at a glance that she wasn't hurt, not even annoyed, but simply curious. He didn't bother to apologize. "Damn sheep in the road."

Bryan hauled herself up and looked out the windshield. There were three of them lined unconcernedly across the road, nearly head to tail. One of them turned its head and glanced up at the van, then looked away again.

"They look like they're waiting for a bus," she decided, then grabbed Shade's wrist before he could lean on the horn. "No, wait a minute. I've never touched one."

Before Shade could comment, she was out of the van and walking toward them. One of them shied a few inches away as she approached, but for the most part, the sheep couldn't have cared less. Shade's annoyance began to fade as she leaned over and touched one. He thought another woman might look the same as she stroked a sable at a furrier. Pleased, tentative and oddly sexual. And the light was good. Taking his camera, he selected a filter.

"How do they feel?"

"Soft—not as soft as I'd thought. Alive. Nothing like a lamb's-wool coat." Still bent over, one hand on the sheep, Bryan looked up. It surprised her to be facing a camera. "What's that for?"

"Discovery." He'd already taken two shots, but he wanted more. "Discovery has a lot to do with summer. How do they smell?"

Intrigued, Bryan leaned closer to the sheep. He framed her when her face was all but buried in the wool. "Like sheep," she said with a laugh, and straightened. "Want to play with the sheep and I'll take your picture?"

"Maybe next time."

She looked as if she belonged there, on the long deserted road surrounded by stretches of empty land, and it puzzled him. He'd thought she set well in L.A., in the center of the glitz and illusions.

"Something wrong?" She knew he was thinking of her, only of her, when he looked at her like that. She wished she could've taken it a step further, yet was oddly relieved that she couldn't.

"You acclimate well."

Her smile was hesitant. "It's simpler that way. I told you I don't like complications."

He turned back to the truck, deciding he was thinking about her too much. "Let's see if we can get these sheep to move."

"But, Shade, you can't just leave them on the side of the road." She jogged back to the van. "They'll wander right back out. They might get run over."

He gave her a look that said he clearly wasn't interested. "What do you expect me to do? Round 'em up?"

"The least we can do is get them back over the fence." As if he'd agreed wholeheartedly, Bryan turned around and started back to the sheep. As he watched, she reached down, hauled one up and nearly toppled over. The other two bleated and scattered.

"Heavier than they look," she managed, and began to stagger toward the fence strung along the shoulder of the road while the sheep she carried bleated, kicked and struggled. It wasn't easy, but after a test of wills and brute strength, she dropped the sheep over the fence. With one hand, she swiped at the sweat on her forehead as she turned to scowl at Shade. "Well, are you going to help or not?"

He'd enjoyed the show, but he didn't smile as he leaned against the van. "They'll probably find the hole in the fence again and be back on the road in ten minutes."

"Maybe they will," Bryan said between her teeth as she headed for the second sheep. "But I'll have done what should be done."

"Idealist," he said again.

With her hands on her hips, she whirled around. "Cynic."

"As long as we understand each other." Shade straightened. "I'll give you a hand."

The others weren't as easily duped as the first. It took Shade several exhausting minutes to catch number two, with Bryan running herd. Twice he lost his concentration and his quarry because her sudden husky laughter distracted him.

"Two down and one to go," he announced as he set the sheep free in pasture.

"But this one looks stubborn." From opposite sides of the road, the rescuers and the rescuee studied each other. "Shifty eyes," Bryan murmured. "I think he's the leader."

"She."

"Whatever. Look, just be nonchalant. You walk around that side, I'll walk around this side. When we have her in the middle, wham!"

Shade sent her a cautious look. "Wham?"

"Just follow my lead." Tucking her thumbs in her back pockets, she strolled across the road, whistling.

"Bryan, you're trying to outthink a sheep."

She sent him a bland look over her shoulder. "Maybe between the two of us we can manage to."

He wasn't at all sure she was joking. His first urge was to simply get back in the van and wait until she'd finished making a fool of herself. Then again, they'd already wasted enough time. Shade circled around to the left as Bryan moved to the right. The sheep eyed them both, swiveling her head from side to side.

"Now!" Bryan shouted, and dived.

Without giving himself the chance to consider the absurdity, Shade lunged from the other side. The sheep danced delicately away. Momentum carrying them both, Shade and Bryan collided, then rolled together onto the soft shoulder of the road. Shade felt the rush of air as they slammed into each other, and the soft give of her body as they tumbled together.

With the breath knocked out of her, Bryan lay on her back, half under Shade. His body was very hard and very male. She might not have had her wind, but Bryan had her wit. She knew if they stayed like this, things were going to get complicated. Drawing in air, she stared up into his face just above her.

His look was contemplative, considering and not altogether friendly. He wouldn't be a friendly lover, that she knew instinctively. It was in his eyes—those dark, deepset eyes. He was definitely a man to avoid having a personal involvement with. He'd overwhelm quickly, completely, and there'd be no turning back. She had to remind herself that she preferred easy relationships, as her heart started a strong, steady rhythm.

"Missed," she managed to say, but didn't try to move away.

"Yeah." She had a stunning face, all sharp angles and soft skin. Shade could nearly convince himself that his interest in it was purely professional. She'd photograph wonderfully from any angle, in any light. He could make her look like a queen or a peasant, but she'd always look like a woman a man would want. The lazy sexuality he could sense in her would come across in the photograph.

Just looking at her, he could plot half a dozen settings he'd like to shoot her in. And he could think of dozens of ways he'd like to make love to her. Here was first, on the cool grass along the roadside with the sun setting behind them and no sound.

She saw the decision in his eyes, saw it in time to avoid the outcome. But she didn't. She had only to shift away, only to protest with one word or a negative movement. But she didn't. Her mind told her to, arguing with an urge that was unarguably physical. Later, Bryan would wonder why she hadn't listened. Now, with the air growing cool and the sky darkening, she wanted the experience. She couldn't admit that she wanted him.

When he lowered his mouth to hers, there wasn't any of the light experimentation of the first time. Now he knew her and wanted the full impact of her passion. Their mouths met greedily, as if each one were racing the other to delirium.

Her body heated so quickly that the grass seemed to shimmer like ice beneath her. She wondered it didn't melt. It was a jolt that left her bewildered. With a small sound in her throat, Bryan reached for more. His fingers were in her hair, tangled in the restriction of her braid as if he didn't choose, or didn't dare, to touch her yet. She moved under him, not in retreat but in advance. Hold me, she seemed to demand. Give me more. But he continued to make love only to her mouth. Devastatingly.

She could hear the breeze; it tickled through the grass beside her ear and taunted her. He'd give sparingly of himself. She could feel it in the tenseness of his body. He'd hold back. While his mouth stripped away her defenses, one by one, he held himself apart. Frustrated, Bryan ran her hands up his back. She'd seduce.

Shade wasn't used to the pressure to give, to the desire to. She drew from him a need for merging he'd thought he'd beaten down years before. There seemed to be no pretenses in her—her mouth was warm and eager, tasting of generosity. Her body was soft and agile, tempting. Her scent drifted around him, sexual, uncomplicated. When she said his name, there seemed to be no hidden meaning. For the first time in too long for him to remember, he wanted to give, unheedingly, boundlessly.

He held himself back. Pretenses, he knew, could be well hidden. But he was losing to her. Even though Shade was fully aware of it, he couldn't stop it. She drew and drew from him, with a simplicity that couldn't be blocked. He might've sworn against it, cursed her, cursed himself, but his mind was beginning to swim. His body was throbbing.

They both felt the ground tremble, but it didn't occur to either of them that it was anything but their own passion. They heard the noise, the rumble, growing louder and louder, and each thought it was inside his or her own head. Then the wind rocketed by them and the truck driver gave one long, rude blast of the horn. It was enough to jolt them back to sanity. Feeling real panic for the first time, Bryan scrambled to her feet.

"We'd better take care of that sheep and get going." She swore at the breathiness of her own voice and wrapped her arms protectively around herself. There was a chill in the air, she thought desperately. That was all. "It's nearly dark."

Shade hadn't realized how deep the twilight had become. He'd lost track of his surroundings—something he never allowed to happen. He'd forgotten that they were on the side of the road, rolling in the grass like a couple of brainless teenagers. He felt the lick of anger, but stemmed it. He'd nearly lost control once. He wouldn't lose it now.

She caught the sheep on the other side of the road, where it grazed, certain that both humans had lost interest. It bleated in surprised protest as she scooped it up. Swearing under his breath, Shade stalked over and grabbed the sheep from her before Bryan could take another tumble. He dumped it unceremoniously in the pasture.

"Satisfied now?" he demanded.

She could see the anger in him, no matter how tightly he reined it in. Her own bubbled. She'd had her share of frustrations as well. Her body was pulsing, her legs were unsteady. Temper helped her to forget them.

"No," she tossed back. "And neither are you. It seems to me that should prove to both of us that we'd better keep a nice, clean distance."

He grabbed her arm as she started to swing past. "I didn't force you into anything, Bryan."

"Nor I you," she reminded him. "I'm responsible for my own actions, Shade." She glanced down at the hand that was curled around her arm. "And my own mistakes. If you like to shift blame, it's your prerogative."

His fingers tightened on her arm, briefly, but long enough for her eyes to widen in surprise at the strength and the depth of his anger. No, she wasn't used to wild swings of mood in herself or to causing them in others.

Slowly, and with obvious effort, Shade loosened his grip. She'd hit it right on the mark. He couldn't argue with honesty.

"No," he said a great deal more calmly. "I'll take my share, Bryan. It'll be easier on both of us if we agree to that nice, clean distance."

She nodded, steadier. Her lips curved into a slight smile. "Okay." Lighten up, she warned herself, for everyone's sake. "It'd have been easier from the beginning if you'd been fat and ugly."

He'd grinned before he'd realized it. "You too."

"Well, since I don't suppose either of us is willing to do anything about that particular problem, we just have to work around it. Agreed?" She held out her hand.

"Agreed."

Their hands joined. A mistake. Neither of them had recovered from the jolt to their systems. The contact, however casual, only served to accentuate it. Bryan linked her hands behind her back. Shade dipped his into his pockets.

"Well…" Bryan began, with no idea where to go.

"Let's find a diner before we head into camp. Tomorrow's going to start early."

She wrinkled her nose at that but started toward her side of the truck. "I'm starving," she announced, and pretended she was in control by propping her feet on the dash.

"Think we'll find something decent to eat soon, or should I fortify myself with a candy bar?"

"There's a town about ten miles down this road." Shade turned on the ignition. His hand was steady, he told himself. Or nearly. "Bound to be a restaurant of some kind. Probably serve great lamb chops."

Bryan looked at the sheep grazing beside them, then sent Shade a narrowed-eyed glance. "That's disgusting."

"Yeah, and it'll keep your mind off your stomach until we eat."

They bumped back onto the road and drove in silence. They'd made it over a hump, but each of them knew there'd be mountains yet to struggle over. Steep, rocky mountains.

Chapter 4

Bryan recorded vacationers floating like corks in the Great Salt Lake. When the shot called for it, she used a long or a wide-angle lens to bring in some unusual part of the landscape. But for the most part, Bryan concentrated on the people.

In the salt flats to the west, Shade framed race car enthusiasts. He angled for the speed, the dust, the grit. More often than not, the people included in his pictures would be anonymous, blurred, shadowy. He wanted only the essence.

Trips to large cities and through tidy suburbs used up rolls of film. There were summer gardens, hot, sweaty traffic jams, young girls in thin dresses, shirtless men, and babies in strollers being pushed along sidewalks and in shopping malls.

Their route through Idaho and Utah had been winding, but steady. Neither was displeased with the pace or the subjects. For a time, after the turbulent detour on the country road in Idaho, Bryan and Shade worked side by side in relative harmony. They concentrated on their own subjects, but they did little as a team.

They'd already taken hundreds of pictures, a fraction of which would be printed and still a smaller fraction published. Once it occurred to Bryan that the pictures they'd taken far outnumbered the words they'd spoken to each other.

They drove together up to eight hours a day, stopping along the way whenever it was necessary or desirable to work. And they worked as much as they drove. Out of each twenty-four hours, they were together an average of twenty. But they grew no closer. It was something either of them might have accomplished with the ease of a friendly gesture or a few casual words. It was something both of them avoided.

Bryan learned it was possible to keep an almost obsessive emotional distance from someone while sharing a limited space. She also learned a limited space made it very difficult to ignore what Shade had once termed chemistry. To balance the two, Bryan kept her conversations light and brief and almost exclusively centered on the assignment. She asked no more questions. Shade volunteered no more information.

By the time they crossed the border into Arizona, at the end of the first week, she was already finding it an uncomfortable way to work.

It was hot. The sun was merciless. The van's air-conditioning helped, but just looking out at the endless desert and faded sage made the mouth dry. Bryan had an enormous paper cup filled with soda and ice. Shade drank bottled iced tea as he drove.

She estimated that they hadn't exchanged a word for

fifty-seven miles. Nor had they spoken much that morning when they'd set up to shoot, each in separate territory, at Glen Canyon in Utah. Bryan might be pleased with the study she'd done of the cars lined up at the park's entrance, but she was growing weary of their unspoken agreement of segregation.

The magazine had hired them as a team, she reminded herself. Each of them would take individual pictures, naturally, but there had to be some communication if the photo essay were to have any cohesion. There had to be some blending if the final result was the success both of them wanted. Compromise, she remembered with a sigh. They'd forgotten the operative word.

Bryan thought she knew Shade well enough at this point to be certain he'd never make the first move. He was perfectly capable of driving thousands of miles around the country without saying her name more than once a day. As in, Pass the salt, Bryan.

She could be stubborn. Bryan thought about it as she brooded out the window at the wide stretches of Arizona. She could be just as aloof as he. And, she admitted with a grimace, she could bore herself to death within another twenty-four hours.

Contact, she decided. She simply couldn't survive without some kind of contact. Even if it was with a hard-edged, casually rude cynic. Her only choice was to swallow her pride and make the first move herself. She gritted her teeth, gnawed on ice and thought about it for another ten minutes.

"Ever been to Arizona?"

Shade tossed his empty bottle into the plastic can they used for trash. "No."

Bryan pried off one sneaker with the toe of the other. If

at first you don't succeed, she told herself. "They filmed *Outcast* in Sedona. Now that was a tough, thinking-man's Western," she mused, and received no response. "I spent three days there covering the filming for *Celebrity*." After adjusting her sun visor, she sat back again. "I was lucky enough to miss my plane and get another day. I spent it in Oak Creek Canyon. I've never forgotten it—the colors, the rock formations."

It was the longest speech she'd made in days. Shade negotiated the van around a curve and waited for the rest.

Okay, she thought, she'd get more than one word out of him if she had to use a crowbar. "A friend of mine settled there. Lee used to work for *Celebrity*. Now she's a novelist with her first book due out in the fall. She married Hunter Brown last year."

"The writer?"

Two words, she thought, smug. "Yes, have you read his stuff?"

This time Shade merely nodded and pulled a cigarette out of his pocket. Bryan began to sympathize with dentists who had to coax a patient to open wide.

"I've read everything he's written, then I hate myself for letting his books give me nightmares."

"Good horror fiction's supposed to make you wake up at 3:00 a.m. and wonder if you've locked your doors."

This time she grinned. "That sounds like something Hunter would say. You'll like him."

Shade merely moved his shoulders. He'd agreed to the stop in Sedona already, but he wasn't interested in taking flattering, commercial pictures of the occult king and his family. It would, however, give Shade the break he needed. If he could dump Bryan off for a day or two with her friends, he could take the time to get his system back to normal.

He hadn't had an easy moment since the day they'd started out of L.A. Every day that went by only tightened his nerves and played havoc with his libido. He'd tried, but it wasn't possible to forget she was there within arm's reach at night, separated from him only by the width of the van and the dark.

Yes, he could use a day away from her, and that natural, easy sexuality she didn't even seem aware of.

"You haven't seen them for a while?" he asked her.

"Not in months." Bryan relaxed, more at ease now that they'd actually begun a two-way conversation. "Lee's a good friend. I've missed her. She'll have a baby about the same time her book comes out."

The change in her voice had him glancing over. There was something softer about her now. Almost wistful.

"A year ago, we were both still with *Celebrity*, and now..." She turned to him, but the shaded glasses hid her eyes. "It's odd thinking of Lee settled down with a family. She was always more ambitious than me. It used to drive her crazy that I took everything with such a lack of intensity."

"Do you?"

"Just about everything," she murmured. Not you, she thought to herself. I don't seem to be able to take you easily. "It's simpler to relax and live," she went on, "than to worry about how you'll be living next month."

"Some people have to worry *if* they'll be living next month."

"Do you think the fact they worry about it changes things?" Bryan forgot her plan to make contact, forgot the fact that she'd been groping for some sort of compromise from him. He'd seen more than she'd seen of the world, of life. She had to admit that he'd seen more than she wanted to see. But how did he feel about it?

"Being aware can change things. Looking out for yourself's a priority some of us haven't a choice about."

Some of us. She noted the phrase but decided not to pounce on it. If he had scars, he was entitled to keep them covered until they'd faded a bit more.

"Everyone worries from time to time," she decided. "I'm just not very good at it. I suppose it comes from my parents. They're..." She trailed off and laughed. It occurred to him he hadn't heard her laugh in days, and that he'd missed it. "I guess they're what's termed bohemians. We lived in this little house in Carmel that was always in varying states of disrepair. My father would get a notion to take out a wall or put in a window, then in the middle of the project, he'd get an inspiration, go back to his canvases and leave the mess where it lay."

She settled back, no longer aware that she was doing all the talking and Shade all the listening. "My mother liked to cook. Trouble was, you'd never know what mood she'd be in. You might have grilled rattlesnake one day, cheeseburgers the next. Then, when you least expected it, there'd be gooseneck stew."

"Gooseneck stew?"

"I ate at the neighbors' a lot." The memory brought on her appetite. Taking out two candy bars, she offered one to Shade. "How about your parents?"

He unwrapped the candy absently while he paced his speed to the state police car in the next lane. "They retired to Florida. My father fishes and my mother runs a craft shop. Not as colorful as yours, I'm afraid."

"Colorful." She thought about it, and approved. "I never knew they were unusual until I'd gone away to college and realized that most kids' parents were grown-up and sensible. I guess I never realized how much I'd been influenced by them until Rob pointed out things like most people preferring to eat dinner at six, rather than scrounging for popcorn or peanut butter at ten o'clock at night."

"Rob?"

She glanced over quickly, then straight ahead. Shade listened too well, she decided. It made it too easy to say more than you intended. "My ex-husband." She knew she shouldn't still see the "ex" as a stigma; these days it was nearly a status symbol. For Bryan, it was the symbol that proved she hadn't done what was necessary to keep a promise.

"Still sore?" He'd asked before he could stop himself. She made him want to offer comfort, when he'd schooled himself not to become involved in anyone's life, anyone's problem.

"No, it was years ago." After a quick shrug, she nibbled on her candy bar. Sore? she thought again. No, not sore, but perhaps she'd always be just a little tender. "Just sorry it didn't work out, I suppose."

"Regrets are more a waste of time than worrying."

"Maybe. You were married once, too."

"That's right." His tone couldn't have been more dismissive. Bryan gave him a long, steady look.

"Sacred territory?"

"I don't believe in rehashing the past."

This wound was covered with scar tissue, she mused.

She wondered if it troubled him much, or if he'd truly filed it away. In either case, it wasn't her business, nor was it the way to keep the ball rolling between them.

"When did you decide to become a photographer?" That was a safe topic, she reflected. There shouldn't be any tender points.

"When I was five and got my hands on my father's new thirty-five-millimeter. When he had the film developed, he discovered three close-ups of the family dog. I'm told he didn't know whether to congratulate me or give me solitary confinement when they turned out to be better than any of his shots."

Bryan grinned. "What'd he do?"

"He bought me a camera of my own."

"You were way ahead of me," she commented. "I didn't have any interest in cameras until high school. Just sort of fell into it. Up until then, I'd wanted to be a star."

"An actress?"

"No." She grinned again. "A star. Any kind of a star, as long as I had a Rolls, a gold lamé dress and a big tacky diamond."

He had to grin. She seemed to have the talent for forcing it out of him. "An unassuming child."

"No, materialistic." She offered him her drink, but he shook his head. "That stage coincided with my parents' return-to-the-earth period. I guess it was my way of rebelling against people who were almost impossible to rebel against."

He glanced down at her ringless hands and her faded jeans. "Guess you got over it."

"I wasn't made to be a star. Anyway, they needed someone to take pictures of the football team." Bryan finished off the candy bar and wondered how soon they could stop for lunch. "I volunteered because I had a crush on one of the players." Draining her soda, she dumped the cup in with Shade's bottle. "After the first day, I fell in love with the camera and forgot all about the defensive lineman."

"His loss."

Bryan glanced over, surprised by the offhand compliment. "That was a nice thing to say, Colby. I didn't think you had it in you."

He didn't quite defeat the smile. "Don't get used to it."

"Heaven forbid." But she was a great deal more pleased than his casual words warranted. "Anyway, my parents were thrilled when I became an obsessive photographer. They'd lived with this deadly fear that I had no creative drives and would end up being a smashing business success instead of an artist."

"So now you're both."

She thought about it a moment. Odd how easy it was to forget about one aspect of her work when she concentrated so hard on the other. "I suppose you're right. Just don't mention it to Mom and Dad."

"They won't hear it from me."

They both saw the construction sign at the same time. Whether either of them realized it, their minds followed the same path. Bryan was already reaching for her camera when Shade slowed and eased off the road. Ahead of them, a road crew patched, graded and sweated under the high Arizona sun.

Shade walked off to consider the angle that would show the team and machinery battling against the erosion of the road. A battle that would be waged on roads across the country each summer as long as roads existed. Bryan homed in on one man.

He was bald and had a yellow bandanna tied around his head to protect the vulnerable dome of his scalp. His face and neck were reddened and damp, his belly sagging over the belt of his work pants. He wore a plain white T-shirt, pristine compared to the colorful ones slashed with sayings and pictures the workmen around him had chosen.

To get in close she had to talk to him and deal with the comments and grins from the rest of the crew. She did so with an aplomb and charm that would've caused a public relations expert to rub his hands together. Bryan was a firm believer that the relationship between the photographer and the subject showed through in the final print. So first, in her own way, she had to develop one.

Shade kept his distance. He saw the men as a team— the sunburned, faceless team that worked roads across the country and had done so for decades. He wanted no relationship with any of them, nothing that would color the way he saw them as they stood, bent and dug.

He took a telling shot of the grime, dust and sweat. Bryan learned that the foreman's name was Al and he'd worked for the road commission for twenty-two years.

It took her a while to ease her way around his self-consciousness, but once she got him talking about what the miserable winter had done to his road, everything clicked. Sweat dribbled down his temple. When he reached up with one beefy arm to swipe at it, Bryan had her picture.

The impulsive detour took them thirty minutes. By the time they piled back in the van, they were sweating as freely as the laborers.

"Are you always so personal with strangers?" Shade

asked her as he switched on the engine and the air-conditioning.

"When I want their picture, sure." Bryan opened the cooler and pulled out one of the cold cans she'd stocked, and another bottle of iced tea for Shade. "You get what you wanted?"

"Yeah."

He'd watched her at work. Normally they separated, but this time he'd been close enough to see just how she went about her job. She'd treated the road man with more respect and good humor than many photographers showed their hundred-dollar-an-hour models. And she hadn't done it just for the picture, though Shade wasn't sure she realized it. She'd been interested in the man—who he was, what he was and why.

Once, a long time before, Shade had had that kind of curiosity. Now he strapped it down. Knowing involved you. But it wasn't easy, he was discovering, to strap down his curiosity about Bryan. Already she'd told him more than he'd have asked. Not more than he wanted to know, but more than he'd have asked. It still wasn't enough.

For nearly a week he'd backed off from her—just as far as it was possible under the circumstances. He hadn't stopped wanting her. He might not like to rehash the past, but it wasn't possible to forget that last molten encounter on the roadside.

He'd closed himself off, but now she was opening him up again. He wondered if it was foolish to try to fight it, and the attraction they had for each other. It might be better, simpler, more logical, to just let things progress to the only possible conclusion.

They'd sleep together, burn the passion out and get back to the assignment.

Cold? Calculated? Perhaps, but he'd do nothing except follow the already routed course. He knew it was important to keep the emotions cool and the mind sharp.

He'd let his emotions fuddle his logic and his perception before. In Cambodia, a sweet face and a generous smile had blinded him to treachery. Shade's fingers tightened on the wheel without his realizing it. He'd learned a lesson about trust then—it was only the flip side of betrayal.

"Where've you gone?" Bryan asked quietly. A look had come into his eyes that she didn't understand, and wasn't certain she wanted to understand.

He turned his head. For an instant she was caught in the turmoil, in the dark place he remembered too well and she knew nothing about. Then it was over. His eyes were remote and calm. His fingers eased on the wheel.

"We'll stop in Page," he said briefly. "Get some shots of the boats and tourists on Lake Powell before we go down to the canyon."

"All right."

He hadn't been thinking of her. Bryan could comfort herself with that. She hoped the look that had come into his eyes would never be applied to her. Even so, she was determined that sooner or later she'd discover the reason for it.

She could've gotten some good technical shots of the dam. But as they passed through the tiny town of Page, heading for the lake, Bryan saw the high golden arches shimmering behind waves of heat. It made her grin. Cheeseburgers and fries weren't just summer pastimes. They'd become a way of life. Food for all seasons. But she couldn't resist the sight of the familiar building settled low below the town, almost isolated, like a mirage in the middle of the desert.

She rolled down her window and waited for the right angle. "Gotta eat," she said as she framed the building. "Just gotta." She clicked the shutter.

Resigned, Shade pulled into the lot. "Get it to go," he ordered as Bryan started to hop out. "I want to get to the marina."

Swinging her purse over her shoulder, she disappeared inside. Shade didn't have the chance to become impatient before she bounded back out again with two white bags. "Cheap, fast and wonderful," she told him as she slid back into her seat. "I don't know how I'd make it through life if I couldn't get a cheeseburger on demand."

She pulled out a wrapped burger and handed it to him.

"I got extra salt," she said over her first taste of fries. "Mmm, I'm starving."

"You wouldn't be if you'd eat something besides a candy bar for breakfast."

"I'd rather be awake when I eat," she mumbled, involved in unwrapping her burger.

Shade unwrapped his own. He hadn't asked her to bring him anything. He'd already learned it was typical of her to be carelessly considerate. Perhaps the better word was *naturally.* But it wasn't typical of him to be moved by the simple offer of a piece of meat in a bun. He reached in a bag and brought out a paper napkin. "You're going to need this."

Bryan grinned, took it, folded her legs under her and dug in. Amused, Shade drove leisurely to the marina.

They rented a boat, what Bryan termed a putt-putt. It

was narrow, open and about the size of a canoe. It would, however, carry them, and what equipment they chose, out on the lake.

She liked the little marina, with its food stands and general stores with displays of suntan oil and bathing suits. The season was in full swing; people strolled by dressed in shorts and cover-ups, in hats and sunglasses. She spotted a teenage couple, brown and gleaming, on a bench, licking at dripping ice-cream cones. Because they were so involved with each other, Bryan was able to take some candid shots before the paperwork on the rental was completed.

Ice cream and suntans. It was a simple, cheerful way to look at summer. Satisfied, she secured her camera in its bag and went back to Shade.

"Do you know how to drive a boat?"

He sent her a mild look as they walked down the dock. "I'll manage."

A woman in a neat white shirt and shorts gave them a rundown, pointing out the life jackets and explaining the engine before she handed them a glossy map of the lake. Bryan settled herself in the bow and prepared to enjoy herself.

"The nice thing about this," she called over the engine, "is it's so unexpected." She swept one arm out to indicate the wide expanse of blue.

Red-hued mesas and sheer rock walls rose up steeply to cradle the lake, settled placidly where man had put it. The combination was fascinating to her. Another time, she might've done a study on the harmony and power that could result in a working relationship between human imagination and nature.

It wasn't necessary to know all the technical details of

the dam, of the labor force that built it. It was enough that it was, that they were here—cutting through water that had once been desert, sending up a spray that had once been sand.

Shade spotted a tidy cabin cruiser and veered in its direction. For the moment, he'd navigate and leave the camera work to Bryan. It'd been a long time since he'd spent a hot afternoon on the water. His muscles began to relax even as his perception sharpened.

Before he was done, he'd have to take some pictures of the rocks. The texture in them was incredible, even in their reflection on the water. Their colors, slashed against the blue lake, made them look surreal. He'd make the prints sharp and crisp to accent the incongruity. He edged a bit closer to the cabin cruiser as he planned the shot for later.

Bryan took out her camera without any definite plan. She hoped there'd be a party of people, perhaps greased up against the sun. Children maybe, giddy with the wind and water. As Shade steered, she glanced toward the stern and lifted the camera quickly. It was too good to be true.

Poised at the stern of the cruiser was a hound—Bryan couldn't think of any other description for the floppy dog. His big ears were blowing back, and his tongue was lolling as he stared down at the water. Over his chestnut fur was a bright orange life vest.

"Go around again!" she yelled to Shade.

She waited impatiently for the angle to come to her again. There were people on the boat, at least five of them, but they no longer interested her. Just the dog, she thought, as she gnawed on her lip and waited. She wanted nothing but the dog in the life jacket leaning out and staring down at the water.

There were towering mesas just behind the boat. Bryan had to decide quickly whether to work them in or frame them out. If she'd had more time to think… She opted against the drama and settled on the fun. Shade had circled the trim little cruiser three times before she was satisfied.

"Wonderful!" With a laugh, Bryan lowered her camera. "That one print's going to be worth the whole trip."

He veered off to the right. "Why don't we see what else we can dig up, anyway?"

They worked for two hours, shifting positions after the first. Stripped to the waist as defense against the heat, Shade knelt at the bow and focused in on a tour boat. The rock wall rose in the background, the water shimmered cool and blue. Along the rail the people were no more than a blur of color. That's what he wanted. The anonymity of tours, and the power of what drew the masses to them.

While Shade worked, Bryan kept the speed low and looked at everything. She'd decided after one glimpse of his lean, tanned torso that it'd be wiser for her to concentrate on the scenery. If she hadn't, she might've missed the cove and the rock island that curved over it.

"Look." Without hesitating, she steered toward it, then cut the engines until the boat drifted in its own wake. "Come on, let's take a swim." Before he could comment, she'd hopped out in the ankle-deep water and was securing the lines with rocks.

Wearing a snug tank top and drawstring shorts, Bryan dashed down to the cove and sank in over her head. When she surfaced, laughing, Shade was standing on the island above her. "Fabulous," she called out. "Come on, Shade, we haven't taken an hour to play since we started."

She was right about that. He'd seen to it. Not that he

hadn't needed to relax, but he'd thought it best not to around her. He knew, even as he watched her smoothly treading in the rock-shadowed water, that it was a mistake. Yet he'd told himself it was logical to stop fighting what would happen between them. Following the logic, he walked down to the water.

"It's like opening a present," she decided, shifting onto her back to float briefly. "I had no idea I was being slowly boiled until I stepped in here." With a sigh, she dipped under the water and rose again so that it flowed from her face. "There was a pond a few miles away from home when I was a kid. I practically lived there in the summer."

The water was seductive, almost painfully so. As Shade lowered himself into it, he felt the heat drain, but not the tension. Sooner or later, he knew, he'd have to find an outlet for it.

"We did a lot better here than I expected to." Lazily she let the water play through her fingers. "I can't wait to get to Sedona and start developing." She tossed her dripping braid behind her back. "And sleep in a real bed."

"You don't seem to have any trouble sleeping." One of the first things he'd noticed was that she could fall asleep anywhere, anytime, and within seconds of shutting her eyes.

"Oh, it's not the sleeping, it's the waking up." And waking up only a few feet away from him, morning after morning—seeing his face shadowed by a night's growth of beard, dangerously attractive, seeing his muscles ripple as he stretched, dangerously strong. No, she couldn't deny that the accommodations occasionally gave her a few twinges.

"You know," she began casually, "the budget could handle a couple of motel rooms every week or so—nothing outrageous. A real mattress and a private shower, you know. Some of those campgrounds we've stopped in advertise hot water with their tongues in their cheeks."

He had to smile. It hadn't given him much pleasure to settle for tepid water after a long day on the road. But there was no reason to make it too easy on her. "Can't handle roughing it, Bryan?"

She stretched out on her back again, deliberately kicking water up and over him. "Oh, I don't mind roughing it," she said blandly. "I just like to do it on my own time. And I'm not ashamed to say I'd rather spend the weekend at the Beverly Wilshire than rubbing two sticks together in the wilderness." She closed her eyes and let her body drift. "Wouldn't you?"

"Yeah." With the admission, he reached out, grabbed her braid and tugged her head under.

The move surprised her, but it pleased her as well, even as she came up sputtering. So he was capable of a frivolous move from time to time. It was something else she could like him for.

"I'm an expert on water games," she warned him as she began to tread again.

"Water suits you." When had he relaxed? He couldn't pinpoint the moment when the tension began to ease from him. There was something about her—laziness? No, that wasn't true. She worked every bit as hard as he, though in her own fashion. *Easiness* was a better word, he decided. She was an easy woman, comfortable with herself and whatever surroundings she found herself in.

"It looks pretty good on you, too." Narrowing her eyes, Bryan focused on him—something she'd avoided for several days. If she didn't allow herself a clear look, it helped bank down on the feelings he brought out in her. Many of them weren't comfortable, and Shade had been right. She was a woman who liked to be comfortable. But now, with the water lapping cool around her and the only sound that of boats putting in the distance, she wanted to enjoy him.

His hair was damp and tangled around his face, which was as relaxed as she'd ever seen it. There didn't seem to be any secrets in his eyes just now. He was nearly too lean, but there were muscles in his forearms, in his back. She already knew just how strong his hands were. She smiled at him because she wasn't sure just how many quiet moments they'd share.

"You don't let up on yourself enough, Shade."

"No?"

"No. You know..." She floated again, because treading took too much effort. "I think deep down, really deep down, there's a nice person in you."

"No, there isn't."

But she heard the humor in his voice. "Oh, it's buried in there somewhere. If you let me do your portrait, I'd find it."

He liked the way she floated in the water; there was absolutely no energy expended. She lay there, trusting buoyancy. He was nearly certain that if she lay quietly for five minutes, she'd be asleep. "Would you?" he murmured. "I think we can both do without that."

She opened her eyes again, but had to squint against the sun to see him. It was at his back, glaring. "Maybe you can, but I've already decided to do it—once I know you better."

He circled her ankle with his finger, lightly. "You have to have my cooperation to do both."

"I'll get it." The contact was more potent than she could handle. She'd tensed before she could stop it. And so, she realized after a long ten seconds, had he. Casually, she let her legs drop. "The water's getting cold." She swam toward the boat with smooth strokes and a racing heart.

Shade waited a moment. No matter what direction he took with her, he always ended up in the same place. He wanted her, but wasn't certain he could handle the consequences of acting on that desire. Worse now, she was perilously close to becoming his friend. That wouldn't make things any easier on either of them.

Slowly, he swam out of the cove and toward the boat, but she wasn't there. Puzzled, he looked around and started to call, but then he saw her perched high on the rock.

She'd unbraided her hair and was brushing it dry in the sun. Her legs were folded under her, her face tilted up. The thin summer clothes she wore were drenched and clung to every curve. She obviously didn't care. It was the sun she sought, the heat, just as she'd sought the cool water only moments before.

Shade reached in his camera bag and attached his long lens. He wanted her to fill the viewfinder. He focused and framed her. For the second time, her careless sexuality gave him a staggering roundhouse punch. He was a professional, Shade reminded himself as he set the depth of field. He was shooting a subject, that was all.

But when she turned her head and her eyes met his through the lens, he felt the passion sizzle—from himself and from her. They held each other there a moment, separated, yet irrevocably joined. He took the picture, and as he did, Shade knew he was recording a great deal more than a subject.

A bit steadier, Bryan rose and worked her way down the curve of the rock. She had to remind herself to play it lightly—something that had always come easily to her. "You didn't get a release form, Colby," she reminded him as she dropped her brush into her oversize bag.

Reaching out, he touched her hair. It was damp, hanging rich and heavy to her waist. His fingers curled into it, his eyes locked on hers. "I want you."

She felt her legs liquefy, and heat started somewhere in the pit of her stomach and spread out to her fingertips. He was a hard man, Bryan reminded herself. He wouldn't give, but take. In the end, she'd need him to do both.

"That's not good enough for me," she said steadily. "People want all the time—a new car, a color TV. I have to have more than that."

She stepped around him and into the boat. Without a word, Shade joined her and they drifted away from the cove. As the boat picked up speed, both of them wondered if Shade could give any more than what he'd offered.

Chapter 5

Bryan had romanticized Oak Creek Canyon over the years since she'd been there. When she saw it again, she wasn't disappointed. It had all the rich strength, all the colors, she'd remembered.

Campers would be pocketed through it, she knew. They'd be worth some time and some film. Amateur and serious fishermen by the creek, she mused, with their intense expressions and colorful lures. Evening campfires with roasting marshmallows. Coffee in tin cups. Yes, it would be well worth the stop.

They planned to stay for three days, working, developing and printing. Bryan was itching to begin. But before they drove into town to handle the details, they'd agreed to stop in the canyon where Bryan could see Lee and her family.

"According to the directions, there should be a little dirt road leading off to the right just beyond a trading post."

Shade watched for it. He, too, was anxious to begin. Some of the shots he'd taken were pulling at him to bring them to life. He needed the concentration and quiet of a darkroom, the solitude of it. He needed to let his creativity flow, and hold in his hands the results.

The picture of Bryan sitting on the island of rock. He didn't like to dwell on that one, but he knew it would be the first roll he developed.

The important thing was that he'd have the time and the distance he'd promised himself. Once he dropped her at her friends'—and he was certain they'd want her to stay with them—he could go into Sedona, rent a darkroom and a motel room for himself. After living with her for twenty-four hours a day, he was counting on a few days apart to steady his system.

They'd each work on whatever they chose—the town, the canyon, the landscape. That gave him room. He'd work out a schedule for the darkroom. With luck, they wouldn't so much as see each other for the next three days.

"There it is," Bryan told him, though he'd already seen the narrow road and slowed for it. She looked at the steep, tree-lined road and shook her head. "God, I'd never have pictured Lee here. It's so wild and rough and she's…well, elegant."

He'd known a few elegant women in his life. He'd lived with one. Shade glanced at the terrain. "What's she doing here, then?"

"She fell in love," Bryan said simply, and leaned forward. "There's the house. Fabulous."

Glass and style. That's what she thought of it. It wasn't the distinguished town house she would have imagined for Lee, but Bryan could see how it would suit her friend. There were flowers blooming, bright red-orange blossoms she couldn't identify. The grass was thick, the trees leafy.

In the driveway were two vehicles, a dusty late-model Jeep and a shiny cream-colored sedan. As they pulled up behind the Jeep, a huge silver-gray form bounded around the side of the house. Shade swore in sheer astonishment.

"That must be Santanas." Bryan laughed, but gave the dog a wary once-over with her door firmly closed.

Fascinated, Shade watched the muscles bunch as the dog moved. But the tail was wagging, the tongue lolling. Some pet, he decided. "It looks like a wolf."

"Yeah." She continued to look out the window as the dog paced up and down the side of the van. "Lee tells me he's friendly."

"Fine. You go first."

Bryan shot him a look that he returned with a casual smile. Letting out a deep breath, Bryan opened the door. "Nice dog," she told him as she stepped out, keeping one hand on the handle of the door. "Nice Santanas."

"I read somewhere that Brown raised wolves," Shade said carelessly as he stepped out of the opposite side.

"Cute," Bryan mumbled, and cautiously offered her hand for the dog to sniff.

He did so, and obviously liked her, because he knocked her to the ground in one bounding leap. Shade was around the van before Bryan had a chance to draw a breath. Fear and fury had carried him, but whatever he might've done was stopped by the sound of a high whistle.

"Santanas!" A young girl darted around the house, braids flying. "Cut it out right now. You're not supposed to knock people down."

Caught in the act, the huge dog plopped down on his belly and somehow managed to look innocent. "He's sorry." The girl looked at the tense man looming over the dog and the breathless woman sprawled beside him. "He just gets excited when company comes. Are you Bryan?"

Bryan managed a nod as the dog dropped his head on her arm and looked up at her.

"It's a funny name. I thought you'd look funny too, but you don't. I'm Sarah."

"Hello, Sarah." Catching her wind, Bryan looked up at Shade. "This is Shade Colby."

"Is that a real name?" Sarah demanded.

"Yeah." Shade looked down as the girl frowned up at him. He wanted to scold her for not handling her dog, but found he couldn't. She had dark, serious eyes that made him want to crouch down and look into them from her level. A heartbreaker, he decided. Give her ten years, and she'll break them all.

"Sounds like something from one of my dad's books. I guess it's okay." She grinned down at Bryan and shuffled her sneakers in the dirt. Both she and her dog looked embarrassed. "I'm really sorry Santanas knocked you down. You're not hurt or anything, are you?"

Since it was the first time anyone had bothered to ask, Bryan thought about it. "No."

"Well, maybe you won't say anything to my dad." Sarah flashed a quick smile and showed her braces. "He gets mad when Santanas forgets his manners."

Santanas swiped an enormous pink tongue over Bryan's shoulder.

"No harm done," she decided.

"Great. We'll go tell them you're here." She was off in a bound. The dog clambered up and raced after her without giving Bryan a backward look.

"Well, it doesn't look like Lee's settled for a dull life," Bryan commented.

Shade reached down and hauled her to her feet. He'd been frightened, he realized. Seriously frightened for the first time in years, and all because a little girl's pet had knocked down his partner.

"You okay?"

"Yeah." With quick swipes, she began to brush the dirt off her jeans. Shade ran his hands up her arms, stopping her cold.

"Sure?"

"Yes, I…" She trailed off as her thoughts twisted into something incoherent. He wasn't supposed to look at her like that, she thought. As though he really cared. She wished he'd look at her like that again, and again. His fingers were barely touching her arms. She wished he'd touch her like that again. And again.

"I'm fine," she managed finally. But it was hardly more than a whisper, and her eyes never left his.

He kept his hands on her arms. "That dog had to weigh a hundred and twenty."

"He didn't mean any harm." Why, she wondered vaguely, were they talking about a dog, when there really wasn't anything important but him and her?

"I'm sorry." His thumb skimmed over the inside of her elbow, where the skin was as soft as he'd once imagined. Her pulse beat like an engine. "I should've gotten out first instead of playing around." If she'd been hurt… He wanted to kiss her now, right now, when he was thinking only of her and not the reasons that he shouldn't.

"It doesn't matter," she murmured, and found that her hands were resting on his shoulders. Their bodies were close, just brushing. Who had moved? "It doesn't matter," she said again, half to herself, as she leaned closer. Their lips hovered, hesitated, then barely touched. From the house came the deep, frantic sound of barking. They drew back from each other with something close to a jerk.

"Bryan!" Lee let the door slam behind her as she came onto the porch. It wasn't until she'd already called out that she noticed how intent the two people in her driveway were on each other.

With a quick shudder, Bryan took another step back before she turned. Too many feelings, was all she could think. Too many feelings, too quickly.

"Lee." She ran over, or ran away—she wasn't certain. All she knew was, at that moment she needed someone. Grateful, she felt herself closed in Lee's arms. "Oh, God, it's so good to see you."

The greeting was just a little desperate. Lee took a long look over Bryan's shoulder at the man who remained several paces back. Her first impression was that he wanted to stay that way. Separate. What had Bryan gotten herself into? she wondered, and gave her friend a fierce hug.

"I've got to look at you," Bryan insisted, laughing now as the tension drained. The elegant face, the carefully styled hair—they were the same. But the woman wasn't. Bryan could feel it before she glanced down to the rounded swell beneath Lee's crisp summer dress.

"You're happy." Bryan gripped Lee's hands. "It shows. No regrets?"

"No regrets." Lee took a long, hard study. Bryan looked the same, she decided. Healthy, easy, lovely in a way that seemed exclusively her own. The same, she thought, but for the slightest hint of trouble in her eyes. "And you?"

"Things are good. I've missed you, but I feel better about it after seeing you here."

With a laugh, Lee slipped her arm around Bryan's waist. If there was trouble, she'd find the source. Bryan was hopeless at hiding anything for long. "Come inside. Sarah and Hunter are making iced tea." She sent a significant look in Shade's direction and felt Bryan tense. Just a little, but Lee felt it and knew she'd already found the source.

Bryan cleared her throat. "Shade."

He moved forward, Lee thought, like a man who was used to testing the way.

"Lee Radcliffe—Lee Radcliffe Brown," Bryan corrected, and relaxed a bit. "Shade Colby. You remember when I spent the money I'd saved for a new car on one of his prints."

"Yes, I told you you were crazy." Lee extended her hand and smiled, but her voice was cool. "It's nice to meet you. Bryan's always admired your work."

"But you haven't," he returned, with more interest and respect than he'd intended to feel.

"I often find it harsh, but always compelling," Lee said simply. "Bryan's the expert, not me."

"Then she'd tell you that we don't take pictures for experts."

Lee nodded. His handshake had been firm—not gentle, but far from cruel. His eyes were precisely the same. She'd have to reserve judgment for now. "Come inside, Mr. Colby."

He'd intended to simply drop Bryan off and move along, but he found himself accepting. It wouldn't hurt, he rationalized, to cool off a bit before he drove into town. He followed the women inside.

"Dad, if you don't put more sugar in it, it tastes terrible."

As they walked into the kitchen, they saw Sarah with her hands on her hips, watching her father mop up around a pitcher of tea.

"Not everyone wants to pour sugar into their system the way you do."

"I do." Bryan grinned when Hunter turned. She thought his work brilliant—often cursing him for it in the middle of the night, when it kept her awake. She thought he looked like a man one of the Brontë sisters would have written about—strong, dark, brooding. But more, he was the man who loved her closest friend. Bryan opened her arms to him.

"It's good to see you again." Hunter held her close, chuckling when he felt her reach behind him to the plate of cookies Sarah had set out. "Why don't you gain weight?"

"I keep trying," Bryan claimed, and bit into the chocolate chip cookie. "Mmm, still warm. Hunter, this is Shade Colby."

Hunter put down his dishcloth. "I've followed your work," he told Shade as they shook hands. "It's powerful."

"That's the word I'd use to describe yours."

"Your latest had me too paranoid to go down to the basement laundry room for weeks," Bryan accused Hunter. "I nearly ran out of clothes."

Hunter grinned, pleased. "Thanks."

She glanced around the sunlit kitchen. "I guess I expected your house to have cobwebs and creaking boards."

"Disappointed?" Lee asked.

"Relieved."

With a laugh, Lee settled at the kitchen table with Sarah

on her left and Bryan across from her. "So how's the project going?"

"Good." But Lee noticed she didn't look at Shade as she spoke. "Maybe terrific. We'll know more once we develop the film. We've made arrangements with one of the local papers for the use of a darkroom. All we have to do is drive into Sedona, check in and get a couple of rooms. Tomorrow, we work."

"Rooms?" Lee set down the glass Hunter handed her. "But you're staying here."

"Lee." Bryan gave Hunter a quick smile as he offered the plate of cookies. "I wanted to see you, not drop in bag and baggage. I know both you and Hunter are working on new books. Shade and I'll be up to our ears in developing fluid."

"How are we supposed to visit if you're in Sedona?" Lee countered. "Damn it, Bryan, I've missed you. You're staying here." She laid a hand on her rounded stomach. "Pregnant women have to be pampered."

"You should stay," Shade put in before Bryan could comment. "It might be the last chance for quite a while for a little free time."

"We've a lot of work to do," Bryan reminded him.

"It's a short drive into town from here. That won't make any difference. We're going to need to rent a car, in any case, so we can both be mobile."

Hunter studied the man across the room. Tense, he thought. Intense. Not the sort of man he'd have picked for the free-rolling, slow-moving Bryan, but it wasn't his place to judge. It was his place, and his talent, to observe. What was between them was obvious to see. Their reluctance to accept it was just as obvious. Calmly, he picked up his tea and drank.

"The invitation applies to both of you."

Shade glanced over with an automatic polite refusal on the tip of his tongue. His eyes met Hunter's. They were both intense, internalized men. Perhaps that's why they understood each other so quickly.

I've been there before, Hunter seemed to say to him with a hint of a smile. *You can run fast but only so far.*

Shade sensed something of the understanding, and something of the challenge. He glanced down to see Bryan giving him a long, cool look.

"I'd love to stay," he heard himself say. Shade crossed to the table and sat.

Lee looked over the prints in her precise, deliberate way. Bryan paced up and down the terrace, ready to explode.

"Well?" she demanded. "What do you think?"

"I haven't finished looking through them yet."

Bryan opened her mouth, then shut it again. It wasn't like her to be nervous over her work. She knew the prints were good. Hadn't she put her sweat and her heart into each of them?

More than good, she told herself as she yanked a chocolate bar out of her pocket. These prints ranked with her best work. It might've been the competition with Shade that had pushed her to produce them. It might've been the need to feel a bit smug after some of the comments he'd made on her particular style of work. Bryan didn't like to think she was base enough to resort to petty rivalry, but she had to admit that now she was. And she wanted to win.

She and Shade had lived in the same house, worked in

the same darkroom for days, but had managed to see almost nothing of each other. A neat trick, Bryan thought ruefully. Perhaps it had worked so well because they'd both played the same game. Hide and don't seek. Tomorrow they'd be back on the road.

Bryan found that she was anxious to go even while she dreaded it. And she wasn't a contrary person, Bryan reminded herself almost fiercely. She was basically straightforward and...well, yes, she was amiable. It was simply her nature to be. So why wasn't she with Shade?

"Well."

Bryan whirled around as Lee spoke. "Well?" she echoed, waiting.

"I've always admired your work, Bryan. You know that." In her tidy way, Lee folded her hands on the wrought-iron table.

"But?" Bryan prompted.

"But these are the best." Lee smiled. "The very best you've ever done."

Bryan let out the breath she'd been holding and crossed to the table. Nerves? Yes, she had them. She didn't care for them. "Why?"

"I'm sure there're a lot of technical reasons—the light and the shading, the cropping."

Impatiently, Bryan shook her head. "Why?"

Understanding, Lee chose a print. "This one of the old woman and the little girl on the beach. Maybe it's my condition," she said slowly as she studied it again, "but it makes me think of the child I'll have. It also makes me remember I'll grow old, but not too old to dream. This picture's powerful because it's so basically simple, so straightforward and so incredibly full of emotion. And this one…"

She shuffled the prints until she came to the one of the road worker. "Sweat, determination, honesty. You know when you look at this face that the man believes in hard work and paying his bills on time. And here, these teen-agers. I see youth just before those inevitable changes of adulthood. And this dog." Lee laughed as she looked at it. "The first time I looked, it just struck me as cute and funny, but he looks so proud, so, well, human. You could almost believe the boat was his."

While Bryan remained silent, Lee tidied the prints again. "I could go over each one of them with you, but the point is, each one of them tells a story. It's only one scene, one instant of time, yet the story's there. The feelings are there. Isn't that the purpose?"

"Yes." Bryan smiled as her shoulders relaxed. "That's the purpose."

"If Shade's pictures are half as good, you'll have a wonderful essay."

"They will be," Bryan murmured. "I saw some of his negatives in the darkroom. They're incredible."

Lee lifted a brow and watched Bryan devour chocolate. "Does that bother you?"

"What? Oh, no, no, of course not. His work is his work—and in this case it'll be part of mine. I'd never have agreed to work with him if I hadn't admired him."

"But?" This time Lee prompted with a raised brow and half smile.

"I don't know, Lee, he's just so—so perfect."

"Really?"

"He never fumbles," Bryan complained. "He always

knows exactly what he wants. When he wakes up in the morning, he's perfectly coherent, he never misses a turn on the road. He even makes decent coffee."

"Anyone would detest him for that," Lee said dryly.

"It's frustrating, that's all."

"Love often is. You are in love with him, aren't you?"

"No." Genuinely surprised, Bryan stared over at Lee. "Good God, I hope I've more sense than that. I have to work hard at even liking him."

"Bryan, you're my friend. Otherwise what I'm calling concern would be called prying."

"Which means you're going to pry," Bryan put in.

"Exactly. I've seen the way the two of you tiptoe around each other as if you're terrified that if you happened to brush up against each other there'd be spontaneous combustion."

"Something like that."

Lee reached out and touched her hand. "Bryan, tell me."

Evasions weren't possible. Bryan looked down at the joined hands and sighed. "I'm attracted," she admitted slowly. "He's different from anyone I've known, mostly because he's just not the type of man I'd normally socialize with. He's very remote, very serious. I like to have fun. Just fun."

"Relationships have to be made up of more than just fun."

"I'm not looking for a relationship." On this point she was perfectly clear. "I date so I can go dancing, go to a party, listen to music or see a movie. That's it. The last thing I want is all the tension and work that goes into a relationship."

"If someone didn't know you, they'd say that was a pretty shallow sentiment."

"Maybe it is," Bryan tossed back. "Maybe I am."

Lee said nothing, just tapped a finger on the prints.

"That's my work," Bryan began, then gave up. A lot of people might take what she said at face value, not Lee. "I don't want a relationship," she repeated, but in a quieter tone. "Lee, I've been there before, and I'm lousy at it."

"Relationship equals two," Lee pointed out. "Are you still taking the blame?"

"Most of the blame was mine. I was no good at being a wife."

"At being a certain kind of wife," Lee corrected.

"I imagine there's only a handful of definitions in the dictionary."

Lee only raised a brow. "Sarah has a friend whose mother is wonderful. She keeps not just a clean house, but an interesting one. She makes jelly, takes the minutes at the P.T.A. and runs a Girl Scout troop. The woman can take colored paper and some glue and create a work of art. She's lovely and helps herself stay that way with exercise classes three times a week. I admire her a great deal, but if Hunter had wanted those things from me, I wouldn't have his ring on my finger."

"Hunter's special," Bryan murmured.

"I can't argue with that. And you know why I nearly ruined it with him—because I was afraid I'd fail at building and maintaining a relationship."

"It's not a matter of being afraid." Bryan shrugged her shoulders. "It's more a matter of not having the energy for it."

"Remember who you're talking to," Lee said mildly.

With a half laugh, Bryan shook her head. "All right, maybe it's a matter of being cautious. *Relationship*'s a very weighty word. *Affair*'s lighter," she said consideringly. "But an affair with a man like Shade's bound to have tremendous repercussions."

That sounded so cool, Bryan mused. When had she started to think in such logical terms? "He's not an easy man, Lee. He has his own demons and his own way of dealing with them. I don't know whether he'd share them with me, or if I'd want him to."

"He works at being cold," Lee commented. "But I've seen him with Sarah. I admit the basic kindness in him surprised me, but it's there."

"It's there," Bryan agreed. "It's just hard to get to."

"Dinner's ready!" Sarah yanked open the screen door and let it hit the wall with a bang. "Shade and I made spaghetti, and it's terrific."

It was. During the meal, Bryan watched Shade. Like Lee, she'd noticed his easy relationship with Sarah. It was more than tolerance, she decided as she watched him laugh with the girl. It was affection. It hadn't occurred to her that Shade could give his affection so quickly or with so few restrictions.

Maybe I should be a twelve-year-old with braces, she decided, then shook her head at her own thought pattern. She didn't want Shade's affection. His respect, yes.

It wasn't until after dinner that she realized she was wrong. She wanted a great deal more.

It was the last leisurely evening before the group separated. On the front porch they watched the first stars come out and listened to the first night sounds begin. By that time the next evening, Shade and Bryan would be in Colorado.

Lee and Hunter sat on the porch swing with Sarah nestled between them. Shade stretched out in a chair just to the side, relaxed, a little tired, and mentally satisfied after his long hours in the darkroom. Still, as he sat talking easily to the Browns, he realized that he'd needed this visit as much as, perhaps more than, Bryan.

He'd had a simple childhood. Until these past days, he'd nearly forgotten just how simple, and just how solid. The things that had happened to him as an adult had blocked a great deal of it out. Now, without consciously realizing it, Shade was drawing some of it back.

Bryan sat on the first step, leaning back against a post. She joined in the conversation or distanced herself from it as she chose. There was nothing important being said, and the easiness of the conversation made the scene that much more appealing. A moth battered itself against the porch light, crickets called, and the breeze rippled through the full leaves of the surrounding trees. The sounds made a soothing conversation of their own.

She liked the way Hunter had his arm across the back of the swing. Though he spoke to Shade, his fingers ran lightly over his wife's hair. His daughter's head rested against his chest, but once in a while, she'd reach a hand over to Lee's stomach as if to test for movement. Though she hadn't been consciously setting the scene, it grew in front of her eyes. Unable to resist, Bryan slipped inside.

When she returned a few moments later, she had her camera, tripod and light stand.

"Oh, boy." Sarah took one look and straightened primly. "Bryan's going to take our picture."

"No posing," Bryan told her with a grin. "Just keep talking," she continued before anyone could protest. "Pretend I'm not even here. It's so perfect," she began to mutter to herself as she set up. "I don't know why I didn't see it before."

"Let me give you a hand."

Bryan glanced up at Shade in surprise, and nearly refused before she stopped the words. It was the first time he'd made any attempt to work with her. Whether it was a gesture to her or to the affection he'd come to feel for her friends, she wouldn't toss it back at him. Instead, she smiled and handed him her light meter.

"Give me a reading, will you?"

They worked together as though they'd been doing so for years. Another surprise, for both of them. She adjusted her light, already calculating her exposure as Shade gave her the readings. Satisfied, Bryan checked the angle and framing through the viewfinder, then stepped back and let Shade take her place.

"Perfect." If she was looking for a lazy summer evening and a family content with it and one another, she could've done no better. Stepping back, Shade leaned against the wall of the house. Without thinking about it, he continued to help by distracting the trio on the swing.

"What do you want, Sarah?" he began as Bryan moved behind the camera again. "A baby brother or a sister?"

As she considered, Sarah forgot her enchantment with being photographed. "Well…" Her hand moved to Lee's stomach again. Lee's hand closed over it spontaneously. Bryan clicked the shutter. "Maybe a brother," she decided. "My cousin says a little sister can be a real pain."

As Sarah spoke Lee leaned her head back, just slightly,

until it rested on Hunter's arm. His fingers brushed her hair again. Bryan felt the emotion well up in her and blur her vision. She took the next shot blindly.

Had she always wanted that? she wondered as she continued to shoot. The closeness, the contentment that came with commitment and intimacy? Why had it waited to slam into her now, when her feelings toward Shade were already tangled and much too complicated? She blinked her eyes clear and opened the shutter just as Lee turned her head to laugh at something Hunter said.

Relationship, she thought as the longing rose up in her. Not the easy, careless friendships she'd permitted herself, but a solid, demanding, sharing relationship. That was what she saw through the viewfinder. That was what she discovered she needed for herself. When she straightened from the camera, Shade was beside her.

"Something wrong?"

She shook her head and reached over to switch off the light. "Perfect," she announced with a casualness that cost her. She gave the family on the swing a smile. "I'll send you a print as soon as we stop and develop again."

She was trembling. Shade was close enough to see it. He turned and dealt with the camera and tripod himself. "I'll take this up for you."

She turned to tell him no, but he was already carrying it inside. "I'd better pack my gear," she said to Hunter and Lee. "Shade likes to leave at uncivilized hours."

When she went inside, Lee leaned her head against Hunter's arm again. "They'll be fine," he told her. "She'll be fine."

Lee glanced toward the doorway. "Maybe."

Shade carried Bryan's equipment up to the bedroom

she'd been using and waited. The moment she came in with the light, he turned to her. "What's wrong?"

Bryan opened the case and packed her stand and light. "Nothing. Why?"

"You were trembling." Impatient, Shade took her arm and turned her around. "You're still trembling."

"I'm tired." In its way, it was true. She was tired of having her emotions sneak up on her.

"Don't play games with me, Bryan. I'm better at it than you."

God, could he have any idea just how much she wanted to be held at that moment? Would he have any way of understanding how much she'd give if only he'd hold her now? "Don't push it, Shade."

She should've known he wouldn't listen. With one hand, he cupped her chin and held her face steady. The eyes that saw a great deal more than he was entitled to looked into hers. "Tell me."

"No." She said it quietly. If she'd been angry, insulted, cold, he'd have dug until he'd had it all. He couldn't fight her this way.

"All right." He backed off, dipping his hands into his pockets. He'd felt something out on the porch, something that had pulled at him, offered itself to him. If she'd made one move, the slightest move, he might have given her more at that moment than either of them could imagine. "Maybe you should get some sleep. We'll leave at seven."

"Okay." Deliberately she turned away to pack up the rest of her gear. "I'll be ready."

He was at the door before he felt compelled to turn around again. "Bryan, I saw your prints. They're exceptional."

She felt the first tears stream down her face and was

appalled. Since when did she cry because someone acknowledged her talent? Since when did she tremble because a picture she was taking spoke to her personally?

She pressed her lips together for a moment and continued to pack without turning around. "Thanks."

Shade didn't linger any longer. He closed the door soundlessly on his way out.

Chapter 6

By the time they'd passed through New Mexico and into
Colorado, Bryan felt more in tune with herself. In part, she
thought that the break in Oak Creek Canyon had given her
too much time for introspection. Though she often relied
heavily on just that in her work, there were times when it
could be self-defeating.

At least that's what she'd been able to convince herself
of after she and Shade had picked up the routine of drive
and shoot and drive some more.

They weren't looking for cities and major events on
this leg. They sought out small, unrecognizable towns and
struggling ranches. Families that worked with the land
and one another to make ends meet. For them, summer
was a time of hard, endless work to prepare for the rigors
of winter. It wasn't all fun, all games, all sun and sand. It
was migrant workers waiting to pick August peaches, and
gardens being weeded and tended to offset the expense of
winter vegetables.

They didn't consider Denver, but chose instead places like Antonito. They didn't go after the big, sprawling cattle spreads, but the smaller, more personal operations.

Bryan had her first contact with a cattle branding on a dusty little ranch called the Bar T. Her preconception of sweaty, loose-limbed cowboys rounding 'em up and heading 'em out wasn't completely wrong. It just didn't include the more basic aspects of branding—such as the smell of burned flesh and the splash of blood as potential bulls were turned into little steers.

She was, she discovered as her stomach heaved, a city girl at heart.

But they got their pictures. Cowboys with bandannas over their faces and spurs on their boots. Some of them laughed, some of them swore. All of them worked.

She learned the true meaning of *workhorse* as she watched the men push their mounts through their paces. The sweat of a horse was a heavy, rich smell. It hung thickly in the air with the sweat of men.

Bryan considered her best shot a near-classic study of a man taking hold of his leisure time with both hands. The young cowboy was rangy and ruddy, which made him perfect for what she was after. His chambray shirt was dark with patches of sweat down the front, down the back and spreading from under the arms. More sweat mixed with dust ran down his face. His work boots were creased and caked with grime. The back pocket of his jeans was worn from the constant rub against a round can of chewing tobacco. With his hat tilted back and his bandanna tied loosely around his throat, he straddled the fence and lifted an icy can of beer to his lips.

Bryan thought when the picture was printed you'd

almost be able to see his Adam's apple move as he swallowed. And every woman who looked at it, she was certain, would be half in love. He was the mystic, the swashbuckler, the last of the knights. Having that picture in her camera nearly made up for almost losing her lunch over the branding.

She'd seen Shade home right in on it and known his pictures would be gritty, hard and detailed. Yet she'd also seen him focusing in on a young boy of eleven or twelve as he'd ridden in his first roundup with all the joy and innocence peculiar to a boy of that age. His choice had surprised her, because he rarely went for the lighter touch. It was also, unfortunately for her state of mind, something else she could like him for. There were others.

He hadn't made any comment when she'd turned green and distanced herself for a time from what was going on in the small enclosed corral where calves bawled for their mothers and let out long, surprised wails when knife and iron were applied. He hadn't said a word when she'd sat down in the shade until she was certain her stomach would stay calm. Nor had he said a word when he'd handed her a cold drink. Neither had she.

That night they camped on Bar T land. Shade had given her space since they'd left Arizona, because she suddenly seemed to need it. Oddly, he found he didn't. In the beginning, it had always been Bryan who'd all but forced him into conversations when he'd have been content to drive in silence for hours. Now he wanted to talk to her, to hear her laugh, to watch the way her hands moved when she became enthusiastic about a certain point. Or to watch the way she stretched, easily, degree by inching degree, as her voice slowed.

Something undefinable had shifted in both of them during their time in Oak Creek. Bryan had become remote, when she'd always been almost too open for his comfort. He found he wanted her company, when he'd always been solitary. He wanted, though he didn't fully comprehend why, her friendship. It was a shift he wasn't certain he cared for, or even understood. In any case, because the opposing shifts had happened in both of them simultaneously, it brought them no closer.

Shade had chosen the open space near a fast-running creek for a campsite for no reason other than that it appealed to him. Bryan immediately saw other possibilities.

"Look, I'm going down to wash off." She was as dusty as the cowboys she'd focused on all afternoon. It occurred to her, not altogether pleasantly, that she might smell a bit too much like the horses she'd watched. "It's probably freezing, so I'll make it fast and you can have a turn."

Shade pried the top off a beer. Perhaps they hadn't rounded up cattle, but they'd been on their feet and in the sun for almost eight hours. "Take your time."

Bryan grabbed a towel and a cake of soap and dashed off. The sun was steadily dropping behind the mountains to the west. She knew enough of camping by now to know how quickly the air would cool once the sun went down. She didn't want to be wet and naked when it did.

She didn't bother to glance around before she stripped off her shirt. They were far enough away from the ranch house that none of the men would wander out that way at sunset. Shade and she had already established the sanctity of privacy without exchanging a word on the subject.

Right now, she thought as she wiggled out of her jeans, the cowboys they'd come to shoot were probably sitting down to an enormous meal—red meat and potatoes, she mused. Hot biscuits with plenty of butter. Lord knows they deserved it, after the day they'd put in. And me, too, she decided, though she and Shade were making do with cold sandwiches and a bag of chips.

Slim, tall and naked, Bryan took a deep breath of the pine-scented air. Even a city girl, she thought as she paused a moment to watch the sunset, could appreciate all this.

Gingerly she stepped into the cold knee-high water and began to rinse off the dust. Strange, she didn't mind the chill as much as she once had. The drive across America was bound to leave its mark. She was glad of it.

No one really wanted to stay exactly the same throughout life. If her outlook changed and shifted as they traveled, she was fortunate. The assignment was giving her more than the chance for professional exposure and creative expression. It was giving her experiences. Why else had she become a photographer, but to see things and understand them?

Yet she didn't understand Shade any better now than when they'd started out. Had she tried? In some ways, she thought, as she glided the soap over her arms. Until what she saw and understood began to affect her too deeply and too personally. Then she'd backed off fast.

She didn't like to admit it. Bryan shivered and began to wash more swiftly. The sun was nearly set. Self-preservation, she reminded herself. Perhaps her image was one of take what comes and make the best of it, but she had her phobias as well. And she was entitled to them.

It had been a long time since she'd been hurt, and that was because of her own deceptively simple maneuvering. If she stood at a crossroads and had two routes, one smooth, the other rocky, with a few pits, she'd take the smooth one. Maybe it was less admirable, but she'd always felt you ended up in the same place with less energy expended. Shade Colby was a rocky road.

In any case, it wasn't just a matter of her choice. They could have an affair—a physically satisfying, emotionally shallow affair. It worked well for a great many people. But...

He didn't want to be involved with her any more than she did with him. He was attracted, just as she was, but he wasn't offering her any more than that. If he ever did... She dropped that line of thought like a stone. Speculation wasn't always healthy.

The important thing was that she felt more like herself again. She was pleased with the work she'd done since they'd left Arizona, and was looking forward to crossing over into Kansas the next day. The assignment, as they'd both agreed from the outset, was the first priority.

Wheat fields and tornadoes, she thought with a grin. Follow the yellow brick road. That was what Kansas brought to her mind. She knew better now, and looked forward to finding the reality. Bryan was beginning to enjoy having her preconceptions both confirmed and blown to bits.

That was for tomorrow. Right now it was dusk and she was freezing.

Agile, she scrambled up the small bank and reached for the towel. Shade could wash up while she stuffed herself with whatever was handy in the cupboards. She pulled on a long-sleeved oversize shirt and reached up to button it. That's when she saw the eyes.

For a moment she only stared with her hands poised at the top button. Then she saw there was more to it than a pair of narrow yellow eyes peering out of the lowering light. There was a sleek, muscled body and a set of sharp, white teeth only a narrow creek bed away.

Bryan took two steps back, tripped over her own tangled jeans and let out a scream that might've been heard in the next county.

Shade was stretched out in a folding chair beside the small campfire he'd built on impulse. He'd enjoyed himself that day—the rough-and-ready atmosphere, the baking sun and cold beer. He'd always admired the camaraderie that went hand in hand with people who work outdoors.

He needed the city—it was in his blood. For the most part, he preferred the impersonal aspects of people rushing to their own places, in their own time. But it helped to touch base with other aspects of life from time to time.

He could see now, even after only a few weeks on the road, that he'd been getting stale. He hadn't had the challenge of his early years. That get-the-shot-and-stay-alive sort of challenge. He didn't want it. But he'd let himself become too complacent with what he'd been doing.

This assignment had given him the chance to explore himself as well as his country. He thought of his partner with varying degrees of puzzlement and interest. She wasn't nearly as simple or laid-back as he'd originally believed. Still, she was nearly 180 degrees removed from him. He was beginning to understand her. Slowly, but he was beginning to.

She was sensitive, emotional and inherently kind. He was rarely kind, because he was careful not to be. She was comfortable with herself, easily amused and candid. He'd learned long ago that candor can jump back on you with teeth.

But he wanted her—because she was different or in spite of it, he wanted her. Forcing himself to keep his hands off her in all the days and nights that had passed since that light, interrupted kiss in Hunter Brown's driveway was beginning to wear on him. He had his control to thank for the fact that he'd been able to, the control that he honed so well that it was nearly a prison.

Shade tossed his cigarette into the fire and leaned back. He wouldn't lose that control, or break out of that prison, but that didn't mean that sooner or later he and Bryan wouldn't be lovers. He meant it to happen. He would simply bide his time until it happened his way. As long as he was holding the reins, he wouldn't steer himself into the mire.

When he heard her scream, a dozen agonizing images rushed into his head, images that he'd seen and lived through, images that only someone who had could conjure up. He was out of the chair and running before he'd fully realized they were only memories.

When he got to her, Bryan was scrambling up from the tumble she'd taken. The last thing she expected was to be hauled up and crushed against Shade. The last thing she expected was exactly what she needed. Gasping for air, she clung to him.

"What happened?" Her own panic muffled her ears to the thread of panic in his voice. "Bryan, are you hurt?"

"No, no. It scared me, but it ran away." She pushed her face against his shoulder and just breathed. "Oh, God, Shade."

"What?" Gripping her by the elbows, he pulled her back far enough to see her face. "What scared you?"

"A cat."

He wasn't amused. His fear turned to fury, tangibly

enough that Bryan could see the latter even before he cursed her. "Damn it! What kind of fool are you?" he demanded. "Letting out a scream like that over a cat."

She drew air in and out, in and out, and concentrated on her anger—genuine fear was something she didn't care for. "Not a house cat," she snapped. She was still shaken, but not enough to sit back and be called a fool. "It was one of those...I don't know." She lifted a hand to push at her hair and dropped it again when it trembled. "I have to sit down." She did so with a plop on the grass.

"A bobcat?" Calmer, Shade crouched down beside her.

"I don't know. Bobcat, cougar—I wouldn't know the difference. It was a hell of a lot bigger than any tabby." She lowered her head to her knees. Maybe she'd been frightened before in her life, but she couldn't remember anything to compare with this. "He just stood over there, staring at me. I thought—I thought he was going to jump over the creek. His teeth..." She shuddered and shut her eyes. "Big," she managed, no longer caring if she sounded like a simpleminded fool. "Real big."

"He's gone now." His fury turned inward. He should've known she wasn't the kind of woman who jumped at shadows. He knew what it was to be afraid and to feel helpless with it. This time he cursed himself as he slipped an arm around her. "The way you screamed, he's ten miles away and still running."

Bryan nodded but kept her face buried against her knees. "I guess he wasn't that big, but they look different out of the zoo. I just need a minute to pull myself together."

"Take your time."

He found he didn't mind offering comfort, though it was something he hadn't done in a long time. The air was cool, the night still. He could hear the sound of the water rushing by in the creek. For a moment he had a quick flash of the Browns' porch, of the easy family portrait on the swing. He felt a touch of the same contentment here, with his arm around Bryan and night closing in.

Overhead a hawk screeched, out for its first flight of the night. Bryan jolted.

"Easy," Shade murmured. He didn't laugh at her reaction, or even smile. He soothed

"I guess I'm a little jumpy." With a nervous laugh, she lifted her hand to push at her hair again. It wasn't until then that Shade realized she was naked beneath the open, billowing shirt.

The sight of her slim, supple body beneath the thin, fluttering material sent the contentment he'd felt skyrocketing into need. A need, he discovered only in that instant, that was somehow exclusively for her—not just for a woman with a lovely face, a desirable body, but for Bryan.

"Maybe we should get back and..." She turned her head and found her eyes only inches from his. In his, she saw everything he felt. When she started to speak again, he shook his head.

No words. No words now. Only needs, only feelings. He wanted that with her. As his mouth closed over hers, he gave her no choice but to want it as well.

Sweetness? Where had it come from and how could she possibly turn away from it? They'd been together nearly a month, but she'd never suspected he had sweetness in him. Nor had she known just how badly she'd needed to find it there.

His mouth demanded, but so slowly, so subtly, that she was giving before she was aware of it. Once she'd given, she couldn't take away again. She felt his hand, warm and firm on her bare skin, but she sighed in pleasure, not in protest. She'd wanted him to touch her, had waited for it, had denied her waiting. Now she leaned closer. There'd be no denying.

He'd known she'd feel like this—slim, strong, smooth. A hundred times, he'd imagined it. He hadn't forgotten that she'd taste like this—warm, tempting, generous. A hundred times, he'd tried not to remember.

This time she smelled of the creek, fresh and cool. He could bury his face in her throat and smell the summer night on her. He kissed her slowly, leaving her lips for her throat, her throat for her shoulder. As he lingered there, he gave himself the pleasure of discovering her body with his fingertips.

It was torture. Exquisite. Agonizing. Irresistible. Bryan wanted it to go on, and on and on. She drew him closer, loving the hard, lean feel of his body against hers, the brush of his clothes against her skin, the whisper of his breath across it. And through it all, the quick, steady beat of his heart near hers.

She could smell the work of the day on him, the faint tang of healthy sweat, the traces of dust he hadn't yet washed off. It excited her with memories of the way his muscles had bunched beneath his shirt when he'd climbed onto a fence for a better angle. She could remember exactly how he'd looked then, though she'd pretended to herself that she hadn't seen, hadn't needed to.

She wanted his strength. Not the muscles, but the inner strength she'd sensed in him from the start. The strength that had carried him through what he'd seen, what he'd lived with.

Yet wasn't it that strength that helped to harden him, to separate him emotionally from the people around him? With her mind whirling, her body pulsing, she struggled to find the answer she needed.

Wants weren't enough. Hadn't she told him so herself? God, she wanted him. Her bones were melting from the desire for him. But it wasn't enough. She only wished she knew what was.

"Shade…" Even when she tried to speak, he cut her off with another long, draining kiss.

She wanted him to drain her. Mind, body, soul. If he did, there'd be no question and no need for answers. But the questions were there. Even as she held him to her, they were there.

"Shade," she began again.

"I want to make love with you." He lifted his head, and his eyes were so dark, so intense, it was almost impossible to believe his hands were so gentle. "I want to feel your skin under my hand, feel your heart race, watch your eyes."

The words were quiet, incredibly calm when his eyes were so passionate. More than the passion and demand in his eyes, the words frightened her.

"I'm not ready for this." She barely managed the words as she drew away from him.

He felt the needs rise and the anger begin. It took all his skill to control both. "Are you saying you don't want me?"

"No." She shook her head as she drew her shirt together. When had it become so cold? she wondered. "No, lying's foolish."

"So's backing away from something we both want to happen."

"I'm not sure I do. I can't be logical about this, Shade."

She gathered her clothes quickly and hugged them against her as she stood. "I can't think something like this through step-by-step the way you do. If I could, it'd be different, but I can only go with my feelings, my instincts."

There was a deadly calm around him when he rose. The control he'd nearly forfeited to her was back in place. Once more he accepted the prison he'd built for himself. "And?"

She shivered without knowing if it was from the cold without or the cold within. "And my feelings tell me I need more time." When she looked up at him again, her face was honest, her eyes were eloquent. "Maybe I do want this to happen. Maybe I'm just a little afraid of how much I want you."

He didn't like her use of the word *afraid*. She made him feel responsible, obliged. Defensive. "I've no intention of hurting you."

She gave herself a moment. Her breathing was easier, even if her pulse was still unsteady. Whether he knew it or not, Shade had already given her the distance she needed to resist him. Now she could look at him, calmer. Now she could think more clearly.

"No, I don't think you do, but you could, and I have a basic fear of bruises. Maybe I'm an emotional coward. It's not a pretty thought, but it might be true." With a sigh, she lifted both hands to her hair and pushed it back. "Shade, we've a bit more than two months left on the road. I can't afford to spend it being torn up inside because of you. My instincts tell me you could very easily do that to me, whether you planned on it or not."

She knew how to back a man into a corner, he thought in frustration. He could press, relieve the knot she'd tightened in his stomach. And by doing so, he'd run the risk of having her words echo back at him for a long time to come. It'd only taken a few words from her to remind him what it felt like to be responsible for someone else.

"Go back to the van," he told her, turning away to strip off his shirt. "I have to clean up."

She started to speak, then realized there was nothing more she could say. Instead, she left him to follow the thin, moonlit trail back to the van.

Chapter 7

Wheat fields. Bryan's preconception wasn't slashed as they drove through the Midwest, but reinforced. Kansas was wheat fields.

Whatever else Bryan saw as they crossed the state, it was the endless, rippling gold grass that captivated her, first and last. Color, texture, shape, form. Emotion. There were towns, of course, cities with modern buildings and plush homes, but in seeing basic Americana, grain against sky, Bryan saw it all.

Some might have found the continuous spread of sun-ripened grain waving, acre after acre, monotonous. Not Bryan. This was a new experience for a woman of the city. There were no jutting mountains, no glossy towering buildings, no looping freeways, to break the lines. Here was space, just as awesome as the terrain of Arizona, but lusher, and somehow calmer. She could look at it and wonder.

In the fields of wheat and acres of corn, Bryan saw the heart and the sweat of the country. It wasn't always an idyllic scene. There were insects, dirt, grimy machinery. People worked here with their hands, with their backs.

In the cities, she saw the pace and energy. On the farms, she saw a schedule that would have made a corporate executive wilt. Year after year, the farmer gave himself to the land and waited for the land to give back.

With the right angle, the proper light, she could photograph a wheat field and make it seem endless, powerful. With evening shadows, she could give a sense of serenity and continuity. It was only grass, after all, only stalks growing to be cut down, processed, used. But the grain had a life and a beauty of its own. She wanted to show it as she saw it.

Shade saw the tenuous, inescapable dependence of man on nature. The planter, keeper and harvester of the wheat, was irrevocably tied to the land. It was both his freedom and his prison. The man riding the tractor in the Kansas sunlight, damp with healthy sweat, lean from years of labor, was as dependent on the land as the land was on him. Without man, the wheat might grow wild, it might flourish, but then it would wither and die. It was the tie Shade sensed, and the tie he meant to record.

Still, perhaps for the first time since they'd left L.A., he and Bryan weren't shooting as separate entities. They might not have realized it yet, but their feelings, perceptions and needs were drawing them closer to the same mark.

They made each other think. How did she see this scene? How did he feel about this setting? Where before each of them had considered their photographs separately, now subtly, unconsciously, they began to do two things that would improve the final result: compete and consult.

They'd spent a day and a night in Dodge City for the Fourth of July celebrations in what had once been a Wild West town. Bryan thought of Wyatt Earp, of Doc Holliday and the desperadoes who had once ridden through town, but she'd been drawn to the street parade that might've been in Anytown, U.S.A.

It was here, caught up in the pageantry and the flavor, that she'd asked Shade his opinion of the right angle for shooting a horse and rider, and he in turn had taken her advice on capturing a tiny, bespangled majorette.

The step they'd taken had been lost in the moment to both of them. But they'd stood side by side on the curb as the parade had passed, music blaring, batons flying. Their pictures had been different—Shade had looked for the overview of holiday parades while Bryan had wanted individual reactions. But they'd stood side by side.

Bryan's feelings for Shade had become more complex, more personal. When the change had begun or how, she couldn't say. But because her work was most often a direct result of her emotions, the pictures she took began to reflect both the complexity and the intimacy. Their view of the same wheat field might be radically different, but Bryan was determined that when their prints were set side by side, hers would have equal impact.

She'd never been an aggressive person. It just wasn't her style. But Shade had tapped a need in her to compete—as a photographer, and as a woman. If she had to travel in close quarters for weeks with a man who ruffled her professional feathers and stirred her feminine needs, she had to deal with him directly—on both counts. Directly, she decided, but in her own fashion and her own time. As the days went on, Bryan wondered if it would be possible to have both success and Shade without losing something vital.

She was so damn calm! It drove him crazy. Every day, every hour, they spent together pushed Shade closer to the edge. He wasn't used to wanting anyone so badly. He didn't enjoy finding out he could, and that there was nothing he could do about it. Bryan put him in the position of needing, then having to deny himself. There were times he nearly believed she did so purposely. But he'd never known anyone less likely to scheme than Bryan. She wouldn't think of it—and if she did, she'd consider it too much bother.

Even now, as they drove through the Kansas twilight, she was stretched out in the seat beside him, sound asleep. It was one of the rare times she'd left her hair loose. Full, wavy and lush, it was muted to a dull gold in the lowering light. The sun had given her skin all the color it needed. Her body was relaxed, loose like her hair. Shade wondered if he'd ever had the capability to let his mind and body go so enviably limp. Was it that that tempted him, that drove at him? Was he simply pushed to find that spark of energy she could turn on and off at will? He wanted to set it to life. For himself.

Temptation. The longer he held himself back, the more intense it became. To have her. To explore her. To absorb her. When he did—he no longer used the word *if*—what cost would there be? Nothing was free.

Once, he thought as she sighed in sleep. Just once. His way. Perhaps the cost would be high, but he wouldn't be the one to pay it. His emotions were trained and disciplined. They wouldn't be touched. There wasn't a woman alive who could make him hurt.

His body and his mind tensed as Bryan slowly woke. Groggy and content to be so, she yawned. The scent of smoke and tobacco stung the air. On the radio was low, mellow jazz. The windows were half open, so that when she shifted, the slap of wind woke her more quickly than she'd have liked.

It was fully dark now. Surprised, Bryan stretched and stared out the window at a moon half covered by clouds. "It's late," she said on another yawn. The first thing she remembered as her mind cleared of sleep was that they hadn't eaten. She pressed a hand to her stomach. "Dinner?"

He glanced at her just long enough to see her shake back her hair. It rippled off her shoulders and down her back. As he watched, he had to fight back the urge to touch it. "I want to get over the border tonight."

She heard it in his voice—the tension, the annoyance. Bryan didn't know what had prompted it, nor at the moment did she want to. Instead, she lifted a brow. If he was in a hurry to get to Oklahoma and was willing to drive into the night to get there, it was his business. She'd stocked a cabinet in the back of the van with a few essentials just for moments like this. Bryan started to haul herself out of her seat when she heard the long blare of a horn and the rev of an engine.

The scarred old Pontiac had a hole in the muffler you could've tossed a baseball through. The sound of the engine clattered like a badly tuned plane. It swerved around the van at a dangerous speed, fishtailed, then bolted ahead, radio blaring. As Shade swore, Bryan got a glimpse that revealed the dilapidated car was packed with kids.

"Saturday night in July," she commented.

"Idiots," he said between his teeth as he watched the taillights weave.

"Yeah." She frowned as she watched the car barrel ahead, smoke streaming. "They were just kids, I hope they don't..."

Even as she thought it, it happened. The driver decided to press his luck by passing another car over the double yellow lines. The truck coming toward him laid on the horn and swerved. Bryan felt her blood freeze.

Shade was already hitting the brakes as the Pontiac screeched back into its own lane. But it was out of control. Skidding sideways, the Pontiac kissed the fender of the car it had tried to pass, then flipped into a telephone pole.

The sound of screaming tires, breaking glass and smashing metal whirled in her head. Bryan was up and out of the van before Shade had brought it to a complete stop. She could hear a girl screaming, others weeping. Even as the sounds shuddered through her, she told herself it meant they were alive.

The door on the passenger's side was crushed against the telephone pole. Bryan rushed to the driver's side and wrenched at the handle. She smelled the blood before she saw it. "Good God," she whispered as she managed to yank the door open on the second try. Then Shade was beside her, shoving her aside.

"Get some blankets out of the van," he ordered without looking at her. It had only taken him one glance at the driver to tell him it wasn't going to be pretty. He shifted enough to block Bryan's view, then reached in to check the pulse in the driver's throat as he heard her run back to the van. Alive, he thought, then blocked out everything but what had to be done. He worked quickly.

The driver was unconscious. The gash on his head was serious, but it didn't worry Shade as much as the probability of internal injuries. And nothing worried him as much as the smell of gas that was beginning to sweeten the air. Under other circumstances, Shade would've been reluctant to move the boy. Now there was no choice. Locking his arms under the boy's arms, Shade hauled him out. Even as Shade began to drag him, the driver of the truck ran over and took the boy's legs.

"Got a CB in the truck," he told Shade breathlessly. "Called for an ambulance."

With a nod, Shade laid the boy down. Bryan was already there with the first blanket.

"Stay here. The car's going to go up." He said it calmly. Without a backward glance, he went back to the crippled Pontiac.

Terror jolted through her. Within seconds, Bryan was at the car beside him, helping to pull the others out of the wreck.

"Get back to the van!" Shade shouted at her as Bryan half carried a sobbing girl. "Stay there!"

Bryan spoke soothingly, covered the girl with a blanket, then rushed back to the car. The last passenger was also unconscious. A boy, Bryan saw, of no more than sixteen. She had to half crawl into the car to reach him. By the time she'd dragged him to the open door, she was drenched and exhausted. Both Shade and the truck driver carried the other injured passengers. Shade had just set a young girl on the grass when he turned and saw Bryan struggling with the last victim.

Fear was instant and staggering. Even as he started to run, his imagination worked on him. In his mind, Shade could see the flash of the explosion, hear the sound of bursting metal and shattering, flying glass. He knew exactly what it would smell like the moment the gas ignited. When he reached Bryan, Shade scooped up the unconscious boy as though he were weightless.

"Run!" he shouted at her. Together, they raced away from the Pontiac.

Bryan didn't see the explosion. She heard it, but more, she felt it. The whoosh of hot air slammed into her back and sent her sprawling onto the grassy shoulder of the road. There was a whistle of metal as something hot and twisted and lethal flew overhead. One of the teenagers screamed and buried her face in her hands.

Stunned, Bryan lay prone a moment, waiting to catch her breath. Over the sound of fire, she could hear the whine of sirens.

"Are you hurt?" Shade half dragged her up to her knees. He'd seen the flying slice of metal whiz by her head. Hands that had been rock steady moments before trembled as they gripped her.

"No." Bryan shook her head and, finding her balance, turned to the whimpering girl beside her. A broken arm, she realized as she tucked the blanket under the girl's chin. And the cut on her temple would need stitches. "Take it easy," Bryan murmured, pulling out a piece of gauze from the first-aid box she'd brought from the van. "You're going to be fine. The ambulance is coming. Can you hear it?"

As she spoke, she pressed the gauze against the wound to stop the bleeding. Her voice was calm, but her fingers trembled.

"Bobby." Tears ran down the girl's face as she clung to Bryan. "Is Bobby all right? He was driving."

Bryan glanced over and looked directly at Shade before she lowered her gaze to the unconscious boy. "He's going to be fine," she said, and felt helpless.

Six young, careless children, she thought as she scanned those sitting or lying on the grass. The driver of the other car sat dazedly across from them, holding a rag to the cut on his own head. For a moment, a long, still moment, the night was quiet—warm, almost balmy. Stars were brilliant overhead. Moonlight was strong and lovely. Thirty feet away, what was left of the Pontiac crackled with flame. Bryan slipped her arm around the shoulders of the girl and watched the lights of the ambulance speed up the road.

As the paramedics began to work, another ambulance and the fire department were called. For twenty minutes, Bryan sat by the young girl, talking to her, holding her hand while her injuries were examined and tended to.

Her name was Robin. She was seventeen. Of the six teenagers in the car, her boyfriend, Bobby, was the oldest at nineteen. They'd only been celebrating summer vacation.

As Bryan listened and soothed, she glanced up to see Shade calmly setting his camera. Astonished, she watched as he carefully focused and framed in the injured. Dispassionately, he recorded the scene of the accident, the victims and what was left of the car. As astonishment faded, Bryan felt the fury bubble inside her. When Robin was carried to the second ambulance, Bryan sprang up.

"What the hell are you doing?" She grabbed his shoulder, spoiling a shot. Still calm, Shade turned to her and gave her one quick study.

She was pale. Her eyes showed both strain and fury. And, he thought, a dull sheen of shock. For the first time since he'd known her, Shade saw how tense her body could be. "I'm doing my job," he said simply, and lifted the camera again.

"Those kids are bleeding!" Bryan grabbed his shoulder again, swinging herself around until she was face-to-face with him. "They've got broken bones. They're hurt and they're frightened. Since when is your job taking pictures of their pain?"

"Since I picked up a camera for pay." Shade let the camera swing by its strap. He'd gotten enough, in any case. He didn't like the feeling in his own stomach, the tension behind his eyes. Most of all, he didn't like the look in Bryan's as she stared at him. Disgust. He shrugged it off.

"You're only willing to take pictures of fun in the sun for this assignment, Bryan. You saw the car, those kids. That's part of it too. Part of life. If you can't handle it, you'd better stick to your celebrity shots and leave the real world alone."

He'd taken two steps toward the van when Bryan was on him again. She might avoid confrontations as a matter of habit, take the line of least resistance as often as possible, but there were times when she'd fight. When she did, she used everything.

"I can handle it." She wasn't pale any longer; her face glowed with anger. Her eyes gleamed with it. "What I can't handle are the vultures who love picking at bones, making a profit off misery in the name of art. There were six people in that car. *People,*" she repeated, hissing at him. "Maybe they were foolish, maybe they deserved what happened, but I'll be damned if I'm going to judge. Do you think it makes you a better photographer, a better artist, because you're cold enough, you're *professional* enough, to freeze their pain on printing paper? Is this the way you look for another Pulitzer nomination?"

She was crying now, too angry, too churned up by what she'd seen, to be aware of the tears streaming down her cheeks. Yet somehow the tears made her look stronger. They thickened her voice and gave it impact. "I'll tell you what it makes you," she went on when Shade remained silent. "It makes you empty. Whatever compassion you were born with died somewhere along the way, Shade. I'm sorry for you."

She left him standing in the middle of the road by the shell of the car.

It was nearly 3:00 a.m. Shade had learned that the mind was at its most helpless in those early hours of the morning. The van was dark and quiet, parked in a small campground just over the Oklahoma border. He and Bryan hadn't exchanged a word since the accident. Each had prepared for bed in silence, and though both of them had lain awake for some time, neither had spoken. Now they slept, but only Bryan slept dreamlessly.

There'd been a time, during the first months after his return from Cambodia, that Shade had had the dream regularly. Over the years it had come to him less and less. Often he could force himself awake and fight the dream off before it really took hold. But now, in the tiny Oklahoma campground, he was powerless.

He knew he was dreaming. The moment the figures and shapes began to form in his mind, Shade understood it wasn't real—that it wasn't real any longer. It didn't stop the panic or the pain. The Shade Colby in the dream would go through the same motions he'd gone through all those years ago, leading to the same end. And in the dream there were no soft lines, no mists to lessen the impact. He saw it as it had happened, in strong sunlight.

Shade came out of the hotel and onto the street with Dave, his assistant. Between them, they carried all their luggage and equipment. They were going home. After four months of hard, often dangerous work in a city torn, ravaged and smoldering, they were going home. It had occurred to Shade that they were calling it close— but he'd called it close before. Every day they stayed on added to the risk of getting out at all. But there'd always been one more picture to take, one more statement to make. And there'd been Sung Lee.

She'd been so young, so eager, so wise. As a contact in the city, she'd been invaluable. She'd been just as invaluable to Shade personally. After a bumpy, unpleasant divorce from a wife who'd wanted more glamour and less reality, Shade had needed the long, demanding assignment. And he'd needed Sung Lee.

She was devoted, sweet, undemanding. When he'd taken her to bed, Shade had finally been able to block out the rest of the world and relax. His only regret in going back home was that she wouldn't leave her country.

As they'd stepped out on the street, Shade had been thinking of her. They'd said their goodbyes the night before, but he was thinking of her. Perhaps if he hadn't been, he'd have sensed something. He'd asked himself that hundreds of times in the months that followed.

The city was quiet, but it wasn't peaceful. The tension in the air could erupt at any time. Those who were getting out were doing so in a hurry. Tomorrow, the next day, the doors might be closed. Shade took one last look around as they started toward their car. One last picture, he'd thought, of the calm before the storm.

A few careless words to Dave and he was alone, standing on the curb pulling his camera out of its case. He laughed as Dave swore and struggled with the luggage on his way to the car. Just one last picture. The next time he lifted his camera to shoot, it would be on American soil.

"Hey, Colby!" Young, grinning, Dave stood beside the car. He looked like a college student on spring break. "How about taking one of a future award-winning photographer on his way out of Cambodia?"

With a laugh, Shade lifted his camera and framed in his assistant. He remembered exactly the way he'd looked. Blond, tanned, a bit gangly, with a crooked front tooth and a faded USC T-shirt.

He took the shot. Dave turned the key in the lock.

"Let's go home," his assistant yelled the instant before the car exploded.

"Shade. Shade!" Heart pounding, Bryan shook him. "Shade, wake up, it's a dream." He grabbed her hard enough to make bruises, but she kept talking. "It's Bryan, Shade. You're having a dream. Just a dream. We're in Oklahoma, in your van. Shade." She took his face in her hands and felt the skin cold and damp. "Just a dream," she said quietly. "Try to relax. I'm right here."

He was breathing too quickly. Shade felt himself straining for air and forced himself to calm. God, he was cold. He felt the warmth of Bryan's skin under his hands, heard her voice, calm, low, soothing. With an oath, he dropped back down again and waited for the shuddering to stop.

"I'll get you some water."

"Scotch."

"All right." The moonlight was bright enough. She found the plastic cup and the bottle and poured. Behind her, she heard the flare of his lighter and the hiss as it caught paper and tobacco. When Bryan turned, he was sitting up on the bunk, resting back against the side of the van. She had no experience with whatever trauma haunted Shade, but she did know how to soothe nerves. She handed him the drink, then, without asking, sat beside him. She waited until he'd taken the first sip.

"Better?"

He took another sip, a deeper one. "Yeah."

She touched his arm lightly, but the contact was made. "Tell me."

He didn't want to speak of it, not to anyone, not to her. Even as the refusal formed on his lips, she increased the grip on his arm.

"We'll both feel better if you do. Shade..." She had to wait again, this time for him to turn and look at her. Her heartbeat was steadier now, and so, as her fingers lay over his wrist, was his. But there was still a thin sheen of sweat drying on his skin. "Nothing gets better and goes away if you hold it in."

He'd held it in for years. It'd never gone away. Perhaps it never would. Maybe it was the quiet understanding in her voice, or the late hour, but he found himself talking.

He told her of Cambodia, and though his voice was flat, she could see it as he had. Ripe for explosion, crumbling, angry. Long, monotonous days punctuated by moments of terror. He told her how he'd reluctantly taken on an assistant and then learned to appreciate and enjoy the young man fresh out of college. And Sung Lee.

"We ran across her in a bar where most of the journalists hung out. It wasn't until a long time later that I put together just how convenient the meeting was. She was twenty, beautiful, sad. For nearly three months, she gave us leads she supposedly learned from a cousin who worked at the embassy."

"Were you in love with her?"

"No." He drew on his cigarette until there was nothing left but filter. "But I cared. I wanted to help her. And I trusted her."

He dropped his cigarette into an ashtray and concentrated on his drink. The panic was gone. He'd never realized he could talk about it calmly, think about it calmly. "Things were heating up, and the magazine decided to pull its people out. We were going home. We were coming out of the hotel, and I stopped to take a couple of shots. Like a tourist." He swore and drained the rest of the Scotch. "Dave got to the car first. It'd been booby-trapped."

"Oh, my God." Without realizing it, she moved closer to him.

"He was twenty-three. Carried a picture of the girl he was going to marry."

"I'm sorry." She laid her head against his shoulder, wound her arm around him. "I'm so sorry."

He braced himself against the flood of sympathy. He wasn't ready for it. "I tried to find Sung Lee. She was gone; her apartment was empty. It turned out that I'd been her assignment. The group she'd worked for had let things leak through so I'd relax and trust her. They'd intended to make a statement by blowing away an important American reporter. They'd missed me. An assistant photographer on his first overseas assignment didn't make any impact. The kid died for nothing."

And he'd watched the car explode, she thought. Just as he'd watched the car explode tonight. What had it done to him—then and now? Was that why, she wondered, he'd coolly taken out his camera and recorded it all? He was so determined not to feel.

"You blame yourself," she murmured. "You can't."

"He was a kid. I should've looked out for him."

"How?" She shifted so that they were face-to-face again. His eyes were dark, full of cold anger and frustration. She'd never forget just how they looked at that moment. "How?" she repeated. "If you hadn't stopped to take those pictures, you'd have gotten into the car with him. He'd still be dead."

"Yeah." Suddenly weary, Shade ran his hands over his face. The tension was gone, but not the bitterness. Perhaps that's what he was weary of.

"Shade, after the accident—"

"Forget it."

"No." This time she had his hand caught in hers. "You were doing what you had to, for your own reasons. I said I wouldn't judge those kids, but I was judging you. I'm sorry."

He didn't want her apology, but she gave it. He didn't want her to cleanse him, but she was washing away the guilt. He'd seen so much—too much—of the dark side of human nature. She was offering him the light. It tempted him and it terrified him.

"I'll never see things as you do," he murmured. After a moment's hesitation, he laced his fingers with hers. "I'll never be as tolerant."

Puzzled, she frowned as they stared at each other. "No, I don't think you will. I don't think you have to."

"You were right earlier when you said my compassion

was dead. I haven't any." She started to speak, but he shook his head. "I haven't any patience, very little sympathy."

Did he look at his own pictures? she wondered. Didn't he see the carefully harnessed emotion in them? But she said nothing, letting him make whatever point he needed to.

"I stopped believing in intimacy, genuine intimacy, permanency, between two people a long time ago. But I do believe in honesty."

She might've drawn away from him. There was something in his voice that warned her, but she stayed where she was. Their bodies were close. She could feel his heartbeat steady as hers began to race. "I think permanency works for some people." Was that her voice? she wondered, so calm, so practical. "I stopped looking for it for myself."

Isn't that what he'd wanted to hear? Shade looked down at their joined hands and wondered why her words left him dissatisfied. "Then it's understood that neither of us wants or needs promises."

Bryan opened her mouth, amazed that she wanted to object. She swallowed. "No promises," she managed. She had to think, had to have the distance to manage it. Deliberately she smiled. "I think we both could use some sleep, though."

He tightened his grip on her hand as she started to move. Honesty, he'd said. Though the words weren't easy for him, he'd say what he meant. He looked at her a long time. What was left of the moonlight showered her face and shadowed her eyes. Caught in his, her hand was steady. Her pulse wasn't.

"I need you, Bryan."

There were so many things he could have said, and to any of them she'd have had an answer. Wants—no, wants weren't enough. She'd already told him. Demands could be refused or shrugged off.

Needs. Needs were deeper, warmer, stronger. A need was enough.

He didn't move. He waited. Watching him, Bryan knew he'd let her take the step toward or away. Choices. He was a man who demanded them for himself, yet he was also capable of giving them. How could he know she'd had none the moment he'd spoken?

Slowly, she drew her hand from his. Just as slowly, she lifted both hands to his face and brought her mouth to his. With their eyes open, they shared a long, quiet kiss. It was a move that both offered and took.

She offered, with her hands light on his skin. She took, with her mouth warm and certain. He accepted. He gave. And then in the same instant, they both forgot the rules.

Her lashes fluttered down, her lips parted. Mindlessly he pulled her against him until their bodies were crushed close. She didn't resist, but went with him as they slid from the bunk and onto the rug.

She'd wanted this—the triumph and the weakness of being touched by him. She'd wanted the glory of letting herself go, of allowing her longings freedom. With his mouth hungry on hers, there was no need to think, no need to hold back what she'd wanted so desperately to give him. Only to him.

Take more. Her mind was reeling from the demands of her body. Take all. She could feel him tug at the wide neck of her sleep shirt until her shoulder was bare and vulnerable to his mouth. Still more. She skimmed her hands up his back, naked and warm from the night breeze flowing in the windows.

He wasn't easy as a lover. Hadn't she known it? There was no patience in him. Hadn't he told her? She'd known it before, but she was already aware that she'd never know relaxation with Shade. He drove her quickly, thoroughly. While she experienced all, she had no time to luxuriate in separate sensations. Masses of them swirled around, inside her.

Tastes…his lips, his skin—dark flavor. Scents…flowers, flesh—sweet and pungent. Textures…the nap of the rug rubbing against her legs, the hard brush of his palm, the soft warmth of his mouth. Sounds…her heartbeat pounding in her head, the murmur of her name in his whisper. She could see shadows, moonlight, the gleam of his eyes before his mouth took hers again. Everything merged and mixed together until they were one overpowering sensation. Passion.

He pulled the shirt lower until her arms were pinned. For a moment, she was helpless as he trailed his lips down her breast, pausing to taste, taste thoroughly, with lips, tongue, teeth. Some women would've found him merciless.

Perhaps it was the sound of her moan that made him linger when he was driven to hurry on. She was so slender, so smooth. The moonlight filtered in so that he could see where her tan gave way to paler, more vulnerable skin. Once he'd have turned away from vulnerability, knowing the dangers of it. Now it drew him—the softness of it. Her scent was there, clinging to the underside of her breast where he could taste as well as smell it. Sexy, tempting, subtle. It was as she was, and he was lost.

He felt his control slip, skid away from him. Ruthlessly, he brought it back. They would make love once—a hundred times that night—but he'd stay in control. As he was now, he thought as she arched under him. As he'd promised himself he would be, always. He would drive her, but he would not, could not, be driven by her.

Pulling the material down, he explored every inch of her mercilessly. He would show no mercy to either of them. Already she was beyond thought and he knew it. Her skin was hot, and somehow softer with the heat; her scent intensified with it. He could run those hungry, openmouthed kisses wherever he chose.

Her hands were free. Energy and passion raced together inside her. She tumbled over the first peak, breathless and strong. Now she could touch, now she could enrage him, entice him, weaken him. She moved quickly, demanding when he'd expected surrender. It was too sudden, too frantic, to allow him to brace himself against it. Even as she raced to the next peak, she felt the change in him.

He couldn't stop it. She wouldn't permit him to take without giving. His mind swam. Though he tried to clear it, fought to hold himself back, she seduced. Not his body, he'd have given that freely. She seduced his mind until it reeled with her. Emotion raged through him. Clean, hot, strong.

Tangled together, body and mind, they drove each other higher. They took each other over.

Chapter 8

They were both very careful. Neither Bryan nor Shade wanted to say anything the other could misunderstand. They'd made love, and for each of them it had been more intense, more vital, than anything they'd ever experienced. They'd set rules, and for each of them the need to abide by them was paramount.

What had happened between them had left them both more than a little stunned, and more wary than ever.

For a woman like Bryan, who was used to saying what she wanted, doing as she pleased, it wasn't easy to walk on eggshells twenty-four hours a day. But they'd made themselves clear before making love, she reminded herself. No complications, no commitments. No promises. They'd both failed once at the most important of relationships, marriage. Why should either of them risk failure again?

They traveled in Oklahoma, giving an entire day to a small-town rodeo. Bryan hadn't enjoyed anything as much since the Fourth of July celebrations they'd seen in Kansas.

She enjoyed watching the heat of competition, the pitting of man against animal and man against man and the clock. Every man who'd lowered himself onto a bronc or a bull had been determined to make it to the bell.

Some had been young, others had been seasoned, but all had had one goal. To win, and then to go on to the next round. She'd liked seeing that a game could be turned into a way of life.

Unable to resist, she bought a pair of boots with fancy stitching and a stubby heel. Since the van was too small to permit indiscriminate souvenir buying, she'd restrained herself this far. But there wasn't any point in being a martyr about it. The boots made her happy, but she resisted buying a leather belt with an oversize silver buckle for Shade. It was just the sort of gesture he might misunderstand. No, they wouldn't give each other flowers or trinkets or pretty words.

She drove south toward Texas while Shade read the paper in the seat beside her. On the radio was a raspy Tina Turner number that was unapologetically sexy.

Summer had reached the point when the heat began to simmer. Bryan didn't need the radio announcer to tell her it was ninety-seven and climbing, but both she and Shade had agreed to use the air-conditioning sparingly on the long trips. On the open highway, the breeze was almost enough. In defense, she was wearing a skimpy tank top and shorts while she drove in her bare feet. She thought of Dallas and an air-conditioned hotel room with cool sheets on a soft mattress.

"I've never been to Texas," she said idly. "I can't imagine any place that has cities fifty and sixty miles across. A cab ride across town could cost you a week's pay."

The paper crackled as he flipped the page. "You live in Dallas or Houston, you own a car."

It was like him to give a brief practical answer, and she'd come to accept it. "I'm glad we're taking a couple of days in Dallas to print. Ever spent any time there?"

"A little." He shrugged as he turned the next section of the paper. "Dallas, Houston—those cities are Texas. Big, sprawling, wealthy. Plenty of Tex-Mex restaurants, luxury hotels and a freeway system that leaves the out-of-towner reeling. That's why I routed in San Antonio as well. It's something apart from the rest of Texas. It's elegant, serene, more European."

She nodded, glancing out at the road signs. "Did you have an assignment in Texas?"

"I tried living in Dallas for a couple of years in between the overseas work."

It surprised her. She just couldn't picture him anywhere but L.A. "How'd you like it?"

"Not my style," he said simply. "My ex-wife stayed on and married oil."

It was the first time he'd made any sort of reference to his marriage. Bryan wiped her damp hands on her shorts and wondered how to handle it. "You don't mind going back?"

"No."

"Does it…" She trailed off, wondering if she was getting in deeper than she should.

Shade tossed the paper aside. "What?"

"Well, does it bother you that she's remarried and settled? Don't you ever think back and try to figure out what messed things up?"

"I know what messed things up. There's no use dwelling on it. After you admit you've made a mistake, you've got to go on."

"I know." She pushed at her sunglasses. "I just sometimes wonder why some people can be so happy together, and others so miserable."

"Some people don't belong with each other."

"And yet it often seems like they do before they walk up the aisle."

"Marriage doesn't work for certain kinds of people."

Like us? Bryan wondered. After all, they'd both failed at it. Perhaps he was right, and it was as simple as that. "I made a mess out of mine," she commented.

"All by yourself?"

"Seems that way."

"Then you screwed up and married Mr. Perfect."

"Well, I..." She glanced over and saw him looking at her, one brow raised and a bland look of anticipation on his face. She'd forgotten he could make her laugh as well as ache. "Mr. Nearly Perfect, anyway." She grinned. "I'd have been smarter to look for someone with flaws."

After lighting a cigarette, he rested his feet on the dash as Bryan was prone to do. "Why didn't you?"

"I was too young to realize flaws were easier to deal with. And I loved him." She hadn't realized it would be so painless to say it, to put it in the past tense. "I really did," she murmured. "In a naive, rose-tinted way. At the time I didn't realize I'd have to make a choice between his conception of marriage and my work."

He understood exactly. His wife hadn't been cruel, she hadn't been vindictive. She'd simply wanted things he couldn't give. "So you married Mr. Nearly Perfect and I married Ms. Socially Ambitious. I wanted to take important pictures, and she wanted to join the country club. Nothing wrong with either goal—they just don't mesh."

"But sometimes don't you regret that you couldn't make it fit?"

"Yeah." It came out unexpectedly, surprising him a great deal more than it surprised her. He hadn't realized he had regrets. He hadn't allowed himself to. "You're getting low on gas," he said abruptly. "We'll stop in the next town and fill up."

Bryan had heard of one-horse towns, but nothing fitted the phrase more perfectly than the huddle of houses just over the Oklahoma-Texas border. Everything seemed to be dusty and faded by the heat. Even the buildings looked tired. Perhaps the state was enriched by oil and growth, but this little corner had slept through it.

As a matter of habit, Bryan took her camera as she stepped from the van to stretch her legs. As she walked around the side of the van, the skinny young attendant goggled at her. Shade saw the boy gape and Bryan smile before he walked into the little fan-cooled store behind the pumps.

Bryan found a small, fenced yard just across the street. A woman in a cotton housedress and a faded apron watered the one colorful spot—a splash of pansies along the edge of the house. The grass was yellow, burned by the sun, but the flowers were lush and thriving. Perhaps they were all the woman needed to keep her content. The fence needed painting badly and the screen door to the house had several small holes, but the flowers were a bright, cheerful slash. The woman smiled as she watered them.

Grateful she'd picked up the camera she'd loaded with color film, Bryan tried several angles. She wanted to catch the tired, sun-faded wood of the house and the parched lawn, both a contrast to that bouquet of hope.

Dissatisfied, she shifted again. The light was good, the colors perfect, but the picture was wrong. Why? Stepping back, she took it all in again and asked herself the all-important question. What do I feel?

Then she had it. The woman wasn't necessary, just the illusion of her. Her hand holding the watering can, no more. She could be any woman, anywhere, who needed flowers to complete her home. It was the flowers and the hope they symbolized that were important, and that was what Bryan finally recorded.

Shade came out of the store with a paper bag. He saw Bryan across the street, experimenting with angles. Content to wait, he set the bag in the van, drawing out the first cold can before he turned to pay the attendant for the gas. The attendant, Shade noticed, who was so busy watching Bryan he could hardly screw on the gas cap.

"Nice van," he commented, but Shade didn't think he'd even looked at it.

"Thanks." He allowed his own gaze to follow the boy's until it rested on Bryan's. He had to smile. She was a very distracting sight in the swatch of material she called shorts. Those legs, he mused. They seemed to start at the waist and just kept going. Now he knew just how sensitive they could be—on the inside of the knee, just above the ankle, on the warm, smooth skin high on the thigh.

"You and your wife going far?"

"Hmm?" Shade lost track of the attendant as he became just as fascinated by Bryan.

"You and the missus," the boy repeated, sighing a little as he counted out Shade's change. "Going far?"

"Dallas," he murmured. "She's not..." He started to correct the boy's mistake about their relationship, then found himself stopping. The *missus*. It was a quaint word, and somehow appealing. It hardly mattered if a boy in a border town thought Bryan belonged to him. "Thanks," he said absently and, stuffing the change in his pocket, walked to her.

"Good timing," she told him as she crossed toward him. They met in the middle of the road.

"Find something?"

"Flowers." She smiled, forgetting the unmerciful sun. If she breathed deeply enough, she could just smell them over the dust. "Flowers where they didn't belong. I think it's..." She felt the rest of the words slide back down her throat as he reached out and touched her hair.

He never touched her, not in the most casual of ways. Unless they were making love, and then it was never casual. There was never any easy brush of hands, no gentle squeeze. Nothing. Until now, in the center of the road, between a parched yard and a grimy gas station.

"You're beautiful. Sometimes it stuns me."

What could she say? He never spoke soft words. Now they flowed over her as his fingers trailed to her cheek. His eyes were so dark. She had no idea what he saw when he looked at her, what he felt. She'd never have asked. Perhaps for the first time, he was giving her the opportunity, but she couldn't speak, only stare.

He might have told her that he saw honesty, kindness, strength. He might have told her he felt needs that were growing far beyond the borders he'd set up between him and the rest of the world. If she'd asked, he might have told her that she was making a difference in his life he hadn't foreseen but could no longer prevent.

For the first time, he bent toward her and kissed her, with an uncharacteristic gentleness. The moment demanded it, though he wasn't sure why. The sun was hot and hard, the road dusty, and the smell of gasoline was strong. But the moment demanded tenderness from him. He gave it, surprised that it was in him to offer.

"I'll drive," he murmured as he slipped her hand into his. "It's a long way to Dallas."

His feelings had changed. Not for the city they drove into, but for the woman beside him. Dallas had changed since he'd lived there, but Shade knew from experience that it seemed to change constantly. Even though he'd only lived there briefly, it had seemed as though a new building would grow up overnight. Hotels, office buildings, popped up wherever they could find room, and there seemed to be an endless supply of room in Dallas. The architecture leaned toward the futuristic—glass, spirals, pinnacles. But you never had to look far to find that unique southwestern flavor. Men wore cowboy hats as easily as they wore three-piece suits.

They'd agreed on a midtown hotel because it was within walking distance of the darkroom they'd rented for two days. While one worked in the field, the other would have use of the equipment to develop and print. Then they'd switch.

Bryan looked up at the hotel with something like reverence as they pulled up in front of it. Hot running water, feather pillows. Room service. Stepping out, she began to unload her share of the luggage and gear.

"I can't wait," she said as she hauled out another case

and felt sweat bead down her back. "I'm going to wallow in the bathtub. I might even sleep there."

Shade pulled out his tripod, then hers. "Do you want your own?"

"My own?" She swung the first camera bag strap over her shoulder.

"Tub."

She looked up and met his calm, questioning glance. He wouldn't assume, she realized, that they'd share a hotel room as they shared the van. They might be lovers, but the lack of strings was still very, very clear. Yes, they'd agreed there'd be no promises, but maybe it was time she took the first step. Tilting her head, she smiled.

"That depends."

"On?"

"Whether you agree to wash my back."

He gave her one of his rare spontaneous smiles as he lifted the rest of the luggage. "Sounds reasonable."

Fifteen minutes later, Bryan dropped her cases inside their hotel room. With equal negligence, she tossed down her shoes. She didn't bother to go to the window and check out the view. There'd be time for that later. There was one vital aspect of the room that demanded immediate attention. She flopped lengthwise on the bed.

"Heaven," she decided, and closed her eyes on a sigh. "Absolute heaven."

"Something wrong with your bunk in the van?" Shade stacked his gear in a corner before pulling open the drapes.

"Not a thing. But there's a world of difference between bunk and bed." Rolling onto her back, she stretched across the spread diagonally. "See? It's just not possible to do this on a bunk."

He gave her a mild look as he opened his suitcase. "You won't be able to do that on a bed, either, when you're sharing it with me."

True enough, she thought as she watched him methodically unpack. She gave her own suitcase an absent glance. It could wait. With the same enthusiasm as she'd had when she'd plopped down, Bryan sprang up. "Hot bath," she said, and disappeared into the bathroom.

Shade dropped his shaving kit onto the dresser as he heard the water begin to run. He stopped for a moment, listening. Already, Bryan was beginning to hum. The combination of sounds was oddly intimate—a woman's low voice, the splash of water. Strange that something so simple could make him burn.

Perhaps it'd been a mistake to take only one room in the hotel. It wasn't quite like sharing the van in a campground. Here, they'd had a choice, a chance for privacy and distance. Before the day was over, he mused, her things would be spread around the room, tossed here, flung there. It wasn't like him to freely invite disorder. And yet he had.

Glancing up, he saw himself in the mirror, a dark man with a lean body and a lean face. Eyes a bit too hard, mouth a bit too sensitive. He was too used to his own reflection to wonder what Bryan saw when she looked at him. He saw a man who looked a bit weary and needed a shave. And he didn't want to wonder, though he stared at himself as an artist stares at his subject, if he saw a man who'd already taken one irrevocable step toward change.

Shade looked at his face, reflected against the hotel room behind him. Just inside the door were Bryan's cases and the shoes she'd carried into the room. Fleetingly, he wondered if he took his camera and set the shot to take in his reflection, and that of the room and cases behind, just what kind of picture he'd have. He wondered if he'd be able to understand it. Shaking off the mood, he crossed the room and walked into the bath.

Her head moved, but that was all. Though her breath caught when he strolled into the room, Bryan kept her body still and submerged. This kind of intimacy was new and left her vulnerable. Foolishly, she wished she'd poured in a layer of bubbles so that she'd have some mystique.

Shade leaned against the sink and watched her. If she had plans to wash, she was taking her time about it. The little cake of soap sat wrapped in its dish while she lay naked in the tub. It struck him that it was the first time he'd seen her, really seen her, in the light. Her body was one long, alluring line. The room was small and steamy. He wanted her. Shade wondered if a man could die from wanting.

"How's the water?" he asked her.

"Hot." Bryan told herself to relax, be natural. The water that had soothed her now began to arouse.

"Good." Calmly, he began to strip.

Bryan opened her mouth, but shut it again. She'd never seen him undress. Always they'd held to their own unspoken, strict code of ethics. When they camped, each of them changed in the showers. Since they'd become lovers, they'd fallen into a sense of urgency at the end of the day, undressing themselves and each other in the dark van while they made love. Now, for the first time, she could watch her lover casually reveal his body to her.

She knew how it looked. Her hands had shown her. But it was a far different experience to see the slopes, the contours. Athletic, she thought, in the way of a runner or a hurdler. She supposed it was apt enough. Shade would always expect the next hurdle and be prepared to leap over it.

He left his clothes on the sink but made no comment when he had to step over hers where she'd dropped them.

"You said something about washing your back," he commented as he eased in behind her. Then he swore lightly at the temperature of the water. "You like to take off a couple layers of skin when you bathe?"

She laughed, relaxed and shifted to accommodate him. When his body rubbed and slid against hers, she decided there was something to be said for small tubs. Content, she snuggled back against him, a move that at first surprised him, then pleased.

"We're both a little long," she said as she adjusted her legs. "But it helps that we're on the slim side."

"Keep eating." He gave in to the urge to kiss the top of her head. "It's bound to stick sooner or later."

"Never has." She ran her hand along his thigh, trailing from the knee. It was a light, casual stroke that made his insides churn. "I like to believe I burn up calories just thinking. But you…"

"Me?"

On a quiet sigh, Bryan closed her eyes. He was so complex, so…driven. How could she explain it? She knew so little of what he'd seen and been through. Just one isolated incident, she thought. Just one scar. She didn't have to be told there were others.

"You're very physical," she said at length. "Even your thought pattern has a kind of physical force to it. You don't relax. It's like—" She hesitated for another moment, then plunged. "It's like you're a boxer in the ring. Even between rounds you're tensed and waiting for the bell to ring."

"That's life, isn't it?" But he found himself tracing the line of her neck with his finger. "One long match. A quick breather, then you're up and dancing."

"I've never looked at it that way. It's an adventure," she said slowly. "Sometimes I don't have the energy for it, so I can sit back and watch everyone else go through the moves. Maybe that's why I wanted to be a photographer, so I could pull in little pieces of life and keep them. Think of it, Shade."

Shifting slightly, she turned her head so that she could look at him. "Think of the people we've met, the places we've been and seen. And we're only halfway done. Those rodeo cowboys," she began, eyes brightening. "All they wanted was a plug of tobacco, a bad-tempered horse and a handful of sky. The farmer in Kansas, riding his tractor in the heat of the day, sweating and aching and looking out over acres of his own land. Children playing hopscotch, old men weeding kitchen gardens or playing checkers in the park. That's what life is. It's women with babies on their hips, young girls sunning at the beach and kids splashing in little rubber swimming pools in the side yard."

He touched her cheek. "Do you believe that?"

Did she? It sounded so simplistic…. Idealistic? She wondered. Frowning, she watched the steam rise from the water. "I believe that you have to take what good there is, what beauty there is, and go with it. The rest has to be dealt with, but not every minute of every day. That woman today…"

Bryan settled back again, not sure why it was so important for her to tell him. "The one in the house just across from where we stopped for gas. Her yard was burning up in the sun, the paint was peeling on the fence. I saw arthri-

tis in her hands. But she was watering her pansies. Maybe
she's lived in that tiny little house all her life. Maybe she'll
never know what it's like to sit in a new car and smell the
leather or fly first-class or shop at Saks. But she was watering her pansies. She'd planted, weeded and tended them
because they gave her pleasure. Something of value, one
bright foolish spot she can look at, smile at. Maybe it's
enough."

"Flowers can't grow everywhere."

"Yes, they can. You only have to want them to."

It sounded true when she said it. It sounded like something he'd like to believe. Unconsciously, he rested his
cheek against her hair. It was damp from the steam, warm,
soft. She made him relax. Just being with her, listening to
her, uncurled something in him. But he remembered the
rules, those they'd both agreed on. Keep it easy, he reminded himself. Keep it light.

"Do you always have philosophical discussions in the
tub?"

Her lips curved. It was so rare and so rewarding to hear
that touch of humor in his voice. "I figure if you're going
to have one, you might as well be comfortable. Now, about
my back…"

Shade picked up the soap and unwrapped it. "Do you
want the first shift in the darkroom tomorrow?"

"Mmm." She leaned forward, stretching as he rubbed
the dampened soap over her back. Tomorrow was too far
away to worry about. "Okay."

"You can have it from eight to twelve."

She started to object to the early hour, then subsided.
Some things didn't change. "What're you…" The question

trailed off into a sigh as he skimmed the soap around her waist and up to her throat. "I like being pampered."

Her voice was sleepy, but he traced a soapy finger over her nipple and felt the quick shudder. He ran the soap over her in steady circles, lower, still lower, until all thought of relaxation was over. Abruptly, she twisted until he was trapped beneath her, her mouth fixed on his. Her hands raced over him, taking him to the edge before he had a chance to brace himself.

"Bryan—"

"I love to touch you." She slid down until her mouth could skim over his chest, tasting flesh and water. She nibbled, listening to the thunder of his heart, then rubbed her cheek against his damp flesh just to feel, just to experience. She felt him tremble and lie still a moment. When was the last time he'd let himself be made love to? she wondered. Perhaps this time she'd give him no choice.

"Shade." She let her hands roam where they pleased. "Come to bed with me." Before he could answer, she rose. While the water streamed from her, she smiled down at him and slowly pulled the pins from her hair. As it fell, she shook it back, then reached for a towel. It seemed they were through with words.

She waited until he stepped from the tub, then took another towel and rubbed it over him herself. He made no objection, but she could sense him building up the emotional defense. Not this time, she thought. This time it would be different.

As she dried him, she watched his eyes. She couldn't read his thoughts, she couldn't see beneath the desire. For now, it was enough. Taking his hand, she walked toward the bed.

She would love him this time. No matter how strong, how urgent, the need, she would show him what he made her feel. Slowly, her arms already around him, she lowered herself to the bed. As the mattress gave, her mouth found his.

The need was no less. It tore through him. But this time, Shade found himself unable to demand, unable to pull her to his pace. She was satiating him with the luxury of being enjoyed. Her lips took him deep, deeper, but lazily. He learned that with her, passion could be built, layer by finite layer, until there was nothing else. They smelled of the bath they'd shared, of the soap that had rubbed from his skin to hers. She seemed content to breathe it in, to breathe it out, while slowly driving him mad.

It was pleasure enough to see him in the late-afternoon sunlight. No darkness now, no shadows. To make love in the light, freely and without barriers, was something she hadn't even known she craved. His shoulders were still damp. She could see the sheen of water on them, taste it. When their mouths met, she could watch his eyes and see the desire there that echoed what pulsed inside her. In this they were the same, she told herself. In this, if nothing else, they understood each other.

And when he touched her, when she saw his gaze follow the trail of his hand, she trembled. Needs, his and hers, collided, shuddered, then merged together.

There was more here than they'd allowed themselves or each other before. At last this was intimacy, shared knowledge, shared pleasure. No one led, no one held back. For the first time, Shade dropped all pretenses of keeping that thin emotional barrier between them. She filled him, completed him. This time he wanted her—all of her—more than he'd ever wanted anything. He wanted the fun of her, the joy, the kindness. He wanted to believe it could make a difference.

The sun slanted in across the deep, vivid gray of her eyes, highlighting them as he'd once imagined. Her mouth was soft, yielding. Above him, her hair flowed down, wild, free. The lowering sun seemed trapped in her skin, making it gleam gold. She might have been something he'd only imagined—woman, lean, agile and primitive, woman without restraints, accepting her own passions. If he photographed her this way, would he recognize her? Would he be able to recapture the emotions she could push into him?

Then she tossed back her head and she was young, vibrant, reachable. This woman he'd know, this feeling he'd recognize, if he went away alone for decades. He'd need no photograph to remind him of that one astonishing instant of give and take.

Shade drew her closer, needing her. You, he thought dizzily as their bodies merged and their thoughts twined. Only you. He watched her eyes slowly close as she gave herself to him.

Chapter 9

"I could get used to this."

With her camera settled comfortably in her lap, Bryan stretched back in the pirogue, the trim little dugout canoe they'd borrowed from a family who lived on the bayou. A few miles away was the bustling city of Lafayette, Louisiana, but here was a more slumberous view of summer.

Bees humming, shade spreading, birds trilling. Dragonflies. One whisked by, too fast for her camera, but slow enough to appreciate. Spanish moss hung overhead, shading and dipping toward the river as the water moved slowly. Why hurry? It was summer, fish were there for catching, flowers were there for picking. Cypress trees thrust their way out of the water, and an occasional frog stirred himself enough to plop from his pad and take a swim.

Why hurry, indeed? Life was there to be enjoyed.

As Shade had once pointed out, Bryan was adaptable. In the rush of Dallas, she'd worked long hours in the darkroom and on the street. All business. When the moment called for it, she could be efficient, quick and energetic. But here, where the air was heavy and the living slow, she was content to lie back, cross her ankles and wait for whatever came.

"We're supposed to be working," he pointed out.

She smiled. "Aren't we?" While she swung one foot in lazy circles, she wished they'd thought to borrow a fishing pole as well. What did it feel like to catch a catfish? "We took dozens of pictures before we got in the boat," she reminded him.

It'd been her idea to detour into the bayou, though she was all but certain Shade had topped her with his pictures of the family who'd welcomed them. She might've charmed them into the use of their boat, but Shade had won hands down with camera work.

"The one you took of Mrs. Bienville shelling beans has to be fabulous. Her hands." Bryan shook her head and relaxed. "I've never seen such hands on a woman. I imagine she could make the most elegant of soufflés right before she went out and cut down a tree."

"Cajuns have their own way of life, their own rules."

She tilted her head as she studied him. "You like that."

"Yeah." He rowed, not because they needed to get anywhere, but because it felt so good. It warmed his muscles and relaxed his mind. He nearly smiled, thinking that being with Bryan accomplished almost the same thing. "I like the independence and the fact that it works."

Bryan lay back, listening to the buzz and hum of insects, the sounds of the river. They'd walked along another river in San Antonio, but the sounds had been different there. Soft Spanish music from musicians, the clink of silver on china from the outdoor cafés. It had been fabulous at night, she remembered. The lights had glowed on the water, the water had rippled from the river taxis, the taxis had been full of people content with the Texas version of a gondola. She'd taken a picture of two young lovers, newlyweds perhaps, huddled together on one of the arched stone bridges above the water.

When they'd driven into Galveston, she'd seen yet another kind of Texas, one with white sand beaches, ferries and bicycle surreys. It'd been easier to talk Shade into renting one than she'd imagined. With a smile, she thought of just how far they'd come, and not only in miles. They were working together, and when he could be distracted, they played.

In Malibu, they'd gone their separate ways on the beach. In Galveston, after two hours of work, they'd walked hand in hand along the shore. A small thing for many people, Bryan mused, but not for either of them.

Each time they made love, there seemed to be something more. She didn't know what it was, but she didn't question it. It was Shade she wanted to be with, laugh with, talk with. Every day she discovered something new, something different, about the country and the people. She discovered it with Shade. Perhaps that was all the answer she needed.

What was it about him? Whether she chose to or not, there were times she wondered. What was it about Shade Colby that made her happy? He wasn't always patient. One moment he might be generous and something close to sweet, and the next he could be as cool and aloof as a stranger. Being with him wasn't without its frustrations for a woman accustomed to less fluctuating moods. But being with him was exactly what she wanted.

At the moment, he was relaxed. He wasn't often, she

knew, but the mood of the river seemed to have seeped into him. Still, he was watching. Someone else might have floated down the river, glancing at the scenery, appreciating the overall effect. Shade dissected it.

This she understood, because it was her way as well. A tree might be studied for the texture of its leaves, the grain in the wood, the pattern of shade and light it allowed to fall on the ground. A layman might take a perfectly competent picture of the tree, but it would be only that. When Bryan took the picture, she wanted it to pull feelings out of the viewer.

She specialized in people, Bryan remembered as she watched Shade draw the oars through the water. Landscapes, still lifes, she considered a change of pace. It was the human element that fascinated her, and always would. If she wanted to understand her feelings about Shade, maybe it was time to treat him as she would any other subject.

Under half-lowered lashes, she studied and dissected. He had very dominating physical looks, she mused. Being dominated was definitely not her ambition in life. Perhaps that was why she was so often drawn to his mouth, because it was sensitive, vulnerable.

She knew his image—cool, distant, pragmatic. Part of it was true, she thought, but part of it was illusion. Once she'd thought to photograph him in shadows. Now she wondered what sort of study she'd get if she photographed him in quiet sunlight. Without giving herself a chance to think, she lifted her camera, framed him in and shot.

"Just testing," she said lightly when he arched a brow. "And after all, you've already taken a couple of me."

"So I have." He remembered the picture he'd taken of her brushing her hair on the rock in Arizona. He hadn't told her that he'd sent the print back to the magazine, even though he had no doubt it would be used in the final essay. Nor had he told her it was a print he intended to keep in his private collection.

"Hold it a minute." With brisk, professional movements, she changed her lens, adjusted for distance and depth and focused on a heron perched on top of a cypress knee. "A place like this," she murmured as she took two more insurance shots, "makes you think summer just goes on and on."

"Maybe we should take another three months traveling back and do autumn."

"It's tempting." She stretched back again. "Very tempting. A study on all seasons."

"Your clients might get testy."

"Unfortunately true. Still..." She let her fingers dip into the water. "We miss the seasons in L.A. I'd like to see spring in Virginia and winter in Montana." Tossing her braid back, she sat up. "Have you ever thought of chucking it, Shade? Just packing up and moving to, oh, say, Nebraska, and setting up a little studio. Wedding and graduation pictures, you know."

He gave her a long steady look. "No."

With a laugh, she flopped back. "Me either."

"You wouldn't find many megastars in Nebraska."

She narrowed her eyes but spoke mildly. "Is that another subtle shot at my work?"

"Your work," he began as he gently turned the boat back, "is uniformly excellent. Otherwise, we wouldn't be working together."

"Thank you very much. I think."

"And because of the quality of your work," he continued, "I wonder why you limit yourself to the pretty people."

"It's my specialty." She saw a clump of wildflowers on the mossy, muddy edge of the river. Carefully she adjusted her camera again. "And a great many of my subjects are far from pretty—physically or emotionally. They interest me," she said before he could comment. "I like to find out what's under the image and give a glimpse of it."

And she was well skilled at it, he decided. In truth, he'd discovered he admired her for it—not only for her skill, but for her perception. He simply couldn't rationalize her following the glitz trail. "Culture art?"

If he'd meant it as an insult, however mild, it missed its mark. "Yes. And if you asked, I'd say Shakespeare wrote culture art. Are you hungry?"

"No." Fascinating woman, he thought, as reluctant as ever to be fascinated. He craved her, it was true. Her body, her company. But he couldn't resolve the constant fascination she held for him, mind to mind. "You had a bowl of shrimp and rice big enough to feed a family of four before we started out."

"That was hours ago."

"Two, to be exact."

"Picky," she mumbled, and stared up at the sky. So peaceful, she mused. So simple. Moments like this were meant to be savored. Lowering her gaze, she smiled at him. "Ever made love in a pirogue?"

He had to grin. She made it impossible to do otherwise. "No, but I don't think we should ever refuse a new experience."

Bryan touched her tongue to her top lip. "Come here."

They left the lazy, insect-humming air of the bayou behind and landed in bustling, raucous New Orleans. Sweating trumpet players on Bourbon Street, merchants fanning themselves in the Farmers Market, artists and tourists around Jackson Square—it was a taste of the South, they both agreed, that was as far apart from the South as San Antonio had been apart from Texas.

From there, they traveled north to Mississippi for a touch of July in the Deep South. Heat and humidity. Tall, cool drinks and precious shade. Life was different here. In the cities, men sweated in white shirts and loosened ties. In the rural districts, farmers worked under the sweltering sun. But they moved more slowly than their counterparts to the north and west. Perhaps temperatures soaring to a hundred and more caused it, or perhaps it was just a way of life.

Children exercised the privilege of youth and wore next to nothing. Their bodies were browned and damp and dusty. In a city park, Bryan took a close-up of a grinning boy with mahogany skin cooling himself in a fountain.

The camera didn't intimidate him. As she homed in, he laughed at her, squealing as the water cascaded over him, white and cool, until he looked encased in glass.

In a small town just northwest of Jackson, they stumbled across a Little League game. It wasn't much of a field, and the bleachers looked as if they'd object to more than fifty people at a time, but they pulled off and parked between a pickup and a rusted-out sedan.

"This is great." Bryan grabbed her camera bag.

"You just smell hot dogs."

"That too," she agreed easily. "But this *is* summer. We might get to a Yankee game in New York, but we'll get better pictures here today." She hooked her arm through his before he could get too far away. "I'll reserve judgment on the hot dogs."

Shade took a long, sweeping view. The crowd was spread out, on the grass, in folding chairs, on the bleachers. They cheered, complained, gossiped and gulped iced drinks. He was all but certain everyone there knew one another by name or by sight. He watched an old man in a baseball cap casually spit out a plug of tobacco before he berated the umpire.

"I'm going to wander around a bit," he decided, considering a seat on the bleachers too limiting for the moment.

"Okay." Bryan had taken her own scan and considered the bleachers the focal point for what she wanted.

They separated, Shade moving toward the old man who'd already captured his attention. Bryan walked to the bleachers, where she and the onlookers would have a solid view of the game.

The players wore white pants, already grass-stained and dusty, with bright red or blue shirts emblazoned with team names. A good many of them were too small for the uniforms, and the mitts looked enormous on the ends of gangling arms. Some wore spikes, some wore sneakers. A few had batting gloves hung professionally from their back pocket.

It was the hats, she decided, that told of the individual's personality. One might wear it snug or tipped back, another tilted rakishly over the eyes. She wanted an action shot, something that would bring the color and the personalities together with the sport itself. Until something formed for her, Bryan contented herself with taking a shot of the second baseman, who passed the time until the batter stepped into the box by kicking his spikes against the bag and blowing bubbles with his wad of gum.

Scooting up another step, she tried her long lens. Better, she decided, and was pleased to see that her second baseman had a face full of freckles. Above her, someone snapped gum and whistled when the umpire called a strike.

Bryan lowered her camera and allowed herself to become involved in the game. If she wanted to portray the atmosphere, she had to let herself feel it. It was more than the game, she thought, it was the feeling of community. As the batters came up, people in the crowd called them by name, tossing out casual remarks that indicated a personal knowledge. But the sides were definitely drawn.

Parents had come to the game from work, grandparents had pushed away from an early dinner, and neighbors had chosen the game against an evening by the TV. They had their favorites, and they weren't shy about rooting for them.

The next batter interested Bryan mainly because she was a strikingly pretty girl of about twelve. At a glance, Bryan would've set her more easily at a ballet bar than home plate. But when she watched the way the girl gripped the bat and bent into her stance, Bryan lifted her camera. This was one to watch.

Bryan caught her in the first swing on a strike. Though the crowd moaned, Bryan was thrilled with the flow of movement. She might be shooting a Little League game in a half-forgotten town in Mississippi, but she thought of her studio work with the prima ballerina. The batter poised for the pitch, and Bryan poised for the next shot. She had to wait, growing impatient, through two balls.

"Low and outside," she heard someone mumble beside her. All she could think was, if the girl walked, she'd lose the picture she wanted.

Then it came over, too fast for Bryan to judge the placement of the ball, but the girl connected with a solid swing.

The batter took off, and using the motor drive, Bryan followed her around the bases. When she rounded second, Bryan homed in on her face. Yes, Maria would understand that look, Bryan thought. Strain, determination and just plain guts. Bryan had her as she slid into third with a storm of dust and a swing of body.

"Wonderful!" She lowered the camera, so thrilled that she didn't even realize she'd spoken out loud. "Just wonderful!"

"That's our girl."

Distracted, Bryan glanced over to the couple beside her. The woman was her own age, perhaps a year or two older. She was beaming. The man beside her was grinning over a wad of gum.

Perhaps she hadn't heard properly. They were so young. "She's your daughter?"

"Our oldest." The woman slipped a hand into her husband's. Bryan saw the plain twin wedding bands. "We've got three others running around here, but they're more interested in the concession stand than the game."

"Not our Carey." The father looked out to where his daughter took a short lead on third. "She's all business."

"I hope you don't mind my taking her picture."

"No." The woman smiled again. "Do you live in town?"

It was a polite way to find out who she was. Bryan hadn't a doubt the woman knew everyone within ten miles. "No, I'm traveling." She paused as the next batter blooped to right field and brought Carey home. "Actually, I'm a freelance photographer on assignment for *Life-style*. Perhaps you've heard of it."

"Sure." The man jerked a head at his wife as he kept his eyes on the game. "She picks it up every month."

Pulling a release form out of her bag, she explained her interest in using Carey's picture. Though she kept it short and her voice low, word spread throughout the bleachers. Bryan found herself answering questions and dealing with curiosity. In order to handle it all in the simplest fashion, she climbed down from the bleachers, changed to a wide-angle lens and took a group shot. Not a bad study, she decided, but she didn't want to spend the next hour having people pose for her. To give the baseball fans time to shift their attention back to the game, she wandered to the concession stand.

"Any luck?"

She swiveled her head around to see Shade fall into step beside her. "Yeah. You?"

He nodded, then leaned on the counter of the stand. There was no relief from the heat, though the sun was lowering. It promised to be as sweltering a night as it had a day. He ordered two large drinks and two hot dogs.

"Know what I'd love?" she asked as she began to bury her hot dog under relish.

"A shovel?"

Ignoring him, she piled on mustard. "A long, cool dip in an enormous pool, followed closely by an iced margarita."

"For now you'll have to settle for the driver's seat of the van. It's your turn."

She shrugged. A job was a job. "Did you see the girl who hit the triple?" They walked over the uneven grass toward the van.

"Kid that ran like a bullet?"

"Yes. I sat next to her parents in the stands. They have four kids."

"So?"

"Four kids," she repeated. "And I'd swear she wasn't more than thirty. How do people do it?"

"Ask me later and I'll show you."

With a laugh, she jabbed him with her elbow. "That's not what I meant—though I like the idea. What I mean is, here's this couple—young, attractive. You could tell they even liked each other."

"Amazing."

"Don't be cynical," she ordered as she pulled open the door to the van. "A great many couples don't, especially when they've got four kids, a mortgage and ten or twelve years of marriage under their belts."

"Now who's being cynical?"

She started to speak and frowned instead. "I guess I am," she mused as she turned on the engine. "Maybe I've picked a world that's tilted my outlook, but when I see a happily married couple with a track record, I'm impressed."

"It is impressive." Carefully, he stored his camera bag under the dash before he sat back. "When it really works."

"Yeah."

She fell silent, remembering the jolt of envy and longing she'd felt when she'd framed the Browns in her viewfinder. Now, weeks and miles later, it was another jolt for Bryan to realize she hadn't brushed off that peculiar feeling. She had managed to put it aside, somewhere to the back of her mind, but it popped out again now as she thought of the couple in the bleachers of a small-town park.

Family, cohesion. Bonding. Did some people just keep promises better than others? she wondered. Or were some people simply unable to blend their lives with someone else's, make those adjustments, the compromises?

When she looked back, she believed both she and Rob

had tried, but in their own ways. There'd been no meeting of the minds, but two separate thought patterns making decisions that never melded with each other. Did that mean that a successful marriage depended on the mating of two people who thought along the same lines?

With a sigh, she turned onto the highway that would lead them into Tennessee. If it was true, she decided, she was much better off single. Though she'd met a great many people she liked and could have fun with, she'd never met anyone who thought the way she did. Especially the man seated next to her with his nose already buried in the newspaper. There alone they were radically different.

He'd read that paper and every paper in every town they stopped in from cover to cover, devouring the words. She'd skim the headlines, glance over the style or society pages and go straight for the comics. If she wanted news, she'd rather have it in spurts on the radio or blurbs on televisions. Reading was for relaxation, and relaxation was not an analysis of détente.

Relationships. She thought back on the discussion she'd had with Lee just weeks before. No, she simply wasn't cut out for relationships on a long-term basis. Shade himself had pointed out that some people just weren't capable of permanency. She'd agreed, hadn't she? Why should the truth suddenly depress her?

Whatever her feelings were for Shade, and she'd yet to define them satisfactorily, she wasn't going to start smelling orange blossoms. Maybe she had a few twinges when she saw couples together who seemed to complete each other rather than compete, but that was only natural. After all, she didn't want to start making adjustments in her life-style to accommodate someone else at this stage. She was perfectly content the way things were.

If she was in love… Bryan felt the twinge again and ignored it. *If* she was, it would complicate things. The fact was, she was very happy with a successful career, her freedom and an attractive, interesting lover. She'd be crazy if she wasn't happy. She'd be insane to change one single thing.

"And it doesn't have anything to do with being afraid," she said aloud.

"What?"

She turned to Shade and, to his astonishment and hers, blushed. "Nothing," she muttered. "Thinking out loud."

He gave her a long, quiet look. Her expression came very close to a baffled sort of pout. Giving in to the urge, he leaned over and touched a hand to her cheek. "You're not eating your hot dog."

She could have wept. For some absurd reason, she wanted to stop the van, drop her head on the steering wheel and drown herself in hot, violent tears. "Not hungry," she managed.

"Bryan." He watched her snatch her sunglasses from the dash and push them on, though the sun was riding low. "Are you all right?"

"Fine." She took a deep breath and kept her eyes straight ahead. "I'm fine."

No, she wasn't. Though strain in her voice was rare, he recognized it. Only a few weeks before, he'd have shrugged and turned back to his reading. Deliberately, he dropped the paper on the floor at his feet. "What is it?"

"Nothing." She cursed herself and turned up the radio. Shade simply switched it off.

"Pull over."

"What for?"

"Just pull over."

With more violence than necessary, Bryan swung the van toward the shoulder, slowed and stopped. "We won't make very good time if we stop ten minutes after we start."

"We won't be making any time at all until you tell me what's wrong."

"Nothing's wrong!" Then she gritted her teeth and sat back. It wasn't any use saying nothing was wrong if you snarled at the same time. "I don't know," she evaded. "I'm edgy, that's all."

"You?"

She turned on him with a vengeance. "I've a right to foul moods, Colby. You don't have a patent on them."

"You certainly have," he said mildly. "Since it's the first one I've witnessed, I'm interested."

"Don't be so damn patronizing."

"Wanna fight?"

She stared through the windshield. "Maybe."

"Okay." Willing to oblige, he made himself comfortable. "About anything in particular?"

She swung her head around, ready to pounce on anything. "Do you have to bury your face in a paper every time I get behind the wheel?"

He smiled maddeningly. "Yes, dear."

A low sound came from her throat as she stared through the windshield again. "Never mind."

"I could point out that you have a habit of falling asleep when you sit in this seat."

"I said never mind." She reached for the key. "Just never mind. You make me sound like a fool."

He put his hand over hers before she could turn the key. "You sound foolish skirting around whatever's bothering you." He wanted to reach her. Without being aware when, he'd passed the point where he could tell himself not to get involved and follow the advice. Whether he wanted it or not, whether she accepted it or not, he was involved. Slowly, he lifted her hand to his lips. "Bryan, I care."

She sat there stunned that a simple statement could spin through her with such force. *I care*. He'd used the same word when he'd spoken about the woman who'd caused his nightmare. Along with the pleasure his words brought her came an inescapable sense of responsibility. He wouldn't allow himself to care indiscriminately. Glancing up, she met his eyes, patient, puzzled, as they studied her face.

"I care too," she said quietly. She twined her fingers with his, only briefly, but it unsettled them both.

Shade took the next step carefully, not certain of her, or himself. "Is that what's bothering you?"

She let out a long breath, as wary as he now. "Some. I'm not used to it...not like this."

"Neither am I."

She nodded, watching the cars breeze by. "I guess we'd both better take it easy then."

"Sounds logical." And next to impossible, he thought. Right now he wanted to gather her close, forget where they were. Just hold her, he realized. It was all he wanted to do. With an effort, he drew back. "No complications?"

She managed to smile. Rule number one was the most important, after all. "No complications," she agreed. Again she reached for the key. "Read your paper, Colby," she said lightly. "I'll drive until dark."

Chapter 10

They took a slice out of Tennessee—Nashville, Chattanooga—caught the eastern corner of Arkansas—mountains and legends—and headed up through Twain's Missouri to Kentucky. There they found tobacco leaves, mountain laurel, Fort Knox and Mammoth Cave, but when Bryan thought of Kentucky, she thought of horses. Kentucky was sleek, glossy Thoroughbreds grazing on rich grass. It made her think of long-legged foals running in wide pastures and wide-chested colts pounding the track at Churchill Downs.

As they crossed the state toward Louisville, she saw much more. Tidy suburban homes bordered the larger cities and smaller towns as they did in every state across the country. Farms spread acre after acre—tobacco, horses, grain. Cities rose with their busy office buildings and harried streets. So much was the same as it had been to the west and to the south, and yet so much was different.

"Daniel Boone and the Cherokees," Bryan murmured as they traveled down another long, monotonous highway.

"What?" Slade glanced up from the map he'd been checking. When Bryan was driving, it didn't hurt to keep an eye on the navigation.

"Daniel Boone and the Cherokees," Bryan repeated. She increased the speed to pass a camper loaded down with bikes on the back bumper and fishing poles on the front. And where were they going? she wondered. Where had they come from? "I was thinking maybe it's the history of a place that makes it different from another. Maybe it's the climate, the topography."

Shade glanced back down at the map, idly figuring the time and mileage. He didn't give the camper rolling along behind them more than a passing thought. "Yes."

Bryan shot him an exasperated smile. One and one always added up to two for Shade. "But people are basically the same, don't you think? I imagine if you took a cross section of the country and polled, you'd find out that most people want the same things. A roof over their heads, a good job, a couple weeks off a year to play."

"Flowers in the garden?"

"All right, yes." She gave a careless little shrug and refused to believe it sounded foolish. "I think most peoples' wants are fairly simple. Italian shoes and a trip to Barbados might add in, but it's the basic things that touch everyone. Healthy children, a nest egg, a steak on the grill."

"You've a way of simplifying things, Bryan."

"Maybe, but I don't see any reason to complicate them."

Interested, he set down the map and turned to her. Perhaps he'd avoided digging too deeply into her, leery of what he might find. But now, behind his sunglasses, his eyes were direct. So was his question. "What do you want?"

"I..." She faltered a moment, frowning as she took the van around a long curve. "I don't know what you mean."

He thought she did, but they always seemed to end up fencing. "A roof over your head, a good job? Are those the most important things to you?"

Two months before, she might've shrugged and agreed. Her job came first, and gave her whatever she needed. That was the way she'd planned it, the way she'd wanted it. She wasn't sure any longer. Since she'd left L.A., she'd seen too much, felt too much. "I have those things," she said evasively. "Of course I want them."

"And?"

Uncomfortable, she shifted. She hadn't meant to have her idle speculation turned back on her. "I wouldn't turn down a trip to Barbados."

He didn't smile as she'd hoped he would, but continued to watch her from behind the protection of tinted glasses. "You're still simplifying."

"I'm a simple person."

Her hands were light and competent on the wheel, and her hair was scooped back in its habitual braid. She wore no makeup, a pair of faded cut-offs and a T-shirt two sizes too large for her. "No," he decided after a moment, "you're not. You only pretend to be."

Abruptly wary, she shook her head. Since her outburst in Mississippi, Bryan had managed to keep herself level, and to keep herself, she admitted, from thinking too deeply. "You're a complicated person, Shade, and you see complications where there aren't any."

She wished she could see his eyes. She wished she could see the thoughts behind them.

"I know what I see when I look at you, and it isn't simple."

She shrugged carelessly, but her body had begun to tense. "I'm easily read."

He corrected her with a short, concise word calmly spoken. Bryan blinked once, then gave her attention to the road. "Well, I'm certainly not full of mysteries."

Wasn't she? Shade watched the thin gold loops sway at her ears. "I wonder what you're thinking when you lie beside me after we've made love—in those minutes after passion and before sleep. I often wonder."

She wondered, too. "After we've made love," she said in a tolerably steady voice, "I have a hard time thinking at all."

This time he did smile. "You're always soft and sleepy," he murmured, making her tremble. "And I wonder what you might say, what I might hear if you spoke your thoughts aloud."

That I might be falling in love with you. That every day we have together takes us a day closer to the end. That I can't imagine what my life will be like when I don't have you there to touch, to talk to. Those were her thoughts, but she said nothing.

She had her secrets, Shade thought. Just as he did. "One day, before we're finished, you'll tell me."

He was easing her into a corner; Bryan felt it, but she didn't know why. "Haven't I told you enough already?"

"No." Giving in to the urge that came over him more and more often, he touched her cheek. "Not nearly."

She tried to smile, but she had to clear her throat to

speak. "This is a dangerous conversation to have when I'm driving on an interstate at sixty miles an hour."

"It's a dangerous conversation in any case." Slowly, he drew his hand away. "I want you, Bryan. I can't look at you and not want you."

She fell silent, not because he was saying things she didn't want to hear, but because she no longer knew how to deal with them, and with him. If she spoke, she might say too much and break whatever bond had begun to form. She couldn't tell him so, but it was a bond she wanted.

He waited for her to speak, needing her to say something after he'd all but crossed over the line they'd drawn in the beginning. Risk. He'd taken one. Couldn't she see it? Needs. He needed her. Couldn't she feel it? But she remained silent, and the step forward became a step back.

"Your exit's coming up," he told her. Picking up the map, he folded it carefully. Bryan switched lanes, slowed down and left the highway.

Kentucky had made her think of horses; horses led them to Louisville, and Louisville to Churchill Downs. The Derby was long over, but there were races and there were crowds. If they were going to include in their glimpse of summer those who spent an afternoon watching races and betting, where else would they go?

The moment Bryan saw it, she thought of a dozen angles. There were cathedrallike domes and clean white buildings that gave a quiet elegance to the frenzy. The track was the focal point, a long oval of packed dirt. Stands rose around it. Bryan walked about, wondering just what kind of person would come there, or to any track, to plop down two dollars—or two hundred—on a race that would take only minutes. Again, she saw the variety.

There was the man with reddened arms and a sweaty T-shirt who pored over a racing form, and another in casually elegant slacks who sipped something long and cool. She saw women in quietly expensive dresses holding field glasses and families treating their children to the sport of kings. There was a man in a gray hat with tattoos snaking up both arms and a boy laughing on top of his father's shoulders.

They'd been to baseball games, tennis matches, drag races across the country. Always she saw faces in the crowd that seemed to have nothing in common except the game. The games had been invented, Bryan mused, and turned into industries. It was an interesting aspect of human nature. But people kept the games alive; they wanted to be amused, they wanted to compete.

She spotted one man leaning against the rail, watching a race as though his life depended on the outcome. His body was coiled, his face damp. She caught him in profile.

A quick scan showed her a woman in a pale rose dress and summer hat. She watched the race idly, distanced from it the way an empress might've been from a contest in a coliseum. Bryan framed her as the crowd roared the horses down the stretch.   ·

Shade rested a hip on the rail and shot the horses in varying positions around the track, ending with the final lunge across the finish line. Before, he'd framed in the odds board, where numbers flashed and tempted. Now he waited until the results were posted and focused on it again.

Before the races were over, Shade saw Bryan standing at the two-dollar window. With her camera hanging around her neck and her ticket in her hand, she walked back toward the stands.

"Haven't you got any willpower?" he asked her.

"No." She'd found a vending machine, and she offered Shade a candy bar that was already softening in the heat. "Besides, there's a horse in the next race called Made in the Shade." When his eyebrow lifted up, she grinned. "How could I resist?"

He wanted to tell her she was foolish. He wanted to tell her she was unbearably sweet. Instead, he drew her sunglasses down her nose until he could see her eyes. "What's his number?"

"Seven."

Shade glanced over at the odds board and shook his head. "Thirty-five to one. How'd you bet?"

"To win, of course."

Taking her arm, he led her down to the rail again. "You can kiss your two bucks goodbye, hotshot."

"Or I can win seventy." Bryan pushed her glasses back in place. "Then I'll take you out to dinner. If I lose," she continued as the horses were led to the starting gate, "I've always got plastic. I can still take you out to dinner."

"Deal," Shade told her as the bell rang.

Bryan watched the horses lunge forward. They were nearly to the first turn before she managed to find number 7, third from the back. She glanced up to see Shade shake his head.

"Don't give up on him yet."

"When you bet on a long shot, love, you've got to be ready to lose."

A bit flustered by his absent use of the endearment, she turned back to the race. Shade rarely called her by name, much less one of those sweetly intimate terms. A long shot, she agreed silently. But she wasn't altogether sure she was as prepared to lose as she might've been.

"He's moving up," she said quickly as number 7 passed three horses with long, hard-driving strides. Forgetting herself, she leaned on the rail and laughed. "Look at him! He's moving up." Lifting her camera, she used the telephoto lens like a field glass. "God, he's beautiful," she murmured. "I didn't know he was so beautiful."

Watching the horse, she forgot the race, the competition. He was beautiful. She could see the jockey riding low in a blur of color that had a style of its own, but it was the horse, muscles bunching, legs pounding, that held her fascinated. He wanted to win; she could feel it. No matter how many races he'd lost, how many times he'd been led back to the stables sweating, he wanted to win.

Hope. She sensed it, but she no longer heard the call of the crowd around her. The horse straining to overtake the leaders hadn't lost hope. He believed he could win, and if you believed hard enough… With a last burst of speed, he nipped by the leader and crossed the wire like a champion.

"I'll be damned," Shade murmured. He found he had his arm around Bryan's shoulders as they watched the winner take his victory lap in long, steady strides.

"Beautiful." Her voice was low and thick.

"Hey." Shade tipped up her chin when he heard the tears. "It was only a two-dollar bet."

She shook her head. "He did it. He wanted to win, and he just didn't give up until he did."

Shade ran a finger down her nose. "Ever hear of luck?"

"Yeah." More composed, she took his hand in hers. "And this had nothing to do with it."

For a moment, he studied her. Then, with a shake of his head, he lowered his mouth to hers lightly, sweetly. "And this from a woman who claims to be simple."

And happy, she thought as her fingers laced with his. Ridiculously happy. "Let's go collect my winnings."

"There was a rumor," he began as they worked their way through the stands, "about you buying dinner."

"Yeah. I heard something about it myself."

She was a woman of her word. That evening, as the sky flashed with lightning and echoed with the thunder of a summer storm, they stepped into a quiet, low-lighted restaurant.

"Linen napkins," Bryan murmured to Shade as they were led to a table.

He laughed in her ear as he pulled out her chair. "You're easily impressed."

"True enough," she agreed, "but I haven't seen a linen napkin since June." Picking it off her plate, she ran it through her hands. It was smooth and rich. "There isn't a vinyl seat or a plastic light in this place. There won't be any little plastic containers of ketchup either." With a wink, she knocked a finger against a plate and let it ring. "Try that with paper and all you get is a thump."

Shade watched her experiment with the water glass next. "All this from the queen of fast food?"

"A steady diet of hamburgers is all right, but I like a change of pace. Let's have champagne," she decided as their waiter came over. She glanced at the list, made her choice and turned back to Shade again.

"You just blew your winnings on a bottle of wine."

"Easy come, easy go." Cupping her chin on her hands,

she smiled at him. "Did I mention you look wonderful by candlelight?"

"No." Amused, he leaned forward as well. "Shouldn't that be my line?"

"Maybe, but you didn't seem in a rush to come out with it. Besides, I'm buying. However..." She sent him a slow, simmering look. "If you'd like to say something flattering, I wouldn't be offended."

Lazily, she ran a finger along the back of his hand, making him wonder why any man would object to the benefits of women's liberation. It wasn't a hardship to be wined and dined. Nor would it be a hardship to relax and be seduced. All the same, Shade decided as he lifted her hand to his lips, there was something to be said for partnership.

"I might say that you always look lovely, but tonight..." He let his gaze wander over her face. "Tonight, you take my breath away."

Momentarily flustered, she allowed her hand to stay in his. How was it he could say such things so calmly, so unexpectedly? And how could she, when she was used to casual, inconsequential compliments from men, deal with one that seemed so serious? Carefully, she warned herself. Very carefully.

"In that case I'll have to remember to use lipstick more often."

With a quick smile, he kissed her fingers again. "You forgot to put any on."

"Oh." Stuck, Bryan stared at him.

"Madame?" The wine steward held out the bottle of champagne, label up.

"Yes." She let out a quiet breath. "Yes, that's fine."

Still watching Shade, she heard the cork give in to pressure and the wine bubble into her glass. She sipped, closing her eyes to enjoy it. Then, with a nod, she waited until the steward filled both glasses. Steadier, Bryan lifted her glass and smiled at Shade.

"To?"

"One summer," he said, and touched his rim to hers. "One fascinating summer."

It made her lips curve again, so that her eyes reflected the smile as she sipped. "I expected you to be a terrible bore to work with."

"Really." Shade let the champagne rest on his tongue a moment. Like Bryan, it was smooth and quiet, with energy bubbling underneath. "I expected you to be a pain in the—"

"However," she interrupted dryly. "I've been pleased that my preconception didn't hold true." She waited a moment. "And yours?"

"Did," he said easily, then laughed when she narrowed her eyes at him. "But I wouldn't have enjoyed you nearly as much if it'd been otherwise."

"I liked your other compliment better," she mumbled, and picked up her menu. "But I suppose since you're stingy with them, I have to take what I get."

"I only say what I mean."

"I know." She pushed back her hair as she skimmed the menu. "But I — Oh look, they've got chocolate mousse."

"Most people start at the appetizers."

"I'd rather work backward, then I can gauge how much I want to eat and still have room for dessert."

"I can't imagine you turning down anything chocolate."

"Right you are."

"What I can't understand is how you can shovel it in the way you do and not be fat."

"Just lucky, I guess." With the menu open over her plate, she smiled at him. "Don't you have any weaknesses, Shade?"

"Yeah." He looked at her until she was baffled and flustered again. "A few." And one of them, he thought as he watched her eyes, was becoming more and more acute.

"Are you ready to order?"

Distracted, Bryan looked up at the well-mannered waiter. "What?"

"Are you ready to order?" he repeated. "Or would you like more time?"

"The lady'll have the chocolate mousse," Shade said smoothly.

"Yes, sir." Unflappable, the waiter marked it down. "Will that be all?"

"Not by a long shot," Shade told him, and picked up his wine again.

With a laugh, Bryan worked her way through the menu.

"Stuffed," Bryan decided over an hour later, as they drove through a hard, driving rain. "Absolutely stuffed."

Shade cruised through an amber light. "Watching you eat is an amazing way to pass the time."

"We're here to entertain," she said lightly. Snuggled back in her seat with champagne swimming in her head and thunder grumbling in a bad-tempered sky, she was content to ride along wherever he chose to go. "It was sweet of you to let me have a bite of your cheesecake."

"Half," Shade corrected her. Deliberately he turned away from the campground they'd decided on that afternoon. The wipers made quick swishing sounds against the windshield. "But you're welcome."

"It was lovely." She let out a sigh, quiet and sleepy. "I like being pampered. Tonight should get me through another month of fast-food chains and diners with stale doughnuts." Content, she glanced around at the dark, wet streets, the puddles at the curbs. She liked the rain, especially at night, when it made everything glisten. Watching it, she fell to dreaming, rousing herself only when he turned into the lot of a small motel.

"No campground tonight," he said before she could question. "Wait here while I get a room."

She didn't have time to comment before he was out of the van and dashing through the rain. No campground, she thought, looking over her shoulder at the narrow twin bunks on either side of the van. No skinny, makeshift beds and trickling showers.

With a grin, she jumped up and began to gather his equipment and hers. She never gave the suitcases a thought.

"Champagne, linen napkins and now a bed." She laughed as he climbed back into the van, soaking wet. "I'm going to get spoiled."

He wanted to spoil her. There was no logic to it, only fact. Tonight, if only for tonight, he wanted to spoil her. "Room's around the back." When Bryan dragged the equipment forward, he drove slowly around, checking numbers on the lines of doors. "Here." He strapped camera bags over his shoulder. "Wait a minute." She'd grabbed another bag and her purse by the time he'd pulled open her door from the outside. To her astonishment, she found herself lifted into his arms.

"Shade!" But the rain slapped into her face, making her gasp as he dashed across the lot to an outside door.

"Least I could do after you sprang for dinner," he told her as he maneuvered the oversize key into the lock. Bryan was laughing as he struggled to open the door holding her, the camera bags and tripods.

Kicking the door closed with his foot, he fastened his mouth on hers. Still laughing, Bryan clung to him.

"Now we're both wet," she murmured, running a hand through his hair.

"We'll dry off in bed." Before she knew his intention, Bryan was falling through the air and landing with two bounces full-length onto the mattress.

"So romantic," she said dryly, but her body stayed limp. She lay there, smiling, because he'd made a rare frivolous gesture and she intended to enjoy it.

Her dress clung to her, her hair fanned out. He'd seen her change for dinner and knew she wore a thin teddy cut high at the thigh, low over her breasts, and sheer, sheer stockings. He could love her now, love her for hours. It wouldn't be enough. He knew how relaxed, how pliant, her body could be. How full of fire, strength, vibrancy. He could want all of it, have all of it. It wouldn't be enough.

He was an expert at capturing the moment, the emotions, the message. Letting his own feelings hum, he reached for his camera bag.

"What're you doing?"

When she started to sit up, Shade turned back. "Stay there a minute."

Intrigued and wary, she watched him set his camera. "I don't—"

"Just lie back like you were," he interrupted. "Relaxed and rather pleased with yourself."

His intention was obvious enough now. Bryan lifted a brow. An obsession, she thought, amused. The camera was an obsession for both of them. "Shade, I'm a photographer, not a model."

"Humor me." Gently, he pushed her back on the bed.

"I've too much champagne in my system to argue with you." She smiled up at him as he held the camera over his face. "You can play if you like, or take serious pictures if you must. As long as I don't have to do anything."

She did nothing but smile, and he began to throb. So often he'd used the camera as a barrier between himself and his subject, other times as a conductor for his emotion, emotion he refused to let loose any other way. Now, it was neither. The emotion was already in him, and barriers weren't possible.

He framed her quickly and shot, but was unsatisfied.

"That's not what I want." He was so businesslike that Bryan didn't see it as a defense, only as his manner. But when he came over, pulled her into a sitting position and unzipped her dress, her mouth fell open.

"Shade!"

"It's that lazy sex," he murmured as he slipped the dress down over one shoulder. "Those incredible waves of sensuality that take no effort at all, but just are. It's the way your eyes look." But when his came back to hers, she forgot the joke she'd been about to make. "The way they look when I touch you—like this." Slowly, he ran a hand over her naked shoulder. "The way they look just after I kiss you—like this." He kissed her, lingering over it while her mind emptied of thought and her body filled with sensation.

"Like this," he whispered, more determined than ever to capture that moment, make it tangible so that he could hold it in his hands and see it. "Just like this," he said again, backing off one step, then two. "The way you look just before we make love. The way you look just after."

Helplessly aroused, Bryan stared into the lens of the camera as he lifted it. He caught her there, like a quarry in the crosshairs of a scope, empty of thoughts, jumbled with feeling. At the same time, he caught himself.

For an instant her heart was in her eyes. The shutter opened, closed and captured it. When he printed the photograph, he thought as he carefully set down his camera, would he see what she felt? Would he be certain of his own feelings?

Now she sat on the bed, her dress disarrayed, her hair tumbled, her eyes clouded. Secrets, Shade thought again. They both had them. Was it possible he'd locked a share of each of their secrets on film inside his camera?

When he looked at her now, he saw a woman aroused, a woman who aroused. He could see passion and pliancy and acceptance. He could see a woman whom he'd come to know better than anyone else. Yet he saw a woman he'd yet to reach—one he'd avoided reaching.

He went to her in silence. Her skin was damp but warm, as he'd known it would be. Raindrops clung to her hair. He touched one, then it was gone. Her arms lifted.

While the storm raged outside, he took her and himself where there was no need for answers.

Chapter 11

If they had more time…

As August began to slip by, that was the thought that continued to run through Bryan's mind. With more time, they could have stayed longer at each stop. With more time, they might have passed through more states, more towns, more communities. There was so much to see, so much to record, but time was running out.

In less than a month, the school she'd photographed empty and waiting in the afternoon light would be filled again. Leaves that were full and green would take on those vibrant colors before they fell. She would be back in L.A., back in her studio, back to the routine she'd established. For the first time in years, the word *alone* had a hollow ring.

How had it happened? Shade Colby had become her partner, her lover, her friend. He'd become, though it was frightening to admit, the most important person in her life. Somehow she'd become dependent on him, for his opinion, his company, for the nights they spent involved only with each other.

She could imagine how it would be when they returned to L.A. and went their separate ways. Separate parts of the city, she thought, separate lives, separate outlooks.

The closeness that had so slowly, almost painfully, developed between them would dissolve. Wasn't that what they'd both intended from the start? They'd made a bargain with each other, just as they'd made the bargain to work together. If her feelings had changed, she was responsible for them, for dealing with them. As the odometer turned over on the next mile, as the next state was left behind, she wondered how to begin.

Shade had his own thoughts to deal with. When they'd crossed into Maryland, they'd crossed into the East. The Atlantic was close, as close as the end of summer. It was the end that disturbed him. The word no longer seemed to mean finished, but over. He began to realize he was far from ready to draw that last line. There were ways to rationalize it. He tried them all.

They'd missed too much. If they took their time driving back, rather than sticking to their plan of going straight across the country, they could detour into so many places they'd eliminated on the way out. It made sense. They could stay in New England a week, two weeks after Labor Day. After long days in the van and the intense work they'd both put in, they deserved some time off. It was reasonable.

They should work their way back, rather than rush. If they weren't preoccupied with making time, making miles, how many pictures would come out of it? If one of them was special, it would be worth it. That was professional.

When they returned to L.A., perhaps Bryan could move

in with him, share his apartment as they'd shared the van. It was impossible. Wasn't it?

She didn't want to complicate their relationship. Hadn't she said so? He didn't want the responsibility of committing himself to one person. Hadn't he made himself clear? Perhaps he'd come to need her companionship on some level. And it was true he'd learned to appreciate the way she could look at anything and see the fun and the beauty of it. That didn't equal promises, commitments or complications.

With a little time, a little distance, the need was bound to fade. The only thing he was sure of was that he wanted to put off that point for as long as possible.

Bryan spotted a convertible—red, flashy. Its driver had one arm thrown over the white leather seat while her short blond hair flew in the wind. Grabbing her camera, Bryan leaned out the open window. Half kneeling, half crouching, on the seat, she adjusted for depth.

She wanted to catch it from the rear, elongating the car into a blur of color. But she didn't want to lose the arrogant angle of the driver's arm, or the negligent way her hair streamed back. Already she knew she would dodge the plain gray highway and the other cars in the darkroom. Just the red convertible, she thought as she set her camera.

"Try to keep just this distance," she called to Shade. She took one shot and, dissatisfied, leaned out farther for the next. Though Shade swore at her, Bryan got her shot before she laughed and flopped back on her seat.

He was guilty of the same thing, he knew. Once the camera was in place, you tended to think of it as a shield. Nothing could happen to you—you simply weren't part of what was happening. Though he'd known better, it had happened to him often enough, even after his first stint overseas. Perhaps it was the understanding that made his voice mild, though he was annoyed.

"Don't you have more sense than to climb out the window of a moving car?"

"Couldn't resist. There's nothing like a convertible on an open highway in August. I'm always toying with the idea of getting one myself."

"Why don't you?"

"Buying a new car is hard work." She looked at the green-and-white road signs as she'd looked at so many others that summer. There were cities, roads and routes she'd never heard of. "I can hardly believe we're in Maryland. We've come so far and yet, I don't know, it doesn't seem like two months."

"Two years?"

She laughed. "Sometimes. Other times it seems like days. Not enough time," she said, half to herself. "Never enough."

Shade didn't give himself the chance to think before he took the opening. "We've had to leave out a lot."

"I know."

"We went through Kansas, but not Nebraska, Mississippi, and not the Carolinas. We didn't go to Michigan or Wisconsin."

"Or Florida, Washington State, the Dakotas." She shrugged, trying not to think of what was left behind. Just today, Bryan told herself. Just take today.

"I've been thinking about tying them in on the way back."

"On the way back?" Bryan turned to him as he reached for a cigarette.

"We'd be on our own time." The van's lighter glowed red against the tip. "But I think we could both take a month or so and finish the job."

More time. Bryan felt the quick surge of hope, then ruthlessly toned it down. He wanted to finish the job his way. It was his way, she reminded herself, to do things thoroughly. But did the reason really matter? They'd have more time. Yes, she realized as she stared out the side window. The reason mattered a great deal too much.

"The job's finished in New England," she said lightly. "Summer's over, and it's back to business. My work at the studio will be backed up for a month. Still..." She felt herself weakening, though he said nothing, did nothing, to persuade her. "I wouldn't mind a few detours on the trip back."

Shade kept his hands easy on the wheel, his voice casual. "We'll think about it," he said, and let the subject they both wanted to pursue drop.

Weary of the highway, they took to the back roads. Bryan took her pictures of kids squirting each other with garden hoses, of laundry drying in the breeze, of an elderly couple sitting on a porch glider. Shade took his of sweating construction workers spreading tar on roofs, of laborers harvesting peaches and, surprisingly, of two ten-year-old businessmen hawking lemonade in their front yard.

Touched, Bryan accepted the paper cup Shade handed her. "That was sweet."

"You haven't tasted it yet," he commented, and climbed into the passenger's seat. "To keep down the overhead, they used a light hand on the sugar."

"I meant you." On impulse, she leaned over and kissed him, lightly, comfortably. "You can be a very sweet man."

As always, she moved him, and he couldn't stop it. "I can give you a list of people who'd disagree."

"What do they know?" With a smile, she touched her lips to his again. She drove down the neat, shady street appreciating the trim lawns, flower gardens and dogs barking in the yards. "I like the suburbs," she said idly. "To look at, anyway. I've never lived in one. They're so orderly." With a sigh, she turned right at the corner. "If I had a house here, I'd probably forget to fertilize the lawn and end up with crab grass and dandelions. My neighbors would take up a petition. I'd end up selling my house and moving into a condo."

"So ends Bryan Mitchell's career as a suburbanite."

She made a face at him. "Some people aren't cut out for picket fences."

"True enough."

She waited, but he said nothing that made her feel inadequate—nothing that made her feel as though she should be. She laughed delightedly, then grabbed his hand and squeezed. "You're good for me, Shade. You really are."

He didn't want to let her hand go, and released it reluctantly. Good for her. She said it so easily, laughing. Because she did, he knew she had no idea just what it meant to him to hear it. Maybe it was time he told her. "Bryan—"

"What's that?" she said abruptly, and swung toward the curb. Excited, she inched the car forward until she could read the colorful cardboard poster tacked to a telephone pole. "Nightingale's Traveling Carnival." Pulling on the brake, she nearly climbed over Shade to see it more clearly. "Voltara, the Electric Woman." With a half whoop, she nudged closer to Shade. "Terrific, just terrific. Sampson, the Dancing Elephant. Madame Zoltar, Mystic. Shade, look, it's their last night in town. We can't miss it. What's summer without a carny? Thrilling rides, games of skill and chance."

"And Dr. Wren, the Fire Eater."

It was easy to ignore the dry tone. "Fate." She scrambled back to her own seat. "It has to be fate that we turned down this road. Otherwise, we might've missed it."

Shade glanced back at the sign as Bryan pulled away from the curb. "Think of it," he murmured. "We might've gotten all the way to the coast without seeing a dancing elephant."

A half hour later, Shade leaned back in his seat, calmly smoking, his feet on the dash. Frazzled, Bryan swung the van around the next turn.

"I'm not lost."

Shade blew out a lazy stream of smoke. "I didn't say a word."

"I know what you're thinking."

"That's Madame Zoltar's line."

"And you can stop looking so smug."

"Was I?"

"You always look smug when I get lost."

"You said you weren't."

Bryan gritted her teeth and sent him a killing look. "Why don't you just pick up that map and tell me where we are?"

"I started to pick it up ten minutes ago and you snarled at me."

Bryan let out a long breath. "It was the *way* you picked it up. You were smirking, and I could hear you thinking—"

"You're stepping into Madame Zoltar's territory again."

"Damn it, Shade." But she had to choke back a laugh

as she drove down the long, unlit country road. "I don't mind making a fool of myself, but I hate it when someone lifts an eyebrow over it."

"Did I?"

"You know you did. Now, if you'd just—"

Then she caught the first glimmer of red, blue, green lights flickering. A Ferris wheel, she thought. It had to be. The sound of tinny music came faintly through the summer dusk. A calliope. This time it was Bryan who looked smug. "I knew I'd find it."

"I never had a doubt."

She might've had something withering to say to that, but the lights glowing in the early-evening dusk, and the foolish piping music held her attention. "It's been years," she murmured. "Just years since I've seen anything like this. I've got to watch the fire eater."

"And your wallet."

She shook her head as she turned off the road onto the bumpy field where cars were parked. "Cynic."

"Realist." He waited until she maneuvered the van next to a late-model pickup. "Lock the van." Shade gathered his bag and waited outside the van until Bryan had hers. "Where first?"

She thought of pink cotton candy but restrained herself. "Why don't we just wander around a bit? We might want some shots now, but at night they'd have more punch."

Without the dark, without the bright glow of colored lights, the carnival looked too much like what it was—a little weary, more than a little tawdry. Its illusions were too easily unmasked now, and that wasn't why Bryan had come. Carnivals, like Santa Claus, had a right to their mystique. In another hour, when the sun had completely set behind those rolling, blue-tinted hills to the west, the carnival would come into its own. Peeling paint wouldn't be noticed.

"Look, there's Voltara." Bryan grabbed Shade's arm and swung him around to see a life-size poster that gave her lavish curves and scant cover as she was being strapped into what looked like a homemade electric chair.

Shade looked at the painted spangles over generous cleavage. "Might be worth watching after all."

With a quick snort, Bryan pulled him toward the Ferris wheel. "Let's take a ride. From the top we'll be able to see the whole layout."

Shade pulled a bill out of his wallet. "That's the only reason you want to ride."

"Don't be ridiculous." They walked over, waiting while the attendant let a couple off. "It's a good way of covering ground and sitting down at the same time," she began as she took the vacated seat. "It's sure to be an excellent angle for some aerial pictures, and..." She slipped a hand into his as they started the slow swing up. "It's the very best place to neck at a carnival."

When he laughed, she wrapped her arms around him and silenced his lips with hers. They reached the top where the evening breeze flowed clean and hung there one moment—two—aware only of each other. On the descent, the speed picked up and the drop had her stomach shivering, her mind swimming. It was no different from the sensation of being held by him, loved by him. They held tight and close through two revolutions.

Gathering her against his shoulder, Shade watched the carnival rush up toward them. It'd been years since he'd held someone soft and feminine on a Ferris wheel. High school? he wondered. He could hardly remember. Now he realized he'd let his youth slip by him because so many other things had seemed important at the time. He'd let it go freely, and though he wouldn't, couldn't, ask for the whole of it back, perhaps Bryan was showing him how to recapture pieces of it.

"I love the way this feels," she murmured. She could watch the sun go down in a last splashy explosion of arrogance, hear the music, the voices, ebb and fade as the wheel spun around. She could look down and be just removed enough from the scene to enjoy it, just separate enough to understand it. "A ride on a Ferris wheel should be required once a year, like a routine physical."

With her head against Shade's shoulder, she examined the scene below, the midway, the concessions, the booths set up for games of skill. She wanted to see it all, close up. She could smell popcorn, grilling meat, sweat, the heavy-handed after-shave of the attendant as their car swung by him. It gave her the overall view. This was life, a sidelong glance at it. This was the little corner of life where children could see wonders and adults could pretend for just a little while.

Taking her camera, she angled down through the cars and wires to focus in on the attendant. He looked a bit bored as he lifted the safety bar for one couple and lowered it for the next. A job for him, Bryan thought, a small thrill for the rest. She sat back, content to ride.

When it was dark, they went to work. There were people gathered around the wheel of fortune, plopping down a dollar for a chance at more. Teenagers showed off for their girls or their peers by hurling softballs at stacked bottles. Toddlers hung over the rope and tossed Ping-Pong balls at fishbowls, hoping to win a goldfish whose life expectancy was short at best. Young girls squealed on the fast-spinning Octopus, while young boys goggled at the posters along the midway.

Bryan took one telling shot of a woman carrying a baby on one hip while a three-year-old dragged her mercilessly along. Shade took another of a trio of boys in muscle shirts standing apart and doing their best to look tough and aloof.

They ate slices of pizza with rubber crusts as they watched with the rest of the crowd as Dr. Wren, Fire Eater, came out of his tent to give a quick, teasing demonstration of his art. Like the ten-year-old boy who watched beside her, Bryan was sold.

With an agreement to meet back at the entrance to the midway in thirty minutes, they separated. Caught up, Bryan wandered. She wasn't able to resist Voltara, and slipped into part of the show to see the somewhat weary, glossy-faced woman strapped into a chair that promised to zap her with two thousand volts.

She pulled it off well enough, Bryan thought, closing her eyes and giving a regal nod before the lever was pulled. The special effects weren't top-notch, but they worked. Blue light shimmered up the chair and around Voltara's head. It turned her skin to the color of summer lightning. At fifty cents a shot, Bryan decided as she stepped back out, the audience got their money's worth.

Intrigued, she wandered around in back of the midway to where the carnival workers parked their trailers. No colorful lights here, she mused as she glanced over the small caravan. No pretty illusions. Tonight, they'd pack up the equipment, take down the posters and drive on.

The moonlight hit the metal of a trailer and showed the

scratches and dents. The shades were drawn at the little windows, but there was faded lettering on the side. Nightingale's.

Bryan found it touching and crouched to shoot.

"Lost, little lady?"

Surprised, Bryan sprang up and nearly collided with a short, husky man in T-shirt and work pants. If he worked for the carnival, Bryan thought quickly, he'd been taking a long break. If he'd come to watch, the lights and sideshows hadn't held his interest. The smell of beer, warm and stale, clung to him.

"No." She gave him a careful smile and kept a careful distance. Fear hadn't entered into it. The move had been automatic and mild. There were lights and people only a few yards away. And she thought he might give her another angle for her photographs. "Do you work here?"

"Woman shouldn't wander around in the dark alone. 'Less she's looking for something."

No, fear hadn't been her first reaction, nor did it come now. Annoyance did. It was that that showed in her eyes before she turned away. "Excuse me."

Then he had her arm, and it occurred to her that the lights were a great deal farther away than she'd have liked. Brazen it out, she told herself. "Look, I've people waiting for me."

"You're a tall one, ain't you?" His fingers were very firm, if his stance wasn't. He weaved slightly as he looked Bryan over. "Don't mind looking eye to eye with a woman. Let's have a drink."

"Some other time." Bryan put her hand on his arm to push it away and found it solid as a concrete block. That's when the fear began. "I came back here to take some pictures," she said as calmly as she could. "My partner's waiting for me." She pushed at his arm again. "You're hurting me."

"Got some more beer in my truck," he mumbled as he began to drag her farther away from the lights.

"No." Her voice rose on the first wave of panic. "I don't want any beer."

He stopped a moment, swaying. As Bryan took a good look in his eyes, she realized he was as drunk as a man could get and still stand. Fear bubbled hot in her throat. "Maybe you want something else." He skimmed down her thin summer top and brief shorts. "Woman usually wants something when she wanders around half naked."

Her fear ebbed as cold fury rushed in. Bryan glared. He grinned.

"You ignorant ass," she hissed just before she brought her knee up, hard. His breath came out in a whoosh as he dropped his hand. Bryan didn't wait to see him crouch over. She ran.

She was still running when she rammed straight into Shade.

"You're ten minutes late," he began, "but I've never seen you move that fast."

"I was just— I had to..." She trailed off, breathless, and leaned against him. Solid, dependable, safe. She could have stayed just like that until the sun rose again.

"What is it?" He could feel the tension before he drew her away and saw it on her face. "What happened?"

"Nothing really." Disgusted with herself, Bryan dragged her hair back from her face. "I just ran into some jerk who wanted to buy me a drink whether I was thirsty or not."

His fingers tightened on her arms, and she winced

as they covered the same area that was already tender. "Where?"

"It was nothing," she said again, furious with herself that she hadn't taken the time to regain her composure before she ran into him. "I went around back to get a look at the trailers."

"Alone?" He shook her once, quickly. "What kind of idiot are you? Don't you know carnivals aren't just cotton candy and colored lights? Did he hurt you?"

It wasn't concern she heard in his voice, but anger. Her spine straightened. "No, but you are."

Ignoring her, Shade began to drag her through the crowds toward the parking section. "If you'd stop looking at everything through rose-colored glasses, you'd see a lot more clearly. Do you have any idea what might've happened?"

"I can take care of myself. I did take care of myself." When they reached the van, she swung away from him. "I'll look at life any way I like. I don't need you to lecture me, Shade."

"You need something." Grabbing the keys from her, he unlocked the van. "It's brainless to go wandering around alone in the dark in a place like this. Looking for trouble," he muttered as he climbed into the driver's seat.

"You sound remarkably like the idiot I left sprawled on the grass with his hands between his legs."

He shot her a look. Later, when he was calm, he might admire the way she'd dealt with an obnoxious drunk, but now he couldn't see beyond her carelessness. Independence aside, a woman was vulnerable. "I should've known better than to let you go off alone."

"Now just a minute." She whirled around in her seat.

"You don't *let* me do anything, Colby. If you've got it in your head that you're my keeper or anything of the sort, then you'd better get it right out again. I answer to myself. Only myself."

"For the next few weeks, you answer to me as well."

She tried to control the temper that pushed at her, but it wasn't possible. "I may work with you," she said, pacing her words. "I may sleep with you. But I don't answer to you. Not now. Not ever."

Shade punched in the van's lighter. "We'll see about that."

"Just remember the contract." Shaking with fury, she turned away again. "We're partners on this job, fifty-fifty."

He gave his opinion of what she could do with the contract. Bryan folded her arms, shut her eyes and willed herself to sleep.

He drove for hours. She might sleep, but there was too much churning inside him to allow him the same release. So he drove, east toward the Atlantic.

She'd been right when she'd said she didn't answer to him. That was one of the first rules they'd laid down. He was damned sick of rules. She was her own woman. His strings weren't on her any more than hers were on him. They were two intelligent, independent people who wanted it that way.

But he'd wanted to protect her. When everything else was stripped away, he'd wanted to protect her. Was she so dense that she couldn't see he'd been furious not with her but with himself for not being there when she'd needed him?

She'd tossed that back in his face, Shade thought grimly

as he ran a hand over his gritty eyes. She'd put him very clearly, very concisely, in his place. And his place, he reminded himself, no matter how intimate they'd become, was still at arm's length. It was best for both of them.

With his window open, he could just smell the tang of the ocean. They'd crossed the country. They'd crossed more lines than he'd bargained for. But they were a long way from crossing the final one.

How did he feel about her? He'd asked himself that question time after time, but he'd always managed to block out the answer. Did he really want to hear it? But it was three o'clock in the morning, that hour he knew well. Defenses crumbled easily at three o'clock in the morning. Truth had a way of easing its way in.

He was in love with her. It was too late to take a step back and say no thanks. He was in love with her in a way that was completely foreign to him. Unselfishly. Unlimitedly.

Looking back, he could almost pinpoint the moment when it had happened to him, though he'd called it something else. When he'd stood on the rock island in the Arizona lake, he'd desired her, desired her more intensely than he'd desired anything or anyone. When he'd woken from the nightmare and had found her warm and solid beside him, he'd needed her, again more than anything or anyone.

But when he'd looked across the dusty road on the Oklahoma border and seen her standing in front of a sad little house with a plot of pansies, he'd fallen in love.

They were a long way from Oklahoma now, a long way from that moment. Love had grown, overwhelming him. He hadn't known how to deal with it then. He hadn't a clue what to do about it now.

He drove toward the ocean where the air was moist. When he pulled the van between two low-rising dunes, he could just see the water, a shadow with sound in the distance. Watching it, listening to it, he slept.

Bryan woke when she heard the gulls. Stiff, disoriented, she opened her eyes. She saw the ocean, blue and quiet in the early light that wasn't quite dawn. At the horizon, the sky was pink and serene. Misty. Waking slowly, she watched gulls swoop over the shoreline and soar to sea again.

Shade slept in the seat beside her, turned slightly in his seat, his head resting against the door. He'd driven for hours, she realized. But what had driven him?

She thought of their argument with a kind of weary tolerance. Quietly, she slipped from the van. She wanted the scent of the sea.

Had it only been two months since they'd stood on the shore of the Pacific? Was this really so different? she wondered as she stepped out of her shoes and felt the sand, cool and rough under her feet. He'd driven through the night to get here, she mused. To get here, one step closer to the end. They had only to drive up the coast now, winding their way through New England. A quick stop in New York for pictures and darkroom work, then on to Cape Cod, where summer would end for both of them.

It might be best, she thought, if they broke there completely. Driving back together, touching on some of the places they'd discovered as a team, might be too much to handle. Perhaps when the time came, she'd make some excuse and fly back to L.A. It might be best, she reflected, to start back to those separate lives when summer ended.

They'd come full circle. Through the tension and annoyance of the beginning, into the cautious friendship, the frenzied passion, and right back to the tension again.

Bending, Bryan picked up a shell small enough to fit into the palm of her hand, but whole.

Tension broke things, didn't it? Cracked the whole until pressure crumbled it into pieces. Then whatever you'd had was lost. She didn't want that for Shade. With a sigh, she looked out over the ocean, where the water was green, then blue. The mist was rising.

No, she didn't want that for him. When they turned from each other, they should do so as they'd turned to each other. As whole, separate people, standing independently.

She kept the shell in her hand as she walked back toward the van. The weariness was gone. When she saw him standing beside the van watching her, with his hair ruffled by the wind, his face shadowed, eyes heavy, her heart turned over.

The break would come soon enough, she told herself. For now, there should be no pressure.

Smiling, she went to him. She took his hand and pressed the shell into it. "You can hear the ocean if you listen for it."

He said nothing, but put his arm around her and held her. Together they watched the sun rise over the east.

Chapter 12

On a street corner in Chelsea, five enterprising kids loosened the bolts on a fire hydrant and sent water swooshing. Bryan liked the way they dived through the stream, soaking their sneakers, plastering their hair. It wasn't necessary to think long about her feelings toward the scene. As she lifted her camera and focused, her one predominant emotion was envy, pure and simple.

Not only were they cool and delightfully wet while she was limp from the heat, but they hadn't a care in the world. They didn't have to worry if their lives were heading in the right direction, or any direction at all. It was their privilege in these last breathless weeks of summer to enjoy— their youth, their freedom and a cool splash in city water.

If she was envious, there were others who felt the same way. As it happened, Bryan's best shot came from incorporating one passerby in the scene. The middle-aged deliveryman in the sweaty blue shirt and dusty work shoes looked over his shoulder as one of the children lifted his arms up to catch a stream. On one face was pleasure, pure and giddy. On the other was amusement, laced with regret for something that couldn't be recaptured.

Bryan walked on, down streets packed with bad-tempered traffic, over sidewalks that tossed up heat like insults. New York didn't always weather summer with a smile and a wave.

Shade was in the darkroom they'd rented, while she'd opted to take the field first. She was putting it off, she admitted, as she skirted around a sidewalk salesman and his array of bright-lensed plastic sunglasses. Putting off coping with the last darkroom session she'd have before they returned to California. After this brief stop in New York, they'd head north for the final weekend of summer in Cape Cod.

And she and Shade had gone back to being almost unbearably careful with each other. Since that morning when they'd woken at the beach, Bryan had taken a step back. Deliberately, she admitted. She'd discovered all too forcibly that he could hurt her. Perhaps it was true that she'd left herself wide open. Bryan wouldn't deny that somewhere along the way she'd lost her determination to maintain a certain distance. But it wasn't too late to pull back just enough to keep from getting battered. She had to accept that the season was nearly over, and when it was, her relationship with Shade ended with it.

With this in mind, she took a slow, meandering route back toward midtown and the rented darkroom.

Shade already had ten rows of proofs. Sliding a strip under the enlarger, he methodically began to select and eliminate. As always, he was more ruthless, more critical with his own work than he'd have been with anyone else's.

He knew Bryan would be back shortly, so any printing he did would have to wait until the following day. Still, he wanted to see one now, for himself.

He remembered the little motel room they'd taken that rainy night just outside of Louisville. He remembered the way he'd felt then—involved, a little reckless. That night had been preying on his mind, more and more often, as he and Bryan seemed to put up fences again. There'd been no boundaries between them that night.

Finding the print he was looking for, he brought the magnifier closer. She was sitting on the bed, her dress falling off her shoulders, raindrops clinging to her hair. Soft, passionate, hesitant. All those things were there in the way she held herself, in the way she looked at the camera. But her eyes…

Frustrated, he narrowed his own. What was in her eyes? He wanted to enlarge the proof now, to blow it up so that he could see and study and understand.

She was holding back now. Every day he could feel it, sense it. Just a little bit more distance every day. But what had been in her eyes on that rainy night? He had to know. Until he did, he couldn't take a step, either toward her or away.

When the knock came on the door, he cursed it. He wanted another hour. With another hour, he could have the print, and perhaps his answer. He found it a simple matter to ignore the knock.

"Shade, come on. Time for the next shift."

"Come back in an hour."

"An hour!" On the other side of the door, Bryan pounded again. "Look, I'm melting out there. Besides, I've already given you twenty minutes more than your share."

The moment he yanked open the door, Bryan felt the waves of impatience. Because she wasn't in the mood to wrestle with it, she merely lifted a brow and skirted around him. If he wanted to be in a foul mood, fine. As long as he took it outside with him. Casually she set down her camera and a paper cup filled with soft drink and ice.

"So how'd it go?"

"I'm not finished."

With a shrug, she began to set out the capsules of undeveloped film she'd stored in her bag. "You've tomorrow for that."

He didn't want to wait until tomorrow, not, he discovered, for another minute. "If you'd give me the rest of the time I want, I wouldn't need tomorrow."

Bryan began to run water in a shallow plastic tub. "Sorry, Shade. I've run out of steam outside. If I don't get started in here, the best I'll do is go back to the hotel and sleep the rest of the afternoon. Then I'll be behind. What's so important?"

He stuffed his hands in his pockets. "Nothing. I just want to finish."

"And I've got to start," she murmured absently as she checked the temperature of the water.

He watched her a moment, the competent way she set up, arranging bottles of chemicals to her preference. Little tendrils of her hair curled damply around her face from the humidity. Even as she set up to work, she slipped out of her shoes. He felt a wave of love, of need, of confusion, and reached out to touch her shoulder. "Bryan—"

"Hmm?"

He started to move closer, then stopped himself. "What time will you be finished?"

There were touches of amusement and annoyance in her voice. "Shade, will you stop trying to push me out?"

"I want to come back for you."

She stopped long enough to look over her shoulder. "Why?"

"Because I don't want you walking around outside after it's dark."

"For heaven's sake." Exasperated, she turned completely around. "Do you have any idea how many times I've been to New York alone? Do I look stupid?"

"No."

Something in the way he said it had her narrowing her eyes. "Look—"

"I want to come back for you," he repeated, and this time touched her cheek. "Humor me."

She let out a long breath, tried to be annoyed and ended by lifting her hand to his. "Eight, eight-thirty."

"Okay. We can grab something to eat on the way back."

"There's something we can agree on." She smiled and lowered her hand before she could give in to the urge to move closer. "Now go take some pictures, will you? I've got to get to work."

He lifted his camera bag and started out. "Any longer than eight-thirty and you buy dinner."

Bryan locked the door behind him with a decisive click. She didn't lose track of time while she worked. Time was too essential. In the dark she worked briskly. In the amber light, her movements flowed with the same rhythm. As one set of negatives was developed and hung to dry, she went on to the next, then the next. When at length she could switch on the overhead light, Bryan arched her back, stretched her shoulders and relaxed.

An idle glance around showed her that she'd forgotten the carryout drink she'd picked up on the way. Unconcerned, she took a long gulp of lukewarm, watered-down soda.

The work satisfied her—the precision it required. Now her thoughts were skipping ahead to the prints. Only then would the creativity be fully satisfied. She had time, she noticed as she took a quick glance at her watch, to fuss with the negatives a bit before he came back. But then she'd end up putting herself in the same position she'd put him in—leaving something half done. Instead, mildly curious, she walked over to study his proofs.

Impressive, she decided, but then she'd expected no less. She might just be inclined to beg for a blowup of the old man in the baseball cap. Not Shade's usual style, she mused as she bent over the strip. It was so rare that he focused in on one person and let the emotions flow. The man who'd taken it had once told her he had no compassion. Bryan shook her head as she skimmed over other proofs. Did Shade believe that, or did he simply want the rest of the world to?

Then she saw herself and stopped with a kind of dazed wonder. Of course she remembered Shade setting up that picture, amusing, then arousing her while he changed angles and f-stops. The way he'd touched her… It wasn't something she'd forget, so it shouldn't surprise her to see the proof. Yet it did more than surprise her.

Not quite steady, Bryan picked up a magnifying glass and held it over one tiny square. She looked…pliant. She heard her own nervous swallow as she looked deeper. She looked…soft. It could be her imagination or, more likely, the skill of the photographer. She looked…in love.

Slowly, Bryan set down the glass and straightened. The skill of the photographer, she repeated, fighting to believe it. A trick of the angle, of the light and shadows. What a photographer captured on film wasn't always the truth. It was often illusion, often that vague blur between truth and illusion.

A woman knew when she loved. That's what Bryan told herself. A woman knew when she'd given her heart. It wasn't something that could happen and not be felt.

She closed her eyes a moment and listened to the quiet. Was there anything she hadn't felt when it came to Shade? How much longer was she going to pretend that passion, needs, longings, stood on their own? Love had bound them together. Love had cemented them into something solid and strong and undeniable.

She turned to where her negatives hung. There was one she'd managed to ignore. There was one tiny slice of film she'd taken on impulse and then buried because she'd come to be afraid of the answer she'd find. Now, when she had the answer already, Bryan stared at it.

It was reversed, so that his hair was light, his face dark. The little sliver of river in the corner was white, like the oars in his hands. But she saw him clearly.

His eyes were too intense, though his body seemed relaxed. Would he ever allow his mind true rest? His face was hard, lean, with the only tangible sensitivity around his mouth. He was a man, Bryan knew, who'd have little patience with mistakes—his own or others'. He was a man with a rigid sense of what was important. And he was a man who was capable of harnessing his own emotions and denying them to another. What he gave, when he gave, would be on his terms.

She knew, and understood, and loved regardless.

She'd loved before, and love had made more sense then. At least it had seemed to. Still, in the end, love hadn't been enough. What did she know about making love work? Could she possibly believe that when she'd failed once, she could succeed with a man like Shade?

She loved now, and told herself she was wise enough, strong enough, to let him go.

Rule number one, Bryan reminded herself as she put the darkroom in order. No complications. It was a litany she had running through her head until Shade knocked on the door. When she opened it for him, she nearly believed it.

They'd reached the last stop, the last day. Summer was not, as some would wish it, endless. Perhaps the weather would stay balmy for weeks longer. Flowers might still bloom defiantly, but just as Bryan had considered the last day of school summer's conception, so did she consider the Labor Day weekend its demise.

Clambakes, beach parties, bonfires. Hot beaches and cool water. That was Cape Cod. There were volleyball games in the sand and blasting portable radios. Teenagers perfected the tans they'd show off during those first few weeks of school. Families took to the water in a last, frantic rush before autumn signaled the end. Backyard barbecues smoked. Baseball hung on gamely before football could push its way through. As if it knew its time was limited, summer poured on the heat.

Bryan didn't mind. She wanted this last weekend to be everything summer could be—hot, hazy, torrid. She wanted her last weekend with Shade to reflect it. Love could be disguised with passion. She could let herself flow with it. Long, steamy days led to long, steamy nights, and Bryan held on to them.

If her lovemaking was a little frantic, if her desires were a little desperate, she could blame it on the heat. While Bryan became more aggressive, Shade became more gentle.

He'd noticed the change. Though he'd said nothing, Shade had noticed it the night he'd come back to meet her at the darkroom. Perhaps because she rarely had nerves, Bryan thought she hid them well. Shade could almost see them jump every time he looked at her.

Bryan had made a decision in the darkroom—a decision she felt would be best for both herself and for Shade. Shade had made a decision in the darkroom as well, the day after, when he'd watched the print of Bryan slowly come to life.

On the ride east, they'd become lovers. Now he had to find a way on the ride west to court her, as a man does the woman he wants to spend his life with.

Gentleness came first, though he wasn't an expert at it. Pressure, if it came to that, could be applied later. He was more experienced there.

"What a day." After long hours walking, watching and shooting, Bryan dropped down on the back of the van where the doors were open wide to let in the breeze. "I can't believe how many half-naked people I've seen." Grinning at Shade, she arched her back. She wore nothing but her sleek red bathing suit and a loose white cover-up that drooped over one shoulder.

"You seem to fit right in."

Lazily, she lifted one leg and examined it. "Well, it's nice to know that this assignment hasn't ruined my tan." Yawning, she stretched. "We've got a couple more hours of sun. Why don't you put on something indecent and walk down to the beach with me?" She rose, lifting her arms so they could wind easily around his neck. "We could cool off in the water." She touched her lips to his, teasing, taunting. "Then we could come back and heat up again."

"I like the second part." He turned the kiss into something staggering with an increase of pressure and change of angle. Beneath his hands, he felt her sigh. "Why don't you go ahead down, do the cooling-off? I've got some things to do."

With her head resting against his shoulder, Bryan struggled not to ask again. She wanted him to go with her, be with her every second they had left. Tomorrow she'd have to tell him that she'd made arrangements to fly back to the Coast. This was their last night, but only she knew it.

"All right." She managed to smile as she drew away. "I can't resist the beach when we're camped so close. I'll be back in a couple hours."

"Have fun." He gave her a quick, absent kiss and didn't watch as she walked away. If he had, he might've seen her hesitate and start back once, only to turn around again and walk on.

The air had cooled by the time Bryan started back to the van. It chilled her skin, a sure sign that summer was on its last legs. Bonfires were set and ready to light down on the beach. In the distance, Bryan heard a few hesitant, amateur guitar chords. It wouldn't be a quiet night, she decided as she passed two other campsites on the way to the van.

She paused a moment to look toward the water, tossing her hair back. It was loose from its braid and slightly damp from her dip in the Atlantic. Idly she considered grabbing her shampoo out of the van and taking a quick trip to the showers. She could do that before she threw together a cold sandwich. In an hour or two, when the bonfires were going steadily, and the music was at its peak, she and Shade would go back down and work.

For the last time, she thought as she reached for the door of the van.

At first, she stood blinking, confused by the low, flickering light. Candles, she saw, baffled. Candles and white linen. There on the little collapsible table they sometimes set between the bunks were a fresh, snowy cloth and two red tapers in glass holders. There were red linen napkins folded at angles. A rosebud stood in a narrow, clear glass vase. On the little radio in the back was low, soft music.

At the narrow makeshift counter was Shade, legs spread as he added a sprinkling of alfalfa to a salad.

"Have a nice swim?" he said casually, as if she'd climbed into the van every evening to just such a scene.

"Yeah, I… Shade, where did you get all this?"

"Took a quick trip into town. Hope you like your shrimp spicy. I made it to my taste."

She could smell it. Over the scent of candle wax, under the fragrance of the single rose, was the rich, ripe aroma of spiced shrimp. With a laugh, Bryan moved to the table and ran a finger down one of the tapers. "How did you manage all this?"

"I've been called adept occasionally." She looked up from the candle to him. Her face was lovely, clean-lined. In the soft light, her eyes were dark, mysterious. But above all he saw her lips curve hesitantly as she reached out for him.

"You did this for me."

He touched her, lightly, just a hand to her hair. Both of them felt something shimmer. "I intend to eat, too."

"I don't know what to say." She felt her eyes fill and didn't bother to blink the tears back. "I really don't."

He lifted her hand and, with a simplicity he'd never shown, kissed her fingers, one by one. "Try thanks."

She swallowed and whispered. "Thanks."

"Hungry?"

"Always. But…" In a gesture that always moved him, she lifted her hands to his face. "Some things are more important."

Bryan brought her lips to his. It was a taste he could drown in—a taste he could now admit he wanted to drown in. Moving slowly, gently, he brought her into his arms.

Their bodies fit. Bryan knew it was so, and ached from the knowledge. Even their breathing seemed to merge until she was certain their hearts beat at precisely the same rhythm. He ran his hands under her shirt, along her back, where the skin was still damp from the sea.

Touch me. She drew him closer, as if her body could shout the words to him.

Savor me. Her mouth was suddenly avid, hot and open, as if with lips alone she could draw what she needed from him.

Love me. Her hands moved over him as if she could touch the emotion she wanted. Touch it, hold it, keep it— if only for one night.

He could smell the sea on her, and the summer and the evening. He could feel the passion as her body pressed against his. Needs, demands, desires—they could be tasted as his mouth drew from hers. But tonight he found he needed to hear the words. Too soon, his mind warned as he began to lose himself. It was too soon to ask, too soon to tell. She'd need time, he thought, time and more finesse than he was accustomed to employing.

But even when he drew her away, he wasn't able to let go. Looking down at her, he saw his own beginning. Whatever he'd seen and done in the past, whatever memories he had, were unimportant. There was only one vital thing in his life, and he held it in his arms.

"I want to make love with you."

Her breath was already unsteady, her body trembling. "Yes."

His hands tightened on her as he tried to be logical. "Room's at a premium."

This time she smiled and drew him closer. "We have the floor." She pulled him down with her.

Later, when her mind was clearer and her blood cooler, Bryan would remember only the tumult of feeling, only the flood of sensation. She wouldn't be able to separate the dizzying feel of his mouth on her skin from the heady taste of his under hers.

She'd know that his passion had never been more intense, more relentless, but she wouldn't be able to say how she'd known. Had it been the frantic way he'd said her name? Had it been the desperate way he'd pulled the snug suit down her body, exploiting, ravishing, as he went?

She understood that her own feelings had reached an apex she could never express with words. Words were inadequate. She could only show him. Love, regrets, desires, wishes, had all culminated to whirl inside her until she'd clung to him. And when they'd given each other all they could, she clung still, holding the moment to her as she might a photograph faded after years of looking.

As she lay against him, her head on his chest, she smiled. They had given each other all they could. What more could anyone ask? With her eyes still closed, she pressed her lips against his chest. Nothing would spoil the night. Tonight they'd have candlelight and laughter. She'd never forget it.

"I hope you bought plenty of shrimp," she murmured. "I'm starving."

"I bought enough to feed an average person and a greedy one."

Grinning, she sat up. "Good." With a rare show of energy, she struggled back into the bulky cover-up and sprang up. Bending over the pot of shrimp, she breathed deep. "Wonderful. I didn't know you were so talented."

"I decided it was time I let you in on some of my more admirable qualities."

With a half smile, she looked back to see him slipping on his shorts. "Oh?"

"Yeah. After all, we've got to travel a long way together yet." He sent her a quiet, enigmatic look. "A long way."

"I don't—" She stopped herself and turned to toy with the salad. "This looks good," she began, too brightly.

"Bryan." He stopped her before she could reach in the cupboard above for bowls. "What is it?"

"Nothing." Did he always have to see? she demanded. Couldn't she hide anything from him?

He stepped over, took her arms and held her face to face. "What?"

"Let's talk about it tomorrow, all right?" The brightness was still there, straining. "I'm really hungry. The shrimp's cool by now, so—"

"Now." With a quick shake, he reminded both of them that his patience only stretched so far.

"I've decided to fly back," she blurted out. "I can get a flight out tomorrow afternoon."

He went very still, but she was too busy working out her explanation to notice just how dangerously still. "Why?"

"I've had to reschedule like crazy to fit in this assignment. The extra time I'd get would ease things." It sounded weak. It was weak.

"Why?"

She opened her mouth, prepared to give him a variation on the same theme. One look from him stopped her. "I just want to get back," she managed. "I know you'd like company on the drive, but the assignment's finished. Odds are you'll make better time without me."

He fought back the anger. Anger wasn't the way. If he'd given in to it, he'd have shouted, raged, threatened. That wasn't the way. "No," he said simply, and left it at that.

"No?"

"You're not flying back tomorrow." His voice was calm, but his eyes said a great deal more. "We go together, Bryan."

She braced herself. An argument, she decided, would be easy. "Now look—"

"Sit down."

Haughtiness came to her rarely, but when it did, it was exceptional. "I beg your pardon?"

For an answer, Shade gave her a quick shove onto the bench. Without speaking, he pulled open a drawer and took out the manila envelope that held his most recently developed prints. Tossing them onto the table, he pulled out the one of Bryan.

"What do you see?" he demanded.

"Myself." She cleared her throat. "I see myself, of course."

"Not good enough."

"That's what I see," she tossed back, but she didn't look down at the print again. "That's all there is."

Perhaps fear played a part in his actions. He didn't want to admit it. But it was fear, fear that he'd imagined something that wasn't there. "You see yourself, yes. A beautiful woman, a desirable woman. A woman," he continued slowly, "looking at the man she loves."

He'd stripped her. Bryan felt it as though he'd actually peeled off layer after layer of pretense, defense, disguise. She'd seen the same thing in the image he'd frozen on film. She'd seen it, but what gave him the right to strip her?

"You take too much," she said in a quiet voice. Rising, she turned away from him. "Too damned much."

Relief poured through him. He had to close his eyes on it for a moment. Not imagination, not illusion, but truth. Love was there, and with it, his beginning. "You've already given it."

"No." Bryan turned back, holding on to what she had left. "I haven't given it. What I feel is my responsibility. I haven't asked you for anything, and I won't." She took a deep breath. "We agreed, Shade. No complications."

"Then it looks like we both reneged, doesn't it?" He grabbed her hand before she could move out of reach. "Look at me." His face was close, candlelight flickering over it. Somehow the soft light illuminated what he'd seen, what he'd lived through, what he'd overcome. "Don't you see anything when you look at me? Can you see more in a stranger on the beach, a woman in a crowd, a kid on a street corner, than you do when you look at me?"

"Don't—" she began, only to be cut off.

"What do you see?"

"I see a man," she said, speaking quickly, passionately. "A man who's had to see more than he should. I see a man who's learned to keep his feelings carefully controlled because he isn't quite sure what would happen if he let loose. I see a cynic who hasn't been able to completely stamp out his own sensitivity, his own empathy."

"True enough," he returned evenly, though it was both more and less than he'd wanted to hear. "What else?"

"Nothing," she told him, close to panic. "Nothing."

It wasn't enough. The frustration came through; she could feel it in his hands. "Where's your perception now? Where's the insight that takes you under the glitter of some temperamental leading man to the core? I want you to see into me, Bryan."

"I can't." The words came out on a shudder. "I'm afraid to."

Afraid? He'd never considered it. She took emotions in stride, sought them, dug for them. He loosened his grip on her and said the words that were the most difficult for him to speak. "I love you."

She felt the words slam into her, knocking her breathless. If he said them, he meant them, of that she could be sure. Had she been so caught up in her own feelings that she hadn't seen his? It was tempting, it would be easy, to simply go into his arms and take the risk. But she remembered that they'd both risked before, and failed.

"Shade…" She tried to think calmly, but his words of love still rang in her head. "I don't—you can't—"

"I want to hear you say it." He held her close again. There was no place to go. "I want you to look at me, knowing everything you've said about me is true, and tell me."

"It couldn't work," she began quickly, because her knees

were shaking. "It couldn't, don't you see? I'd want it all because I'm just idiot enough to think maybe this time— with you... Marriage, children, that's not what you want, and I understand. I didn't think I wanted them either, until everything got so out of control."

He was calmer now, as she became more frazzled. "You haven't told me yet."

"All right." She nearly shouted it. "All right then, I love you, but I—"

He closed his mouth over hers so there could be no excuses. For now, he could simply drink in the words and all they meant to him. Salvation. He could believe in it.

"You've a hell of a nerve," he said against her mouth, "telling me what I want."

"Shade, please." Giving in to the weakness, she dropped her head on his shoulder. "I didn't want to complicate things. I don't want to now. If I fly back, it'll give us both time to put things back in perspective. My work, your work—"

"Are important," he finished. "But not as important as this." He waited until her eyes slowly lifted to his. Now his voice was calm again. His grip eased, still holding her but without the desperation. "Nothing is, Bryan. You didn't want it, maybe I thought I didn't, but I know better now. Everything started with you. Everything important. You make me clean." He ran a hand through her hair. "God, you make me hope again, believe again. Do you think I'm going to let you take all that away from me?"

The doubts began to fade, quietly, slowly. Second chances? Hadn't she always believed in them? Long shots, she remembered. You only had to want to win badly enough.

"No," she murmured. "But I need a promise. I need the promise, Shade, and then I think we could do anything."

So did he. "I promise to love you, to respect you. To care for you whether you like it or not And I promise that what I am is yours." Reaching up, he flipped open the cupboard door. Speechless, Bryan watched him draw out a tiny cardboard pot of pansies. Their scent was light and sweet and lasting.

"Plant them with me, Bryan."

Her hands closed over his. Hadn't she always believed life was as simple as you made it? "As soon as we're home."

Epilogue

"Cooperate, will you?"

"No." Amused, but not altogether pleased, Shade watched Bryan adjust the umbrellas beside and behind him. It seemed to him she'd been fiddling with the lighting a great deal longer than necessary.

"You said I could have anything I wanted for Christmas," she reminded him as she held the light meter up to his face. "I want this picture."

"It was a weak moment," he mumbled.

"Tough." Unsympathetic, Bryan stepped back to study the angles. There, the lighting was perfect, the shadows just where they should be. But... A long-suffering sigh came out. "Shade, stop glowering, will you?"

"I said you could take the picture. I didn't say it'd be pretty."

"No chance of that," she said under her breath.

Exasperated, she brushed at her hair, and the thin gold band on her left hand caught the light. Shade watched it glimmer with the same sort of odd pleasure he always felt when it hit him that they were a team, in every way. With a grin, he joined his left hand with hers, so that the twin rings they wore touched lightly.

"Sure you want this picture for Christmas? I'd thought of buying you ten pounds of French chocolate."

She narrowed her eyes, but her fingers laced with his. "A low blow, Colby. Dead low." Refusing to be distracted, she backed off. "I'll have my picture," she told him. "And if you want to be nasty, I'll buy my own chocolate. Some husbands," she continued as she walked back to the camera set on a tripod, "would cater to their wife's every whim when she's in my delicate condition."

He glanced down at the flat stomach under baggy overalls. It still dazed him that there was life growing there. Their life. When summer came again, they'd hold their first child. It wouldn't do to let her know he had to fight the urge to pamper her, to coddle her every moment. Instead, Shade shrugged and dipped his hands in his pockets.

"Not this one," he said lightly. "You knew what you were getting when you married me."

She looked at him through the viewfinder. His hands were in his pockets, but he wasn't relaxed. As always, his body was ready to move, his mind moving already. But in his eyes she saw the pleasure, the kindness and the love. Together they were making it work. He didn't smile, but Bryan did as she clicked the shutter.

"So I did," she murmured.

* * * * *

Island of Flowers

For my mother and father

Chapter 1

Laine's arrival at Honolulu International Airport was traditional. She would have preferred to melt through the crowd, but it appeared traveling tourist class categorized her as just that. Golden-skinned girls with ivory smiles and vivid sarongs bestowed brilliant colored leis. Accepting both kiss and floral necklace, Laine wove through the milling crowd and searched for an information desk. The girth of a fellow passenger hampered her journey. His yellow and orange flowered shirt and the twin cameras which joined the lei around his neck attested to his determination to enjoy his vacation. Under different circumstances, his appearance would have nudged at her humor, but the tension in Laine's stomach stifled any amusement. She had not stood on American soil in fifteen years. The ripe land with cliffs and beaches which she had seen as the plane descended brought no sense of homecoming.

The America Laine pictured came in sporadic patches of memory and through the perspective of a child of seven.

America was a gnarled elm tree guarding her bedroom window. It was a spread of green grass where buttercups scattered gold. It was a mailbox at the end of a long, winding lane. But most of all, America was the man who had taken her to imaginary African jungles and desert islands. However, there were orchids instead of daisies. The graceful palms and spreading ferns of Honolulu were as foreign to Laine as the father she had traveled half the world to find. It seemed a lifetime ago that divorce had pulled her away from her roots.

Laine felt a quiet desperation that the address she had found among her mother's papers would lead to emptiness. The age of the small, creased piece of paper was unknown to her. Neither did she know if Captain James Simmons still lived on the island of Kauai. There had only been the address tossed in among her mother's bills. There had been no correspondence, nothing to indicate the address was still a vital one. To write to her father was the practical thing to do, and Laine had struggled with indecision for nearly a week. Ultimately, she had rejected a letter in favor of a personal meeting. Her hoard of money would barely see her through a week of food and lodging, and though she knew the trip was impetuous, she had not been able to prevent herself. Threading through her doubts was the shimmering strand of fear that rejection waited for her at the end of her journey.

There was no reason to expect anything else, she lectured herself. *Why should the man who had left her fatherless during her growing-up years care about the woman she had become?* Relaxing the grip on the handle of her handbag, Laine reasserted her vow to accept whatever waited at her journey's end. She had learned long ago to adjust to whatever life offered. She concealed her feelings with the habit developed during her adolescence.

Quickly, she adjusted the white, soft-brimmed hat over a halo of flaxen curls. She lifted her chin. No one would have guessed her underlying anxiety as she moved with unconscious grace through the crowds. She looked elegantly aloof in her inherited traveling suit of ice blue silk, altered to fit her slight figure rather than her mother's ample curves.

The girl at the information desk was deep in an enjoyable conversation with a man. Standing to one side, Laine watched the encounter with detached interest. The man was dark and intimidatingly tall. Her pupils would undoubtedly have called him *séduisant*. His rugged features were surrounded by black hair in curling disorder, while his bronzed skin proved him no stranger to the Hawaiian sun. There was something rakish in his profile, some basic sensuality which Laine recognized but did not fully comprehend. She thought perhaps his nose had been broken at one time, but rather than spoiling the appeal of the profile, the lack of symmetry added to it. His dress was casual, the jeans well worn and frayed at the cuffs, and a denim work shirt exposed a hard chest and corded arms.

Vaguely irritated, Laine studied him. She observed the easy flow of charm, the indolent stance at the counter, the tease of a smile on his mouth. *I've seen his type before,* she thought with a surge of resentment, *hovering around Vanessa like a crow around carrion.* She remembered, too, that when her mother's beauty had become only a shadow, the flock had left for younger prey. At that moment, Laine could feel only gratitude that her contacts with men had been limited.

He turned and encountered Laine's stare. One dark brow rose as he lingered over his survey of her. She was too unreasonably angry with him to look away. The simplicity of her suit shouted its exclusiveness, revealing the tender elegance of young curves. The hat half shaded a fragile, faintly aristocratic face with well-defined planes, straight nose, unsmiling mouth and morning-sky eyes. Her lashes were thick and gold, and he took them as too long for authenticity. He assessed her as a cool, self-possessed woman, recognizing only the borrowed varnish.

Slowly, and with deliberate insolence, he smiled. Laine kept her gaze steady and struggled to defeat a blush. The clerk, seeing her companion's transfer of attention, shifted her eyes in Laine's direction and banished a scowl.

"May I help you?" Dutifully, she affixed her occupational smile. Ignoring the hovering male, Laine stepped up to the counter.

"Thank you. I need transportation to Kauai. Could you tell me how to arrange it?" A whisper of France lingered in her voice.

"Of course, there's a charter leaving for Kauai in..." The clerk glanced at her watch and smiled again. "Twenty minutes."

"I'm leaving right now." Laine glanced over and gave the loitering man a brief stare. She noted that his eyes were as green as Chinese jade. "No use hanging around the airport, and," he continued as his smile became a grin, "my Cub's not as crowded or expensive as the charter."

Laine's disdainful lift of brow and dismissing survey had been successful before, but did not work this time. "Do you have a plane?" she asked coldly.

"Yeah, I've got a plane." His hands were thrust in his

pockets, and in his slouch against the counter, he still managed to tower over her. "I can always use the loose change from picking up island hoppers."

"Dillon," the clerk began, but he interrupted her with another grin and a jerk of his head.

"Rose'll vouch for me. I run for Canyon Airlines on Kauai." He presented Rose with a wide smile. She shuffled papers.

"Dillon...Mr. O'Brian is a fine pilot." Rose cleared her throat and sent Dillon a telling glance. "If you'd rather not wait for the scheduled charter, I can guarantee that your flight will be equally enjoyable with him."

Studying his irreverent smile and amused eyes, Laine was of the opinion that the trip would be something less than enjoyable. However, her funds were low and she knew she must conserve what she had.

"Very well, Mr. O'Brian, I will engage your services." He held out his hand, palm up, and Laine dropped her eyes to it. Infuriated by his rudeness, she brought her eyes back to his. "If you will tell me your rate, Mr. O'Brian, I shall be happy to pay you when we land."

"Your baggage check," he countered, smiling. "Just part of the service, lady."

Bending her head to conceal her blush, Laine fumbled through her purse for the ticket.

"O.K., let's go." He took both the stub and her arm, propelling her away as he called over his shoulder in farewell to the information clerk, "See you next time, Rose."

"Welcome to Hawaii," Rose stated out of habit, then, with a sigh, pouted after Dillon's back.

Unused to being so firmly guided, and hampered by a stride a fraction of his, Laine struggled to maintain her composure while she trotted beside him. "Mr. O'Brian, I hope I don't have to jog to Kauai." He stopped and grinned at her. She tried, and failed, not to pant. His grin, she discovered, was a strange and powerful weapon, and one for which she had not yet developed a defense.

"Thought you were in a hurry, Miss…" He glanced at her ticket, and she watched the grin vanish. When his eyes lifted, all remnants of humor had fled. His mouth was grim. She would have retreated from the waves of hostility had not his grip on her arm prevented her. "Laine Simmons?" It was more accusation than question.

"Yes, you've read it correctly," she said.

Dillon's eyes narrowed. She found her cool façade melting with disconcerting speed. "You're going to see James Simmons?"

Her eyes widened. For an instant, a flash of hope flickered on her face. But his expression remained set and hostile. She smothered the impulse to ask hundreds of questions as she felt his tightening fingers bruise her arm.

"I don't know how that concerns you, Mr. O'Brian," she began, "but yes. Do you know my father?" She faltered over the final word, finding the novelty of its use bittersweet.

"Yes, I know him…a great deal better than you do. Well, Duchess—" he released her as if the contact was offensive "—I doubt if fifteen years late is better than never, but we'll see. Canyon Airlines is at your disposal." He inclined his head and gave Laine a half bow. "The trip's on the house. I can hardly charge the owner's prodigal daughter." Dillon retrieved her luggage and stalked from the terminal in thunderous silence. In the wake of the storm, Laine followed, stunned by his hostility and by his information.

Her father owned an airline. She remembered James Simmons only as a pilot, with the dream of his own planes a distant fantasy. When had the dream become reality? Why did this man, who was currently tossing her mother's elegant luggage like so many duffel bags into a small, streamlined plane, turn such hostility on her at the discovery of her name? How did he know fifteen years had spanned her separation from her father? She opened her mouth to question Dillon as he rounded the nose of the plane. She shut it again as he turned and captured her with his angry stare.

"Up you go, Duchess. We've got twenty-eight minutes to endure each other's company." His hands went to her waist, and he hoisted her as if she were no more burden than a feather pillow. He eased his long frame into the seat beside her. She became uncomfortably aware of his virility and attempted to ignore him by giving intense concentration to the buckling of her safety belt. Beneath her lashes, she watched as he flicked at the controls before the engine roared to life.

The sea opened beneath them. Beaches lay white against its verge, dotted with sun worshipers. Mountains rose, jagged and primitive, the eternal rulers of the islands. As they gained height, the colors in the scene below became so intense that they seemed artificial. Soon the shades blended. Browns, greens and blues softened with distance. Flashes of scarlet and yellow merged before fading. The plane soared with a surge of power, then its wings tilted as it made a curving arch and hurtled into the sky.

"Kauai is a natural paradise," Dillon began in the tone of a tour guide. He leaned back in his seat and lit a cigarette. "It offers, on the North Shore, the Wailua River which ends at Fern Grotto. The foliage is exceptional. There are miles of beaches, fields of cane and pineapple. Opeakea Falls, Hanalei Bay and Na Pali Coast are also worth seeing. On the South Shore," he continued, while Laine adopted the air of attentive listener, "we have Kokie State Park and Waimea Canyon. There are tropical trees and flowers at Olopia and Menehune Gardens. Water sports are exceptional almost anywhere around the island. Why the devil did you come?"

The question, so abrupt on the tail of his mechanical recital, caused Laine to jolt in her seat and stare. "To…to see my father."

"Took your own sweet time about it," Dillon muttered and drew hard on his cigarette. He turned again and gave her a slow, intimate survey. "I guess you were pretty busy attending that elegant finishing school."

Laine frowned, thinking of the boarding school which had been both home and refuge for nearly fifteen years. She decided Dillon O'Brian was crazed. There was no use contradicting a lunatic. "I'm glad you approve," she returned coolly. "A pity you missed the experience. It's amazing what can be done with rough edges."

"No thanks, Duchess." He blew out a stream of smoke. "I prefer a bit of honest crudeness."

"You appear to have an adequate supply."

"I get by. Island life can be a bit uncivilized at times." His smile was thin. "I doubt if it's going to suit your tastes."

"I can be very adaptable, Mr. O'Brian." She moved her shoulders with gentle elegance. "I can also overlook a certain amount of discourtesy for short periods of time. Twenty-eight minutes is just under my limit."

"Terrific. Tell me, Miss Simmons," he continued with exaggerated respect, "how is life on the Continent?"

"Marvelous." Deliberately, she tilted her head and looked at him from under the brim of her hat. "The French are so cosmopolitan, so urbane. One feels so..." Attempting to copy her mother's easy polish, she gestured and gave the next word the French expression. "*Chez soi* with people of one's own inclinations."

"Very true." The tone was ironic. Dillon kept his eyes on the open sky as he spoke. "I doubt if you'll find many people of your own inclinations on Kauai."

"Perhaps not." Laine pushed the thought of her father aside and tossed her head. "Then again, I may find the island as agreeable as I find Paris."

"I'm sure you found the men agreeable." Dillon crushed out his cigarette with one quick thrust. Laine found his fresh anger rewarding. The memory of the pitifully few men with whom she had had close contact caused her to force back a laugh. Only a small smile escaped.

"The men of my acquaintance—" she apologized mentally to elderly Father Rennier "—are men of elegance and culture and breeding. They are men of high intellect and discerning tastes who possess the manners and sensitivity which I currently find lacking in their American counterparts."

"Is that so?" Dillon questioned softly.

"That, Mr. O'Brian," said Laine firmly, "is quite so."

"Well, we wouldn't want to spoil our record." Switching over to automatic pilot, he turned in his seat and captured her. Mouth bruised mouth before she realized his intent.

She was locked in his arms, her struggles prevented by his strength and by her own dazed senses. She was overwhelmed by the scent and taste and feel of him. He increased the intimacy, parting her lips with his tongue. To escape from sensations more acute than she had thought possible, she clutched at his shirt.

Dillon lifted his face, and his brows drew straight at her look of stunned, young vulnerability. She could only stare, her eyes filled with confused new knowledge. Pulling away, he switched back to manual control and gave his attention to the sky. "It seems your French lovers haven't prepared you for American technique."

Stung, and furious with the weakness she had just discovered, Laine turned in her seat and faced him. "Your technique, Mr. O'Brian, is as crude as the rest of you."

He grinned and shrugged. "Be grateful, Duchess, that I didn't simply shove you out the door. I've been fighting the inclination for twenty minutes."

"You would be wise to suppress such inclinations," Laine snapped, feeling her temper bubbling at an alarming speed. *I will not lose it,* she told herself. She would not give this detestable man the satisfaction of seeing how thoroughly he had unnerved her.

The plane dipped into an abrupt nosedive. The sea hurtled toward them at a terrifying rate as the small steel bird performed a series of somersaults. The sky and sea were a mass of interchangeable blues with the white of clouds and the white of breakers no longer separate. Laine clutched at her seat, squeezing her eyes shut as the sea and sky whirled in her brain. Protest was impossible. She had lost both her voice and her heart at the first circle. She clung and prayed for her stomach to remain stationary. The plane leveled, then cruised right side up, but inside her head the world still revolved. Laine heard her companion laugh whole-heartedly.

"You can open your eyes now, Miss Simmons. We'll be landing in a minute."

Turning to him, Laine erupted with a long, detailed analysis of his character. At length, she realized she was stating her opinion in French. She took a deep breath. "You, Mr. O'Brian," she finished in frigid English, "are the most detestable man I have ever met."

"Thank you, Duchess." Pleased, he began to hum.

Laine forced herself to keep her eyes open as Dillon began his descent. There was a brief impression of greens and browns melding with blue, and again the swift rise of mountains before they were bouncing on asphalt and gliding to a stop. Dazed, she surveyed the hangars and lines of aircraft, Piper Cubs and cabin planes, twin engines and passenger jets. *There's some mistake,* she thought. *This cannot belong to my father.*

"Don't get any ideas, Duchess," Dillon remarked, noting her astonished stare. His mouth tightened. "You've forfeited your share. And even if the captain was inclined to be generous, his partner would make things very difficult. You're going to have to look someplace else for an easy ride."

He jumped to the ground as Laine stared at him with disbelief. Disengaging her belt, she prepared to lower herself to the ground. His hands gripped her waist before her feet made contact. For a moment, he held her suspended. With their faces only inches apart, Laine found his eyes her jailer. She had never known eyes so green or so compelling.

"Watch your step," he commanded, then dropped her to the ground.

Laine stepped back, retreating from the hostility in his voice. Gathering her courage, she lifted her chin and held her ground. "Mr. O'Brian, would you please tell me where I might find my father?"

He stared for a moment, and she thought he would simply refuse and leave her. Abruptly, he gestured toward a small white building. "His office is in there," he barked before he turned to stride away.

Chapter 2

The building which Laine approached was a midsize hut. Fanning palms and flaming anthurium skirted its entrance. Hands trembling, Laine entered. She felt as though her knees might dissolve under her, as though the pounding of her heart would burst through her head. What would she say to the man who had left her floundering in loneliness for fifteen years? What words were there to bridge the gap and express the need which had never died? Would she need to ask questions, or could she forget the whys and just accept?

Laine's image of James Simmons was as clear and vivid as yesterday. It was not dimmed by the shadows of time. *He would be older,* she reminded herself. *She was older as well.* She was not a child trailing after an idol, but a woman meeting her father. They were neither one the same as they had been. Perhaps that in itself would be an advantage.

The outer room of the hut was deserted. Laine had a vague impression of wicker furnishings and woven mats.

She stared around her, feeling alone and unsure. Like a ghost of the past, his voice reached out, booming through an open doorway. Approaching the sound, Laine watched as her father talked on the phone at his desk.

She could see the alterations which age had made on his face, but her memory had been accurate. The sun had darkened his skin and laid its lines upon it, but his features were no stranger to her. His thick brows were gray now, but still prominent over his brown eyes. The nose was still strong and straight over the long, thin mouth. His hair remained full, though as gray as his brows, and she watched as he reached up in a well-remembered gesture and tugged his fingers through it.

She pressed her lips together as he replaced the receiver, then swallowing, Laine spoke in soft memory. "Hello, Cap."

He twisted his head, and she watched surprise flood his face. His eyes ran a quick gamut of emotions, and somewhere between the beginning and the end she saw the pain. He stood, and she noted with a small sense of shock that he was shorter than her child's perspective had made him.

"Laine?" The question was hesitant, colored by a reserve which crushed her impulse to rush toward him. She sensed immediately that his arms would not be open to receive her, and this rejection threatened to destroy her tentative smile.

"It's good to see you." Hating the inanity, she stepped into the room and held out her hand.

After a moment, he accepted it. He held her hand briefly, then released it. "You've grown up." His survey was slow, his smile touching only his mouth. "You've the look of your mother. No more pigtails?"

The smile illuminated her face with such swift impact, her father's expression warmed. "Not for some time. There was no one to pull them." Reserve settled over him again. Feeling the chill, Laine fumbled for some new line of conversation. "You've got your airport; you must be very happy. I'd like to see more of it."

"We'll arrange it." His tone was polite and impersonal, whipping across her face like the sting of a lash.

Laine wandered to a window and stared out through a mist of tears. "It's very impressive."

"Thank you, we're pretty proud of it." He cleared his throat and studied her back. "How long will you be in Hawaii?"

She gripped the windowsill and tried to match his tone. Even at their worst, her fears had not prepared her for this degree of pain. "A few weeks perhaps, I have no definite plans. I came...I came straight here." Turning, Laine began to fill the void with chatter. "I'm sure there are things I should see since I'm here. The pilot who flew me over said Kauai was beautiful, gardens and..." She tried and failed to remember the specifics of Dillon's speech. "And parks." She settled on a generality, keeping her smile fixed. "Perhaps you could recommend a hotel?"

He was searching her face, and Laine struggled to keep her smile from dissolving. "You're welcome to stay with me while you're here."

Burying her pride, she agreed. She knew she could not afford to stay anywhere else. "That's kind of you. I should like that."

He nodded and shuffled some papers on his desk. "How's your mother?"

"She died," Laine murmured. "Three months ago."

Cap glanced up sharply. Laine watched the pain flicker over his face. He sat down. "I'm sorry, Laine. Was she ill?"

"There was…" She swallowed. "There was a car accident."

"I see." He cleared his throat, and his tone was again impersonal. "If you had written, I would have flown over and helped you."

"Would you?" She shook her head and turned back to the window. She remembered the panic, the numbness, the mountain of debts, the auction of every valuable. "I managed well enough."

"Laine, why did you come?" Though his voice had softened, he remained behind the barrier of his desk.

"To see my father." Her words were devoid of emotion.

"Cap." At the voice Laine turned, watching as Dillon's form filled the doorway. His glance scanned her before returning to Cap. "Chambers is leaving for the mainland. He wants to see you before he takes off."

"All right. Laine," Cap turned and gestured awkwardly, "this is Dillon O'Brian, my partner. Dillon, this is my daughter."

"We've met." Dillon smiled briefly.

Laine managed a nod. "Yes, Mr. O'Brian was kind enough to fly me from Oahu. It was a most…fascinating journey."

"That's fine then." Cap moved to Dillon and clasped a hand to his shoulder. "Run Laine to the house, will you, and see she settles in? I'm sure she must be tired."

Laine watched, excluded from the mystery of masculine understanding as looks were exchanged. Dillon nodded. "My pleasure."

"I'll be home in a couple of hours." Cap turned and regarded Laine in awkward silence.

"All right." Her smile was beginning to hurt her cheeks, so Laine let it die. "Thank you." Cap hesitated, then walked through the door leaving her staring at emptiness. *I will not cry,* she ordered herself. *Not in front of this man.* If she had nothing else left, she had her pride.

"Whenever you're ready, Miss Simmons."

Brushing past Dillon, Laine glanced back over her shoulder. "I hope you drive a car with more discretion than you fly a plane, Mr. O'Brian."

He gave an enigmatic shrug. "Why don't we find out?"

Her bags were sitting outside. She glanced down at them, then up at Dillon. "You seem to have anticipated me."

"I had hoped," he began as he tossed the bags into the rear of a sleek compact, "to pack both them and you back to where you came from, but that is obviously impossible now." He opened his door, slid into the driver's seat and started the engine. Laine slipped in beside him, unaided. Releasing the brake, he shot forward with a speed which jerked her against the cushions.

"What did you say to him?" Dillon demanded, not bothering with preliminaries as he maneuvered skillfully through the airport traffic.

"Being my father's business partner does not entitle you to an account of his personal conversations with me," Laine answered. Her voice was clipped and resentful.

"Listen, Duchess, I'm not about to stand by while you drop into Cap's life and stir up trouble. I didn't like the way he looked when I walked in on you. I gave you ten minutes, and you managed to hurt him. Don't make me stop the car and persuade you to tell me." He paused and

lowered his voice. "You'd find my methods unrefined."
The threat vibrated in his softly spoken words.

Suddenly Laine found herself too tired to argue. Nights
with only patches of sleep, days crowded with pressures
and anxiety, and the long, tedious journey had taken their
toll. With a weary gesture, she pulled off her hat. Resting her head against the seat, she closed her eyes. "Mr.
O'Brian, it was not my intention to hurt my father. In the
ten minutes you allowed, we said remarkably little. Perhaps it was the news that my mother had died which upset
him, but that is something he would have learned eventu-
ally at any rate." Her tone was hollow, and he glanced at
her, surprised by the sudden frailty of her unframed face.
Her hair was soft and pale against her ivory skin. For the
first time, he saw the smudges of mauve haunting her eyes.

"How long ago?"

Laine opened her eyes in confusion as she detected a
whisper of sympathy in his voice. "Three months." She
sighed and turned to face Dillon more directly. "She ran
her car into a telephone pole. They tell me she died instantly." *And painlessly,* she added to herself, *anesthetized
with several quarts of vintage champagne.*

Dillon lapsed into silence, and she was grateful that he
ignored the need for any trite words of sympathy. She had
had enough of those already and found his silence more
comforting. She studied his profile, the bronzed chiseled
lines and unyielding mouth, before she turned her attention back to the scenery.

The scent of the Pacific lingered in the air. The water
was a sparkling blue against the crystal beaches. Screw
pines rose from the sand and accepted the lazy breeze, and
monkeypods, wide and domelike, spread their shade in

invitation. As they drove inland, Laine caught only brief glimpses of the sea. The landscape was a myriad of colors against a rich velvet green. Sun fell in waves of light, offering its warmth so that flowers did not strain to it, but rather basked lazily in its glory.

Dillon turned up a drive which was flanked by two sturdy palms. As they approached the house, Laine felt the first stir of pleasure. It was simple, its lines basic and clean, its walls cool and white. It stood two stories square, sturdy despite its large expanses of glass. Watching the windows wink in the sun, Laine felt her first welcoming.

"It's lovely."

"Not as fancy as you might have expected," Dillon countered as he halted at the end of the drive, "but Cap likes it." The brief truce was obviously at an end. He eased from the car and gave his attention to her luggage.

Without comment, Laine opened her door and slipped out. Shading her eyes from the sun, she stood for a moment and studied her father's home. A set of stairs led to a circling porch. Dillon climbed them, nudged the front door open and strode into the house. Laine entered unescorted.

"Close my door; flies are not welcome."

Laine glanced up and saw, with stunned admiration, an enormous woman step as lightly down the staircase as a young girl. Her girth was wrapped in a colorful, flowing muumuu. Her glossy black hair was pulled tight and secured at the back of her head. Her skin was unlined, the color of dark honey. Her eyes were jet, set deep and widely spaced. Her age might have been anywhere from thirty to sixty. The image of an island priestess, she took a long, uninhibited survey of Laine when she reached the foot of the stairs.

"Who is this?" she asked Dillon as she folded her thick arms over a tumbling bosom.

"This is Cap's daughter." Setting down the bags, he leaned on the banister and watched the exchange.

"Cap Simmons's daughter." Her mouth pursed and her eyes narrowed. "Pretty thing, but too pale and skinny. Don't you eat?" She circled Laine's arm between her thumb and forefinger.

"Why, yes, I…"

"Not enough," she interrupted and fingered a sunlit curl with interest. "Mmm, very nice, very pretty. Why do you wear it so short?"

"I…"

"You should have come years ago, but you are here now." Nodding, she patted Laine's cheek. "You are tired. I will fix your room."

"Thank you. I…"

"Then you eat," she ordered, and hefted Laine's two cases up the stairs.

"That was Miri," Dillon volunteered and tucked his hands in his pockets. "She runs the house."

"Yes, I see." Unable to prevent herself, Laine lifted her hand to her hair and wondered over the length. "Shouldn't you have taken the bags up for her?"

"Miri could carry me up the stairs without breaking stride. Besides, I know better than to interfere with what she considers her duties. Come on." He grabbed her arm and pulled her down the hall. "I'll fix you a drink."

With casual familiarity, Dillon moved to a double-doored cabinet. Laine flexed her arm and surveyed the cream-walled room. Simplicity reigned here as its outer shell had indicated, and she appreciated Miri's obvious diligence with polish and broom. There was, she noted with a sigh, no room for a woman here. The furnishings shouted with masculinity, a masculinity which was well established and comfortable in its solitary state.

"What'll you have?" Dillon's question brought Laine back from her musings. She shook her head and dropped her hat on a small table. It looked frivolous and totally out of place.

"Nothing, thank you."

"Suit yourself." He poured a measure of liquor into a glass and dropped down on a chair. "We're not given to formalities around here, Duchess. While you're in residence, you'll have to cope with a more basic form of existence."

She inclined her head, laying her purse beside her hat. "Perhaps one may still wash one's hands before dinner?"

"Sure," he returned, ignoring the sarcasm. "We're big on water."

"And where, Mr. O'Brian, do you live?"

"Here." He stretched his legs and gave a satisfied smile at her frown. "For a week or two. I'm having some repairs done to my house."

"How unfortunate," Laine commented and wandered the room. "For both of us."

"You'll survive, Duchess." He toasted her with his glass. "I'm sure you've had plenty of experience in surviving."

"Yes, I have, Mr. O'Brian, but I have a feeling you know nothing about it."

"You've got guts, lady, I'll give you that." He tossed back his drink and scowled as she turned to face him.

"Your opinion is duly noted and filed."

"Did you come for more money? Is it possible you're that greedy?" He rose in one smooth motion and crossed the room, grabbing her shoulders before she could back away from his mercurial temper. "Haven't you squeezed enough out of him? Never giving anything in return. Never even disturbing yourself to answer one of his letters. Letting the years pile up without any acknowledgment. What the devil do you want from him now?"

Dillon stopped abruptly. The color had drained from her face, leaving it like white marble. Her eyes were dazed with shock. She swayed as though her joints had melted, and he held her upright, staring at her in sudden confusion. "What's the matter with you?"

"I...Mr. O'Brian, I think I would like that drink now, if you don't mind."

His frown deepened, and he led her to a chair before moving off to pour her a drink. Laine accepted with a murmured thanks, then shuddered at the unfamiliar burn of brandy. The room steadied, and she felt the mists clearing.

"Mr. O'Brian, I...am I to understand..." She stopped and shut her eyes a moment. "Are you saying my father wrote to me?"

"You know very well he did." The retort was both swift and annoyed. "He came to the islands right after you and your mother left him, and he wrote you regularly until five years ago when he gave up. He still sent money," Dillon added, flicking on his lighter. "Oh yes, the money kept right on coming until you turned twenty-one last year."

"You're lying!"

Dillon looked over in astonishment as she rose from her chair. Her cheeks were flaming, her eyes flashing. "Well, well, it appears the ice maiden has melted." He blew out a stream of smoke and spoke mildly. "I never lie, Duchess. I find the truth more interesting."

"He never wrote to me. Never!" She walked to where Dillon sat. "Not once in all those years. All the letters I sent came back because he had moved away without even telling me where."

Slowly, Dillon crushed out his cigarette and rose to face her. "Do you expect me to buy that? You're selling to the wrong person, Miss Simmons. I saw the letters Cap sent, *and* the checks every month." He ran a finger down the lapel of her suit. "You seem to have put them to good use."

"I tell you I never received any letters." Laine knocked his hand away and tilted her head back to meet his eyes. "I have not had one word from my father since I was seven years old."

"Miss Simmons, I mailed more than one letter myself, though I was tempted to chuck them into the Pacific. Presents, too; dolls in the early years. You must have quite a collection of porcelain dolls. Then there was the jewelry. I remember the eighteenth birthday present very clearly. Opal earrings shaped like flowers."

"Earrings," Laine whispered. Feeling the room tilt again, she dug her teeth into her lip and shook her head.

"That's right." His voice was rough as he moved to pour himself another drink. "And they all went to the same place: 17 rue de la Concorde, Paris."

Her color ebbed again, and she lifted a hand to her temple. "My mother's address," she murmured, and turned away to sit before her legs gave way. "I was in school; my mother lived there."

"Yes." Dillon took a quick sip and settled on the sofa again. "Your education was both lengthy and expensive."

Laine thought for a moment of the boarding school with its plain, wholesome food, cotton sheets and leaking roof.

She pressed her fingers to her eyes. "I was not aware that my father was paying for my schooling."

"Just who did you think was paying for your French pinafores and art lessons?"

She sighed, stung by the sharpness of his tone. Her hands fluttered briefly before she dropped them into her lap. "Vanessa...my mother said she had an income. I never questioned her. She must have kept my father's letters from me."

Laine's voice was dull, and Dillon moved with sudden impatience. "Is that the tune you're going to play to Cap? You make it very convincing."

"No, Mr. O'Brian. It hardly matters at this point, does it? In any case, I doubt that he would believe me any more than you do. I will keep my visit brief, then return to France." She lifted her brandy and stared into the amber liquid, wondering if it was responsible for her numbness. "I would like a week or two. I would appreciate it if you would not mention this discussion to my father; it would only complicate matters."

Dillon gave a short laugh and sipped from his drink. "I have no intention of telling him any part of this little fairy tale."

"Your word, Mr. O'Brian." Surprised by the anxiety in her voice, Dillon glanced up. "I want your word." She met his eyes without wavering.

"My word, Miss Simmons," he agreed at length.

Nodding, she rose and lifted her hat and bag from the table. "I would like to go up to my room now. I'm very tired."

He was frowning into his drink. Laine, without a backward glance, walked to her room.

Chapter 3

Laine faced the woman in the mirror. She saw a pale face, dominated by wide, shadowed eyes. Reaching for her rouge, she placed borrowed color in her cheeks.

She had known her mother's faults: the egotism, the shallowness. As a child, it had been easy to overlook the flaws and prize the sporadic, exciting visits with the vibrant, fairy-tale woman. Ice-cream parfaits and party dresses were such a contrast to home-spun uniforms and porridge. As Laine had grown older, the visits had become further spaced and shorter. It became routine for her to spend her vacations from school with the nuns. She had begun to see, through the objectivity of distance, her mother's desperation for youth, her selfish grip on her own beauty. A grown daughter with firm limbs and unlined skin had been more of an obstacle than an accomplishment. A grown daughter was a reminder of one's own mortality.

She was always afraid of losing, Laine thought. Her looks, her youth, her friends, her men. All the creams and potions. She sighed and shut her eyes. All the dyes and lotions. There had been a collection of porcelain dolls, Laine remembered. Vanessa's dolls, or so she had thought. Twelve porcelain dolls, each from a different country. She thought of how beautiful the Spanish doll had been with its high comb and mantilla. And the earrings...Laine tossed down her brush and whirled around the room. Those lovely opal earrings that looked so fragile in Vanessa's ears. I remember seeing her wear them, just as I remember listing them and the twelve porcelain dolls for auction. *How much more that was mine did she keep from me?* Blindly, Laine stared out her window. The incredible array of island blossoms might not have existed.

What kind of woman was she to keep what was mine for her own pleasure? To let me think, year after year, that my father had forgotten me? She kept me from him, even from his words on paper. I resent her for that, how I resent her for that. Not for the money, but for the lies and the loss. She must have used the checks to keep her apartment in Paris, and for all those clothes and all those parties. Laine shut her eyes tight on waves of outrage. At least I know now why she took me with her to France: as an insurance policy. She lived off me for nearly fifteen years, and even then it wasn't enough. Laine felt tears squeezing through her closed lids. Oh, how Cap must hate me. How he must hate me for the ingratitude and the coldness. He would never believe me. She sighed, remembering her father's reaction to her appearance. *"You've the look of your mother."* Opening her eyes, she walked back and studied her face in the mirror.

It was true, she decided as she ran her fingertips along her cheeks. The resemblance was there in the bone structure, in the coloring. Laine frowned, finding no pleasure in her inheritance. He's only to look at me to see her. He's only to look at me to remember. He'll think as Dillon O'Brian thinks. How could I expect anything else? For a few moments, Laine and her reflection merely stared at one another. But perhaps, she mused, her bottom lip thrust forward in thought, with a week or two I might salvage something of what used to be, some portion of the friendship. I would be content with that. But he must not think I've come for money, so I must be careful he not find out how little I have left. More than anything, I shall have to be careful around Mr. O'Brian.

Detestable man, she thought on a fresh flurry of anger. He is surely the most ill-bred, mannerless man I have ever met. He's worse, much worse, than any of Vanessa's hangers-on. At least they managed to wear a light coat of respectability. Cap probably picked him up off the beach out of pity and made him his partner. He has insolent eyes, she added, lifting her brush and tugging it through her hair. Always looking at you as if he knew how you would feel in his arms. He's nothing but a womanizer. Tossing down the brush, she glared at the woman in the glass. He's just an unrefined, arrogant womanizer. Look at the way he behaved on the plane.

The glare faded as she lifted a finger to rub it over her lips. The memory of their turbulent capture flooded back. You've been kissed before, she lectured, shaking her head against the echoing sensations. *Not like that,* a small voice insisted. *Never like that.*

"Oh, the devil with Dillon O'Brian!" she muttered aloud, and just barely resisted the urge to slam her bedroom door on her way out.

Laine hesitated at the sound of masculine voices. It was a new sound for one generally accustomed to female company, and she found it pleasant. There was a mixture of deep blends, her father's booming drum tones and Dillon's laconic drawl. She heard a laugh, an appealing, uninhibited rumble, and she frowned as she recognized it as Dillon's. Quietly, she came down the rest of the steps and moved to the doorway.

"Then, when I took out the carburetor, he stared at it, muttered a stream of incantations and shook his head. I ended up fixing it myself."

"And a lot quicker than the Maui mechanic or any other would have." Cap's rich chuckle reached Laine as she stepped into the doorway.

They were seated easily. Dillon was sprawled on the sofa, her father in a chair. Pipe smoke rose from the tray beside him. Both were relaxed and so content in each other's company that Laine felt the urge to back away and leave them undisturbed. She felt an intruder into some long established routine. With a swift pang of envy, she took a step in retreat.

Her movement caught Dillon's attention. Before she could leave, his eyes held her motionless just as effectively as if his arms had reached out to capture her. She had changed from the sophisticated suit she had worn for the flight into a simple white dress from her own wardrobe. Unadorned and ingenue, it emphasized her youth and her slender innocence. Following the direction of Dillon's unsmiling survey, Cap saw Laine and rose. As he stood, his ease transformed into awkwardness.

"Hello, Laine. Have you settled in all right?"

Laine forced herself to shift her attention from Dillon

to her father. "Yes, thank you." The moistening of her lips was the first outward sign of nerves. "The room is lovely. I'm sorry. Did I interrupt?" Her hands fluttered once, then were joined loosely as if to keep them still.

"No…ah, come in and sit down. Just a little shoptalk." She hesitated again before stepping into the room.

"Would you like a drink?" Cap moved to the bar and jiggled glasses. Dillon remained silent and seated.

"No, nothing, thank you." Laine tried a smile. "Your home is beautiful. I can see the beach from my window." Taking the remaining seat on the sofa, Laine kept as much distance between herself and Dillon as possible. "It must be marvelous being close enough to swim when the mood strikes you."

"I don't get to the water as much as I used to." Cap settled down again, tapping his pipe against the tray. "Used to scuba some. Now, Dillon's the one for it." Laine heard the affection in his voice, and caught it again in his smiling glance at the man beside her.

"I find the sea and the sky have a lot in common," Dillon commented, reaching forward to lift his drink from the table. "Freedom and challenge." He sent Cap an easy smile. "I taught Cap to explore the fathoms; he taught me to fly."

"I suppose I'm more of a land creature," Laine replied, forcing herself to meet his gaze levelly. "I haven't much experience in the air or on the sea."

Dillon swirled his drink idly, but his eyes held challenge. "You do swim, don't you?"

"I manage."

"Fine." He took another swallow of his drink. "I'll teach you to snorkel." Setting down the glass, he resumed his relaxed position. "Tomorrow. We'll get an early start."

His arrogance shot up Laine's spine like a rod. Her tone became cool and dismissive. "I wouldn't presume to impose on your time, Mr. O'Brian."

Unaffected by the frost in her voice, Dillon continued. "No trouble. I've got nothing scheduled until the afternoon. You've got some extra gear around, haven't you, Cap?"

"Sure, in the back room." Hurt by the apparent relief in his voice, Laine shut her eyes briefly. "You'll enjoy yourself, Laine. Dillon's a fine teacher, and he knows these waters."

Laine gave Dillon a polite smile, hoping he could read between the lines. "I'm sure you know how much I appreciate your time, Mr. O'Brian."

The lifting of his brows indicated that their silent communication was proceeding with perfect understanding. "No more than I your company, Miss Simmons."

"Dinner." Miri's abrupt announcement startled Laine. "You." She pointed an accusing finger at Laine, then crooked it in a commanding gesture. "Come eat, and don't pick at your food. Too skinny," she muttered and whisked away in a flurry of brilliant colors.

Laine's arm was captured as they followed in the wake of Miri's waves. Dillon slowed her progress until they were alone in the corridor. "My compliments on your entrance. You were the picture of the pure young virgin."

"I have no doubt you would like to offer me to the nearest volcano god, Mr. O'Brian, but perhaps you would allow me to have my last meal in peace."

"Miss Simmons." He bowed with exaggerated gallantry and increased his hold on her arm. "Even I can stir myself on occasion to escort a lady into dinner."

"Perhaps with a great deal of concentration, you could accomplish this spectacular feat without breaking my arm."

Laine gritted her teeth as they entered the glass-enclosed dining room. Dillon pulled out her chair. She glanced coldly up at him. "Thank you, Mr. O'Brian," she murmured as she slid into her seat. Detestable man!

Inclining his head politely, Dillon rounded the table and dropped into a chair. "Hey, Cap, that little cabin plane we've been using on the Maui run is running a bit rough. I want to have a look at it before it goes up again."

"Hmm. What do you think's the problem?"

There began a technical, and to Laine unintelligible, discussion. Miri entered, placing a steaming tray of fish in front of Laine with a meaningful thump. To assure she had not been misunderstood, Miri pointed a finger at the platter, then at Laine's empty plate before she swirled from the room.

The conversation had turned to the intricacies of fuel systems by the time Laine had eaten all she could of Miri's fish. Her silence during the meal had been almost complete as the men enjoyed their mutual interest. She saw, as she watched him, that her father's lack of courtesy was not deliberate, but rather the result of years of living alone. He was, she decided, a man comfortable with men and out of his depth with feminine company. Though she felt Dillon's rudeness was intentional, it was her father's unconscious slight which stung.

"You will excuse me?" Laine rose during a brief lull in the conversation. She felt a fresh surge of regret as she read the discomfort in her father's eyes. "I'm a bit tired. Please." She managed a smile as she started to rise. "Don't disturb yourself, I know the way." As she turned to go, she could almost hear the room sigh with relief at her exit.

Later that evening, Laine felt stifled in her room. The house was quiet. The tropical moon had risen and she could see the curtains flutter with the gentle whispers of perfumed air. Unable to bear the loneliness of the four walls any longer, she stole quietly downstairs and into the night. As she wandered without regard for destination, she could hear the night birds call to each other, piercing the stillness with a strange, foreign music. She listened to the sea's murmur and slipped off her shoes to walk across the fine layer of sand to meet it.

The water fringed in a wide arch, frothing against the sands and lapping back into the womb of midnight blue. Its surface winked with mirrored stars. Laine breathed deeply of its scent, mingling with the flowered air.

But this paradise was not for her. Dillon and her father had banished her. It was the same story all over again. She remembered how often she had been excluded on her visits to her mother's home in Paris. *Again an intruder,* Laine decided, and wondered if she had either the strength or the will to pursue the smiling masquerade for even a week of her father's company. Her place was not with him any more than it had been with Vanessa. Dropping to the sand, Laine brought her knees to her chest and wept for the years of loss.

"I don't have a handkerchief, so you'll have to cope without one."

At the sound of Dillon's voice, Laine shuddered and hugged her knees tighter. "Please, go away."

"What's the problem, Duchess?" His voice was rough

and impatient. If she had had more experience, Laine might have recognized a masculine discomfort with feminine tears. "If things aren't going as planned, sitting on the beach and crying isn't going to help. Especially if there's no one around to sympathize."

"Go away," she repeated, keeping her face buried. "I want you to leave me alone. I want to be alone."

"You might as well get used to it," he returned carelessly. "I intend to keep a close eye on you until you're back in Europe. Cap's too soft to hold out against the sweet, innocent routine for long."

Laine sprang up and launched herself at him. He staggered a moment as the small missile caught him off guard. "He's my father, do you understand? My *father*. I have a right to be with him. I have a right to know him." With useless fury, she beat her fists against his chest. He weathered the attack with some surprise before he caught her arms and dragged her, still swinging, against him.

"There's quite a temper under the ice! You can always try the routine about not getting his letters—that should further your campaign."

"I don't want his pity, do you hear?" She pushed and shoved and struck out while Dillon held her with minimum effort. "I would rather have his hate than his disinterest, but I would rather have his disinterest than his pity."

"Hold still, blast it," he ordered, losing patience with the battle. "You're not going to get hurt."

"I will not hold still," Laine flung back. "I am not a puppy who washed up on his doorstep and needs to be dried off and given a corner and a pat on the head. I *will* have my two weeks, and I won't let you spoil it for me." She tossed back her head. Tears fell freely, but her eyes now held fury rather than sorrow. "Let me go! I don't want you to touch me." She began to battle with new enthusiasm, kicking and nearly throwing them both onto the sand.

"All right, that's enough." Swiftly, he used his arms to band, his mouth to silence.

He was drawing her into a whirlpool, spinning and spinning, until all sense of time and existence was lost in the current. She would taste the salt of her own tears mixed with some tangy, vital flavor which belonged to him. She felt a swift heat rise to her skin and fought against it as desperately as she fought against his imprisoning arms. His mouth took hers once more, enticing her to give what she did not yet understand. All at once she lost all resistance, all sense of self. She went limp in his arms, her lips softening in surrender. Dillon drew her away and without even being aware of what she was doing, Laine dropped her head to his chest. She trembled as she felt his hand brush lightly through her hair, and nestled closer to him. Suddenly warm and no longer alone, she shut her eyes and let the gamut of emotions run its course.

"Just who are you, Laine Simmons?" Dillon drew her away again. He closed a firm hand under her chin as she stubbornly fought to keep her head lowered. "Look at me," he commanded. The order was absolute. With his eyes narrowed, he examined her without mercy.

Her eyes were wide and brimming, the tears trembling down her cheeks and clinging to her lashes. All layers of her borrowed sophistication had been stripped away, leaving only the vulnerability. His search ended on an impatient oath. "Ice, then fire, now tears. No, don't," he commanded as she struggled to lower her head again. "I'm not in the mood to test my resistance." He let out a deep breath and shook his head. "You're going to be nothing but trouble, I should have seen that from the first look. But you're here, and we're going to have to come to terms."

"Mr. O'Brian..."

"Dillon, for pity's sake. Let's not be any more ridiculous than necessary."

"Dillon," Laine repeated, sniffling and despising herself. "I don't think I can discuss terms with any coherence tonight. If you would just let me go, we could draw up a contract tomorrow."

"No, the terms are simple because they're all mine."

"That sounds exceedingly reasonable." She was pleased that irony replaced tears.

"While you're here," Dillon continued mildly, "we're going to be together like shadow and shade. I'm your guardian angel until you go back to the Left Bank. If you make a wrong move with Cap, I'm coming down on you so fast you won't be able to blink those little-girl eyes."

"Is my father so helpless he needs protection from his own daughter?" She brushed furiously at her lingering tears.

"There isn't a man alive who doesn't need protection from you, Duchess." Tilting his head, he studied her damp, glowing face. "If you're an operator, you're a good one. If you're not, I'll apologize when the time comes."

"You may keep your apology and have it for breakfast. With any luck, you'll strangle on it."

Dillon threw back his head and laughed, the same appealing rumble Laine had heard earlier. Outraged both with the laughter and its effect on her, she swung back her hand to slap his face.

"Oh, no." Dillon grabbed her wrist. "Don't spoil it. I'd

just have to hit you back, and you look fabulous when you're spitting fire. It's much more to my taste than the cool mademoiselle from Paris. Listen, Laine." He took an exaggerated breath to control his laughter, and she found herself struggling to deal with the stir caused by the way her name sounded on his lips. "Let's try a truce, at least in public. Privately, we can have a round a night, with or without gloves."

"That should suit you well enough." Laine wriggled out of his loosened hold and tossed her head. "You have a considerable advantage—given your weight and strength."

"Yeah." Dillon grinned and moved his shoulders. "Learn to live with it. Come on." He took her hand in a friendly gesture which nonplussed her. "Into bed; you've got to get up early tomorrow. I don't like to lose the morning."

"I'm not going with you tomorrow." She tugged her hand away and planted her bare heels in the sand. "You'll probably attempt to drown me, then hide my body in some cove."

Dillon sighed in mock exasperation. "Laine, if I have to drag you out of bed in the morning, you're going to find yourself learning a great deal more than snorkeling. Now, are you going to walk back to the house, or do I carry you?"

"If they could bottle your arrogance, Dillon O'Brian, there would be no shortage of fuel in this country!"

With this, Laine turned and fled. Dillon watched until the darkness shrouded her white figure. Then he bent down to retrieve her shoes.

Chapter 4

The morning was golden. As usual, Laine woke early. For a moment, she blinked in puzzlement. Cool green walls had replaced her white ones, louvered shades hung where she expected faded striped curtains. Instead of her desk stood a plain mahogany bureau topped with a vase of scarlet blossoms. But it was the silence which most confused her. There were no giggles, no rushing feet outside her door. The quiet was broken only by a bird who sang his morning song outside her window. Memory flooded back. With a sigh, Laine lay back against the pillow and wished she could go to sleep again. The habit of early rising was too ingrained. She rose, showered and dressed.

A friend had persuaded her to accept the loan of a swimsuit, and Laine studied the two tiny pieces. She slipped on what had been described as a modified bikini. The silvery blue was flattering, highlighting her subtle curves, but no amount of adjustment could result in a more substantial coverage. There was definitely too much of her and too little suit.

"Silly," Laine muttered and adjusted the halter strings a last time. "Women wear these things all the time, and I've hardly the shape for drawing attention."

Skinny. With a grimace, she recalled Miri's judgment. Laine gave the top a last, hopeless tug. *I don't think all the fish in the Pacific are going to change this inadequacy.* Pulling on white jeans and a scarlet scoop-necked top, she reminded herself that cleavage was not what she needed for dealing with Dillon O'Brian.

As she wandered downstairs, Laine heard the stirrings which accompany an awakening house. She moved quietly, half afraid she would disturb the routine. In the dining room, the sun poured like liquid gold through the windows. Standing in its pool, Laine stared out at soft ferns and brilliant poppies. Charmed by the scene, she decided she would let nothing spoil the perfection of the day. There would be time enough later, on some drizzling French morning, to think of rejections and humiliations, but today the sun was bright and filled with promise.

"So, you are ready for breakfast." Miri glided in from the adjoining kitchen. She managed to look graceful despite her size, and regal despite the glaring flowered muu-muu.

"Good morning, Miri." Laine gave her the first smile of the day and gestured toward the sky. "It's beautiful."

"It will bring some color to your skin." Miri sniffed and ran a finger down Laine's arm. "Red if you aren't careful. Now, sit and I will put flesh on your skinny bones." Imperiously, she tapped the back of a chair, and Laine obeyed.

"Miri, have you worked for my father long?"

"Ten years." Miri shook her head and poured steaming coffee into a cup. "Too long a time for a man not to have a wife. Your mother," she continued, narrowing her dark eyes, "she was skinny too?"

"Well, no, I wouldn't say... That is..." Laine hesitated in an attempt to gauge Miri's estimation of a suitable shape.

Rich laughter shot out. Miri's bosom trembled under pink and orange flowers. "You don't want to say she was not as much woman as Miri." She ran her hands over her well-padded hips. "You're a pretty girl," she said unexpectedly and patted Laine's flaxen curls. "Your eyes are too young to be sad." As Laine stared up at her, speechless under the unfamiliar affection, Miri sighed. "I will bring your breakfast, and you will eat what I give you."

"Make it two, Miri." Dillon strolled in, bronzed and confident in cutoff denims and a plain white T-shirt. "Morning, Duchess. Sleep well?" He dropped into the chair opposite Laine and poured himself a cup of coffee. His movements were easy, without any early-morning lethargy, and his eyes were completely alert. Laine concluded that Dillon O'Brian was one of those rare creatures who moved from sleep to wakefulness instantly. It also occurred to her, in one insistent flash, that he was not only the most attractive man she had ever known, but the most compelling. Struggling against an unexplained longing, Laine tried to mirror his casualness.

"Good morning, Dillon. It appears it's going to be another lovely day."

"We've a large supply of them on this side of the island."

"On this side?" Laine watched as he ran a hand through his hair, sending it into a state of appealing confusion.

"Mmm. On the windward slopes it rains almost every

day." He downed half his coffee in one movement, and Laine found herself staring at his long, brown fingers. They looked strong and competent against the cream-colored earthenware. Suddenly, she remembered the feel of them on her chin. "Something wrong?"

"What?" Blinking, she brought her attention back to his face. "No, I was just thinking...I'll have to tour the island while I'm here," she improvised, rushing through the words. "Is your...is your home near here?"

"Not far." Dillon lifted his cup again, studying her over its rim. Laine began to stir her own coffee as if the task required enormous concentration. She had no intention of drinking it, having had her first—and, she vowed, last—encounter with American coffee aboard the plane.

"Breakfast," Miri announced, gliding into the room with a heaping tray. "You will eat." With brows drawn, she began piling portions onto Laine's plate. "And then you go out so I can clean my house. You!" She shook a large spoon at Dillon who was filling his own plate with obvious appreciation. "Don't bring any sand back with you to dirty my floors."

He responded with a quick Hawaiian phrase and a cocky grin. Miri's laughter echoed after her as she moved from the room and into the kitchen.

"Dillon," Laine began, staring at the amount of food on her plate, "I could never eat all of this."

He forked a mouthful of eggs and shrugged. "Better make a stab at it. Miri's decided to fatten you up, and even if you couldn't use it—and you can," he added as he buttered a piece of toast, "Miri is not a lady to cross. Pretend it's bouillabaisse or escargots."

The last was stated with a tangible edge, and Laine

stiffened. Instinctively, she put up her defenses. "I have no complaints on the quality of the food, but on the quantity."

Dillon shrugged. Annoyed, Laine attacked her breakfast. The meal progressed without conversation. Fifteen minutes later, she searched for the power to lift yet another forkful of eggs. With a sound of impatience, Dillon rose and pulled her from her chair.

"You look like you'll keel over if you shovel in one more bite. I'll give you a break and get you out before Miri comes back."

Laine gritted her teeth, hoping it would help her to be humble. "Thank you."

As Dillon pulled Laine down the hall toward the front door, Cap descended the stairs. All three stopped as he glanced down from man to woman. "Good morning. It should be a fine day for your snorkeling lesson, Laine."

"Yes, I'm looking forward to it." She smiled, straining for a naturalness she was unable to feel in his presence.

"That's good. Dillon's right at home in the water." Cap's smile gained warmth as he turned to the man by her side. "When you come in this afternoon, take a look at the new twin-engine. I think the modifications you specified worked out well."

"Sure. I'm going to do a bit of work on that cabin plane. Keep Tinker away from it, will you?"

Cap chuckled as they enjoyed some personal joke. When he turned to Laine, he had a remnant of his smile and a polite nod. "I'll see you tonight. Have a good time."

"Yes, thank you." She watched him move away and, for a moment, her heart lifted to her eyes. Looking back, she found Dillon studying her. His expression was indrawn and brooding.

"Come on," he said with sudden briskness as he captured her hand. "Let's get started." He lifted a faded, long-stringed bag and tossed it over his shoulder as they passed through the front door. "Where's your suit?"

"I have it on." Preferring to trot alongside rather than be dragged, Laine scrambled to keep pace.

The path he took was a well-worn dirt track. Along its borders, flowers and ferns crept to encroach on the walkway. Laine wondered if there was another place on earth where colors had such clarity or where green had so many shades. The vanilla-scented blossoms of heliotrope added a tang to the moist sea air. With a high call, a skylark streaked across the sky and disappeared. Laine and Dillon walked in silence as the sun poured unfiltered over their heads.

After a ten-minute jog, Laine said breathlessly, "I do hope it isn't much farther. I haven't run the decathlon for years."

Dillon turned, and she braced herself for his irritated retort. Instead, he began to walk at a more moderate pace. Pleased, Laine allowed herself a small smile. She felt even a minor victory in dealing with Dillon O'Brian was an accomplishment. Moments later, she forgot her triumph.

The bay was secluded, sheltered by palms and laced with satin-petaled hibiscus. In the exotic beauty of Kauai, it was a stunning diamond. The water might have dripped from the sky that morning. It shone and glimmered like a multitude of fresh raindrops.

With a cry of pleasure, Laine began to pull Dillon through the circling palms and into the white heat of sun and sand. "Oh, it's beautiful!" She turned two quick circles as if to insure encompassing all the new wonders. "It's perfect, absolutely perfect."

She watched his smile flash like a brisk wind. It chased away the clouds and, for one precious moment, there was understanding rather than tension between them. It flowed from man to woman with an ease which was as unexpected as it was soothing. His frown returned abruptly, and Dillon crouched to rummage through the bag. He pulled out snorkels and masks.

"Snorkeling's easy once you learn to relax and breathe properly. It's important to be both relaxed and alert." He began to instruct in simple terms, explaining breathing techniques and adjusting Laine's mask.

"There is no need to be quite so didactic," she said at length, irked by his patronizing tone and frowning face. "I assure you, I have a working brain. Most things don't have to be repeated more than four or five times before I grasp the meaning."

"Fine." He handed her both snorkel and mask. "Let's try it in the water." Pulling off his shirt, he dropped it on the canvas bag. He stood above her adjusting the strap on his own mask.

A fine mat of black hair lay against his bronzed chest. His skin was stretched tight over his rib cage, then tapered down to a narrow waist. The faded denim hung low over his lean hips. With some astonishment, Laine felt an ache start in her stomach and move warmly through her veins. She dropped her eyes to an intense study of the sand.

"Take off your clothes." Laine's eyes widened. She took a quick step in retreat. "Unless you intend to swim in them," Dillon added. His lips twitched before he turned and moved toward the water.

Embarrassed, Laine did her best to emulate his casualness. Shyly, she stripped off her top. Pulling off her jeans, she folded both and followed Dillon toward the bay. He waited for her, water lapping over his thighs. His eyes traveled over every inch of her exposed skin before they rested on her face.

"Stay close," he commanded when she stood beside him. "We'll skim the surface for a bit until you get the hang of it." He pulled the mask down over her eyes and adjusted it.

Easily, they moved along the shallows where sunlight struck the soft bottom and sea lettuce danced and swayed. Forgetting her instructions, Laine breathed water instead of air and surfaced choking.

"What happened?" Dillon demanded, as Laine coughed and sputtered. "You're going to have to pay more attention to what you're doing," he warned. Giving her a sturdy thump on the back, he pulled her mask back over her eyes. "Ready?" he asked.

After three deep breaths, Laine managed to speak. "Yes." She submerged.

Little by little, she explored deeper water, swimming by Dillon's side. He moved through the water as a bird moves through the air, with inherent ease and confidence. Before long, Laine learned to translate his aquatic hand signals and began to improvise her own. They were joined in the liquid world by curious fish. As Laine stared into round, lidless eyes, she wondered who had come to gape at whom.

The sun flickered through with ethereal light. It nurtured the sea grass and caused shells and smooth rocks to glisten. It was a silent world, and although the sea bottom teemed with life, it was somehow private and free. Pale pink fingers of coral grouped together to form a hiding place for vivid blue fish. Laine watched in fascination as a hermit crab slid out of its borrowed shell and scurried away. There was a pair of orange starfish clinging contentedly to a rock, and a sea urchin nestled in spiny solitude.

Laine enjoyed isolation with this strange, moody man. She did not pause to appraise the pleasure she took in sharing her new experiences with him. The change in their relationship had been so smooth and so swift, she had not even been aware of it. They were, for a moment, only man and woman cloaked in a world of water and sunlight. On impulse, she lifted a large cone-shaped shell from its bed, its resident long since evicted. First holding it out for Dillon to view, she swam toward the dancing light on the surface.

Shaking her head as she broke water, Laine splattered Dillon's mask with sundrops. Laughing, she pushed her own mask to the top of her head and stood in the waist-high water. "Oh, that was wonderful! I've never seen anything like it." She pushed damp tendrils behind her ears. "All those colors, and so many shades of blue and green molded together. It feels…it feels as if there were nothing else in the world but yourself and where you are."

Excitement had kissed her cheeks with color, her eyes stealing the blue from the sea. Her hair was dark gold, clinging in a sleek cap to her head. Now, without the softening of curls, her face seemed more delicately sculptured, the planes and hollows more fragile. Dillon watched her in smiling silence, pushing his own mask atop his head.

"I've never done anything like that before. I could have stayed down there forever. There's so much to see, so much to touch. Look what I found. It's beautiful." She held the shell in both hands, tracing a finger over its amber lines. "What is it?"

Dillon took it for a moment, turning it over in his hands before giving it back to her. "A music volute. You'll find scores of shells around the island."

"May I keep it? Does this place belong to anyone?"

Dillon laughed, enjoying her enthusiasm. "This is a private bay, but I know the owner. I don't think he'd mind."

"Will I hear the sea? They say you can." Laine lifted the shell to her ear. At the low, drifting echo, her eyes widened in wonder. *"Oh, c'est incroyable."* In her excitement, she reverted to French, not only in speech, but in mannerisms. Her eyes locked on his as one hand held the shell to her ear and the other gestured with her words. *"On entend le bruit de la mer. C'est merveilleux! Dillon, écoute."*

She offered the shell, wanting to share her discovery. He laughed as she had heard him laugh with her father. "Sorry, Duchess, you lost me a few sentences back."

"Oh, how silly. I wasn't thinking. I haven't spoken English in so long." She brushed at her damp hair and offered him a smile. "It's marvelous, I can really hear the sea." Her words faltered as his eyes lost their amusement. They were darkened by an emotion which caused her heart to jump and pound furiously against her ribs. Her mind shouted quickly to retreat, but her body and will melted as his arms slid around her. Her mouth lifted of its own accord to surrender to his.

For the first time, she felt a man's hands roam over her naked skin. There was nothing between them but the satin rivulets of water which clung to their bodies. Under the streaming gold sun, her heart opened, and she gave. She accepted the demands of his mouth, moved with the caresses of his hands until she thought they would never become separate. She wanted only for them to remain one until the sun died, and the world was still.

Dillon released her slowly, his arms lingering, as if reluctant to relinquish possession. Her sigh was mixed with pleasure and the despair of losing a newly discovered treasure. "I would swear," he muttered, staring down into her face, "you're either a first-rate actress or one step out of a nunnery."

Immediately, the helpless color rose, and Laine turned to escape to the sand of the beach. "Hold on." Taking her arm, Dillon turned her to face him. His brows drew close as he studied her blush. "That's a feat I haven't seen in years. Duchess, you amaze me. Either way," he continued, and his smile held mockery but lacked its former malice, "calculated or innocent, you amaze me. Again," he said simply and drew her into his arms.

This time the kiss was gentle and teasing. But she had less defense against tenderness than passion, and her body was pliant to his instruction. Her hands tightened on his shoulders, feeling the ripple of muscles under her palms as he drew every drop of response from her mouth. With no knowledge of seduction, she became a temptress by her very innocence. Dillon drew her away and gave her clouded eyes and swollen mouth a long examination.

"You're a powerful lady," he said at length, then let out a quick breath. "Let's sit in the sun awhile." Without waiting for her answer, he took her hand and moved toward the beach.

On the sand, he spread a large beach towel and dropped onto it. When Laine hesitated, he pulled her down to join him. "I don't bite, Laine, I only nibble." Drawing a cigarette from the bag beside them, he lit it, then leaned back on his elbows. His skin gleamed with water and sun.

Feeling awkward, Laine sat very still with the shell in her hands. She tried not only to understand what she had felt in Dillon's arms, but why she had felt it. It had been important, and somehow, she felt certain it would remain important for the rest of her life. It was a gift that did not yet have a name. Suddenly, she felt as happy as when the shell had spoken in her ear. Glancing at it, Laine smiled with unrestrained joy.

"You treat that shell as though it were your firstborn." Twisting her head, she saw Dillon grinning. She decided she had never been happier.

"It is my first souvenir, and I've never dived for sunken treasure before."

"Just think of all the sharks you had to push out of the way to get your hands on it." He blew smoke at the sky as she wrinkled her nose at him.

"Perhaps you're only jealous because you didn't get one of your own. I suppose it was selfish of me not to have gotten one for you."

"I'll survive."

"You don't find shells in Paris," she commented, feeling at ease and strangely fresh. "The children will treasure it as much as they would gold doubloons."

"Children?"

Laine was examining her prize, exploring its smooth surface with her fingers. "My students at school. Most of them have never seen anything like this except in pictures."

"You teach?"

Much too engrossed in discovering every angle of the shell, Laine missed the incredulity in his voice. She answered absently, "Yes, English to the French students and French to the English girls who board there. After I graduated, I stayed on as staff. There was really nowhere else to go, and it had always been home in any case. Dillon, do you suppose I could come back sometime and find one or two others, a different type perhaps? The girls would be fascinated; they get so little entertainment."

"Where was your mother?"

"What?" In the transfer of her attention, she saw he was sitting up and staring at her with hard, probing eyes. "What did you say?" she asked again, confused by his change of tone.

"I said, where was your mother?"

"When…when I was in school? She was in Paris." The sudden anger in his tone threw her into turmoil. She searched for a way to change the topic. "I would like to see the airport again; do you think I…"

"Stop it."

Laine jerked at the harsh command, then quickly tried to slip into her armor. "There's no need to shout. I'm quite capable of hearing you from this distance."

"Don't pull that royal routine on me, Duchess. I want some answers." He flicked away his cigarette. Laine saw both the determination and fury in his face.

"I'm sorry, Dillon." Rising and stepping out of reach, Laine remained outwardly calm. "I'm really not in the mood for a cross-examination."

With a muttered oath, Dillon swung to his feet and captured her arms with a swiftness which left her stunned. "You can be a frosty little number. You switch on and off so fast, I can't make up my mind which is the charade. Just who the devil are you?"

"I'm tired of telling you who I am," she answered quietly. "I don't know what you want me to say; I don't know what you want me to be."

Her answer and her mild tone seemed only to make him more angry. He tightened his hold and gave her a quick shake. "What was this last routine of yours?"

She was yanked against him in a sudden blaze of fury, but before punishment could be meted out, someone called his name. With a soft oath Dillon released her, and turned as a figure emerged from a narrow tunnel of palms.

Laine's first thought was that a spirit from the island was drifting through the shelter and across the sand. Her skin was tawny gold and smooth against a sarong of scarlet and midnight blue. A full ebony carpet of hair fell to her waist, flowing gently with her graceful movements. Almond-shaped amber eyes were fringed with dark velvet. A sultry smile flitted across an exotic and perfect face. She lifted a hand in greeting, and Dillon answered.

"Hello, Orchid."

Her mortality was established in Laine's mind as the beautiful apparition lifted her lips and brushed Dillon's. "Miri said you'd gone snorkeling, so I knew you'd be here." Her voice flowed like soft music.

"Laine Simmons, Orchid King." Dillon's introductions were casual. Laine murmured a response, feeling suddenly as inadequate as a shadow faced with the sun. "Laine's Cap's daughter."

"Oh, I see." Laine was subjected to a more lengthy survey. She saw speculation beneath the practiced smile. "How nice you're visiting at last. Are you staying long?"

"A week or two." Laine regained her poise and met Orchid's eyes. "Do you live on the island?"

"Yes, though I'm off it as often as not. I'm a flight attendant. I'm just back from the mainland, and I've got a few days. I wanted to trade the sky for the sea. I hope you're going back in." She smiled up at Dillon and tucked a hand through his arm. "I would love some company."

Laine watched his charm flow. It seemed he need do nothing but smile to work his own particular magic. "Sure, I've got a couple of hours."

"I think I'll just go back to the house," Laine said quickly, feeling like an intruder. "I don't think I should get too much sun at one time." Lifting her shirt, Laine tugged it on. "Thank you, Dillon, for your time." She bent down and retrieved the rest of her things before speaking again. "It's nice to have met you, Miss King."

"I'm sure we'll see each other again." Undraping her sarong, Orchid revealed an inadequate bikini and a stunning body. "We're all very friendly on this island, aren't we, cousin?" Though it was the standard island form of address, Orchid's use of the word *cousin* implied a much closer relationship.

"Very friendly." Dillon agreed with such ease that Laine felt he must be quite accustomed to Orchid's charms.

Murmuring a goodbye, Laine moved toward the canopy of palms. Hearing Orchid laugh, then speak in the musical tongue of the island, Laine glanced back before the leaves blocked out the view. She watched the golden arms twine around Dillon's neck, pulling his mouth toward hers in invitation.

Chapter 5

The walk back from the bay gave Laine time to reflect on the varying emotions Dillon O'Brian had managed to arouse in the small amount of time she had known him. Annoyance, resentment and anger had come first. Now, there was a wariness she realized stemmed from her inexperience with men. But somehow, that morning, there had been a few moments of harmony. She had been at ease in his company. And, she admitted ruefully, she had never before been totally at ease in masculine company on a one-to-one basis.

Perhaps it had simply been the novelty of her underwater adventure which had been responsible for her response to him. There had been something natural in their coming together, as if body had been created for body and mouth for mouth. She had felt a freedom in his arms, an awakening. It had been as if walls of glass had shattered and left her open to sensations for the first time.

Stopping, Laine plucked a blush-pink hibiscus, then

twirled its stem idly as she wandered up the dirt track. Her tenuous feelings had been dissipated first by Dillon's unexplained anger, then by the appearance of the dark island beauty.

Orchid King, Laine mused. A frown marred her brow as the name of the flirtatious information clerk ran through her brain. *Rose.* Smoothing the frown away, Laine shook off a vague depression. Perhaps Dillon had a predilection for women with flowery names. It was certainly none of her concern. Obviously, she continued, unconsciously tearing off the hibiscus petals, he gave and received kisses as freely as a mouse nibbles cheese. He simply kissed me because I was there. Obviously, she went on doggedly, shredding the wounded blossom without thought, Orchid King has a great deal more to offer than I. She makes me feel like a pale, shapeless wren next to a lush, vibrant flamingo. I would hardly appeal to him as a woman even if he didn't already dislike me. I don't want to appeal to him. Certainly not. The very last thing I want to do is to appeal to that insufferable man. Scowling, she stared down at the mutilated hibiscus. With something between a sigh and a moan, she tossed it aside and increased her pace.

After depositing the shell in her room and changing out of her bathing suit, Laine wandered back downstairs. She felt listless and at loose ends. In the organized system of classes and meals and designated activities, her time had always been carefully budgeted. She found the lack of demand unsettling. She thought of how often during the course of a busy day she had yearned for a free hour to read or simply to sit alone. Now her time was free, and she wished only for occupation. The difference was, she knew, the fear of idle hours and the tendency to think. She found herself avoiding any attempt to sort out her situation or the future.

No one had shown her through the house since her arrival. After a brief hesitation, she allowed curiosity to lead her and gave herself a tour. She discovered that her father lived simply, with no frills or frippery, but with basic masculine comforts. There were books, but it appeared they were little read. She could see by the quantity and ragged appearance of aeronautical magazines where her father's taste in literature lay. Bamboo shades replaced conventional curtains; woven mats took the place of rugs. While far from primitive, the rooms were simply furnished.

Her mind began to draw a picture of a man content with such a basic existence, who lived quietly and routinely; a man whose main outlet was his love of the sky. Now Laine began to understand why her parents' marriage had failed. Her father's lifestyle was as unassuming as her mother's had been pretentious. Her mother would never have been satisfied with her father's modest existence, and he would have been lost in hers. Laine wondered, with a small frown, why she herself did not seem to fit with either one of them.

Laine lifted a black-framed snapshot from a desk. A younger version of Cap Simmons beamed out at her, his arm casually tossed around a Dillon who had not yet reached full manhood. Dillon's smile was the same, however—somewhat cocky and sure. If they had stood in the flesh before her, their affection for each other would have seemed no less real. A shared understanding was revealed in their eyes and their easy stance together. It struck Laine suddenly, with a stab of resentment, that they looked like father and son. The years they had shared could never belong to her.

"It's not fair," she murmured, gripping the picture in both hands. With a faint shudder, she shut her eyes. Who am I blaming? she asked herself. Cap for needing someone? Dillon for being here? Blame won't help, and looking for the past is useless. It's time I looked for something new. Letting out a deep breath, Laine replaced the photograph. She turned away and moved farther down the hall. In a moment, she found herself in the kitchen surrounded by gleaming white appliances and hanging copper kettles. Miri turned from the stove and gave Laine a satisfied smile.

"So you have come for lunch." Miri tilted her head and narrowed her eyes. "You have some color from the sun."

Laine glanced down at her bare arms and was pleased with the light tan. "Why, yes, I do. I didn't actually come for lunch, though." She smiled and made an encompassing gesture. "I was exploring the house."

"Good. Now you eat. Sit here." Miri waved a long knife toward the scrubbed wooden table. "And do not make your bed anymore. That is my job." Miri plopped a glass of milk under Laine's nose, then gave a royal sniff.

"Oh, I'm sorry." Laine glanced from the glass of milk up to Miri's pursed lips. "It's just a habit."

"Don't do it again," Miri commanded as she turned to the refrigerator. She spoke again as she began to remove a variety of contents. "Did you make beds in that fancy school?"

"It isn't actually a fancy school," Laine corrected, watching with growing anxiety as Miri prepared a hefty sandwich. "It's really just a small convent school outside Paris."

"You lived in a convent?" Miri stopped her sandwich-building and looked skeptical.

"Well, no. That is, one might say I lived on the fringes of one. Except, of course, when I visited my mother. Miri..." Daunted by the plate set in front of her, Laine looked up helplessly. "I don't think I can manage all this."

"Just eat, Skinny Bones. Your morning with Dillon, it was nice?"

"Yes, very nice." Laine applied herself to the sandwich as Miri eased herself into the opposite chair. "I never knew there was so much to see underwater. Dillon is an expert guide."

"Ah, that one." Miri shook her head and somehow categorized Dillon as a naughty twelve-year-old boy. "He is always in the water or in the sky. He should keep his feet planted on the ground more often." Leaning back, Miri kept a commanding eye on Laine's progress. "He watches you."

"Yes, I know," Laine murmured. "Like a parole officer. I met Miss King," she continued, lifting her voice. "She came to the bay."

"Orchid King." Miri muttered something in unintelligible Hawaiian.

"She's very lovely...very vibrant and striking. I suppose Dillon has known her for a long time." Laine made the comment casually, surprising herself with the intentional probe.

"Long enough. But her bait has not yet lured the fish into the net." Miri gave a sly smile lost on the woman who stared into her milk. "You think Dillon looks good?"

"Looks good?" Laine repeated and frowned, not understanding the nuance. "Yes, Dillon's a very attractive man. At least, I suppose he is; I haven't known many men."

"You should give him more smiles," Miri advised with

a wise nod. "A smart woman uses smiles to show a man her mind."

"He hasn't given me many reasons to smile at him," Laine said between bites. "And," she continued, finding she resented the thought, "I would think he gets an abundance of smiles from other sources."

"Dillon gives his attention to many women. He is a very generous man." Miri chuckled, and Laine blushed as she grasped the innuendo. "He has not yet found a woman who could make him selfish. Now you..." Miri tapped a finger aside her nose as if considering. "You would do well with him. He could teach you, and you could teach him."

"I teach Dillon?" Laine shook her head and gave a small laugh. "One cannot teach what one doesn't know. In the first place, Miri, I only met Dillon yesterday. All he's done so far is confuse me. From one moment to the next, I don't know how he's going to make me feel." She sighed, not realizing the sound was wistful. "I think men are very strange, Miri. I don't understand them at all."

"Understand?" Her bright laugh rattled through the kitchen. "What need is there to understand? You need only enjoy. I had three husbands, and I never understood one of them. But—" her smile was suddenly young "—I enjoyed. You are very young," she added. "That alone is attractive to a man used to women of knowledge."

"I don't think...I mean, of course, I wouldn't want him to, but..." Laine fumbled and stuttered, finding her thoughts a mass of confusion. "I'm sure Dillon wouldn't be interested in me. He seems to have a very compatible relationship with Miss King. Besides—" Laine shrugged her shoulders as she felt depression growing "—he distrusts me."

"It is a stupid woman who lets what is gone interfere with what is now." Miri placed her fingertips together and leaned back in her chair. "You want your father's love, Skinny Bones? Time and patience will give it to you. You want Dillon?" She held up an imperious hand at Laine's automatic protest. "You will learn to fight as a woman fights." She stood, and the flowers on her muumuu trembled with the movement. "Now, out of my kitchen. I have much work to do."

Obediently, Laine rose and moved to the door. "Miri..." Nibbling her lips, she turned back. "You've been very close to my father for many years. Don't you..." Laine hesitated, then finished in a rush. "Don't you resent me just appearing like this after all these years?"

"Resent?" Miri repeated the word, then ran her tongue along the inside of her mouth. "I do not resent because resent is a waste of time. And the last thing I resent is a child." She picked up a large spoon and tapped it idly against her palm. "When you went away from Cap Simmons, you were a child and you went with your mother. Now you are not a child, and you are here. What do I have to resent?" Miri shrugged and moved back to the stove.

Feeling unexpected tears, Laine shut her eyes on them and drew a small breath. "Thank you, Miri." With a murmur, she retreated to her room.

Thoughts swirled inside Laine's mind as she sat alone in her bedroom. As Dillon's embrace had opened a door to dormant emotions, so Miri's words had opened a door to dormant thoughts. *Time and patience,* Laine repeated silently. Time and patience were Miri's prescription for a daughter's troubled heart. But I have so little time, and little more patience. How can I win my father's love in a matter of days? She shook her head, unable to resolve an answer. *And Dillon,* her heart murmured as she threw herself onto the bed and stared at the ceiling. Why must he complicate an already impossibly complicated situation? Why must he embrace me, making me think and feel as a woman one moment, then push me away and stand as my accuser the next? He can be so gentle when I'm in his arms, so warm. And then… Frustrated, she rolled over, laying her cheek against the pillow. Then he's so cold, and even his eyes are brutal. If only I could stop thinking of him, stop remembering how it feels to be kissed by him. It's only that I have no experience, and he has so much. It's nothing more than a physical awakening. There can be nothing more…nothing more.

The knock on Laine's door brought her up with a start. Pushing at her tousled hair, she rose to answer. Dillon had exchanged cutoffs for jeans, and he appeared as refreshed and alert as she did bemused and heavy-lidded. Laine stared at him dumbly, unable to bring her thoughts and words together. With a frown, he surveyed her sleep-flushed cheeks and soft eyes.

"Did I wake you?"

"No, I…" She glanced back at the clock, and her confusion grew as she noted that an hour had passed since she had first stretched out on the bed. "Yes," she amended. "I suppose the flight finally caught up with me." She reached up and ran a hand through her hair, struggling to orient herself. "I didn't even realize I'd been asleep."

"They're real, aren't they?"

"What?" Laine blinked and tried to sort out his meaning.

"The lashes." He was staring so intently into her eyes, Laine had to fight the need to look away.

Nonchalantly, he leaned against the door and completed his survey. "I'm on my way to the airport. I thought you might want to go. You said you wanted to see it again."

"Yes, I would." She was surprised by his courtesy.

"Well," he said dryly, and gestured for her to come along.

"Oh, I'll be right there. It should only take me a minute to get ready."

"You look ready."

"I need to comb my hair."

"It's fine." Dillon grabbed her hand and pulled her from the room before she could resist further.

Outside she found, to her astonishment, a helmet being thrust in her hands as she faced a shining, trim motorcycle. Clearing her throat, she looked from the helmet, to the machine, to Dillon. "We're going to ride on this?"

"That's right. I don't often use the car just to run to the airport."

"You might find this a good time to do so," Laine advised. "I've never ridden on a motorcycle."

"Duchess, all you have to do is to sit down and hang on." Dillon took the helmet from her and dropped it on her head. Securing his own helmet, he straddled the bike, then kicked the starter into life. "Climb on."

With amazement, Laine found herself astride the purring machine and clutching Dillon's waist as the motorcycle shot down the drive. Her death grip eased slightly as she realized that the speed was moderate, and the motorcycle had every intention of staying upright. It purred along the paved road.

Beside them, a river wandered like an unfurled blue ribbon, dividing patterned fields of taro. There was an excitement in being open to the wind, in feeling the hardness of Dillon's muscles beneath her hands. A sense of liberation flooded her. Laine realized that, in one day, Dillon had already given her experiences she might never have touched. *I never knew how limited my life was,* she thought with a smile. *No matter what happens, when I leave here, nothing will ever be quite the same again.*

When they arrived at the airport, Dillon wove through the main lot, circling to the back and halting in front of a hangar. "Off you go, Duchess. Ride's over."

Laine eased from the bike and struggled with her helmet. "Here." Dillon pulled it off for her, then dropped it to join his on the seat of the bike. "Still in one piece?"

"Actually," she returned, "I think I enjoyed it."

"It has its advantages." He ran his hands down her arms, then captured her waist. Laine stood very still, unwilling to retreat from his touch. He bent down and moved his mouth with teasing lightness over hers. Currents of pleasure ran over her skin. "Later," he said, pulling back. "I intend to finish that in a more satisfactory manner. But at the moment, I've work to do." His thumbs ran in lazy circles over her hips. "Cap's going to take you around; he's expecting you. Can you find your way?"

"Yes." Confused by the urgency of her heartbeat, Laine stepped back. The break in contact did nothing to slow it. "Am I to go to his office?"

"Yeah, the same place you went before. He'll show you whatever you want to see. Watch your step, Laine." His green eyes cooled abruptly, and his voice lost its lightness. "Until I'm sure about you, you can't afford to make any mistakes."

For a moment, she only stared up at him, feeling her skin

grow cold, and her pulse slow. "I'm very much afraid," she admitted sadly, "I've already made one."

Turning, she walked away.

Chapter 6

Laine walked toward the small, palm-flanked building. Through her mind ran all which had passed in twenty-four hours. She had met her father, learned of her mother's deception and was now readjusting her wishes.

She had also, in the brief span of time it takes the sun to rise and fall, discovered the pleasures and demands of womanhood. Dillon had released new and magic sensations. Again, her mind argued with her heart that her feelings were only the result of a first physical attraction. It could hardly be anything else, she assured herself. One does not fall in love in a day, and certainly not with a man like Dillon O'Brian. We're total opposites. He's outgoing and confident, and so completely at ease with people. I envy him his honest confidence. There's nothing emotional about that. I've simply never met anyone like him before. That's why I'm confused. It has nothing to do with emotions. Laine felt comforted as she entered her father's office building.

As she stepped into the outer lobby, Cap strode from his office, glancing over his shoulder at a dark girl with a pad in her hand who was following in his wake.

"Check with Dillon on the fuel order before you send that out. He'll be in a meeting for the next hour. If you miss him at his office, try hangar four." As he caught sight of Laine, Cap smiled and slowed his pace. "Hello, Laine. Dillon said you wanted a tour."

"Yes, I'd love one, if you have the time."

"Of course. Sharon, this is my daughter. Laine, this is Sharon Kumocko, my secretary."

Laine observed the curiosity in Sharon's eyes as they exchanged greetings. Her father's tone during the introductions had been somewhat forced. Laine felt him hesitate before he took her arm to lead her outside. She wondered briefly if she had imagined their closeness during her childhood.

"It's not a very big airport," Cap began as they stepped out into the sun and heat. "For the most part, we cater to island hoppers and charters. We also run a flight school. That's essentially Dillon's project."

"Cap." Impulsively, Laine halted his recital and turned to face him. "I know I've put you in an awkward position. I realize now that I should have written and asked if I could come rather than just dropping on your doorstep this way. It was thoughtless of me."

"Laine…"

"Please." She shook her head at his interruption and rushed on. "I realize, too, that you have your own life, your own home, your own friends. You've had fifteen years to settle into a routine. I don't want to interfere with any of that. Believe me, I don't want to be in the way, and I don't want you to feel..." She made a helpless gesture as the impetus ran out of her words. "I would like it if we could be friends."

Cap had studied her during her speech. The smile he gave her at its finish held more warmth than those he had given her before. "You know," he sighed, tugging his fingers through his hair, "it's sort of terrifying to be faced with a grown-up daughter. I missed all the stages, all the changes. I'm afraid I still pictured you as a bad-tempered pigtailed urchin with scraped knees. The elegant woman who walked into my office yesterday and spoke to me with a faint French accent is a stranger. And one," he added, touching her hair a moment, "who brings back memories I thought I'd buried." He sighed again and stuck his hands in his pockets. "I don't know much about women; I don't think I ever did. Your mother was the most beautiful, confusing woman I've ever known. When you were little, and the three of us were still together, I substituted your friendship for the friendship that your mother and I never had. You were the only female I ever understood. I've always wondered if that was why things didn't work."

Tilting her head, Laine gave her father a long, searching look. "Cap, why did you marry her? There seems to be nothing you had in common."

Cap shook his head with a quick laugh. "You didn't know her twenty years ago. She did a lot of changing, Laine. Some people change more than others." He shook his head again, and his eyes focused on some middle distance. "Besides, I loved her. I've always loved her."

"I'm sorry." Laine felt tears burn the back of her eyes, and she dropped her gaze to the ground. "I don't mean to make things more difficult."

"You're not. We had some good years." He paused until Laine lifted her eyes. "I like to remember them now and again." Taking her arm, he began to walk. "Was your mother happy, Laine?"

"Happy?" She thought a moment, remembering the quicksilver moods, the gay bubbling voice with dissatisfaction always under the surface. "I suppose Vanessa was as happy as she was capable of being. She loved Paris and she lived as she chose."

"Vanessa?" Cap frowned, glancing down at Laine's profile. "Is that how you think of your mother?"

"I always called her by name." Laine lifted her hand to shield her eyes from the sun as she watched the descent of a charter. "She said 'mother' made her feel too old. She hated getting older... I feel better knowing you're happy in the life you've chosen. Do you fly anymore, Cap? I remember how you used to love it."

"I still put in my quota of flight hours. Laine." He took both her arms and turned her to face him. "One question, then we'll leave it alone for a while. Have you been happy?"

The directness of both his questions and his eyes caused her to fumble. She looked away as if fascinated by disembarking passengers. "I've been very busy. The nuns are very serious about education."

"You're not answering my question. Or," he corrected, drawing his thick brows together, "maybe you are."

"I've been content," she said, giving him a smile. "I've learned a great deal, and I'm comfortable with my life. I think that's enough for anyone."

"For someone," Cap returned, "who's reached my age, but not for a very young, very lovely woman." He watched her smile fade into perplexity. "It's not enough, Laine, and

I'm surprised you'd settle for it." His voice was stern, laced with a hint of disapproval which put Laine on the defensive.

"Cap, I haven't had the chance…" She stopped, realizing she must guard her words "I haven't taken the time," she amended, "to chase windmills." She lifted her hands, palms up, in a broad French gesture. "Perhaps I've reached the point in my life when I should begin to do so."

His expression lightened as she smiled up at him. "All right, we'll let it rest for now"

Without any more mention of the past, Cap led Laine through neat rows of planes. He fondled each as if it were a child, explaining their qualities in proud, but to Laine hopelessly technical, terms. She listened, content with his good humor, pleased with the sound of his voice. Occasionally, she made an ignorant comment that made him laugh. She found the laugh very precious.

The buildings were spread out, neat and without pretension; hangars and storage buildings, research and accounting offices, with the high, glass-enclosed control tower dominating all. Cap pointed out each one, but the planes themselves were his consummate interest.

"You said it wasn't big." Laine gazed around the complex and down light-dotted runways. "It looks enormous."

"It's a small, low-activity field, but we do our best to see that it's as well run as Honolulu International."

"What is it that Dillon does here?" Telling herself it was only idle curiosity, Laine surrendered to the urge to question.

"Oh, Dillon does a bit of everything," Cap answered with frustrating vagueness. "He has a knack for organizing. He can find his way through a problem before it becomes one, and he handles people so well they never re-

alize they've been handled. He can also take a plane apart
and put it back together again." Smiling, Cap gave a small
shake of his head. "I don't know what I'd have done without Dillon. Without his drive, I might have been content
to be a crop duster."

"Drive?" Laine repeated, lingering over the word. "Yes,
I suppose he has drive when there is something he wants.
But isn't he..." She searched for a label and settled on a
generality. "Isn't he a very casual person?"

"Island life breeds a certain casualness, Laine, and Dillon was born here." He steered her toward the communica-
tions building. "Just because a man is at ease with himself
and avoids pretension doesn't mean he lacks intelligence
or ability. Dillon has both; he simply pursues his ambi-
tions in his own way."

Later, as they walked toward the steel-domed hangars,
Laine realized she and her father had begun to build a new
relationship. He was more relaxed with her, his smiles
and speech more spontaneous. She knew her shield was
dropped as well, and she was more vulnerable.

"I've an appointment in a few minutes." Cap stopped just
inside the building and glanced at his watch. "I'll have to
turn you over to Dillon now, unless you want me to have
someone take you back to the house."

"No, I'll be fine," she assured him. "Perhaps I can just
wander about. I don't want to be a nuisance."

"You haven't been a nuisance. I enjoyed taking you
through. You haven't lost the curiosity I remember. You
always wanted to know why and how and you always listened. I think you were five when you demanded I explain
the entire control panel of a 707." His chuckle was the same
quick, appealing sound she remembered from childhood.

"Your face would get so serious, I'd swear you had understood everything I'd said." He patted her hand, then smiled over her head. "Dillon, I thought we'd find you here. Take care of Laine, will you? I've got Billet coming in."

"It appears I've got the best of the deal."

Laine turned to see him leaning against a plane, wiping his hand on the loose coveralls he wore.

"Did everything go all right with the union representative?"

"Fine. You can look over the report tomorrow."

"I'll see you tonight, then." Cap turned to Laine, and after a brief hesitation, patted her cheek before he walked away.

Smiling, she turned back to encounter Dillon's brooding stare. "Oh, please," she began, shaking her head. "Don't spoil it. It's such a small thing."

With a shrug, Dillon turned back to the plane. "Did you like your tour?"

"Yes, I did." Laine's footsteps echoed off the high ceiling as she crossed the room to join him. "I'm afraid I didn't understand a fraction of what he told me. He carried on about aprons and funnel systems and became very expansive on wind drag and thrust." She creased her brow for a moment as she searched her memory. "I'm told struts can withstand comprehensive as well as tensile forces. I didn't have the courage to confess I didn't know one force from the other."

"He's happiest when he's talking about planes," Dillon commented absently. "It doesn't matter if you understood as long as you listened. Hand me that torque wrench."

Laine looked down at the assortment of tools, then

searched for something resembling a torque wrench. "I enjoyed listening. Is this a wrench?"

Dillon twisted his head and glanced at the ratchet she offered. With reluctant amusement, he brought his eyes to hers, then shook his head. "No, Duchess. This," he stated, finding the tool himself, "is a wrench."

"I haven't spent a great deal of time under cars or under planes," she muttered. Her annoyance spread as she thought how unlikely it was that he would ask Orchid King for a torque wrench. "Cap told me you've added a flight school. Do you do the instructing?"

"Some."

Pumping up her courage, Laine asked in a rush, "Would you teach me?"

"What?" Dillon glanced back over his shoulder.

"Could you teach me to fly a plane?" She wondered if the question sounded as ridiculous to Dillon as it did to her.

"Maybe." He studied the fragile planes of her face, noting the determined light in her eyes. "Maybe," he repeated. "Why do you want to learn?"

"Cap used to talk about teaching me. Of course—" she spread her hands in a Gallic gesture "—I was only a child, but..." Releasing an impatient breath, Laine lifted her chin and was suddenly very American. "Because I think it would be fun."

The change, and the stubborn set to her mouth, touched off Dillon's laughter. "I'll take one of you up tomorrow." Laine frowned, trying to puzzle out his meaning. Turning back to the plane, Dillon held out the wrench for her to put away. She stared at the grease-smeared handle. Taking his head from the bowels of the plane, Dillon turned back and saw her reluctance. He muttered something she did not attempt to translate, then moved away and pulled another pair of coveralls from a hook. "Here, put these on. I'm going to be a while, and you might as well be useful."

"I'm sure you'd manage beautifully without me."

"Undoubtedly, but put them on anyway." Under Dillon's watchful eye, Laine stepped into the coveralls and slipped her arms into the sleeves. "Good grief, you look swallowed." Crouching down, he began to roll up the pants legs while she scowled at the top of his head.

"I'm sure you'll find me more hindrance than help."

"I figured that out some time ago," he replied. His tone was undeniably cheerful as he rolled up her sleeves half a dozen times. "You shouldn't have quit growing so soon; you don't look more than twelve." He pulled the zipper up to her throat in one swift motion, then looked into her face. She saw his expresion alter. For an instant, she thought she observed a flash of tenderness before he let out an impatient breath. Cursing softly, he submerged into the belly of the plane. "All right," he began briskly, "hand me a screwdriver. The one with the red handle."

Having made the acquaintance of this particular tool, Laine foraged and found it. She placed it in Dillon's outstretched hand. He worked for some time, his conversation limited almost exclusively to the request and description of tools. As time passed, the hum of planes outside became only a backdrop for his voice.

Laine began to ask him questions about the job he was performing. She felt no need to follow his answers, finding pleasure only in the tone and texture of his voice. He was absorbed and she was able to study him unobserved. She surveyed the odd intensity of his eyes, the firm line of his chin and jaw, the bronzed skin which rippled along his arm as he worked. She saw that his chin was shadowed with a day-old beard, that his hair was curling loosely over his collar, that his right brow was lifted slightly higher than his left as he concentrated.

Dillon turned to her with some request, but she could only stare. She was lost in his eyes, blanketed by a fierce and trembling realization.

"What's wrong?" Dillon drew his brows together.

Like a diver breaking water, Laine shook her head and swallowed. "Nothing, I... What did you want? I wasn't paying attention." She bent over the box of tools as if it contained the focus of her world. Silently, Dillon lifted out the one he required and turned back to the engine. Grateful for his preoccupation, Laine closed her eyes. She felt bemused and defenseless.

Love, she thought, *should not come with such quick intensity. It should flow slowly, with tenderness and gentle feelings. It shouldn't stab like a sword, striking without warning, without mercy. How could one love what one could not understand?* Dillon O'Brian was an enigma, a man whose moods seemed to flow without rhyme or reason. And what did she know of him? He was her father's partner, but his position was unclear. He was a man who knew both the sky and the sea, and found it easy to move with their freedom. She knew too that he was a man who knew women and could give them pleasure.

And how, Laine wondered, does one fight love when one has no knowledge of it? Perhaps it was a matter of balance. She deliberately released the tension in her shoulders. I have to find the way to walk the wire without leaning over either side and tumbling off.

"It seems you've taken a side trip," Dillon commented,

pulling a rag from his pocket. He grinned as Laine gave a start of alarm. "You're a miserable mechanic, Duchess, and a sloppy one." He rubbed the rag over her cheek until a black smudge disappeared. "There's a sink over there; you'd better go wash your hands. I'll finish these adjustments later. The fuel system is giving me fits."

Laine moved off as he instructed, taking her time in removing traces of grime. She used the opportunity to regain her composure. Hanging up the borrowed overalls, she wandered about the empty hangar while Dillon packed away tools and completed his own washing up. She was surprised to see that it had grown late during the time she had inexpertly assisted Dillon. A soft dusk masked the day's brilliance. Along the runways, lights twinkled like small red eyes. As she turned back, Laine found Dillon's gaze on her. She moistened her lips, then attempted casualness.

"Are you finished?"

"Not quite. Come here." Something in his tone caused her to retreat a step rather than obey. He lifted his brows, then repeated the order with a soft, underlying threat. "I said come here."

Deciding voluntary agreement was the wisest choice, Laine crossed the floor. Her echoing footsteps seemed to bounce off the walls like thunder. She prayed the sound masked the furious booming of her heart as she stopped in front of him, and that its beating was in her ears only. She stood in silence as he studied her face, wishing desperately she knew what he was looking for, and if she possessed it. Dillon said nothing, but placed his hands on her hips, drawing her a step closer. Their thighs brushed. His grip was firm, and all the while his eyes kept hers a prisoner.

"Kiss me," he said simply. She shook her head in quick protest, unable to look or break away. "Laine, I said kiss me." Dillon pressed her hips closer, molding her shape to his. His eyes were demanding, his mouth tempting. Tentatively, she lifted her arms, letting her hands rest on his shoulders as she rose to her toes. Her eyes remained open and locked on his as their faces drew nearer, as their breaths began to mingle. Softly, she touched her lips to his.

He waited until her mouth lost its shyness and became mobile on his, waited until her arms found their way around his neck to urge him closer. He increased the pressure, drawing out her sigh as he slid his hands under her blouse to the smooth skin of her back. His explorations were slow and achingly gentle. The hands that caressed her taught rather than demanded. Murmuring his name against the taste of his mouth, Laine strained against him, wanting him, needing him. The swift heat of passion was all-consuming. Her lips seemed to learn more quickly than her brain. They began to seek and demand pleasures she could not yet understand. The rest of the world faded like a whisper. At that moment, there was nothing in her life but Dillon and her need for him.

He drew her away. Neither spoke, each staring into the other's eyes as if to read a message not yet written. Dillon brushed a stray curl from her cheek. "I'd better take you home."

"Dillon," Laine began, completely at a loss as to what could be said. Unable to continue, she closed her eyes on her own inadequacy.

"Come on, Duchess, you've had a long day." Dillon circled her neck with his hand and massaged briefly. "We're not dealing on equal footing at the moment, and I like to fight fair under most circumstances."

"Fight?" Laine managed, struggling to keep her eyes open and steady on his. "Is that what this is, Dillon? A fight?"

"The oldest kind," he returned with a small lift to his mouth. His smile faded before it was truly formed, and suddenly his hand was firm on her chin. "It's not over, Laine, and when we have the next round, I might say the devil with the rules."

Chapter 7

When Laine came down for breakfast the next morning, she found only her father. "Hello, Skinny Bones," Miri called out before Cap could greet her. "Sit and eat. I will fix you tea since you do not like my coffee."

Unsure whether to be embarrassed or amused, Laine obeyed. "Thank you, Miri," she said to the retreating back.

"She's quite taken with you." Looking over, Laine saw the light of mirth in Cap's eyes. "Since you've come, she's been so wrapped up with putting pounds on you, she hasn't made one comment about me needing a wife."

With a wry smile, Laine watched her father pour his coffee. "Glad to help. I showed myself around a bit yesterday. I hope you don't mind."

"No, of course not." His smile was rueful. "I guess I should've taken you around the house myself. My manners are a little rusty."

"I didn't mind. Actually," she tilted her head and returned his smile, "wandering around alone gave me a sort of fresh perspective. You said you'd missed all the stages and still thought of me as a child. I think…" Her fingers spread as she tried to clarify her thoughts. "I think I missed them too—that is, I still had my childhood image of you. Yesterday, I began to see James Simmons in flesh and blood."

"Disappointed?" There was more ease in his tone and a lurking humor in his eyes.

"Impressed," Laine corrected. "I saw a man content with himself and his life, who has the love and respect of those close to him. I think my father must be a very nice man."

He gave her an odd smile which spoke both of surprise and pleasure. "That's quite a compliment coming from a grown daughter." He added more coffee to his cup, and Laine let the silence drift.

Her gaze lingered on Dillon's empty seat a moment. "Ah…is Dillon not here?"

"Hmm? Oh, Dillon had a breakfast meeting. As a matter of fact, he has quite a few things to see to this morning." Cap drank his coffee black, and with an enjoyment Laine could not understand.

"I see," she responded, trying not to sound disappointed. "I suppose the airport keeps both of you very busy."

"That it does." Cap glanced at his watch and tilted his head in regret. "Actually, I have an appointment myself very shortly. I'm sorry to leave you alone this way, but…"

"Please," Laine interrupted. "I don't need to be entertained, and I meant what I said yesterday about not wanting to interfere. I'm sure I'll find plenty of things to keep me occupied."

"All right then. I'll see you this evening." Cap rose, then paused at the doorway with sudden inspiration. "Miri can arrange a ride for you if you'd like to do some shopping in town."

"Thank you." Laine smiled, thinking of her limited funds. "Perhaps I will." She watched him stroll away, then sighed, as her gaze fell again on Dillon's empty chair.

Laine's morning was spent lazily. She soon found out that Miri would not accept or tolerate any help around the house. Following the native woman's strong suggestion that she go out, Laine gathered her stationery and set out for the bay. She found it every bit as perfect as she had the day before—the water clear as crystal, the sand white and pure. Spreading out a blanket, Laine sat down and tried to describe her surroundings with words on paper. The letters she wrote to France were long and detailed, though she omitted any mention of her troubled situation.

As she wrote, the sun rose high overhead. The air was moist and ripe. Lulled by the peace and the rays of the sun, she curled up on the blanket and slept.

Her limbs were languid, and behind closed lids was a dull red mist. She wondered hazily how the reverend mother had urged so much heat out of the ancient furnace. Reluctantly, she struggled to toss off sleep as a hand shook her shoulder. *"Un moment, ma soeur,"* she murmured, and sighed with the effort. *"J'arrive."* Forcing open her leaden lids, she found Dillon's face inches above hers.

"I seem to have a habit of waking you up." He leaned back on his heels and studied her cloudy eyes. "Don't you know better than to sleep in the sun with that complexion? You're lucky you didn't burn."

"Oh." At last realizing where she was, Laine pushed herself into a sitting position. She felt the odd sense of guilt of the napper caught napping. "I don't know why I fell asleep like that. It must have been the quiet."

"Another reason might be exhaustion," Dillon countered, then frowned. "You're losing the shadows under your eyes."

"Cap said you were very busy this morning." Laine found his continued survey disconcerting and shuffled her writing gear.

"Hmm, yes, I was. Writing letters?"

She glanced up at him, then tapped the tip of her pen against her mouth. "Hmm, yes, I was."

"Very cute." His mouth twitched slightly as he hauled her to her feet. "I thought you wanted to learn how to fly a plane."

"Oh!" Her face lit up with pleasure. "I thought you'd forgotten. Are you sure you're not too busy? Cap said…"

"No, I hadn't forgotten, and no, I'm not too busy." He cut her off as he leaned down to gather her blanket. "Stop babbling as if you were twelve and I were taking you to the circus for cotton candy."

"Of course," she replied, amused by his reaction.

Dillon let out an exasperated breath before grabbing her hand and pulling her across the sand. She heard him mutter something uncomplimentary about women in general.

Less than an hour later, Laine found herself seated in Dillon's plane. "Now, this is a single prop monoplane with a reciprocating engine. Another time, I'll take you up in the jet, but…"

"You have another plane?" Laine interrupted.

"Some people collect hats," Dillon countered dryly, then pointed to the variety of gauges. "Basically, flying a plane is no more difficult than driving a car. The first thing you have to do is understand your instruments and learn how to read them."

"There are quite a few, aren't there?" Dubiously, Laine scanned numbers and needles.

"Not really. This isn't exactly an X-15." He let out a long breath at her blank expression, then started the engine. "O.K., as we climb, I want you to watch this gauge. It's the altimeter. It…"

"It indicates the height of the plane above sea level or above ground," Laine finished for him.

"Very good." Dillon cleared his takeoff with the tower, and the plane began its roll down the runway. "What did you do, grab one of Cap's magazines last night?"

"No. I remember some of my early lessons. I suppose I stored away all the things Cap used to ramble about when I was a child. This is a compass, and this…" Her brow furrowed in her memory search. "This is a turn and bank indicator, but I'm not sure I remember quite what that means."

"I'm impressed, but you're supposed to be watching the altimeter."

"Oh, yes." Wrinkling her nose at the chastisement, she obeyed.

"All right." Dillon gave her profile a quick grin, then turned his attention to the sky. "The larger needle's going to make one turn of the dial for every thousand feet we climb. The smaller one makes a turn for every ten thousand. Once you learn your gauges, and how to use each one of them, your job's less difficult than driving, and there's generally a lot less traffic."

"Perhaps you'll teach me to drive a car next," Laine suggested as she watched the large needle round the dial for the second time.

"You don't know how to drive?" Dillon demanded. His voice was incredulous.

"No. Is that a crime in this country? I assure you, there are some people who believe me to be marginally intelligent. I'm certain I can learn to fly this machine in the same amount of time it takes any of your other students."

"It's possible," Dillon muttered. "How come you never learned to drive a car?"

"Because I never had one. How did you break your nose?" At his puzzled expression, Laine merely gave him a bland smile. "My question is just as irrelevant as yours."

Laine felt quite pleased when he laughed, almost as though she had won a small victory.

"Which time?" he asked, and it was her turn to look puzzled. "I broke it twice. The first time I was about ten and tried to fly a cardboard plane I had designed off the roof of the garage. I didn't have the propulsion system perfected. I only broke my nose and my arm, though I was told it should've been my neck."

"Very likely," Laine agreed. "And the second time?"

"The second time, I was a bit older. There was a disagreement over a certain girl. My nose suffered another insult, and the other guy lost two teeth."

"Older perhaps, but little wiser," Laine commented. "And who got the girl?"

Dillon flashed his quick grin. "Neither of us. We decided she wasn't worth it after all and went off to nurse our wounds with a beer."

"How gallant."

"Yeah, I'm sure you've noticed that trait in me. I can't seem to shake it. Now, watch your famous turn and bank indicator, and I'll explain its function."

For the next thirty minutes, he became the quintessential teacher, surprising Laine with his knowledge and patience. He answered the dozens of questions she tossed out as flashes of her early lessons skipped through her memory. He seemed to accept her sudden thirst to know as if it were not only natural, but expected. They cruised through a sky touched with puffy clouds and mountain peaks and skimmed the gaping mouth of the multihued Waimea Canyon. They circled above the endless, white-capped ocean. Laine began to see the similarity between the freedom of the sky and the freedom of the sea. She began to feel the fascination Dillon had spoken of, the need to meet the challenge, the need to explore. She listened with every ounce of her concentration, determined to understand and remember.

"There's a little storm behind us," Dillon announced casually. "We're not going to beat it back." He turned to Laine with a faint smile on his lips. "We're going to get tossed around a bit, Duchess."

"Oh?" Trying to mirror his mood, Laine shifted in her seat and studied the dark clouds in their wake. "Can you fly through that?" she asked, keeping her voice light while her stomach tightened.

"Oh, maybe," he returned. She jerked her head around swiftly. When she saw the laughter in his eyes, she let out a long breath.

"You have an odd sense of humor, Dillon. Very unique," she added, then sucked in her breath as the clouds overtook them. All at once, they were shrouded in darkness, rain pelting furiously on all sides. As the plane rocked, Laine felt a surge of panic.

"You know, it always fascinates me to be in a cloud.

Nothing much to them, just vapor and moisture, but they're fabulous." His voice was calm and composed. Laine felt her heartbeat steadying. "Storm clouds are the most interesting, but you really need lightning."

"I think I could live without it," Laine murmured.

"That's because you haven't seen it from up here. When you fly above lightning, you can watch it kicking up inside the clouds. The colors are incredible."

"Have you flown through many storms?" Laine looked out her windows, but saw nothing but swirling black clouds.

"I've done my share. The front of this one'll be waiting for us when we land. Won't last long, though." The plane bucked again, and Laine looked on in bewilderment as Dillon grinned.

"You enjoy this sort of thing, don't you? The excitement, the sense of danger?"

"It keeps the reflexes in tune, Laine." Turning, he smiled at her without a trace of cynicism. "And it keeps life from being boring." The look held for a moment, and Laine's heart did a series of jumping jacks. "There's plenty of stability in life," he continued, making adjustments to compensate for the wind. "Jobs, bills, insurance policies, that's what gives you balance. But sometimes, you've got to ride a roller coaster, run a race, ride a wave. That's what makes life fun. The trick is to keep one end of the scope from overbalancing the other."

Yes, Laine thought. Vanessa never learned the trick. She was always looking for a new game and never enjoyed the one she was playing. And perhaps I've overcompensated by thinking too much of the stability. Too many books, and not enough doing. Laine felt her muscles relax and she turned to Dillon with a hint of a smile. "I haven't ridden a roller coaster for a great many years. One could say that I'm due. Look!" She pressed her face against the side window and peered downward. "It's like something out of *Macbeth,* all misty and sinister. I'd like to see the lightning, Dillon. I really would."

He laughed at the eager anticipation on her face as he began his descent. "I'll see if I can arrange it."

The clouds seemed to swirl and dissolve as the plane lost altitude. Their thickness became pale gray cobwebs to be dusted out of the way. Below, the landscape came into view as they dropped below the mist. The earth was rain-drenched and vivid with color. As they landed, Laine felt her pleasure fade into a vague sense of loss. She felt like a child who had just blown out her last birthday candle.

"I'll take you back up in a couple days if you want," said Dillon, taxiing to a halt.

"Yes, please, I'd like that very much. I don't know how to thank you for..."

"Do your homework," he said as he shut off the engine. "I'll give you some books and you can read up on instrumentation."

"Yes, sir," Laine said with suspicious humility. Dillon glared at her briefly before swinging from the plane. Laine's lack of experience caused her to take more time with her exit. She found herself swooped down before she could complete the journey on her own.

In the pounding rain they stood close, Dillon's hands light on her waist. She could feel the heat of his body through the dampness of her blouse. Dark tendrils of hair fell over his forehead, and without thought, Laine lifted her hand to smooth them back. There was something sweetly ordinary about being in his arms, as if it were a place she had been countless times before and would come back to countless times again. She felt her love bursting to be free.

"You're getting wet," she murmured, dropping her hand to his cheek.

"So are you." Though his fingers tightened on her waist, he drew her no closer.

"I don't mind."

With a sigh, Dillon rested his chin on the top of her head. "Miri'll punch me out if I let you catch a chill."

"I'm not cold," she murmured, finding indescribable pleasure in their closeness.

"You're shivering." Abruptly, Dillon brought her to his side and began to walk. "We'll go into my office, and you can dry out before I take you home."

As they walked, the rain slowed to a mist. Fingers of sunlight began to strain through, brushing away the last stubborn drops. Laine surveyed the complex. She remembered the building which housed Dillon's office from the tour she had taken with her father. With a grin, she pushed damp hair from her eyes and pulled away from Dillon. "Race you," she challenged, and scrambled over wet pavement.

He caught her, laughing and breathless, at the door. With a new ease, Laine circled his neck as they laughed together. She felt young and foolish and desperately in love.

"You're quick, aren't you?" Dillon observed, and she tilted her head back to meet his smile.

"You learn to be quick when you live in a dormitory. Competition for the bath is brutal." Laine thought she saw his smile begin to fade before they were interrupted.

"Dillon, I'm sorry to disturb you."

Glancing over, Laine saw a young woman with classic

bone structure, her raven hair pulled taut at the nape of a slender neck. The woman returned Laine's survey with undisguised curiosity. Blushing, Laine struggled out of Dillon's arms.

"It's all right, Fran. This is Laine Simmons, Cap's daughter. Fran's my calculator."

"He means secretary," Fran returned with an exasperated sigh. "But this afternoon I feel more like an answering service. You have a dozen phone messages on your desk."

"Anything urgent?" As he asked, he moved into an adjoining room.

"No." Fran gave Laine a friendly smile. "Just several people who didn't want to make a decision until they heard from Mount Olympus. I told them all you were out for the day and would get back to them tomorrow."

"Good." Walking back into the room, Dillon carried a handful of papers and a towel. He tossed the towel at Laine before he studied the papers.

"I thought you were supposed to be taking a few days off," Fran stated while Dillon muttered over his messages.

"Um-hum. There doesn't seem to be anything here that can't wait."

"I've already told you that." Fran snatched the papers out of his hand.

"So you did." Unabashed, Dillon grinned and patted her cheek. "Did you ask Orchid what she wanted?"

Across the room, Laine stopped rubbing the towel against her hair, then began again with increased speed.

"No, though after the *third* call, I'm afraid I became a bit abrupt with her."

"She can handle it," Dillon returned easily, then switched his attention to Laine. "Ready?"

"Yes." Feeling curiously deflated, Laine crossed the room and handed Dillon the towel. "Thank you."

"Sure." Casually, he tossed the damp towel to Fran. "See you tomorrow, cousin."

"Yes, master." Fran shot Laine a friendly wave before Dillon hustled her from the building.

With a great deal of effort, Laine managed to thrust Orchid King from her mind during the drive home and throughout the evening meal. The sun was just setting when she settled on the porch with Dillon and her father.

The sky's light was enchanting. The intense, tropical blue was breaking into hues of gold and crimson, the low, misted clouds streaked with pinks and mauves. There was something dreamlike and soothing in the dusk. Laine sat quietly in a wicker chair, thinking over her day as the men's conversation washed over her. Even had she understood their exchange, she was too lazily content to join in. She knew that for the first time in her adult life, she was both physically and mentally relaxed. Perhaps, she mused, it was the adventures of the past few days, the testing of so many untried feelings and emotions.

Mumbling about coffee, Cap rose and slipped inside the house. Laine gave him an absent smile as he passed her, then curled her legs under her and watched the first stars blink into life.

"You're quiet tonight." As Dillon leaned back in his chair, Laine heard the soft click of his lighter.

"I was just thinking how lovely it is here." Her sigh drifted with contentment. "I think it must be the loveliest place on earth."

"Lovelier than Paris?"

Hearing the edge in his voice, Laine turned to look at

him questioningly. The first light of the moon fell gently over her face. "It's very different from Paris," she answered. "Parts of Paris are beautiful, mellowed and gentled with age. Other parts are elegant or dignified. She is like a woman who has been often told she is enchanting. But the beauty here is more primitive. The island is ageless and innocent at the same time."

"Many people tire of innocence." Dillon shrugged and drew deeply on his cigarette.

"I suppose that's true," she agreed, unsure why he seemed so distant and so cynical.

"In this light, you look a great deal like your mother," he said suddenly, and Laine felt her skin ice over.

"How do you know? You never met my mother."

"Cap has a picture." Dillon turned toward her, but his face was in shadows. "You resemble her a great deal."

"She certainly does." Cap sauntered out with a tray of coffee in his hands. Setting it on a round glass table, he straightened and studied Laine. "It's amazing. The light will catch you a certain way, or you'll get a certain expression on your face. Suddenly, it's your mother twenty years ago."

"I'm not Vanessa." Laine sprang up from her seat, and her voice trembled with rage. "I'm nothing like Vanessa." To her distress, tears began to gather in her eyes. Her father looked on in astonishment. "I'm nothing like her. I won't be compared to her." Furious with both the men and herself, Laine turned and slammed through the screen door. On her dash for the stairs, she collided with Miri's substantial form. Stuttering an apology, she streaked up the stairs and into her room.

* * *

Laine was pacing around her room for the third time when Miri strolled in.

"What is all this running and slamming in my house?" Miri asked, folding her arms across her ample chest.

Shaking her head, Laine lowered herself to the bed, then, despising herself, burst into tears. Clucking her tongue and muttering in Hawaiian, Miri crossed the room. Soon Laine found her head cradled against a soft, pillowing bosom. "That Dillon," Miri muttered as she rocked Laine to and fro.

"It wasn't Dillon," Laine managed, finding the maternal comfort new and overwhelming. "Yes, it was…it was both of them." Laine had a sudden desperate need for reassurance. "I'm nothing like her, Miri. I'm nothing like her at all."

"Of course you are not." Miri patted Laine's blond curls. "Who is it you are not like?"

"Vanessa." Laine brushed away tears with the back of her hand. "My mother. Both of them were looking at me, saying how much I look like her."

"What is this? What is this? All these tears because you look like someone?" Miri pulled Laine away by the shoulders and shook her. "Why do you waste your tears on this? I think you're a smart girl, then you act stupid."

"You don't understand." Laine drew up her knees and rested her chin on them. "I won't be compared to her, not to her. Vanessa was selfish and self-centered and dishonest."

"She was your mother," Miri stated with such authority that Laine's mouth dropped open. "You will speak with respect of your mother. She is dead, and whatever she did is over now. You must bury it," Miri commanded, giving

Laine another shake, "or you will never be happy. Did they say you were selfish and self-centered and dishonest?"

"No, but..."

"What did Cap Simmons say to you?" Miri demanded.

Laine let out a long breath. "He said I looked like my mother."

"And do you, or does he lie?"

"Yes, I suppose I do, but..."

"So, your mother was a pretty woman, you are a pretty woman." Miri lifted Laine's chin with her thick fingers. "Do you know who you are, Laine Simmons?"

"Yes, I think I do."

"Then you have no problem." Miri patted her cheek and rose.

"Oh, Miri." Laine laughed and wiped her eyes again. "You make me feel very foolish."

"You make yourself feel foolish," Miri corrected. "I did not slam doors."

Laine sighed over Miri's logic. "I suppose I'll have to go down and apologize."

As Laine stood, Miri folded her arms and blocked her way. "You will do no such thing."

Staring at her, Laine let out a frustrated breath. "But you just said..."

"I said you were stupid, and you were. Cap Simmons and Dillon were also stupid. No woman should be compared to another woman. You are special, you are unique. Sometimes men see only the face." Miri tapped a finger against each of her cheeks. "It takes them longer to see what is inside. So—" she gave Laine a white-toothed smile "—you will not apologize, you will let them apologize. It is the best way."

"I see," Laine said, not seeing at all. Suddenly, she laughed and sat back on the bed. "Thank you, Miri, I feel much better."

"Good. Now go to bed. I will go lecture Cap Simmons and Dillon." There was an unmistakable note of anticipation in her voice.

Chapter 8

The following morning Laine descended the stairs, her Nile-green sundress floating around her, leaving her arms and shoulders bare. Feeling awkward after the previous evening's incident, Laine paused at the doorway of the dining room. Her father and Dillon were already at breakfast and deep in discussion.

"If Bob needs next week off, I can easily take his shift on the charters." Dillon poured coffee as he spoke.

"You've got enough to do at your own place without taking that on, too. Whatever happened to those few days off you were going to take?" Cap accepted the coffee and gave Dillon a stern look.

"I haven't exactly been chained to my desk the past week." Dillon grinned, then shrugged as Cap's expression remained unchanged. "I'll take some time off next month."

"Where have I heard that before?" Cap asked the ceiling. Dillon's grin flashed again.

"I didn't tell you I was retiring next year, did I?" Dillon

sipped coffee casually, but Laine recognized the mischief in his voice. "I'm going to take up hang gliding while you slave away behind a desk. Who are you going to nag if I'm not around every day?"

"When you can stay away for more than a week at a time," Cap countered, "that's when *I'm* going to retire. The trouble with you—" he wagged a spoon at Dillon in admonishment "—is that your mind's too good and you've let too many people find it out. Now you're stuck because nobody wants to make a move without checking with you first. You should've kept that aeronautical-engineering degree a secret. Hang gliding." Cap chuckled and lifted his cup. "Oh, hello, Laine."

Laine jolted at the sound of her name. "Good morning," she replied, hoping that her outburst the evening before had not cost her the slight progress she had made with her father.

"Is it safe to ask you in?" His smile was sheepish, but he beckoned her forward. "As I recall, your explosions were frequent, fierce, but short-lived."

Relieved he had not offered her a stilted apology, Laine took her place at the table. "Your memory is accurate, though I assure you, I explode at very infrequent intervals these days." She offered Dillon a tentative smile, determined to treat the matter lightly. "Good morning, Dillon."

"Morning, Duchess. Coffee?" Before she could refuse, he was filling her cup.

"Thank you," she murmured. "It's hard to believe, but I think today is more beautiful than yesterday. I don't believe I'd ever grow used to living in paradise."

"You've barely seen any of it yet," Cap commented. "You should go up to the mountains, or to the center. You know, the center of Kauai is one of the wettest spots in the world. The rain forest is something to see."

"The island seems to have a lot of variety." Laine toyed with her coffee. "I can't imagine any of it is more beautiful than right here."

"I'll take you around a bit today," Dillon announced. Laine glanced sharply at him.

"I don't want to interfere with your routine. I've already taken up a great deal of your time." Laine had not yet regained her balance with Dillon. Her eyes were both wary and unsure.

"I've a bit more to spare." He rose abruptly. "I'll have things cleared up and be back around eleven. See you later, Cap." He strode out without waiting for her assent.

Miri entered with a full plate and placed it in front of Laine. She scowled at the coffee. "Why do you pour coffee when you aren't going to drink it?" With a regal sniff, she picked up the cup and swooped from the room. With a sigh, Laine attacked her breakfast and wondered how the day would pass. She was to find the morning passed quickly.

As if granting a royal boon, Miri agreed to allow Laine to refresh the vases of flowers which were scattered throughout the house. Laine spent her morning hours in the garden. It was not a garden as Laine remembered from her early American years or from her later French ones. It was a spreading, sprawling, wild tangle of greens and tempestuous hues. The plants would not be organized or dictated to by plot or plan.

Inside again, Laine took special care in the arranging of the vases. Her mind drifted to the daffodils which would be blooming outside her window at school. She found it odd that she felt no trace of homesickness, no longing for the soft French voices of the sisters or the high, eager ones of her students. She knew that she was dangerously close to thinking of Kauai as home. The thought of returning to France and the life she led there filled her with a cold, dull ache.

In her father's den, Laine placed the vase of frangipani on his desk and glanced at the photograph of Cap and Dillon. *How strange,* she thought, *that I should need both of them so badly.* With a sigh, she buried her face in the blossoms.

"Do flowers make you unhappy?"

She whirled, nearly upsetting the vase. For a moment, she and Dillon stared at each other without speaking. Laine felt the tension between them, though its cause and meaning were unclear to her. "Hello. Is it eleven already?'"

"It's nearly noon. I'm late." Dillon thrust his hands in his pockets and watched her. Behind her, the sun poured through the window to halo her hair. "Do you want some lunch?"

"No, thank you," she said with conviction. She saw his eyes smile briefly.

"Are you ready?"

"Yes, I'll just tell Miri I'm going."

"She knows." Crossing the room, Dillon slid open the glass door and waited for Laine to precede him outside.

Laine found Dillon in a silent mood as they drove from the house. She gave his thoughts their privacy and concentrated on the view. Ridges of green mountains loomed on either side. Dillon drove along a sheer precipice where the earth surrendered abruptly to the sky to fall into an azure sea.

"They used to toss Kukui oil torches over the cliffs to

entertain royalty," Dillon said suddenly, after miles of silence. "Legend has it that the menehune lived here. The pixie people," he elaborated at her blank expression. "You see there?" After halting the car, he pointed to a black precipice lined with grooves. "That's their staircase. They built fishponds by moonlight."

"Where are they now?" Laine smiled at him.

Dillon reached across to open her door. "Oh, they're still here. They're hiding."

Laine joined him to walk to the edge of the cliff. Her heart flew to her throat as she stared from the dizzying height down to the frothing power of waves on rock. For an instant, she could feel herself tumbling helplessly through miles of space.

Unaffected by vertigo, Dillon looked out to sea. The breeze teased his hair, tossing it into confusion. "You have the remarkable capacity of knowing when to be quiet and making the silence comfortable," he remarked.

"You seemed preoccupied." The wind tossed curls in her eyes, and Laine brushed them away. "I thought perhaps you were working out a problem."

"Did you?" he returned, and his expression seemed both amused and annoyed. "I want to talk to you about your mother."

The statement was so unexpected that it took Laine a moment to react. "No." She turned away, but he took her arm and held her still.

"You were furious last night. I want to know why."

"I overreacted." She tossed her head as her curls continued to dance around her face. "It was foolish of me, but sometimes my temper gets the better of me." She saw by his expression that her explanation would not placate him.

She wanted badly to tell him how she had been hurt, but the memory of their first discussion in her father's house, and his cold judgment of her, prevented her. "Dillon, all my life I've been accepted for who I am." Speaking slowly, she chose her words carefully. "It annoys me to find that changing now. I do not want to be compared with Vanessa because we share certain physical traits."

"Is that what you think Cap was doing?"

"Perhaps, perhaps not." She tilted her chin yet further. "But that's what you were doing."

"Was I?" It was a question which asked for no answer, and Laine gave none. "Why are you so bitter about your mother, Laine?"

She moved her shoulders and turned back toward the sea. "I'm not bitter, Dillon, not any longer. Vanessa's dead, and that part of my life is over. I don't want to talk about her until I understand my feelings better."

"All right." They stood silent for a moment, wrapped in the wind.

"I'm having a lot more trouble with you than I antici-pated," Dillon muttered.

"I don't know what you mean."

"No," he agreed, looking at her so intently she felt he read her soul. "I'm sure you don't." He walked away, then stopped. After a hesitation too brief to measure, he turned toward her again and held out his hand. Laine stared at it, unsure what he was offering. Finding it did not matter, she accepted.

During the ensuing drive, Dillon spoke easily. His mood had altered, and Laine moved with it. The world was lush with ripe blossoms. Moss clung, green and vi-brant, to cliffs—a carpet on stone. They passed elephant ears whose leaves were large enough to use as a canopy against rain or sun. The frangipani became more varied and more brilliant. When Dillon stopped the car again, Laine did not hesitate to take his hand.

He led her along a path that was sheltered by palms, moving down it as though he knew the way well. Laine heard the rush of water before they entered the clearing. Her breath caught at the sight of the secluded pool circled by thick trees and fed by a shimmering waterfall.

"Oh, Dillon, what a glorious place! There can't be another like it in the world!" Laine ran to the edge of the pool, then dropped down to feel the texture of the water. It was warm silk. "If I could, I would come here to swim in the moonlight." With a laugh, she rose and tossed water to the sky. "With flowers in my hair and nothing else."

"That's the only permissible way to swim in a moonlit pool. Island law."

Laughing again, she turned to a bush and plucked a scarlet hibiscus. "I suppose I'd need long black hair and honey skin to look the part."

Taking the bloom from her, Dillon tucked it behind her ear. After studying the effect, he smiled and ran a finger down her cheek. "Ivory and gold work very nicely. There was a time you'd have been worshiped with all pomp and ceremony, then tossed off a cliff as an offering to jealous gods."

"I don't believe that would suit me." Utterly enchanted, Laine twirled away. "Is this a secret place? It feels like a secret place." Stepping out of her shoes, she sat on the edge of the pool and dangled her feet in the water.

"If you want it to be." Dropping down beside her, Dillon sat Indian-fashion. "It's not on the tourist route, at any rate."

"It feels magic, the same way that little bay feels magic. Do you feel it, Dillon? Do you realize how lovely this all is, how fresh, or are you immune to it by now?"

"I'm not immune to beauty." He lifted her hand, brushing his lips over her fingertips. Her eyes grew wide as currents of pleasure jolted up her arm. Smiling, Dillon turned her hand over and kissed her palm. "You can't have lived in Paris for fifteen years and not have had your hand kissed. I've seen movies."

The lightness of his tone helped her regain her balance. "Actually, everyone's always kissing my left hand. You threw me off when you kissed my right." She kicked water in the air and watched the drops catch the sun before they were swallowed by the pool. "Sometimes, when the rain drizzles in the fall, and the dampness creeps through the windows, I'll remember this." Her voice had changed, and there was something wistful, something yearning in her tone. "Then when spring comes, and the buds flower, and the air smells of them, I'll remember the fragrance here. And when the sun shines on a Sunday, I'll walk near the Seine and think of a waterfall."

Rain came without warning, a shower drenched in sun. Dillon scrambled up, pulling Laine under a sheltering cluster of palms.

"Oh, it's warm." She leaned out from the green ceiling to catch rain in her palm. "It's as if it's dropping from the sun."

"Islanders call it liquid sunshine." Dillon gave an easy tug on her hand to pull her back as she inched forward. "You're getting soaked. I think you must enjoy getting drenched in your clothes." He ruffled her hair and splattered the air with shimmering drops.

"Yes, I suppose I do." She stared out, absorbed with the deepening colors. Blossoms trembled under their shower. "There's so much on the island that remains unspoiled, as if no one had ever touched it. When we stood on the cliff and looked down at the sea, I was frightened. I've always been a coward. But still, it was beautiful, so terrifyingly beautiful I couldn't look away."

"A coward?" Dillon sat on the soft ground and pulled her down to join him. Her head naturally found the curve of his shoulder. "I would have said you were remarkably intrepid. You didn't panic during the storm yesterday."

"No, I just skirted around the edges of panic."

His laugh was full of pleasure. "You also survived the little show in the plane on the way from Oahu without a scream or a faint."

"That's because I was angry." She pushed at her damp hair and watched the thin curtain of rain. "It was unkind of you."

"Yes, I suppose it was. I'm often unkind."

"I think you're kind more often than not. Though I also think you don't like being labeled a kind man."

"That's a very odd opinion for a short acquaintance." Her answering shrug was eloquent and intensely Gallic. A frown moved across his brow. "This school of yours," he began, "what kind is it?"

"Just a school, the same as any other, with giggling girls and rules which must be broken."

"A boarding school?" he probed, and she moved her shoulders again.

"Yes, a boarding school. Dillon, this is not the place to

think of schedules and classes. I shall have to deal with them again soon enough. This is a magic place, and for now I want to pretend I belong here. *Ah, regarde!*" Laine shifted, gesturing in wonder. *"Un arc-en-ciel."*

"I guess that means rainbow." He glanced at the sky, then back at her glowing face.

"There are two! How can there be two?"

They stretched, high and perfect, in curving arches from one mountain ridge to another. The second's shimmering colors were the reverse of the first's. As the sun glistened on raindrops, the colors grew in intensity, streaking across the cerulean sky like a trail from an artist's many-tinted brush.

"Double bows are common here," Dillon explained, relaxing against the base of the palm. "The trade winds blow against the mountains and form a rain boundary. It rains on one side while the sun shines on the other. Then, the sun strikes the raindrops, and..."

"No, don't tell me," Laine interrupted with a shake of her head. "It would spoil it if I knew." She smiled with the sudden knowledge that all things precious should be left unexplained. "I don't want to understand," she murmured, accepting both her love and the rainbows without question, without logic. "I just want to enjoy." Tilting back her head, Laine offered her mouth. "Will you kiss me, Dillon?"

His eyes never left hers. He brought his hands to her face, and gently, his fingers stroked the fragile line of her cheek. In silence, he explored the planes and hollows of her face with his fingertips, learning the texture of fine bones and satin skin. His mouth followed the trail of his fingers, and Laine closed her eyes, knowing nothing had ever been sweeter than his lips on her skin. Still moving slowly, still moving gently, Dillon brushed his mouth over hers in a whisperlike kiss which drugged her senses. He seemed content to taste, seemed happy to sample rather than devour. His mouth moved on, lingering on the curve of her neck, nibbling at the lobe of her ear before coming back to join hers. His tongue teased her lips apart as her heartbeat began to roar in her ears. He took her to the edge of reason with a tender, sensitive touch. As her need grew, Laine drew him closer, her body moving against his in innocent temptation.

Dillon swore suddenly before pulling her back. She kept her arms around his neck, her fingers tangled in his hair as he stared down at her. Her eyes were deep and cloudy with growing passion. Unaware of her own seductive powers, Laine sighed his name and placed a soft kiss on both of his cheeks.

"I want you," Dillon stated in a savage murmur before his mouth crushed hers. She yielded to him as a young willow yields to the wind.

His hands moved over her as if desperate to learn every aspect, every secret, and she who had never known a man's intimate touch delighted in the seeking. Her body was limber under his touch, responsive and eager. She was the student, and he the teacher. Her skin grew hot as her veins swelled with pounding blood. As the low, smoldering fire burst into quick flame, her demands rose with his. She trembled and murmured his name, as frightened of the new sensation as she had been at the edge of the cliff.

Dillon lifted his mouth from hers, resting it on her hair before she could search for the joining again. He held her close, cradling her head against his chest. His heart drummed against her ear, and Laine closed her eyes with the pleasure. Drawing her away, he stood. He moved his hands to his pockets as he turned his back on her.

"It's stopped raining." She thought his voice sounded strange and heard him take a long breath before he turned back to her. "We'd better go."

His expression was unfathomable. Though she searched, Laine could find no words to fill the sudden gap and close the distance which had sprung between them. Her eyes met his, asking questions her lips could not. Dillon opened his mouth as if to speak, then closed it again before he reached down to pull her to her feet. Her eyes faltered. Dillon lifted her chin with his fingertips, then traced the lips still soft from his. Briskly, he shook his head. Without a word, he lay his mouth gently on hers before he led her away from the palms.

Chapter 9

A generous golden ball, the sun dominated the sky as the car moved along the highway. Dillon made easy conversation, as if passion belonged only to a rain-curtained pool. While her brain fidgeted, Laine tried to match his mood.

Men, she decided, must be better able to deal with the demands of the body than women are with those of the heart. He had wanted her; even if he had not said it, she would have known. The urgency, the power of his claim had been unmistakable. Laine felt her color rise as she remembered her unprotesting response. Averting her head as if absorbed in the view, she tried to decide what course lay open to her.

She would leave Kauai in a week's time. Now, she would not only have to abandon the father whom she had longed for all of her life, but the man who held all claim to her heart. Perhaps, she reflected with a small sigh, I'm always destined to love what can never be mine. Miri said I should fight as a woman fights, but I don't know where to begin.

Perhaps with honesty. I should find the place and time to tell Dillon of my feelings. If he knew I wanted nothing from him but his affection, we might make a beginning. I could find a way to stay here at least awhile longer. I could take a job. In time, he might learn to really care for me. Laine's mood lightened at the thought. She focused again on her surroundings.

"Dillon, what is growing there? Is it bamboo?" Acres upon acres of towering stalks bordered the road. Clumps of cylindrical gold stretched out on either side.

"Sugarcane," he answered, without glancing at the fields.

"It's like a jungle." Fascinated, Laine leaned out the window, and the wind buffeted her face. "I had no idea it grew so tall."

"Gets to be a bit over twenty feet, but it doesn't grow as fast as a jungle in this part of the world. It takes a year and a half to two years to reach full growth."

"There's so much." Laine turned to face him, absently brushing curls from her cheeks. "It's a plantation, I suppose, though it's hard to conceive of one person owning so much. It must take tremendous manpower to harvest."

"A bit." Dillon swerved off the highway and onto a hard-packed road. "The undergrowth is burned off, then machines cut the plants. Hand cutting is time consuming so machinery lowers production costs even when labor costs are low. Besides, it's one miserable job."

"Have you ever done it?" She watched a quick grin light his face.

"A time or two, which is why I prefer flying a plane."

Laine glanced around at the infinity of fields, wondering when the harvest began, trying to picture the machines slicing through the towering stalks. Her musings halted as the brilliant white of a house shone in the distance. Tall, with graceful colonial lines and pillars, it stood on lush lawns. Vines dripped from scrolled balconies; the high and narrow windows were shuttered in soft gray. The house looked comfortably old and lived in. Had it not been for South Sea foliage, Laine might have been seeing a plantation house in old Louisiana.

"What a beautiful home. One could see for miles from the balcony." Laine glanced at Dillon in surprise as he halted the car and again leaned over to open her door. "This is a private home, is it not? Are we allowed to walk around?"

"Sure." Opening his own door, Dillon slid out. "It's mine." He leaned against the car and looked down at her. "Are you going to sit there with your mouth open or are you going to come inside?" Quickly, Laine slid out and stood beside him. "I gather you expected a grass hut and hammock?"

"Why, no, I don't precisely know what I expected, but…" With a helpless gesture of her hands, she gazed about. A tremor of alarm trickled through her. "The cane fields," she began, praying she was mistaken. "Are they yours?"

"They go with the house."

Finding her throat closed, Laine said nothing as Dillon led her up stone steps and through a wide mahogany door. Inside, the staircase dominated the hall. Wide and arching in a deep half circle, its wood gleamed. Laine had a quick, confused impression of watercolors and wood carvings as Dillon strode straight down the hall and led her into a parlor.

The walls were like rich cream; the furnishings were

dark and old. The carpet was a delicately faded needle-point over a glistening wood floor. Nutmeg sheers were drawn back from the windows to allow the view of a manicured lawn.

"Sit down." Dillon gestured to a chair. "I'll see about something cold to drink." Laine nodded, grateful for the time alone to organize her scattered thoughts. She listened until Dillon's footsteps echoed into silence.

Her survey of the room was slow. She seated herself in a high-backed chair and let her eyes roam. The room had an undeniable air of muted wealth. Laine had not associated wealth with Dillon O'Brian. Now she found it an insurmountable obstacle. Her protestations of love would never be accepted as pure. He would think his money had been her enticement. She closed her eyes on a small moan of desperation. Rising, she moved to a window and tried to deal with dashed hopes.

What was it he called me once? *An operator.* With a short laugh, she rested her brow against the cool glass. I'm afraid I make a very poor one. I wish I'd never come here, never seen what he has. At least then I could have hung on to hope a bit longer. Hearing Dillon's approach, Laine struggled for composure. As he entered, she gave him a careful smile.

"Dillon, your home is very lovely." After accepting the tall glass he offered, Laine moved back to her chair.

"It serves." He sat opposite her. His brow lifted fractionally at the formality of her tone.

"Did you build it yourself?"

"No, my grandfather." With his customary ease, Dillon leaned back and watched her. "He was a sailor and decided Kauai was the next best thing to the sea."

"So. I thought it looked as if it had known generations." Laine sipped at her drink without tasting it. "But you found planes more enticing than the sea or the fields."

"The fields serve their purpose." Dillon frowned momentarily at her polite, impersonal interest. "They yield a marketable product, assist in local employment and make use of the land. It's a profitable crop and its management takes only a portion of my time." As Dillon set down his glass, Laine thought he appeared to come to some decision. "My father died a couple of months before I met Cap. We were both floundering, but I was angry, and he was..." Dillon hesitated, then shrugged. "He was as he always is. We suited each other. He had a cabin plane and used to pick up island hoppers. I couldn't learn about flying fast enough, and Cap needed to teach. I needed balance, and he needed to give it. A couple of years later, we began planning the airport."

Laine dropped her eyes to her glass. "And it was the money from your fields which built the airport?"

"As I said, the cane has its uses."

"And the bay where we swam?" On a sudden flash of intuition, she lifted her eyes to his. "That's yours, too, isn't it?"

"That's right." She could see no change of expression in his eyes.

"And my father's house?" Laine swallowed the dryness building in her throat. "Is that also on your property?"

She saw annoyance cross his face before he smoothed it away. His answer was mild. "Cap had a fondness for that strip of land, so he bought it."

"From you?"

"Yes, from me. Is that a problem?"

"No," she replied. "It's simply that I begin to see things more clearly. Much more clearly." Laine set down her drink and folded her empty hands. "It appears that you are more my father's son than I shall ever be his daughter."

"Laine…" Dillon let out a short breath, then rose and paced the room with a sudden restlessness. "Cap and I understand each other. We've known each other for nearly fifteen years. He's been part of my life for almost half of it."

"I'm not asking you for justifications, Dillon. I'm sorry if it seemed as if I were." Laine stood, trying to keep her voice steady. "When I return to France next week, it will be good to know that my father has you to rely on."

"Next week?" Dillon stopped pacing. "You're planning to leave next week?"

"Yes." Laine tried not to think of how quickly seven days could pass. "We agreed I would stay for two weeks. It's time I got back to my own life."

"You're hurt because Cap hasn't responded to you the way you'd hoped."

Surprised both by his words and the gentleness of his tone, Laine felt the thin thread of her control straining. She struggled to keep her eyes calm and level with his. "I have changed my mind…on a great many matters. Please don't, Dillon." She shook her head as he started to speak. "I would rather not talk of this; it's only more difficult."

"Laine." He placed his hands on her shoulders to prevent her from turning away. "There are a lot of things that you and I have to talk about, whether they're difficult or not. You can't keep shutting away little parts of yourself. I want…" The ringing of the doorbell interrupted his words. With a quick, impatient oath, he dropped his hands and strode away to answer.

A light, musical voice drifted into the room. When Orchid King entered the parlor on Dillon's arm, Laine met her with a polite smile.

It struck Laine that Orchid and Dillon were a perfectly matched couple. Orchid's tawny, exotic beauty suited his ruggedness, and her fully rounded curves were all the more stunning against his leanness. Her hair fell in an ebony waterfall, cascading down a smooth bare back to the waist of close-fitting pumpkin-colored shorts. Seeing her, Laine felt dowdy and provincial.

"Hello, Miss Simmons." Orchid tightened her hand on Dillon's arm. "How nice to see you again so soon."

"Hello, Miss King." Annoyed by her own insecurities, Laine met Orchid's amusement with eyes of a cool spring morning. "You did say the island was small."

"Yes, I did." She smiled, and Laine was reminded of a tawny cat. "I hope you've been able to see something of it."

"I took Laine around a bit this morning." Watching Laine, Dillon missed the flash of fire in Orchid's amber eyes.

"I'm sure she couldn't find a better guide." Orchid's expression melted into soft appeal. "I'm so glad you were home, Dillon. I wanted to make certain you'd be at the luau tomorrow night." Turning more directly to face him, she subtly but effectively excluded Laine from the conversation. "It wouldn't be any fun without you."

"I'll be there." Laine watched a smile lift one corner of his mouth. "Are you going to dance?"

"Of course." The soft purr of her voice added to Laine's image of a lithesome feline. "Tommy expects it."

Dillon's smile flashed into a grin. He lifted his eyes over Orchid's head to meet Laine's. "Tommy is Miri's nephew.

He's having his annual luau tomorrow. You should find both the food and the entertainment interesting."

"Oh, yes," Orchid agreed. "No tourist should leave the islands without attending a luau. Do you plan to see the other islands during your vacation?"

"I'm afraid that will have to wait for another time. I'm sorry to say I haven't lived up to my obligations as a tourist. The purpose of my visit has been to see my father and his home."

Somewhat impatiently, Dillon disengaged his arm from Orchid's grasp. "I have to see my foreman. Why don't you keep Laine company for a few minutes?"

"Certainly." Orchid tossed a lock of rain-straight hair behind her back. "How are the repairs coming?"

"Fine. I should be able to move back in a couple of days without being in the way." With an inclination of his head for Laine, he turned and strode from the room.

"Miss Simmons, do make yourself at home." Assuming the role of hostess with a graceful wave of her hand, Orchid glided farther into the room. "Would you care for anything? A cold drink perhaps?"

Infuriated at being placed in the position of being Orchid's guest, Laine forced down her temper. "Thank you, no. Dillon has already seen to it."

"It seems you spend a great deal of time in Dillon's company," Orchid commented as she dropped into a chair. She crossed long, slender legs, looking like an advertisement for Hawaii's lush attractions. "Especially for one who comes to visit her father."

"Dillon has been very generous with his time." Laine copied Orchid's action and hoped she was equipped for a feminine battle of words.

"Oh, yes, Dillon's a generous man." Her smile was indulgent and possessive. "It's quite easy to misinterpret his generosity unless one knows him as well as I do. He can be so charming."

"Charming?" Laine repeated, and looked faintly skeptical. "How odd. Charming is not the adjective which comes to my mind. But then," she paused and smiled, "you know him better than I do."

Orchid placed the tips of her fingers together, then regarded Laine over the tips. "Miss Simmons, maybe we can dispense with the polite small talk while we have this time alone."

Wondering if she was sinking over her head, Laine nodded. "Your option, Miss King."

"I intend to marry Dillon."

"A formidable intention," Laine managed as her heart constricted. "I assume Dillon is aware of your goal."

"Dillon knows I want him." Irritation flickered over the exotic face at Laine's easy answer. "I don't appreciate all the time you've been spending with him."

"That's a pity, Miss King." Laine picked up her long-abandoned glass and sipped. "But don't you think you're discussing this with the wrong person? I'm sure speaking to Dillon would be more productive."

"I don't believe that's necessary." Orchid gave Laine a companionable smile, showing just a hint of white teeth. "I'm sure we can settle this between us. Don't you think telling Dillon you wanted to learn to fly a plane was a little trite?"

Laine felt a flush of fury that Dillon had discussed her with Orchid. "Trite?"

Orchid made an impatient gesture. "Dillon's diverted by

you at the moment, perhaps because you're such a contrast to the type of woman he's always preferred. But the milk-and-honey looks won't keep Dillon interested for long." The musical voice hardened. "Cool sophistication doesn't keep a man warm, and Dillon is very much a man."

"Yes, he's made that very clear," Laine could not resist interjecting.

"I'm warning you...once," Orchid hissed. "Keep your distance. I can make things very uncomfortable for you."

"I'm sure you can," Laine acknowledged. She shrugged. "I've been uncomfortable before."

"Dillon can be very vindictive when he thinks he's being deceived. You're going to end up losing more than you bargained for."

"Nom de Dieu!" Laine rose. "Is this how the game is played?" She made a contemptuous gesture with the back of her hand. "I want none of it. Snarling and hissing like two cats over a mouse. This isn't worthy of Dillon."

"We haven't started to play yet." Orchid sat back, pleased by Laine's agitation. "If you don't like the rules, you'd better leave. I don't intend to put up with you any longer."

"Put up with me?" Laine stopped, her voice trembling with rage. "No one, Miss King, no one *puts up* with me. You hardly need concern yourself with a woman who will be gone in a week's time. Your lack of confidence is as pitiful as your threats." Orchid rose at that, her fists clenched by her sides.

"What do you want from me?" Laine demanded. "Do you want my assurance that I won't interfere with your plans? Very well, I give it freely and with pleasure. Dillon is yours."

"That's generous of you." Spinning, Laine saw Dillon

leaning against the doorway. His arms were crossed, his eyes dangerously dark.

"Oh, Dillon, how quick you were." Orchid's voice was faint.

"Apparently not quick enough." His eyes were locked on Laine's. "What's the problem?"

"Just a little feminine talk, Dillon." Recovered, Orchid glided to his side. "Laine and I were just getting to know each other."

"Laine, what's going on?"

"Nothing important. If it's convenient, I should like to go back now." Without waiting for a reply, Laine picked up her bag and moved to the doorway.

Dillon halted her by a hand on her arm. "I asked you a question."

"And I have given you the only answer I intend to give." She wrenched free and faced him. "I will not be questioned any longer. You have no right to question me; I am nothing to you. You have no right to criticize me as you have done from the first moment. You have no right to judge." The anger in her tone was now laced with despair. "You have no right to make love to me just because it amuses you."

She ran in a flurry of flying skirts, and he watched the door slam behind her.

Chapter 10

Laine spent the rest of the day in her room. She attempted not to dwell on the scene in Dillon's home, or on the silent drive which followed it. She was not sure which had been more draining. It occurred to her that she and Dillon never seemed to enjoy a cordial relationship for more than a few hours at a time. It was definitely time to leave. She began to plan for her return to France. Upon a review of her finances, she discovered that she had barely enough for a return ticket.

It would, she realized with a sigh, leave her virtually penniless. Her own savings had been sorely dented in dealing with her mother's debts, and plane fare had eaten at what remained. She could not, she determined, return to France without a franc in her pocket. If there was a complication of any kind, she would be helpless to deal with it. *Why didn't I stop to think before I came here?* she demanded of herself. *Now I've placed myself in an impossible situation.*

Sitting on the bed, Laine rubbed an aching temple and tried to think. She didn't want to ask her father for money. Pride prevented her from wiring to any friends to ask for a loan. She stared down at the small pile of bills in frustration. They won't proliferate of their own accord, she reflected, so I must plan how to increase their number.

She moved to her dresser and opened a small box. For some minutes, she studied the gold locket it contained. It had been a gift from her father to her mother, and Vanessa had given it to her on her sixteenth birthday. She remembered the pleasure she had felt upon receiving something, however indirectly, from her father. She had worn it habitually until she had dressed for her flight to Hawaii. Feeling it might cause her father pain, Laine had placed it in its box, hoping that unhappy memories would be buried. It was the only thing of value she owned, and now she had to sell it.

Her door swung open. Laine held the box behind her back. Miri glided in, a swirling mountain of color. She regarded Laine's flushed face with raised brows.

"Did you mess something up?"

"No."

"Then don't look guilty. Here." She laid a sheath of brilliant blue and sparkling white on the bedspread. "It's for you. You wear this to the luau tomorrow."

"Oh." Laine stared at the exquisite length of silk, already feeling its magic against her skin. "It's beautiful. I couldn't." She raised her eyes to Miri's with a mixture of desire and regret. "I couldn't take it."

"You don't like my present?" Miri demanded imperiously. "You are very rude."

"Oh, no." Struck with alarm at the unintentional offense,

Laine fumbled with an explanation. "It's beautiful…really. It's only that…"

"You should learn to say thank-you and not argue. This will suit your skinny bones." Miri gave a nod of satisfaction encompassing both the woman and the silk. "Tomorrow, I will show you how to wrap it."

Unable to prevent herself, Laine moved over to feel the cool material under her fingers. The combination of longing and Miri's dark, arched brows proved too formidable for pride. She surrendered with a sigh. "Thank you, Miri. It's very good of you."

"That's much better," Miri approved and patted Laine's halo of curls. "You are a pretty child. You should smile more. When you smile, the sadness goes away."

Feeling the small box weighing like a stone in her hand, Laine held it up and opened it. "Miri, I wonder if you might tell me where I could sell this."

One large brown finger traced the gold before Miri's jet eyes lifted. Laine saw the now familiar pucker between her brows. "Why do you want to sell a pretty thing like this? You don't like it?"

"No, no, I like it very much." Helpless under the direct stare, Laine moved her shoulders. "I need the money."

"Money? Why do you need money?"

"For my passage and expenses…to return to France."

"You don't like Kauai?" Her indignant tone caused Laine to smile and shake her head.

"Kauai is wonderful; I'd like nothing better than to stay here forever. But I must get back to my job."

"What do you do in that place?" Miri dismissed France with a regal gesture and settled her large frame into a chair. She folded her hands across the mound of her belly.

"I teach." Laine sat on the bed and closed the lid on the face of the locket.

"Don't they pay you to teach?" Miri pursed her lips in disapproval. "What did you do with your money?"

Laine flushed, feeling like a child who had been discovered spending her allowance on candy. "There...there were debts, and I..."

"You have debts?"

"Well, no, I...not precisely." Laine's shoulders drooped with frustration. Seeing Miri was prepared to remain a permanent fixture of her room until she received an explanation, Laine surrendered. Slowly, she began to explain the financial mountain which she had faced at her mother's death, the necessity to liquidate assets, the continuing drain on her own resources. In the telling, Laine felt the final layers of her resentment fading. Miri did not interrupt the recital, and Laine found that confession had purged her of bitterness.

"Then, when I found my father's address among her personal papers, I took what I had left and came here. I'm afraid I didn't plan things well, and in order to go back..." She shrugged again and trailed off. Miri nodded.

"Why have you not told Cap Simmons? He would not have his daughter selling her baubles. He's a good man, he would not have you in a strange country counting your pennies."

"He doesn't owe me anything."

"He is your father," Miri stated, lifting her chin and peering down her nose at Laine.

"But he's not responsible for a situation brought on by Vanessa's carelessness and my own impulsiveness. He would think... No." She shook her head. "I don't want him to know. It's very important to me that he *not* know. You must promise not to speak of this to him."

"You are a very stubborn girl." Miri crossed her arms and glared at Laine. Laine kept her eyes level. "Very well." Miri's bosom lifted and fell with her sigh. "You must do what you must do. Tomorrow, you will meet my nephew, Tommy. Ask him to come look at your bauble. He is a jeweler and will give you a fair price."

"Thank you, Miri." Laine smiled, feeling a portion of her burden ease.

Miri rose, her muumuu trembling at the movement. "You had a nice day with Dillon?"

"We went by his home," Laine returned evasively. "It's very impressive."

"Very nice place," Miri agreed and brushed an infinitesimal speck of dust from the chair's back. "My cousin cooks there, but not so well as Miri."

"Miss King dropped by." Laine strove for a casual tone, but Miri's brows rose.

"Hmph." Miri stroked the tentlike lines of her flowered silk.

"We had a rather unpleasant discussion when Dillon left us alone. When he came back..." Laine paused and drew her brows together. "I shouted at him."

Miri laughed, holding her middle as if it would split from the effort. For several moments, her mirth rolled comfortably around the room. "So you can shout, Skinny Bones? I would like to have seen that."

"I don't think Dillon found it that amusing." In spite of herself, Laine smiled.

"Oh, that one." She wiped her eyes and shook her head. "He is too used to having his own way with women. He is too good-looking and has too much money." She placed a comforting hand over the barrel of her belly. "He's a fair boss, and he works in the fields when he's needed. He has big degrees and many brains." She tapped her finger on her temple, but looked unimpressed. "He was a very bad boy, with many pranks." Laine saw her lips tremble as she tried not to show amusement at the memories. "He is still a bad boy," she said firmly, regaining her dignity. "He is very smart and *very* important." She made a circling move- ment with both hands to indicate Dillon's importance, but her voice was full of maternal criticism. "But no matter what he thinks, he does not know women. He only knows planes." She patted Laine's head and pointed to the length of silk. "Tomorrow, you wear that and put a flower in your hair. The moon will be full."

It was a night of silver and velvet. From her window, Laine could see the dancing diamonds of moonlight on the sea. Allowing the breeze to caress her bare shoulders, Laine reflected that the night was perfect for a luau under the stars.

She had not seen Dillon since the previous day. He had returned to the house long after she had retired, and had left again before she had awakened. She was determined, however, not to permit their last meeting to spoil the beauty of the evening. If she had only a few days left in his com- pany, she would make every effort to see that they were pleasant.

Turning from her window, Laine gave one final look at the woman in the mirror. Her bare shoulders rose like mar- ble from the brilliant blue of the sarong. She stared at the woman in the glass, recognizing some change, but unable to discern its cause. She was not aware that over the past few days she had moved from girlhood to womanhood. After a final touch of the brush to her hair, Laine left the room. Dillon's voice rose up the staircase, and she moved to meet it. All at once, it seemed years since she had last heard him speak.

"We'll be harvesting next month, but if I know the schedule of meetings far enough in advance, I can..."

His voice trailed away as Laine moved into the doorway. Pausing in the act of pouring a drink, he made a slow survey. Laine felt her pulse triple its rate as his eyes lingered along their route before meeting hers.

Glancing up from filling his pipe, Cap noted Dillon's absorption. He followed his gaze. "Well, Laine." He rose, surprising her by crossing the room and taking both her hands in his. "What a beautiful sight."

"Do you like it?" Smiling first at him, she glanced down at the sarong. "I'm not quite used to the way it feels."

"I like it very much, but I was talking about you. My daughter is a very beautiful woman, isn't she, Dillon?" His eyes were soft and smiled into Laine's.

"Yes." Dillon's voice came from behind him. "Very beautiful."

"I'm glad she's here." He pressed her fingers between the warmth of his hands. "I've missed her." He bent and kissed her cheek, then turned to Dillon. "You two run along. I'll see if Miri's ready, which she won't be. We'll be along later."

Laine watched him stride away. She lifted one hand to her cheek, unable to believe she could be so deeply affected by one small gesture.

"Are you ready?" She nodded, unable to speak, then felt

Dillon's hands descend to her shoulders. "It isn't easy to bridge a fifteen-year gap, but you've made a start."

Surprised by the support in his voice, Laine blinked back tears and turned to face him. "Thank you. It means a great deal to me for you to say that. Dillon, yesterday, I..."

"Let's not worry about yesterday right now." His smile was both an apology and an acceptance of hers. It was easy to smile back. He studied her a moment before lifting her hand to his lips. "You are incredibly beautiful, like a blossom hanging on a branch just out of reach." Laine wanted to blurt out that she was not out of reach, but a thick blanket of shyness covered her tongue. She could do no more than stare at him.

"Come on." Keeping her hand in his, Dillon moved to the door. "You should try everything once." His tone was light again as they slid into his car. "You know, you're a very small lady."

"Only because you look from an intimidating height," she returned, feeling pleased with the ease of their relationship. "What does one do at a luau, Dillon? I'm very much afraid I'll insult a local tradition if I refuse to eat raw fish. But—" resting her head against the seat, she smiled at the stars "—I shall refuse to do so."

"We don't hurl mainlanders into the sea anymore for minor offenses. You haven't much hip," he commented, dropping his eyes for a moment. "But you could have a stab at a hula."

"I'm sure my hips are adequate and will no doubt be more so if Miri has her way." Laine sent him a teasing glance. "Do you dance, Dillon?"

He grinned and met her look. "I prefer to watch. Dancing the hula properly takes years of practice. These dancers are very good."

"I see." She shifted in her seat to smile at him. "Will there be many people at the luau?"

"Mmm." Dillon tapped his finger absently against the wheel. "About a hundred, give or take a few."

"A hundred," Laine echoed. She fought off unhappy memories of her mother's overcrowded, overelegant parties. So many people, so many demands, so many measuring eyes.

"Tommy has a lot of relatives."

"How nice for him," she murmured and considered the advantages of small families.

Chapter 11

The hollow, primitive sound of drums vibrated through air pungent with roasting meat. Torches were set on high stakes, their orange flames shooting flickering light against a black sky. To Laine it was like stepping back in time. The lawn was crowded with guests—some in traditional attire and others, like Dillon, in the casual comfort of jeans. Laughter rose from a myriad of tones and mixed languages. Laine gazed around, enthralled by the scene and the scents.

Set on a huge, woven mat were an infinite variety of mysterious dishes in wooden bowls and trays. Ebony-haired girls in native dress knelt to spoon food onto the plates and serving dishes. Diverse aromas lifted on the night air and lingered to entice. Men, swathed at the waist and bare-chested, beat out pulsating rhythms on high, conical drums.

Introduced to an impossible blur of faces, Laine merely

floated with the mood of the crowd. There seemed to be a universal friendliness, an uncomplicated joy in simply being.

Soon sandwiched between her father and Dillon, Laine sat on the grass and watched her plate being heaped with unknown wonders. A roar of approval rose over the music as the pig was unearthed from the *imu* and carved. Dutifully, she dipped her fingers in poi and sampled. She shrugged her shoulders as Dillon laughed at her wrinkled nose.

"Perhaps it's an acquired taste," she suggested as she wiped her fingers on a napkin.

"Here." Dillon lifted a fork and urged its contents into Laine's reluctant mouth.

With some surprise, she found the taste delightful. "That's very good. What is it?"

"Laulau."

"This is not illuminating."

"If it's good, what else do you have to know?" His logic caused her to arch her brows. "It's pork and butterfish steamed in *ti* leaves," he explained, shaking his head. "Try this." Dillon offered the fork again, and Laine accepted without hesitation.

"Oh, what is it? I've never tasted anything like it."

"Squid," he answered, then roared with laughter at her gasp of alarm.

"I believe," Laine stated with dignity, "I shall limit myself to pork and pineapple."

"You'll never grow hips that way."

"I shall learn to live without them. What is this drink…? No," she decided, smiling as she heard her father's chuckle. "I believe I'm better off not knowing."

Avoiding the squid, Laine found herself enjoying the informal meal. Occasionally, someone stopped and crouched beside them, exchanging quick greetings or a long story. Laine was treated with a natural friendliness which soon put her at her ease. Her father seemed comfortable with her, and though he and Dillon enjoyed an entente which eluded her, she no longer felt like an intruder. Music and laughter and the heady perfume of night swam around her. Laine thought she had never felt so intensely aware of her surroundings.

Suddenly, the drummers beat a rapid tempo, reaching a peak, then halting. Their echo fell into silence as Orchid stepped into view. She stood in a circle of torchlight, her skin glowing under its touch. Her eyes were gold and arrogant. Tantalizing and perfect, her body was adorned only in a brief top and a slight swatch of scarlet silk draped low over her hips. She stood completely still, allowing the silence to build before she began slowly circling her hips. A single drum began to follow the rhythm she set.

Her hair, crowned with a circlet of buds, fell down her bare back. Her hands and lithesome curves moved with a hypnotic power as the bare draping of silk flowed against her thighs. Sensuous and tempting, her gestures moved with the beat, and Laine saw that her golden eyes were locked on Dillon's. The faint smile she gave him was knowledgeable. Almost imperceptibly, her dance grew in speed. As the drum became more insistent, her movements became more abandoned. Her face remained calm and smiling above her undulating body. Then, abruptly, sound and movement halted into stunning silence.

Applause broke out. Orchid threw Laine a look of triumph before she lifted the flower crown from her head and tossed it into Dillon's lap. With a soft, sultry laugh, she retreated to the shadows.

"Looks like you've got yourself an invitation," Cap commented, then pursed his lips in thought. "Amazing. I wonder how many RPMs we could clock her at."

Shrugging, Dillon lifted his glass.

"You like to move like that, Skinny Bones?" Laine turned to where Miri sat in the background. She looked more regal than ever in a high-backed rattan chair. "You eat so you don't rattle, and Miri will teach you."

Flushed with a mixture of embarrassment and the longing to move with such free abandonment, Laine avoided Dillon's eyes. "I don't rattle now, but I think Miss King's ability is natural."

"You might pick it up, Duchess." Dillon grinned at Laine's lowered lashes. "I'd like to sit in on the lessons, Miri. As you well know, I've got a very discerning eye." He dropped his gaze to her bare legs, moving it up the length of blue and white silk, before meeting her eyes.

Miri muttered something in Hawaiian, and Dillon chuckled and tossed back a retort in the same tongue. "Come with me," Miri commanded. Rising, she pulled Laine to her feet.

"What did you say to him?" Laine moved in the wake of Miri's flowing gown.

"I said he is a big hungry cat cornering a small mouse."

"I am not a mouse," Laine returned indignantly.

Miri laughed without breaking stride. "Dillon says no, too. He says you are a bird whose beak is sometimes sharp under soft feathers."

"Oh." Unsure whether to be pleased or annoyed with the description, Laine lapsed into silence.

"I have told Tommy you have a bauble to sell," Miri announced. "You will talk to him now."

"Yes, of course," Laine murmured, having forgotten the locket in the enchantment of the night.

Miri paused in front of the luau's host. He was a spare, dark-haired man with an easy smile and friendly eyes. Laine judged him to be in the later part of his thirties, and she had seen him handle his guests with a practiced charm. "You will talk to Cap Simmons's daughter," Miri commanded as she placed a protective hand on Laine's shoulder. "You do right by her, or I will box your ears."

"Yes, Miri," he agreed, but his subservient nod was not reflected in his laughing eyes. He watched the graceful mountain move off before he tossed an arm around Laine's shoulders. He moved her gently toward the privacy of trees. "Miri is the matriarch of our family," he said with a laugh. "She rules with an iron hand."

"Yes, I've noticed. It's impossible to say no to her, isn't it?" The celebrating sounds of the luau drifted into a murmur as they walked.

"I've never tried. I'm a coward."

"I appreciate your time, Mr. Kinimoko," Laine began.

"Tommy, please, then I can call you Laine." She smiled, and as they walked on, she heard the whisper of the sea. "Miri said you had a bauble to sell. I'm afraid she wasn't any more specific."

"A gold locket," Laine explained, finding his friendly manner had put her at ease. "It's heart-shaped and has a braided chain. I have no idea of its value." She paused, wishing there was another way. "I need the money."

Tommy glanced at the delicate profile, then patted her

shoulder. "I take it you don't want Cap to know? Okay," he continued as she shook her head. "I have some free time in the morning. Why don't I come by and have a look around ten? You'll find it more comfortable than coming into the shop."

Laine heard leaves rustle and saw Tommy glance idly toward the sound. "It's very good of you." He turned back to her and she smiled, relieved that the first hurdle was over. "I hope I'm not putting you to any trouble."

"I enjoy troubling for beautiful wahines." He kept his arm over her shoulders as he led her back toward the sound of drums and guitars. "You heard Miri. You don't want me to get my ears boxed, do you?"

"I would never forgive myself if I were responsible for that. I'll tell Miri you've done right by Cap Simmons's daughter, and your ears will be left in peace." Laughing, Laine tilted her face to his as they broke through the curtain of trees.

"Your sister's looking for you, Tommy." At Dillon's voice, Laine gave a guilty start.

"Thanks, Dillon. I'll just turn Laine over to you. Take good care of her," he advised gravely. "She's under Miri's protection."

"I'll keep that in mind." Dillon watched in silence as Tommy merged back into the crowd, then he turned back to study Laine. "There's an old Hawaiian custom," he began slowly, and she heard annoyance color his tone, "which I have just invented. When a woman comes to a luau with a man, she doesn't walk in monkeypod trees with anyone else."

"Will I be tossed to the sharks if I break the rules?" Her teasing smile faded as Dillon took a step closer.

"Don't, Laine." He circled her neck with his hand. "I haven't had much practice in restraint."

She swayed toward him, giving in to the sudden surging need. "Dillon," she murmured, offering her mouth in simple invitation. She felt the strength of his fingers as they tightened on her neck. She rested her hands against his chest and felt his heartbeat under her palms. The knowledge of his power over her, and her own longing, caused her to tremble. Dillon made a soft sound, a lingering expulsion of breath. Laine watched him struggle with some emotion, watched something flicker in his eyes and fade before his fingers relaxed again.

"A wahine who stands in the shadows under a full moon must be kissed."

"Is this another old Hawaiian tradition?" Laine felt his arms slip around her waist and melted against him.

"Yes, about ten seconds old."

With unexpected gentleness, his mouth met hers. At the first touch, her body went fluid, mists of pleasure shrouding her. As from a distant shore, Laine heard the call of the drums, their rhythm building to a crescendo as did her heartbeat. Feeling the tenseness of Dillon's shoulders under her hands, she stroked, then circled his neck to bring his face closer to hers. Too soon, he lifted his mouth, and his arms relinquished his hold of her.

"More," Laine murmured, unsatisfied, and pulled his face back to hers.

She was swept against him. The power of his kiss drove all but the need from her mind. She could taste the hunger on his lips, feel the heat growing on his flesh. The air seemed to tremble around them. In that moment, her body belonged more to him than to her. If there was a world apart from seeking lips and caressing hands it held no meaning for her. Again, Dillon drew her away, but his voice was low and uneven.

"We'll go back before another tradition occurs to me."

In the morning, Laine lingered under the sun's streaming light, unwilling to leave her bed and the warm pleasure which still clung from the evening before. The taste of Dillon's mouth still lingered on hers, and his scent remained fresh and vital on her senses. She relived the memory of being in his arms. Finally, with a sigh, she abandoned the luxury of her bed and rose to face the day. Just as she was securing the belt of her robe, Miri glided into the room.

"So, you have decided to get up. The morning is half gone while you lay in your bed." Miri's voice was stern, but her eyes twinkled with indulgence.

"It made the night last longer," Laine replied, smiling at the affectionate scold.

"You liked the roast pig and poi?" Miri asked with a wise nod and a whisper of a smile.

"It was wonderful."

With her lilting laugh floating through the room, Miri turned to leave. "I am going to the market. My nephew is here to see your bauble. Do you want him to wait?"

"Oh." Forcing herself back down to earth, Laine ran her fingers through her hair. "I didn't realize it was that late. I don't want to inconvenience him. I…is anyone else at home?"

"No, they are gone."

Glancing down at her robe, Laine decided it was adequate coverage. "Perhaps he could come up and look at it. I don't want to keep him waiting."

"He will give you a fair price," Miri stated as she drifted through the doorway. "Or, you will tell me."

Laine took the small box from her drawer and opened the lid. The locket glinted under a ray of sunshine. There were no pictures to remove but, nonetheless, she opened it and stared at its emptiness.

"Laine."

Turning, she managed to smile at Tommy as he stood in the doorway. "Hello. It was good of you to come. Forgive me, I slept rather late this morning."

"A compliment to the host of the luau." He made a small, rather dapper bow as she approached him.

"It was my first, and I have no doubt it will remain my favorite." Laine handed him the box, then gripped her hands together as he made his examination.

"It's a nice piece," he said at length. Lifting his eyes, Tommy studied her. "Laine, you don't want to sell this— it's written all over your face."

"No." She saw from his manner she need not hedge. "It's necessary that I do."

Detecting the firmness in her voice, Tommy shrugged and placed the locket back in its box. "I can give you a hundred for it, though I think it's worth a great deal more to you."

Laine nodded and closed the lid as he handed the box back to her. "That will be fine. Perhaps you'd take it now. I would rather you kept it."

"If that's what you want." Tommy drew out his wallet and counted out bills. "I brought some cash. I thought you'd find it easier than a check."

"Thank you." After accepting the money, Laine stared down at it until he rested a hand on her shoulder.

"Laine, I've known Cap a long time. Would you take this as a loan?"

"No." She shook her head, then smiled to ease the sharpness of the word. "No. It's very kind of you, but I must do it this way."

"Okay." He took the offered box and pocketed it. "I will, however, hold this for a while in case you have second thoughts."

"Thank you. Thank you for not asking questions."

"I'll see myself out." He took her hand and gave it a small squeeze. "Just tell Miri to get in touch with me if you change your mind."

"Yes, I will."

After he had gone, Laine sat heavily on the bed and stared at the money she held clutched in her hand. There was nothing else I could do, she told herself. It was only a piece of metal. Now, it's done, I can't dwell on it.

"Well, Duchess, it seems you've had a profitable morning."

Laine's head snapped up. Dillon's eyes were frosted like an ice-crusted lake, and she stared at him, unable to clear her thoughts. His gaze raked her scantily clad body, and she reached a hand to the throat of her robe in an automatic gesture. Moving toward her, he pulled the bills from her hand and dropped the money on the nightstand.

"You've got class, Duchess." Dillon pinned her with his eyes. "I'd say that's pretty good for a morning's work."

"What are you talking about?" Her thoughts were scattered as she searched for a way to avoid telling him about the locket.

"Oh, I think that's clear enough. I guess I owe Orchid an apology." He thrust his hands in his pockets and rocked back on his heels. The easy gesture belied the burning temper in his eyes. "When she told me about this little arrangement, I came down on her pretty hard. You're a fast worker, Laine. You couldn't have been with Tommy for more than ten minutes last night; you must have made quite a sales pitch."

"I don't know why you're so angry," she began, confused as to why the sale of her locket would bring on such fury. "I suppose Miss King listened to our conversation last night." Suddenly, Laine remembered the quick rustle of leaves. "But why she should feel it necessary to report to you on my business..."

"How'd you manage to get rid of Miri while you conducted your little business transaction?" Dillon demanded. "She has a rather strict moral code, you know. If she finds out how you're earning your pin money, she's liable to toss you out on your ear."

"What do you..." Realization dawned slowly. *Not my locket,* Laine thought dumbly, *but myself.* All trace of color fled from her face. "You don't really believe that I..." Her voice broke as she read the condemnation in his eyes. "This is despicable of you, Dillon. Nothing you've accused me of, nothing you've said to me since we first met compares with this." The words trembled with emotion as she felt a viselike pressure around her heart. "I won't be insulted this way by you."

"Oh, won't you?" Taking her arm, Dillon dragged Laine to her feet. "Have you a more plausible explanation up your sleeve for Tommy's visit and the wad you're fondling? Go ahead, run it by me. I'm listening."

"Oh, yes, I can see you are. Forgive me for refusing, but Tommy's visit and my money are my business. I owe you no explanation, Dillon. Your conclusions aren't worthy of my words. The fact that you gave enough credence to whatever lie Orchid told you to come check on me, means we have nothing more to say to each other."

"I didn't come here to check on you." He was towering menacingly over her, but Laine met his eyes without flinching. "I came by because I thought you'd want to go up again. You said you wanted to learn to fly, and I said I'd teach you. If you want an apology, all you have to do is give me a reasonable explanation."

"I've spent enough time explaining myself to you. More than you deserve. Questions, always questions. Never *trust*." Her eyes smoldered with blue fire. "I want you to leave my room. I want you to leave me alone for the rest of the time I have in my father's house."

"You had me going." His fingers tightened on her arms, and she caught her breath at the pressure. "I bought it all. The big, innocent eyes, the virginal frailty, the pictures you painted of a woman looking for her father's affection and nothing else. *Trust?*" he flung back at her. "You'd taken me to the point where I trusted you more than myself. You knew I wanted you, and you worked on me. All those trembles and melting bones and artless looks. You played it perfectly, right down to the blushes." He pulled her against him, nearly lifting her off her feet.

"Dillon, you're hurting me." She faltered.

"I wanted you," he went on, as if she had not spoken. "Last night I was aching for you, but I treated you with a restraint and respect I've never shown another woman.

You slip on that innocent aura that drives a man crazy. You shouldn't have used it on me, Duchess."

Terror shivered along her skin. Her breath was rapid and aching in her lungs.

"Game's over. I'm going to collect." He silenced her protest with a hard, punishing kiss. Though she struggled against his imprisoning arms, she made no more ripple than a leaf battling a whirlpool. The room tilted, and she was crushed beneath him on the mattress. She fought against the intimacy as his mouth and hands bruised her. He was claiming her in fury, disposing of the barrier of her robe and possessing her flesh with angry demand.

Slowly, his movements altered in texture. Punishment became seduction as his hands began to caress rather than bruise. His mouth left hers to trail down her throat. With a sob ending on a moan, Laine surrendered. Her body became pliant under his, her will snapping with the weight of sensations never tasted. Tears gathered, but she made no more effort to halt them than she did the man who urged them from her soul.

All movement stopped abruptly, and Dillon lay still. The room was thrown into a tortured silence, broken only by the sound of quick breathing. Lifting his head, Dillon studied the journey of a tear down Laine's cheek. He swore with sudden eloquence, then rose. He tugged a hand through his hair as he turned his back on her.

"This is the first time I've been driven to nearly forcing myself on a woman." His voice was low and harsh as he swung around and stared at her. Laine lay still, emotionally drained. She made no effort to cover herself, but merely stared up at him with the eyes of a wounded child. "I can't deal with what you do to me, Laine."

Turning on his heel, he strode from the room. Laine thought the slamming of her door the loneliest sound she had ever heard.

Chapter 12

It was raining on the new spring grass. From her dormitory window Laine watched the green brighten with its morning bath. Outside her door, she heard girls trooping down the hall toward breakfast, but she did not smile at their gay chattering in French and English. She found smiles still difficult.

It had not yet been two weeks since Miri had met Laine's packed cases with a frown and drawn brows. She had met Laine's sketchy explanations with crossed arms and further questions. Laine had remained firm, refusing to postpone her departure or to give specific answers. The note she had left for her father had contained no more details, only an apology for her abrupt leave-taking and a promise to write once she had settled back in France. As of yet, Laine had not found the courage to put pen to paper.

Memories of her last moments with Dillon continued to haunt her. She could still smell the perfume of island blossoms, still feel the warm, moist air rise from the sea to

move over her skin. Watching the moon wane, she could remember its lush fullness over the heads of palms. She had
hoped her memories would fade with time. She reminded
herself that Kauai and its promises were behind her.

It's better this way, she told herself, picking up her brush
and preparing herself for the day's work. *Better for everyone.* Her father was settled in his life and would be content to exchange occasional letters. One day, perhaps, he
would visit her. Laine knew she could never go back. She,
too, had her own life, a job, the comfort of familiar surroundings. Here, she knew what was expected of her. Her
existence would be tranquil and unmarred by storms of
emotions. She closed her eyes on Dillon's image.

It's too soon, she told herself. Too soon to test her ability
to think of him without pain. Later, when the memory had
dulled, she would open the door. When she allowed herself
to think of him again, it would be to remember the beauty.

It was easier to forget if she followed a routine. Laine
scheduled each day to allow for a minimum of idle time.
Classes claimed her mornings and early afternoons, and
she spent the remainder of her days with chores designed
to keep her mind and hands busy.

Throughout the day, the rain continued. With a musical
plop, the inevitable leak dripped into the basin on Laine's
classroom floor. The school building was old and ram-
bling. Repairs were always either just completed, slated
to be done or in vague consideration for the future. The
windows were shut against the damp, but the gloom crept
into the room. The students were languid and inattentive.
Her final class of the day was made up of English girls
just entering adolescence. They were thoroughly bored

by their hour lesson on French grammar. As it was Saturday, there was only a half day of classes, but the hours dragged. Hugging her navy blazer closer, Laine reflected that the afternoon would be better employed with a good book and a cheerful fire than by conjugating verbs in a rain-dreary classroom.

"Eloise," Laine said, recalling her duty. "One must postpone naps until after class."

The girl's eyes blinked open. She gave a groggy, self-conscious smile as her classmates giggled. "Yes, Mademoiselle Simmons."

Laine bit back a sigh. "You will have your freedom in ten minutes," she reminded them as she perched on the edge of her desk. "If you have forgotten, it is Saturday. Sunday follows."

This information brought murmurs of approval and a few straightened shoulders. Seeing she had at least momentarily captured their attention, Laine went on. *"Maintenant,* the verb *chanter.* To sing. *Attendez, ensuite répétez. Je chante, tu chantes, il chante, nous chantons, vous..."* Her voice faded as she saw the man leaning against the open door in the rear of the classroom.

"Vous chantez."

Laine forced her attention back to young Eloise. *"Oui, vous chantez, et ils chantent. Répétez."*

Obediently, the music of high girlish voices repeated the lesson. Laine retreated behind her desk while Dillon stood calmly and watched. As the voices faded into silence, Laine wracked her brain for the assignment she had planned.

"Bien. You will write, for Monday, sentences using this verb in all its forms. Eloise, we will not consider *'Il chante'* an imaginative sentence."

"Yes, Mademoiselle Simmons."

The bell rang signaling the end of class.

"You will not run," she called over the furious clatter of shuffling desks and scurrying feet. Gripping her hands in her lap, Laine prepared herself for the encounter.

She watched the girls giggle and whisper as they passed by Dillon, and saw, as her heart spun circles, his familiar, easy grin. Crossing the room with his long stride, he stood before her.

"Hello, Dillon." She spoke quickly to cover her confusion. "You seem to have quite an effect on my students."

He studied her face in silence as she fought to keep her smile in place. The flood of emotion threatened to drown her.

"You haven't changed," he said at length. "I don't know why I was afraid you would." Reaching in his pocket, he pulled out the locket and placed it on her desk. Unable to speak, Laine stared at it. As her eyes filled, her hand closed convulsively over the gold heart. "Not a very eloquent apology, but I haven't had a lot of practice. For pity's sake, Laine." His tone shifted into anger so quickly, she lifted her head in shock. "If you needed money, why didn't you tell me?"

"And confirm your opinion of my character?" she retorted.

Turning away, Dillon moved to a window and looked into the insistent mist of rain. "I had that one coming," he murmured, then rested his hands on the sill and lapsed into silence.

She was moved by the flicker of pain that had crossed his face. "There's no purpose in recriminations now, Dillon. It's best to leave all that in the past." Rising, she kept the desk between them. "I'm very grateful to you for taking the time and the trouble to return my locket. It's more important to me than I can tell you. I don't know when I'll be able to pay you. I…"

Dillon whirled, and Laine stepped away from the fury on his face. She watched him struggle for control. "No, don't say anything, just give me a minute." His hands retreated to his pockets. For several long moments, he paced the room. Gradually, his movements grew calmer. "The roof leaks," he said idly.

"Only when it rains."

He gave a short laugh and turned back to her. "Maybe it doesn't mean much, but I'm sorry. No." He shook his head to ward her off as she began to answer. "Don't be so blasted generous. It'll only make me feel more guilty." He started to light a cigarette, remembered where he was and let out a long breath. "After my exhibition of stupidity, I went up for a while. I find that I think more clearly a few thousand feet off the ground. You might find this hard to believe, and I suppose it's even more ridiculous to expect you to forgive me, but I did manage to get a grip on reality. I didn't even believe the things I was saying to you when I was saying them." He rubbed his hands over his face, and Laine noticed for the first time that he looked tired and drawn. "I only know that I went a little crazy from the first minute I saw you.

"I went back to the house with the intention of offering a series of inadequate apologies. I tried to rationalize that all the accusations I tossed at you about Cap were made for his sake." He shook his head, and a faint smile touched his mouth. "It didn't help."

"Dillon…"

"Laine, don't interrupt. I haven't the patience as it is." He paced again, and she stood silent. "I'm not very good at this, so just don't say anything until I'm finished." Restless, he continued to roam around the room as he spoke. "When I got back, Miri was waiting for me. I couldn't get anything out of her at first but a detailed lecture on my character. Finally, she told me you'd gone. I didn't take that news very well, but it's no use going into that now. After a lot of glaring and ancient curses, she told me about the locket. I had to swear a blood oath not to tell Cap. It seems you had her word on that. I've been in France for ten days trying to find you." Turning back, he gestured in frustration. "Ten days," he repeated as if it were a lifetime. "It wasn't until this morning that I traced the maid who worked for your mother. She was very expansive once I settled her into broken English. I got an earful about debts and auctions and the little mademoiselle who stayed in school over Christmas vacations while Madame went to Saint Moritz. She gave me the name of your school." Dillon paused. For a moment there was only the sound of water dripping from the ceiling into the basin. "There's nothing you can say to me that I haven't already said to myself, in more graphic terms. But I figured you should have the chance."

Seeing he was finished, Laine drew a deep breath and prepared to speak. "Dillon, I've thought carefully on how my position would have looked to you. You knew only one side, and your heart was with my father. I find it difficult, when I'm calm, to resent that loyalty or your protection of his welfare. As for what happened on the last morning—" Laine swallowed, striving to keep her voice composed. "I think it was as difficult for you as it was for me, perhaps more difficult."

"You'd make it a whole lot easier on my conscience if you'd yell or toss a few things at me."

"I'm sorry." She managed a smile and lifted her shoulders with the apology. "I'd have to be very angry to do that, especially here. The nuns frown on displays of temper."

"Cap wants you to come home."

Laine's smile faded at his quiet words. He watched her eyes go bleak before she shook her head and moved to the window. "This is my home."

"Your home's in Kauai. Cap wants you back. Is it fair to him to lose you twice?"

"Is it fair to ask me to turn my back on my own life and return?" she countered, trying to block out the pain his words were causing. "Don't talk to me about fair, Dillon."

"Look, be as bitter as you want about me. I deserve it. Cap doesn't. How do you think he feels knowing what your childhood was like?"

"You told him?" She whirled around, and for the first time since he had come into the room, Dillon saw her mask of control slip. "You had no right…"

"I had every right," he interrupted. "Just as Cap had every right to know. Laine, listen to me." She had started to turn away, but his words and quiet tone halted her. "He loves you. He never stopped, not all those years. I guess that's why I reacted to you the way I did." With an impatient sound, he ran his hands through his hair again. "For fifteen years, loving you hurt him."

"Don't you think I know that?" she tossed back. "Why must he be hurt more?"

"Laine, the few days you were with him gave him back his daughter. He didn't ask why you never answered his letters, he never accused you of any of the things I did."

He shut his eyes briefly, and again she noticed fatigue. "He loved you without needing explanations or apologies. It would have been wrong to prolong the lies. When he found you'd left, he wanted to come to France himself to bring you back. I asked him to let me come alone because I knew it was my fault that you left."

"There's no blame, Dillon." With a sigh, Laine slipped the locket into her blazer pocket. "Perhaps you were right to tell Cap. Perhaps it's cleaner. I'll write him myself tonight; it was wrong of me to leave without seeing him. Knowing that he is really my father again is the greatest gift I've ever had. I don't want either one of you to think that my living in France means I hold any resentment. I very much hope that Cap visits me soon. Perhaps you'd carry a note back for me."

Dillon's eyes darkened. His voice was tight with anger when he spoke. "He isn't going to like knowing you're buried in this school."

Laine turned away from him and faced the window.

"I'm not buried, Dillon. The school is my home and my job."

"And your escape?" he demanded impatiently, then swore as he saw her stiffen. He began to pace again. "I'm sorry, that was a cheap shot."

"No more apologies, Dillon. I don't believe the floors can stand the wear."

He stopped his pacing and studied her. Her back was still to him, but he could just see the line of her chin against the pale cap of curls. In the trim navy blazer and white pleated skirt, she looked more student than teacher. He began to speak in a lighter tone. "Listen, Duchess, I'm going to stay around for a couple of days, play tourist.

How about showing me around? I could use someone who speaks the language."

Laine shut her eyes, thinking of what a few days in his company would mean. There was no point in prolonging the pain. "I'm sorry, Dillon, I'd love to take you around, but I haven't the time at the moment. My work here has backed up since I took the time off to visit Kauai."

"You're going to make this difficult, aren't you?"

"I'm not trying to do that, Dillon." Laine turned, with an apologetic smile. "Another time, perhaps."

"I haven't got another time. I'm trying my best to do this right, but I'm not sure of my moves. I've never dealt with a woman like you before. All the rules are different." She saw, with curiosity, that his usual confidence had vanished. He took a step toward her, stopped, then walked to the blackboard. For some moments, he studied the conjugation of several French verbs. "Have dinner with me tonight."

"No, Dillon, I..." He whirled around so swiftly, Laine swallowed the rest of her words.

"If you won't even have dinner with me, how the devil am I supposed to talk you into coming home so I can struggle through this courting routine? Any fool could see I'm no good at this sort of thing. I've already made a mess of it. I don't know how much longer I can stand here and be reasonably coherent. I love you, Laine, and it's driving me crazy. Come back to Kauai so we can be married."

Stunned into speechlessness, Laine stared at him. "Dillon," she began, "did you say you love me?"

"Yes, I said I love you. Do you want to hear it again?" His hands descended to her shoulders, his lips to her hair. "I love you so much I'm barely able to do simple things like eat and sleep for thinking of you. I keep remembering how you looked with a shell held to your ear. You stood there with the water running from your hair, and your eyes the color of the sky and the sea, and I fell completely in love with you. I tried not to believe it, but I lost ground every time you got near me. When you left, it was like losing part of myself. I'm not complete anymore without you."

"Dillon." His name was only a whisper.

"I swore I wasn't going to put any pressure on you." She felt his brow lower to the crown of her head. "I wasn't going to say all these things to you at once like this. I'll give you whatever you need, the flowers, the candlelight. You'd be surprised how conventional I can be when it's necessary. Just come back with me, Laine. I'll give you some time before I start pressuring you to marry me."

"No." She shook her head, then took a deep breath. "I won't come back with you unless you marry me first."

"Listen." Dillon tightened his grip, then with a groan of pleasure lowered his mouth to hers. "You drive a hard bargain," he murmured as he tasted her lips. As if starved for the flavor, he lingered over the kiss.

"I'm not going to give you the opportunity to change your mind." Lifting her arms, Laine circled his neck, then laid her cheek against his. "You can give me the flowers and candlelight after we're married."

"Duchess, you've got a deal. I'll have you married to me before you realize what you're getting into. Some people might tell you I have a few faults—such as, I occasionally lose my temper—"

"Really?" Laine lifted an incredulous face. "I've never known anyone more mild and even-tempered. However—" she trailed her finger down his throat and toyed with the top button of his shirt "—I suppose I should confess that

I am by nature very jealous. It's just something I can't control. And if I ever see another woman dance the hula especially for you, I shall probably throw her off the nearest cliff!"

"Would you?" Dillon gave a self-satisfied masculine grin as he framed her face in his hands. "Then I think Miri should start teaching you as soon as we get back. I warn you, I plan to sit in on every lesson."

"I'm sure I'll be a quick learner." Rising to her toes, Laine pulled him closer. "But right now there are things I would rather learn. Kiss me again, Dillon!"

* * * * *

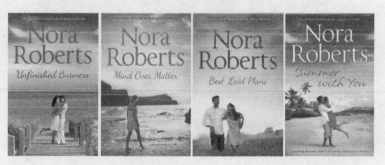

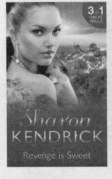

Introducing
Cordina's Royal Family...

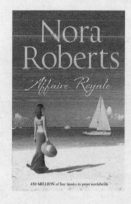

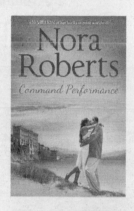

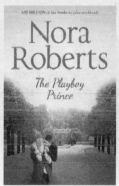

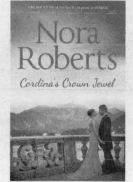

**450 million of her books in
print worldwide**

www.millsandboon.co.uk

**Fall under the spell of *New York Times*
bestselling author**

Nora Roberts

and her MacGregor novels

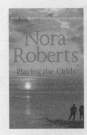
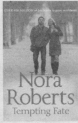
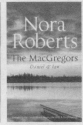
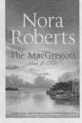
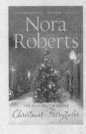
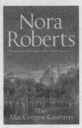
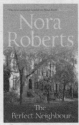

**400 million of her books in
print worldwide**

MACGREGORS

Get ready to meet the MacKade family...

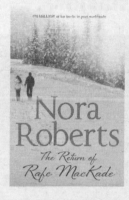

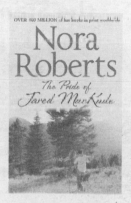

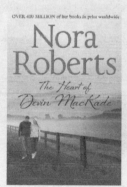

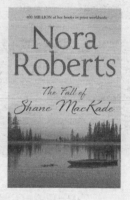

'The most successful
author on planet Earth'
—*Washington Post*

www.millsandboon.co.uk

Introducing
the Stanislaskis...

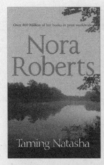
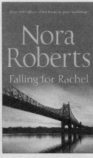
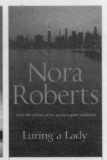
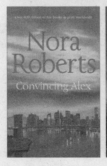
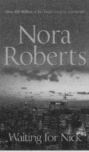
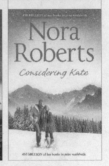